Praise fo

'David Ellis's pages throb with action and suspense'
James Patterson

'A searing and suspenseful tale of law and murder
and long-nurtured revenge . . . The best yet'
Scott Turow

'A triumph for Ellis and a sheer pleasure for the reader'
David Baldacci

'Ellis is a fine writer and does excellent courtroom drama.
An entertaining read'
The Times

'Ellis's intelligent, inventive thriller is a splendid
introduction to his work. More, please!'
Sunday Telegraph

'Grisham's heir apparent . . . A fresh, fast-paced thriller'
Daily Mail

'Ellis conceals and reveals information like a skilled poker player . . .
The plot twists keep readers guessing throughout'
Publishers Weekly

'Filled with tension and twists . . . Ellis ranks among the best
writers in the genre, and this book will keep readers
entertained from start to finish'
Kirkus

David Ellis's previous novels include *Line of Vision* (winner of the Edgar Award for Best First Novel) and *The Hidden Man*. An attorney from Chicago, he currently serves as Chief Counsel to the Speaker of the Illinois House of Representatives. He lives in Illinois.

www.davidellis.com

Also by David Ellis

Jason Kolarich Thrillers

Breach of Trust
The Hidden Man
The Wrong Man

Eye of the Beholder
In the Company of Liars
Jury of One
Life Sentence
Line of Vision

With James Patterson

Guilty Wives
Mistress

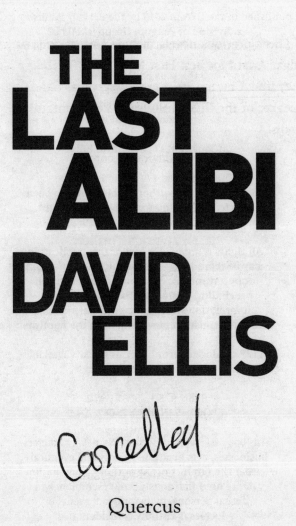

THE LAST ALIBI

DAVID ELLIS

Cancelled

Quercus

First published in the USA in 2013 by the Berkley Publishing Group,
a division of Penguin Group (USA) LLC
This edition published in Great Britain in 2014 by

Quercus Editions Ltd
55 Baker Street
7th Floor, South Block
London W1U 8EW

A CIP catalogue record for this book is available
from the British Library

ISBN 978 1 78087 795 2
EBOOK ISBN 978 1 78087 794 5

10 9 8 7 6 5 4 3 2 1

Printed and bound in Great Britain by Clays Ltd, St Ives plc

Typeset by Ellipsis Books Limited, Glasgow

To Ed Nystrom

THE TRIAL, DAY 1
Monday, December 9

1

Jason

Judge Judith Bialek, from her bench overlooking the court, peers down over her glasses at the defense and prosecution. Until now she has been businesslike, efficient, carefully instructing the twelve jurors and three alternates as to their duties in this case. But this particular case gives her pause, as she is familiar with the parties and tries to emit some kind of acknowledgment of this fact: a grim smile, lips tucked in, a brief nod in the direction of the defense table.

'Please remember, above all,' she says, 'that the defendant has pleaded not guilty, and he is presumed not guilty unless proven otherwise beyond a reasonable doubt.'

Everybody knows that, of course. You've only made it as far as Judge Bialek's courtroom if you've uttered those two words: *Not guilty*. Not guilty by reason of insanity. Self-defense, maybe. But always *Not guilty!*

How many times I've stood in a courtroom like this one, the grand, ornate walnut molding and finishes, the overdone lighting, the walls practically bleeding with the fears and horrors they've absorbed during the seven decades that this building has stood. *Not guilty* are the only words the exhausted and terrified defendants utter prior to trial, but so many more lie just beneath the surface, at the backs of their throats, yearning to gush forth: *I didn't do it. I was set up. This is all a misunderstanding. It's not like it seems. I'm not a criminal. Please, please, before this goes any further, just please hear me out!*

I've lost count of the number of times I've stood here. Over three hundred cases, if you count everything from third-chairing a trial to being the top dog, while I was prosecuting. Nearly fifty cases, surely, as a defense lawyer, standing next to a weak-kneed defendant watching the machinations of the criminal justice system begin to churn against him, the enormity of what is happening crashing down upon him – the judge in a black robe, the steely prosecutor, the sheriff's deputy waiting to handcuff him, the United States flag waving over a courtroom of the public, spectators watching him stand accused by the government, peering at him with a combination of morbid curiosity and vicarious thrill.

'We will now hear opening statements from the prosecution. Mr Ogren.'

'Thank you, Your Honor.' Roger Ogren is a lifer at the office, probably close to twenty-five years in by now. I knew him when I was there. I was surprised, in fact, to learn that he was handling this case. And I was unhappy, too. This is a man who has seen everything, who is surprised by nothing.

He is slim, unusually so to anyone who knows him, after a long illness that many thought would end his career. No longer fitting into his old suits, Roger is wearing new stuff, fashionable threads his wife must have picked out.

As Roger Ogren approaches the podium to address the jury, Shauna Tasker very subtly places her hand over mine. I turn and offer a grim smile. Shauna is my law partner. She is my best friend.

And for this trial, she is my lawyer.

'Ladies and gentlemen,' says Ogren, 'we are here today for one reason and one reason only. This is a murder trial, and the defendant is Jason Kolarich.'

Ogren turns and points his finger at me. I always advise my clients to be ready for that, to have earnest, nonthreatening looks on their faces, and to return the stare. I now understand just how difficult it is.

4

And again I hear the cries of the thousands who have sat in this chair, their silent, desperate wailings: *It wasn't me. They have the wrong guy. You don't understand what happened, just let me explain, please don't do this to me!*

But I say none of those things. I just look at the jurors with my *I didn't kill anybody* face – yes, I practiced before a mirror – searching their eyes, wondering what it is they are seeing in me.

I will probably testify. When I do, I'm not sure it will be convincing enough to establish reasonable doubt. I'm not sure it will do more good than harm.

I'm only sure, in fact, of one thing: When I testify, I will not tell the truth.

SIX MONTHS BEFORE TRIAL
June

2

Jason

I stand up in the courtroom gingerly, still hesitant with the knee, more out of habit than necessity. My mouth is dry and sticky, so I slide the glass of water near the podium in case I need it. Once I start, I don't like interruptions unless I choose one for tactical advantage. It's all about strategy once I walk into a courtroom.

This is war, after all. No other way to look at it. The cop sitting on the witness stand arrested my client for possession of two grams of crack cocaine. My job at this hearing is to show that he had no probable cause to search my client, and therefore the product of that search – the cocaine – must be excluded from evidence. This is technically a preliminary hearing prior to trial, but everyone knows that this is the whole enchilada. If the crack is found admissible, my client is toast; he has no defense left other than claiming that the plastic bags fell from the sky into his pocket, which usually doesn't work. But if, on the other hand, the judge excludes the crack from evidence, my client walks.

My client is William Braden, a nineteen-year-old high school graduate from the posh suburb of Highland Woods who's 'taking a year or two off' before college. Exactly why Billy decided to come down to the city's west side to buy his drugs is anyone's guess. Surely he could have found them at the high school or other places up there;

the lily-white, wealthy suburbs are no longer immune from hard-core drugs. But people do dumb things. If they didn't, I wouldn't have a job.

I cast a glance at Billy's parents, John and Karen, doctors at a prestigious downtown hospital each of them, who are seated behind the defense table, wearing expressions I see all too often – they are overwhelmed, they can't believe this is happening, this isn't where people of their ilk are supposed to find themselves. Not wealthy white people from the suburbs.

I wonder if they know that their son is more than a user – he's a dealer. I certainly can't tell them. And the cops didn't find enough drugs on Billy to charge him with possession with intent to distribute. So to all the world, Billy is simply a clean-cut kid who was experimenting, taking an ill-advised walk on the wild side.

I reach the podium and stop. Three months ago, this small exercise of motor skills would send pain skyrocketing up from my knee.

'Detective Forrest,' I say, 'my name is Jason Kolarich. I represent Billy Braden.' Billy, not William. A kid, a stupid boy, not an adult criminal.

'Counsel,' he says. Nick Forrest has worked undercover narcotics for almost four years. He is thick through the chest and shoulders and maintains a formidable posture. He must, if he works the city's west side.

'You arrested my client walking down Roosevelt Avenue on December eighth of last year, correct?'

'Correct, sir.'

'He was walking west between Girardi and Summerset.'

'That's . . . that's correct.'

'He was alone, as far as you could tell.'

'As far as I could tell.'

'But there were other people on the street, on Roosevelt, yes?'

'There were a few. It was getting close to dusk. People wander out less when it gets to be dark around there.'

'It's a dangerous neighborhood.'

'It can be.'

'Lot of gang activity, right?'

'That's right.' Detective Forrest nods.

'And Billy – Billy was wearing a black wool coat as he walked westbound.'

'He . . . That's right, yes.'

'It was cold out that day, true?'

'It was.'

'Below freezing, you could see your breath, that sort of thing?'

'That's right.'

'Nothing unusual about wearing a black wool coat on a cold day, correct?'

'I didn't say it was unusual.'

I pause. Sometimes judges like to interject when witnesses elaborate, especially at the beginning of their testimony. But Judge Goodson remains mute, his chin resting in his left hand.

'You agree with me, it wasn't unusual.'

'I agree,' he says.

'His hands were in his pockets, correct?'

'I believe they were, yes.'

'Nothing unusual about that, either.'

'Correct.'

'You were in an unmarked Chevy Cavalier, parked on the south side of the street.'

'That's right. I was doing a drive-around.'

Judge Goodson, a former prosecutor, knows what that means, but I have to make my record for the appellate court. 'You were driving around Roosevelt, looking for someone to stop and sell you drugs in your car.'

'Correct.'

'Okay, Detective. And you were in the driver's seat.'

'I was.'

'So you're on the south side of Roosevelt, looking north?'

'That's correct.'

'So Billy, walking west on the opposite side of the street, came up from behind you, so to speak. He wasn't walking toward you, he was walking away from you.'

The detective clears his throat. 'I observed the suspect in my rear-view mirror, walking westbound. Then he passed by my line of sight and continued walking away from me.'

'The suspect,' I say. 'You called him a suspect.'

'Well, the—'

'He was already a suspect, the moment you laid eyes on him in the rearview mirror. That's your testimony.'

Detective Forrest leans forward in his chair, a bit of crimson rising to the surface of his cheeks. Surely he's been warned, over and over again by the prosecutor, not to let me get a rise out of him.

'The block in question is where Buildings A and B of the Eagleton Housing Projects are located,' he says. 'They are known drug houses. It's been well documented that people go to Eagleton to buy crack cocaine.'

'Okay, so he *was* a suspect the moment you saw him walking down the street in a black wool coat with his hands in his pockets.'

'You forgot that he *ran*, Counselor.'

'No, I didn't. I'm not there yet, Detective. I'm at the point in time that you first saw him, in the rearview mirror. For the third time, Detective—'

It's always nice to remind the judge that the witness isn't answering your question.

'—was Billy a suspect at that point in time, or wasn't—'

'And I already told you, Counselor, that he was walking along a route that is known for drug activity.'

'Just walking down Roosevelt? You didn't see my client come out of Building A or B, did you? You were just doing a drive-around when you saw my client, correct?'

He lets out a sigh. 'Correct.'

'So you're saying that simply walking down Roosevelt, between Girardi and Summerset, made Billy automatically a suspect for drug possession.'

12

'I didn't say that.'

'Well, you've already agreed that there were other individuals walking on Roosevelt at that time. Were they all suspects, too?'

'I didn't say that, either.'

I look at the judge, as if I'm bewildered. Judge Goodson actually smirks. My theatrics play better with a jury than with a judge who has seen this act a thousand times.

'So Billy was one of several individuals walking along a *known route for drug activity*,' I say.

'He's the only one who ran,' says Detective Forrest.

'He's the only one you followed in your car,' I answer. 'Right? You drove along after him for almost an entire city block before he started to run. Isn't that true?'

It may or may not be true, but it's what he wrote in his police report, so he's glued to it.

'Yes, that's true.'

'What was so different about Billy versus the other people walking up and down Roosevelt Avenue at that time, Detective? He was wearing a black wool coat and kept his hands in his pockets in the dead of winter. What was so different about him that made you follow him and only him?'

As a technical matter, we tell young lawyers not to ask open-ended questions like this on cross-examination. You're supposed to control the witnesses by asking your preferred questions and getting *yes* or *no* responses. But we're going to get to this point one way or the other when the prosecutor gets to ask him questions, and I want this Q&A on my terms.

Plus, I have his police report, and if he adds facts that weren't contained in that report, I'm going to crucify him. That would make matters even worse for him.

'He was walking quickly and looking around, like he was nervous.'

'Walking quickly in the dead of winter. Looking around nervously while he walked alone in a neighborhood you agreed was dangerous and gang-infested. Walking quickly and acting nervous while an unmarked car, with unknown occupants, *followed* him. *That's* what you're telling the judge struck you as suspicious.'

The detective glances at the judge.

'Anything else, Detective? I'm giving you the floor here. What other facts, Detective, gave you probable cause to believe my client was carrying drugs?' I tick off the points on my hand. 'He was walking on Roosevelt Avenue like several other people, he was wearing a winter coat like several other people, he had his hands in his pockets like several other people, he was looking around nervously and walking quickly while some stranger followed him in a beater Chevy. Is that *it*, Detective?'

The heat has fully reached the detective's face. I'm sure he's the combative sort ordinarily. He'd like to have it out with me behind the courthouse, if he had his druthers.

'He fit a profile,' he answers with a bit less bravado. 'It's a known fact that suburban kids come here to buy drugs.'

'Ah,' I say, like I've discovered gold, like we've finally arrived at the truth. 'He looked like a suburban kid.'

'He did.'

'Because he is white.'

'Because – he looked like a suburban kid.'

I drop my chin a notch and look up at the detective. 'Among the several individuals who were walking along Roosevelt Avenue at that point, isn't it true that Billy Braden was the only white person?'

'I don't recall,' he snaps.

'You picked him out because he was a white kid in a black neighborhood.'

'I didn't.'

Of course, he did. Billy looked like someone who didn't belong. It's not that Detective Forrest was acting illogically. It was somewhat logical. But when it comes to racial profiling, the police department gets very sensitive. They don't want to admit that they single out a white kid in a black neighborhood any more than they want to admit that they single out a black kid in a white neighborhood.

14

And no judge wants to condone racial profiling, either. Judge Goodson is a temperamental sort – if he weren't, he'd have his own felony courtroom by now – but he isn't stupid. Unless the prosecutor cleans this up, the judge will have to toss this one. And I don't think the prosecutor can clean this one up.

He doesn't, not very well at least, during his examination of the detective. I do a recross and lay the racial thing on pretty thick. I don't particularly enjoy doing it, but guess what? My client doesn't pay me for what I enjoy doing. He pays me to win the damn case. And this is the most effective route to winning it.

At the end of the hearing, the judge takes the matter under advisement. We'll find out what he thinks soon. The Bradens thank me more profusely than I deserve. The adrenaline from the court hearing begins its slow leak, my interest in being here along with it. Actually, it's more like the balloon has burst.

I have to leave. I have to get out of here.

Then I hear a woman's voice behind me. 'Mr Kolarich.'

I notice a change in both of the men, father and son alike, their eyes growing, their posture straightening.

I turn. It's the court reporter. The prosecutor's office likes to hire an independent court reporter for these suppression hearings, because when they lose – when their whole case goes in the dumpster because of an evidentiary ruling – they like to appeal the case right away, and the county's court reporters aren't the most reliable.

I quickly understand the reaction of the Braden men. The court reporter has cropped black hair with Cleopatra bangs and large, piercing eyes the color of teal or aqua. Her face is finely etched into a V, with a nicely proportioned figure, from what I can see in her blue suit.

Those are the vital statistics, but there is something more there, something haunting, something electric. Her very presence feels like a dare, a challenge. Like she understands me. *I know you. I know what's wrong with you.*

She hands me her card. 'That has my e-mail and cell on it,' she says. 'I'll have the transcript to you by the end of the week, is that soon enough?'

I look down at the name. *Alexa Himmel.*

'Okay, Alexa Himmel,' I say. Just saying her name makes me feel dirty.

3

Shauna

Tuesday, June 4

I slump into my chair and groan as I look over the files in front of me on my desk. My body is rubbery, fatigued. My brain is still fuzzy, buzzing from the comedown, even though I gave myself a long weekend to shake it out.

Last Friday, on the eve of a jury verdict, we settled our personal injury case, my client an industrial painter who got zapped by an electrical wire while working on a hydraulic lift underneath the train tracks. He survived, but suffered severe nerve damage to his right arm and can no longer hold a toothbrush, much less a sandblaster. We went to trial almost three weeks ago. The general contractor and electric utility blamed each other – the GC said the utility knew the work was going to be performed that day and was supposed to kill the power to those lines; the utility said the work went out of order and nobody told them my client, Joe Mariel, would be blasting by those electrical wires at that location on that day.

We gave it to the jury last Thursday morning. On Friday, while the jury was still deliberating, the general contractor and power company collectively coughed up $650,000 to end the suspense. My client Joe dipped me like a ballroom dancer with his good arm and planted a wet kiss on me when I delivered their final offer to him.

So the law firm of Tasker & Kolarich had a big day – over

$200,000 – and I had my first weekend to myself in a month. No twenty-hour days, no combing over expert reports and witness summaries, no mock direct and cross-examinations, no hair-graying stress wondering if I'd make some crucial mistake that would sink my client's fortunes.

Now the bad news, which, I guess, is also good news: I have another trial starting in five weeks. What are the odds? Civil litigants don't go to trial very often. I hadn't been in front of a jury in almost three years before this PI case. And now two trials within eight weeks? Unheard of. I find myself longing for the old days – before my time, actually – when the caseloads on the judiciary were less oppressive, and judges and lawyers alike tended to schedule everything around their summers. I'm going to lose my June prepping for *Arangold* and my July trying it.

I don't live for these things. I like practicing law (you didn't hear me say *love*) because I like helping people. I enjoy strategizing and the challenge of a good legal argument, too, but I don't relish the fight, the drama, the high-stakes poker.

That's Jason. That's *all* he enjoys. Jason would prefer to be on trial constantly, because it's the only thing that energizes him, the highwire stuff. The preparation and workup in the time before trial are viewed as merely a necessary evil to him, something he tries to delegate as much as he can.

I need Jason, I think to myself. I needed him for the personal injury trial, too, but he was still recuperating from the knee surgery. But the Arangolds are expecting Jason to be the lead trial attorney. They swooned when he came in and did his *aw-shucks* routine while we discussed his successful defense of Senator Almundo on federal RICO charges, his role in the downfall of Governor Snow, and the number of cases he's tried overall, both as a prosecutor and then as a private attorney. I made it clear that Jason would be there when the jury was in the box. I hate to admit it – really hate to – but I don't think I could have landed this case without Jason.

I hear him now, down the hall, and feel an extra skip to my pulse.

I don't think we've been in the office together once in the past month – or if we were, I was too busy huddling with a witness or the client or an expert. He's my law partner and best friend, and I haven't laid eyes on him for weeks. The law firm managed okay while he was laid up, but it felt like an effort, like the entire small firm of Tasker and Kolarich was hobbling on a bad knee along with him.

'Hey, trial lawyer,' he says when he pops into my office. He is glowing from the aftermath of an adversarial hearing himself, some rich kid who got caught with crack cocaine and was looking to Jason to use a legal technicality, also known as the Fourth Amendment.

Glowing, but different. Skinnier, longer hair, dark circles under his eyes. The skinnier part reminds me of high school at Bonaventure, the broad-shouldered, tall kid without much definition to him before Coach Fox got hold of him and he became one of the best football players in school history. The longer hair, of when we were roommates at State, after he got kicked off the football team for fighting and was strongly considering dropping out of school altogether. The dark circles, of the stretch of time two years ago after his wife and daughter missed a turn on a rain-slicked county highway.

I get out of my chair as he walks into my office. I take note of the knee, which doesn't seem to be causing a limp. He wraps one of his bear-arms around my neck and draws me close. He smells like bar soap, exactly as he has ever since Bon-Bon.

'Hey, handsome,' I say, noting that it's not the kind of thing you say to someone you see every day and know like a brother. It's something you say to someone you don't know that well.

'Sorry I missed the celebration,' he says when we pull back. 'Great job on *Marion*. Six-fifty?'

Actually, *Mariel* was my client's last name, but whatever. 'Six-fifty.'

'Wow.'

'I've missed you.' I put a hand on his cheek. 'You look like you could use some sleep.'

'Nah, I'm all good.'

'How's the knee?'

'All good.'

Jason is one of those guys who think it's heroic to be stoic. Nothing ever hurts. Nothing's ever wrong. When Talia and his baby, Emily, died off that county highway, he dropped off the face of the earth for six weeks. He didn't answer his phone, and when he did, he never once told me he was sad. I never once saw him cry, though he assured me he did. I had to drag him to my law office, put him behind a desk, sit a client in front of him, and say, 'Help this person, he needs your help.' That was the only thing that got him back on his feet.

'And how is Richie Rich doing?' I ask. 'Will he be standing trial or whistling on his way home?' I can't tell from his expression whether his hearing went well or not, just that he participated, that post-performance glow.

Jason shrugs. 'Who knows?' That's the funny thing about him. He's all for the fight but little for the glory. I could hold him down and put a knife to his throat and he wouldn't say a nice thing about himself.

Our associate, Bradley John, appears in the doorway looking fresh and bright-eyed. He second-chaired the trial with me. It looks like the long weekend helped him more than it did me. 'Jumping into *Arangold*,' he says. I'd warned him that Tuesday afternoon we'd be back full-throttle in trial preparation.

Jason takes the cue and makes his exit. I watch him leave. There's something not quite right, a couple pieces missing or something.

'You sure you're okay?' I ask.

But I know the answer. 'All good,' we say together.

4

Jason

Tuesday, June 4

I push away the papers on my desk, transcripts from an ATF overhear on a weapons case the feds brought against my client. It can be painful reading, all the starts and stops, the *umms* and *ahhhs*, one talker interrupting the other, and sorting through the nicknames – Combo and Greasy and No-Dope. And best of all, the code words for the product being sold, the automatic weapons. Nobody ever says *gun* or *rifle* or *ammo* over the phone. They think if they code up the whole thing, the ATF agents – and a federal jury – will believe that these gangsters were really talking on their cell phones about the number of tickets they were planning to purchase for the movies that night.

I light the match and hold it upright, the dancing flames inching down the stem to the point where they meet my thumb and ring finger. The fire reaches my fingertips before I can finish the words:

> *I've got tar on my feet and I can't see.*
> *All the birds look down and laugh at me.*

I blow out the flame and toss it into a Styrofoam cup of water, whispers of fleeting smoke curling upward. The flame singed the skin on the tip of my ring finger and turned the corner of the nail black. It hurts more, for some reason, when your eyes are open, when you're watching it happen.

My intercom buzzes. Marie's voice comes over the speaker when I tap it.

'Your three o'clock,' she says.

I didn't know I had an appointment at three o'clock. I didn't know it was three o'clock, either. It's three o'clock?

'I reminded you this morning?' she says in a hushed voice.

Whatever. She probably did. 'Okay.'

I fish through my e-mails and find the calendar reminder for today at three P.M. James Drinker is his name. Okay. Hooray for James Drinker.

He comes in and reaches to shake my hand. I stand cautiously and reach over the desk. The nausea asserts itself, sending a warning message up my throat to the back of my mouth, but it's always a false alarm. Sometimes retching, but never vomiting. It doesn't attack me so much as it stalks me, letting me know it's lurking out there, but never moving in for the kill.

It's not the big pains, my mother said to me about a week before she died. *They've got the medicine for that. It's the knowing, boy. Knowing that it's coming and you can't stop it.*

James Drinker is one of the oddest-looking people I've ever seen, a walking contradiction: big but awkward, a kid's head on a grown-up's developed body. His hair hangs around the sides of his face in tangles, a reddish mop that looks like it doesn't belong, with matching bushy red eyebrows; he is otherwise clean-cut and has a quizzical expression on his face. He wears thick black eyeglasses. His shoulders, chest, and arms suggest he's a workout fiend, but a rounded midsection says he favors Big Macs and chili fries.

The eyes are usually the tell, but they're hard for me to inspect through the thick spectacles. If I were still a prosecutor and he were a suspect in an interview room, I'd make him take them off. My best guess: James Drinker has done some bad things.

'I haven't done anything wrong,' says he.

My mistake. That's a first for me, a client denying his guilt. A first this afternoon, I mean.

'But I'm afraid I'm going to be accused of doing something wrong,' he says.

'What are you going to be accused of doing wrong?'

He pauses. 'This is all confidential, right?'

'Anything you tell me about what happened in the past is confidential,' I say. 'The only thing I can't keep confidential is if you tell me you're going to commit a crime in the future.'

'I'm not going to commit a crime in the future,' he says.

That's always nice to hear. I wave a hand.

'Okay. So James, what crime do you expect to be accused of committing?'

'Murder,' he says, without hesitation.

I sit higher in my chair. Homicides don't walk through the door every day. And here I thought this meeting was going to be boring.

'Two women were killed,' he says. 'I didn't kill them.' Drinker crosses a leg. His sport coat opens as he leans back. Quite the fleshy midsection, this one. Pumps iron and then hits Taco Bell. I raise a fist to my mouth and fight another wave of nausea.

He takes a deep breath. 'I knew each of them,' he says. 'One was a friend of mine. The other one I dated. Two women I knew, two women murdered.'

He's right to be worried. That isn't what the police would call a fanciful coincidence.

'Do the murders appear to be related?' I ask.

He nods, but doesn't answer at first. His eyes are combing my walls, not that there's much to see – some diplomas and certificates, a couple of photographs. It's part of his overall appraisal, checking the schools I attended, equating my stature with the quality of my office.

I pick up a nearby Bic pen, the cap chewed mercilessly, and chew it some more. I hate these cheap pens. I have a fancy Visconti fountain pen my brother, Pete, gave me last Christmas, but it uses replaceable ink cartridges, and I don't want to waste good ink on this guy. The cheap Bic it is.

'Both women were followed home from where they work,' he says. 'And they were both stabbed multiple times.'

The cool deliberation with which he describes the murders sends an icy wave across my back. You can defend all sorts of criminals, but some things you hear, you never get used to. On the bright side, I'm waking up.

'Alicia Corey and Lauren Gibbs,' says Drinker. 'Alicia, I dated a couple of times. Nothing serious. Just a couple of dinners.'

I write down those names with my shitty pen. I hate this pen. I should light the *pen* on fire.

'Is there proof of these dinners?' I ask.

'I . . . I paid for the dinners in cash,' he says.

Interesting. Unusual. Doesn't make him a killer, but most people pay with credit these days. I draw a couple of dollar signs on the pad. Then a smiley face. Then a knife. My mother always said, *You have a flair for art, boy,* but she was talking to my brother, Pete.

'I have a lot of cash,' Drinker explains. 'I'm a mechanic at Higgins Auto Body – over on Delaney? – and sometimes our boss pays us over-time off the books – y'know, in cash.'

Fair enough. A decent explanation to a jury, but not one his employer would want made public – in fact, one he'd probably deny if he thought Uncle Sam might get wind.

'The dinners were on May twelfth and May nineteenth,' he goes on. 'She was murdered the following week. May twenty-second, I think. A Wednesday.'

'You said she was leaving work?'

'She was an exotic dancer,' he says. 'A stripper. Place called Knockers?'

This guy was dating a stripper? There's no accounting for taste, and this guy seems pretty well built, but the goofy red hair down near his shoulders? The fast-food gut? The face made for radio?

'You're surprised,' he says. 'You don't think a stripper would date me.'

'I don't think that.'

'Yes, you do.'

'Tell you what, James.' I lean forward. Again, the vertigo, the feeling I'm tipping to one side. 'I'll make you a deal. Don't tell me what *I* think, and I won't tell you what *you* think. Deal?'

'Deal.' He nods. 'So she left the club at two in the morning and she was murdered at her house when she got home. She was stabbed six or seven times.'

That's a lot of detail for someone who hasn't talked to the police, I think to myself. *And for someone who didn't kill her.*

'Go on,' I say. 'Tell me about the second woman.'

5

Jason

Tuesday, June 4

'The second woman was Lauren, Lauren Gibbs,' James Drinker says. 'She worked at a bank and was trying to build a website design business. Nice woman. Nice woman.' His eyes move away from mine and over to the walls of my office again. 'She was killed two days later, May twenty-fourth, I think. A Friday.'

'And when did you last speak with her?'

He heaves his shoulders. 'Couple of weeks ago?'

'There would be phone records, e-mails, things like that, connecting you to her?'

'Yeah. Phone. Not e-mail. Not Facebook. But phone, yeah. I mean, our friendship wasn't a secret.'

I shift in my chair, but I can't get comfortable. My hand itches, but it's one of those inside itches that my scratching fingernails can't find. I chew the cap on the Bic pen until it's at its breaking point.

'Something wrong?' he asks me.

I take a breath.

'I need a minute,' I say.

I head to the bathroom and splash some cold water on my face. I see dark bags under my eyes. Sleep has been a problem for me. I reach into my pocket, remove my small tin of Altoids, and pop a mint into my mouth. I chew it up and cup some water from the sink.

When I leave the bathroom, Shauna is standing outside Bradley's office and turns to look at me. She reads something in my expression and says, 'What?'

'Nothing,' I answer.

Not interested in prolonging that conversation, I make it back into my office, where James Drinker is standing over by the wall of diplomas and photographs.

'You played football at State, didn't you?' he asks, wagging a finger at a photograph of me catching a football my freshman year.

I ease back into my chair, making noises like an old man getting out of bed. 'Once upon a time,' I say. 'Let's get back to this.'

Drinker resumes his spot in the chair across from me. 'Okay.'

'Do you have alibis, James? For these murders?'

'I was like Macaulay Culkin,' he says.

I stare at him. He stares at me. I'm supposed to understand.

'Home alone,' he says. 'I was home alone. I don't get out too much.'

Now *that* I could believe. 'Any evidence of your being home alone those nights? Did you make phone calls from a landline? Did you send e-mails or go online or order in Chinese food or order a pay-per-view movie? Anything like that?'

His face goes blank. 'I'm not sure. I don't go online a lot, but maybe. I didn't order food or anything. I might have ordered a movie on pay-per-view or something.'

I reach for my pen but can't find it. Must have knocked it off my desk. I bend over to search the carpet, and when I come back up, my body makes me pay: a lightning strike between the ears and a swimming pain in my stomach. I hold my breath and wait it out. Fuck the pen. I'll just memorize the information.

'Good, okay,' I say. 'Think that stuff over. Now, if the police contact—'

'I'm being set up, Mr Kolarich.'

'It may be premature to jump to that—'

'How would you do that?' he asks. 'If it was you? How would you set somebody up for murder?'

27

I sigh, loudly enough for him to get the picture that I'm not very interested in this conversation.

'Please,' he insists. 'I think that's what's happening. How would you frame somebody?'

'How would I . . .' I drum my fingers on the desk. 'Well, okay. The police will usually look for motive, means, and opportunity.'

Drinker scratches at his face, his mouth open in a small O. 'Motive? Why would I wanna kill them?'

From the cops' view, that would be the easiest part of the equation. Boy meets girl. Romance, unrequited love, maybe a little jealousy and obsession sprinkled in. If I put this homely guy next to a hot-body stripper who later wound up with a knife in her chest, first thing I'd think was, *She rebuffed him, he didn't take it so well.* A second girl, same story, or some variation of that story. There can be plenty of variations, but the basic tale is the same – matters of the heart – and the cops see it every day.

'Opportunity,' Drinker says to himself.

'Sounds like you don't have much of an alibi. If someone were framing you, they'd pick a time they knew you had none. Meaning, a time when you're alone. No one to vouch for you.'

Drinker takes a deep breath. That box has been checked, in his case. He was like Macaulay Culkin.

'And *means*?' he says. 'What is that?'

'He'd choose a weapon that you, yourself, had available, too.'

'Like a knife.'

'Sure, like a knife.'

He looks at me with a blank face. 'Well, I have a *knife*,' he says. 'Everybody's got a knife.' He scratches his face again. 'Go on. What else?'

'I don't know what else there is,' I say. 'But if someone wanted to frame you, he might want to help the cops out a little. Leave some clues.'

He shrugs his shoulders. 'I don't know if he did that or not. You mean, like, drop my driver's license there?'

'That, or even more subtle, I suppose. Maybe scrape some grease off the floor of your auto shop and smear it at the scene. Or if he has access to your house, he could take something from your house – a fiber of carpet, some hair from your comb, something like that – and leave it at the crime scene.'

'Damn.' Drinker looks like he's lost a little color. 'Go on. What else?'

I look up at the ceiling. It's been a while since I framed somebody for murder, so I'm a little rusty.

'For that matter,' I say, 'if he had access to your house, he could plant all sorts of things there. The murder weapon. Something from the crime scene. A drop of the victim's blood, even.'

Drinker lets out a shiver. 'I don't think anybody can get into my apartment.'

'You should make sure of that, James. Do you have an alarm system?'

He shakes his head no.

'Get one,' I say. 'It's not that expensive. I have one. But however expensive it may be, it's worth it. If you're serious in thinking that somebody is setting you up, you don't want that person getting into your apartment.'

But he can't be serious about that, can he? He thinks someone's killing women and trying to put him in the soup?

Silence. He studies me. His mind is wandering, and he's not thrilled with where it's going. I can't tell if this guy is for real. Anything's possible, I suppose.

'Guess I got some work to do,' he says.

'I charge three hundred an hour, James. Not counting today. So I'm not cheap.'

He looks up at me, not terribly surprised to hear that number. 'I think I can afford that,' he says. 'I've been saving up.'

I don't comment on the significance of that statement, but he – the innocent man who didn't kill anybody – catches it himself.

'I mean, saving up for a rainy day of some kind,' he clarifies.

Fair enough. I don't know if he's innocent or not, but I do know that if I limited myself to innocent clients, the phone wouldn't ring very often.

'Well, it sounds like it may be raining soon,' I say.

6

Shauna

A late dinner with Jason, just the two of us. My decision and my treat. He looks like he could use a good steak and maybe a stiff drink, but instead he orders some soup and a club soda. Surprising. I've never seen him pass on a drink or a steak. Then it suddenly occurs to me I'm not his mother.

'Is this some kind of diet?' I ask, but he just smirks. Heroically stoic again.

'Anyway, I told Drinker to make a list of anyone who might have a grudge against him and come back tomorrow,' Jason says.

'What a weird meeting. Have you ever had someone come to you and say they think they're being framed?'

He shakes his head. 'When I was a prosecutor, I'd hear that defense. But I've never used it as a defense attorney. And definitely not a guy telling me he's being framed before he's even charged.'

'Maybe he knows he's going to be charged and he wants to lay the table for you.'

'For me?' Jason grimaces. 'He doesn't have to convince his lawyer.'

'Maybe he doesn't know that.'

Jason doesn't respond. He's obliterating a piece of thick bread, shredding it to dust on his plate. But not eating it, I notice. There is a greenish pall to his skin, like he's under the weather.

'So tell me,' I say.

'Tell you what?'

'What's wrong. Are you sick?'

'Nothing's wrong. I'm not sick.'

I sometimes forget that Jason's had a rough time of things, probably because he never lets on about it. Losing your family in a car accident is beyond words, and that was only two years ago. But to make matters worse, he allowed himself a second shot at romance last year, a woman named Tori. Beautiful and elusive, just the way he likes them. I don't know what happened with them. He never shared. But one day she was just gone. And our Jason took it hard. 'Didn't work out' was all he said, but he's easy to read if you know him. He was crushed.

Then a month later, he rips his knee apart on the basketball court, and the jock, the guy who runs fifty miles on a slow week, was laid up for months and hobbling on crutches. His doctor said the pain could last up to a year or longer, depending.

'Either your knee still hurts, you're still pining for Tori, or something else happened while I've been on trial.'

The mention of Tori brings a quick jerk of his eyes, but that's all he gives me. 'Tori is history. My knee hardly ever hurts. Comes and goes.'

He removes a tin of mints from his pocket and pops one in his mouth, chews it up. Not sure why his breath is of concern at the moment. I wasn't planning a make-out session with him after dinner.

'What happened to your hand?' I ask. Each of the fingernails on his right hand has some corner or section blackened, like some kind of gothic manicure. 'Have you been playing with fire?'

He seems to find something interesting, or maybe amusing, in that comment. He lets out a long sigh and leans against the back of the cushioned booth.

Our food comes. Caesar salad for me, French onion soup for the kid. I attack the salad, mixing it up, first picking off the anchovies. Jason stares off into space, his large cauldron of onion soup with the thick slab of Gruyère on top untouched.

'What's with the loss of appetite?' I ask. 'Are you pregnant?'

He doesn't answer, so I don't push. My salad is delicious. Probably loaded with calories, but yummy. I don't work out as much as I should and don't eat as well as I should, but I'm still in shape. Not supermodel thin, but not fat by any stretch. Never have been. But I'm in my mid-thirties now and sometimes I do check myself in the mirror, monitor my butt for signs of sagging and my legs for the first hint of cellulite.

Okay, I check every day. Every single day, after the shower, in front of my full-length mirror. Pure vanity, I guess, or primitive mating behavior. My mother has started asking on a weekly basis about my love life. It's a short conversation. *No, Mom. No, not even a date. Saving myself for Robert Downey, Jr., Mom, but too shy to call him. I left my number on his Facebook page, though.* I have the equivalent of a Ph.D. in brushing off attempts by friends and family to set me up with men who would be absolutely *perfect* for me. It's not that I don't want a man who's absolutely perfect for me. It's that I'm so certain that the people they want me to meet *aren't* that person that I'd rather forgo the stilted, painful dinner conversations and awkward kisses at the door and just wallow in my aloneness. I choose that word deliberately. I'm not lonely. I'm just *alone*. See the difference?

I've become so adept at pretending the lack of romance in my life doesn't bother me that sometimes I even believe my own bullshit.

I'm halfway through my salad when Jason says, 'You look nice.'

I look up from my plate, some dressing on my cheek, a mouthful of lettuce and crouton. 'Huh?'

'I just said you look nice. Blue looks nice on you.'

I make a show of scanning the room behind me, like I can't believe he's saying this to me, a *Who are you and what have you done with Jason?* moment.

'I can't compliment you? You look nice.'

'Um, okay. Thanks?'

I had a go-round with Jason our senior year at Bonaventure High – the prim-and-proper brainiac and the bad-boy athlete, my walk on the wild side – that lasted one night, or more accurately about fifteen minutes, upstairs in Rita Hoffman's bedroom while a hundred kids got drunk or stoned below us. There we were, on top of the covers, our clothes in a bunch on the floor, 'Drive' by R.E.M. blasting below us on the overworked stereo. 'Uh, that was nice,' he said to me when it was over, when he was stripping the condom off and I was pulling on my panties. 'This song sucks' was all I said. 'This whole CD sucks,' he agreed. It was a more intimate moment than the sex. I didn't speak to him again in high school.

I didn't, in fact, even realize we were attending the same university until he became a last-minute addition to our off-campus house at State (when they kick you off the football team, apparently they evict you from the jock dorm, too). He drew the short straw (or one of us did) and got me for a roommate. First thing he said to me, even before hello, seeing me for the first time in almost two years: 'Did you just hate that song, or do you hate R.E.M.?' I said, 'I love R.E.M., but not the newer stuff so much.' He lit up like a Christmas tree. 'Yeah, right, exactly!' And then go-round number two, which lasted about three weeks – sex about ten times, give or take – before we realized that we had to choose between being a full-blown couple or abstain and be buds, it was one or the other in the twelve-by-twelve room we shared. We went with abstinence and buds.

Now we're as close to married as you can be without having sex or living together. He's the only person who can make me laugh out loud, the one who's never left my side, even holding my hand in the doctor's office during that agonizing week that I had the cancer scare (negative, thank you), the one who knows exactly how to navigate my moods when I'm PMS-ing (it's okay if I acknowledge it, not okay for him to so much as mention it).

And now: I look nice. Why would he say something like that? Men don't just say things like that. They pretend they do, but it's not true. There's always a reason.

'Y'know, it's possible Drinker really didn't kill anybody,' he says, digging into his soup, a segue about as delicate as lifting the needle

33

off a Metallica record mid-song. 'This could end up being a really fun case.'

Well, *he's* sure feeling better.

I get the waiter's attention and nod at him. This is going to be an early night.

7

Jason

Wednesday, June 5

'Nobody,' James Drinker says when he returns to see me the next day. 'I can't think of anybody who would have a grudge against me. I don't know why someone would do this to me.'

He's wearing a sport coat again today, over a plaid button-down tucked into blue jeans, highlighting his paunch. Still the disheveled mop of red hair, but he's a bit less apprehensive, less guarded, today.

'Okay, listen, James,' I say. 'We both know that this looks potentially bad for you. The police are going to link these two murders. It shouldn't be hard for them to learn that you dated Alicia Corey or that you were friends with Lauren Gibbs, and even if they only figure out *one* of those two facts, they're going to cross-reference all known acquaintances between the two victims. Frankly, I'm surprised they haven't knocked on your door yet. You with me so far?'

He's listening intently but doesn't seem particularly worried. Surely he's already figured this out independently, but usually when clients hear their lawyer say it looks bad, they start to lose composure. We're the people who are supposed to say, *Don't worry, it's under control, I'm going to make it all better.* When we say, *It doesn't look so good*, they usually freak.

'I understand,' he says.

'Okay. Now. If you're really innocent of these crimes and you think you've been set up, then I can get to work on this for you. You'll have to give me a retainer, and I can start spending it down and billing you by the hour, chasing after the person who is setting you up. I have a great private investigator, and I can do some things from here as well. But if I'm wasting my time, James, if I'm looking for someone who doesn't exist, then I'm wasting your money. Money that you might need for me to defend you in court. If you run out of money – well, I don't work for free. So what I'm saying is, we have to spend your financial resources in a smart way. I'll take your case either way. But don't send me on a wild-goose chase.'

I sit back in my chair.

'So is this a good use of my time?' I ask. 'Or would we be better—'

'I didn't kill those women,' he says. 'I didn't. I really liked Alicia, and Lauren was a friend of mine. I didn't kill them. I don't have a criminal record. I'm – I mean, I'm basically a good person. I'm – I mean . . .' He looks away. Some color reaches his goofy face. He's almost like a cartoon character. 'I know I'm . . . I'm unusual, I guess. Some people think I'm weird. I'm this big goofy guy. I mean, I'm a loner, pretty much.' His eyes return to mine. 'I don't matter to people, Mr Kolarich. I'm nobody to them.'

A little heavy on the dramatic self-pity for my taste. A lot heavy. 'James, I don't care about any of that,' I say. 'I'll defend you whether you're big or small. Whether you're odd or normal.' Cue the music to 'The Star-Spangled Banner.' Jason Kolarich: Give me your tired, your weak, your big and goofy.

I smack my lips. Dry mouth again, the bile in the back of my throat, the slam-dancing going on in my stomach. I pull the Altoids tin out of my pocket and pop one in my mouth. I don't know what the hell to make of this guy.

'Maybe the cops won't even come talk to me,' Drinker speculates, a lilt of unwarranted hope in his voice. 'Maybe they have other suspects.'

'They'll talk to you,' I say. 'And when they do, you tell them you want to talk to your lawyer before you answer a single question. You understand that?'

'Yeah, I got that. But maybe they won't even talk to me. Seriously, that's possible, isn't it?'

I let out a sigh. 'Sure, James. It's possible.'

'Let's do this, Mr Kolarich. Jason. Let's do this: Let's hold tight. Let's see what happens.'

Under the circumstances, that's actually not a terrible idea. If there's a guy in Drinker's past, he'll still be there when Drinker gets pinched.

But.

'James,' I say, 'if this is really happening like we think, then this guy might not stop. He's killing women and he might kill again. Someone else close to you. Or whomever. We should think about going to the police.'

He's nodding along, but then he points at me. I don't really like people pointing at me. 'But isn't that exactly what he wants me to do?'

This is all so odd. But he's not wrong, I have to concede. What he's saying is possible.

'Maybe do it anonymously,' I suggest. 'An anonymous call to the tip line. There must be a tip line.'

'And say what?' Drinker shrugs.

I see his point. *People close to James Drinker are dying – but it wasn't James Drinker who killed them, I swear. And this isn't James Drinker calling, either.*

'I didn't kill anybody, and I'm not going to jail because somebody's trying to frame me,' he says. 'There has to be another way.'

I pinch the bridge of my nose. I'm out of answers.

'Let's hope he's done,' Drinker says. 'He might be done.'

'Okay. Okay, James.' There's nothing else I can say. I can't make him go to the police. And I'd be breaking my oath as an attorney if I called them myself. 'Keep your eyes and ears open, James. And keep my business card with you at all times, just in case.'

He promises to do so. He approaches me and reaches over the table. I shake his hand. It is warm and moist.

He leans into me. 'I hope I'm not nobody to *you*, Jason,' he says.

He gleefully bounds out the door, not waiting for an answer.

8

Shauna

Friday, June 7

Jason and his private investigator, Joel Lightner, are sitting in my office. Lightner has his tie off and his collar open; his week is over. Jason is sitting on the couch in the back of my office, his left leg propped up.

'Come out with us,' Joel says. 'We'll have a few drinks, and who knows? You might finally decide to sleep with me.' Joel is twice divorced, now a committed bachelor and skirt-chaser. If he has sex half as often as he talks about it, his penis should be in the hall of fame.

'It'll be fun,' Jason adds.

'Having drinks with you? Or sleeping with Joel?' I ask.

Jason likes that. He's in a chipper mood, he is, a rosy glow to his cheeks. It's getting harder and harder to predict his moods. A few nights back at dinner, he looked like he was going to toss his cookies, but then he perked up. This morning, walking in the door, he barely lifted his eyes off his feet, and now he's wearing a stupid smirk. And I can't get over the hair, curling out around his ears, bangs hanging across his face. Since college, it was always the high and tight. Who is this person calling himself Jason?

'Come out with us, Shauna,' Joel says again. 'You haven't for a long time.'

That's true; it was the trial. I sacrifice my otherwise diverse and stimulating social life whenever I get close to a trial date. That diverse and stimulating social life consists of dinner at a steak joint with Jason and Joel, who get drunk and insult each other, then heading to a bar where Jason and Joel get drunker and insult each other more and sometimes flirt with women.

I have become one of those women who hang out with men. I didn't used to be. I had a pack of girlfriends, mostly from law school but some from college, whom I ran around with for years. What changed? Marriage. Kids. For them, not me. Nights out at the bars or poetry slams or concerts became quick happy hours before they had to get home, and even the full-scale nights out weren't what they used to be, my friends yawning at eight-thirty, children-tired, or meeting up with their husbands later that night. And then I just got tired of the whole thing, these evenings out with women who were married with kids, who either talk about their kids endlessly (day care / soccer / Music Garden / Chinese lessons / Dora the Explorer) or, worse yet – much worse yet – *catch* themselves doing that and then realize it has the effect of leaving you out, and then they awkwardly stop, the needle screeching off the album mid-chorus, and there is an unstated (God, I *hope* it's unstated) pact not to make Shauna feel worse than she probably already does, and someone forces out a painful segue – 'So, Shauna, are you working on any interesting cases?' – and then you have two choices: (1) acknowledge it and say, 'It's okay, it doesn't make me feel barren and unfulfilled and desperately lonely to hear you talk about your kids and husbands, now what was that you were saying about arts-and-crafts camp?' or (2) let them pity you and tell them about the interesting cases you're working on.

And then you get the sense that it would be easier if you weren't there, and then you realize that they've had the same thought, that they sometimes get together without you, some vague reference to lunch at Alexander's, and they glance at you and say, with a trace of apology, forced casualness, 'It was just a last-minute thing after lacrosse practice.' And so you decide it would be easier to hang out with women just like you, also single, also childless, but then you realize they *aren't* your best friends, but – but – *maybe they can become your best friends*, but then you realize that you're thirty-five and you don't feel like inventing new best buds at that age, and you find yourself probing them, examining them, wondering, *what is it about them, why can't they find someone,* thinking that maybe you can find something in them, some flaw that you have, too, and that if you can just discover that one thing, just that one thing, then suddenly eligible, successful, decent, and handsome men with large penises, who absolutely adore musicals and pinot noir and cunnilingus, will come crawling out of the woodwork competing for your hand in marriage.

And then it turns out it's easier to hang out with Jason and Joel while they get drunk and insult each other.

'The reason she won't come out with us has nothing to do with her dislike for you,' Jason tells Joel. 'She has a trial coming up. How far away?'

'Less than a month,' I say, feeling a shot of dread. 'And you're going to start on it next week, right?' Trials are a bitch. They can be fun, but the workup sucks. Jason has a lot more trial experience than I do, and he's a different personality. He reads a file the day before and goes in there and, damn him, kicks the crap out of witnesses. I don't even enter the courthouse unless I've dissected every single angle of every single question.

My client, Arangold Construction, got into a construction job with the city's civic auditorium that didn't end up so well. The project was delayed, there were problems at the site, ultimately the city replaced Arangold, and the new contractor ran up the bill under the guise of time restraints. So now the city is suing Arangold for twenty million dollars. It's a bet-the-company case. Arangold loses this case and gets hit with a verdict anywhere *near* the number the city wants, the company goes under. Twenty-two employees lose their jobs.

'Yeah, sure. And I can stay tonight if you need some help,' Jason says. 'It's not a problem.'

I look over the overwhelming stacks of paper on the floor in the corner. 'Start fresh on Monday,' I say. 'I can divide out a chunk of the case, a discrete part, and hand it off to you.'

'Sure.'

Marie, our receptionist, pokes her head in the door.

'There she is!' says Joel. He'd sleep with her, too. He'd sleep with a hermit crab.

She points to Jason. 'Court reporter here to see you,' she says. 'Her name's Alexa?'

9

Jason

Friday, June 7

That court reporter from the suppression hearing is standing in my office when I walk in. I remember her. Of course I do. Today she is not dressed for court; she is wearing a blue blouse with frilly sleeves and blue jeans that fit her very snugly, thank you very little.

'Personal delivery?' I ask.

'Personal delivery.'

When it happens with me, it always happens instantly. It doesn't sneak up on me. It doesn't bud and slowly blossom within me. It zaps me like I stuck a paper clip in a socket. When I first met my wife, Talia, back at State, and she suggested that we could study together for the econ final, that moment I first locked eyes with her, I couldn't breathe.

This isn't that. I'll never have that again, what Talia and I shared. But there is something there, lingering between Alexa Himmel and me, something primitive and daring that I can't quite place. *Lust*, if you had to assign it a word, but that feels incomplete. It's more like a connection, something between us that just seems to fit together. *I get you, Jason. I'm like you.*

Those penetrating icy-blue eyes, catching and hanging on to mine for just a beat beyond the required eye contact for a professional conversation, tell me I'm not alone. When we first met, I was coming off a tough cross-examination, I was in courtroom mode, I had clients with me – it was more like a bus nearly plastered me, but I narrowly avoided it and moved on with my life, just an after-rush of adrenaline to show for it. But this time it's just the two of us, and I'm pancaked on the road.

'You seemed like you were in a hurry to get this,' she says, though I'm sure I didn't.

'I was,' I answer, though I wasn't.

'Okay,' she says, like the meeting is about to adjourn. She's taken the first step, after all, a fairly overt one. She came all the way over to my office in person to drop off something that she could have e-mailed. She's not going to take the next step. This is up to me.

She hikes her bag over her shoulder. 'Have a great weekend,' she says.

'Hang on a second,' I say, like I've just come up with a great idea. I wish I had a line to go along with it. *Now I owe you one – how about dinner? At least let me buy you a drink.* A big tough Hungarian lad I am, but I get tongue-tied around the ladies.

'I'm trying to think of a smooth way to ask you on a date,' I say. 'Got any ideas?'

10

Jason

Saturday, June 8

At a quarter to three in the morning, still staring up at the ceiling in my town house, I finally surrender and pull my laptop over and open it. It's always on. I'm supposed to properly turn it off to allow for upgrades or updates or up-somethings, but I never do.

I check out a couple of fitness sites, a marathoner's site being my favorite, even though it will be a long time before I run another marathon. Still, I have to acknowledge, even with the occasional flare-up, my knee is getting better.

This is the worst time, the still of night, shadows jumping across the window, the gentle creaks and groans of the town house's foundation. I'm not so good when I'm left to my own thoughts. A night like this, normally, I'd lace it up and go for a run, no matter the time. I like the city best when I'm alone inside it, when I don't have to share it, when the streets are naked and peaceful.

There is something wrong with me, but that something is nothing. There is nothing inside me. I watch one foot move in front of the other every day. I hear my voice arguing to a judge or jurors or reassuring a client. But it's all nothing, isn't it? The clients will go to prison, and even if I walk them, even if I find some way to win, they'll be back, and sooner or later they'll find a prison cell like metal drawn to a magnet. Everyone's chasing after something, everyone wants something from somebody else, but not me.

There is a tiny earthquake in my stomach. My lips, my mouth, my throat, are dried up, sticky and itchy. I drink from a bottle of water but it doesn't help. I pop an Altoid and chew it up, then slug some more water. Then I jump to the site for our online newspaper, the *Herald*, to hear about the latest stupid thing that Mayor Champion has done, when I'm greeted with this breaking-news headline:

BREAKING: THIRD WOMAN STABBED ON NORTH SIDE

I pop up in bed and click the link. The stabbing just happened. They don't know the victim or too many details. Police responded to a call in the 4200 block of North Riverwood Avenue, a woman bleeding out from a stab wound.

I don't have James Drinker's contact information with me at home, on a Friday night that is technically Saturday morning. I may have brought home my notes from our two meetings. I don't remember. These days I – Well, I don't remember, anyway.

Twenty minutes later, I'm drifting again, the slow downhill nod toward sleep. *Tomorrow,* I think, *tomorrow I'll call James,* a warmth spreading over me, while James Drinker sticks a knife into a woman, pulls it out, and winks at me.

11

Shauna

Saturday, June 8

I dial Jason's cell at a quarter past eight. It's early. He might be sleeping. Before the knee problem, he'd have already completed a twelve-mile run or something crazy, whatever that competitive itch he has that he always needs to scratch.

'Hey,' he says.

'Hey.' I cradle my cell in my shoulder as I scoop butter with a knife. Granola and toast for this working girl. Long day ahead at the office, prepping for the *Arangold* trial. Jason better not fuck me on this trial. Rory Arangold's already been asking about Jason. *He's going to be there, right? He's going to cross-examine their expert?*

'You watching the news?' Jason asks.

He knows I am. I'm a creature of habit.

The woman who was stabbed last night in her apartment is Holly Frazier, a young, attractive woman in the photo they put up over the anchorman's shoulder. A grad student at St. Margaret's. Midtwenties, looks like.

'What the fuck?' Jason mumbles. 'What is it this time? Is she, what, James Drinker's dog walker or something? His study buddy?'

'Ask him,' I say. 'Let's see if this is another coincidence.'

'I fucking will. Is this asshole playing me, Shauna?'

The notion is out there, of course. 'But why would he?' I ask.

'You're his lawyer. Everything he says to you is in confidence. I mean, I hate to say it, but it's possible he's telling you the truth, isn't it?'

'I don't know. I guess.' He mumbles a few more curse words under his breath. 'He said he couldn't think of anyone who'd do this to him, who'd want to taunt him. Fuck with him.'

'So what?' I say. 'It could be anybody. He cut somebody off in an intersection, somebody who turned out to be a sociopath, and he's paying for it now.'

'C'mon, kid.'

'I mean, yeah, it's far-fetched, but people are strange, Jase. They just are. Just because he can't think of anybody who'd want to do him harm doesn't mean there *isn't* somebody.'

I know what Jason's thinking. I know him better than he knows himself. He's thinking about three dead women and wondering if there will be more. And wondering if his client, James Drinker, is the one killing them.

And wondering if that means he has to turn him in.

'Hey, sport,' I say. 'I hate to be the voice of reason, but you can only turn him in for something you *know* he's going to do. Not for something he already did.'

'Right, I know. I know. I can only turn him in if I know he's going to commit a crime in the future, la-de-da-de-da.'

'That's not la-de-da-de-da, kiddo. That's your oath. And you don't know that he's killed *anybody*.'

'I got that part, Shauna. I'm clear on that.'

Snippy, snippy. So it's Moody Jason this morning. Jason doesn't like rules. He doesn't like lines on the road and curbs and stop signs. He likes a fair result, but he doesn't really care if he has to drive over a few front lawns to get there.

'Listen, Jase, if—'

'Hang on.'

'— you think about it—'

47

'Shauna, hold up. My other line's ringing,' Jason says. 'Ten bucks says I know who it is.'

'Monday morning, you start on *Arangold*,' I say to him, but he's already hung up.

12

Jason

Saturday, June 8

No caller ID on the other end. I kill the call with Shauna and answer before my voice mail snatches away the second caller.

'It's James, James Drinker,' he says in a rushed voice. He has my cell phone number from the card I gave him. A defense lawyer has to give out his cell number. He needs to be reachable whenever. 'I didn't kill that girl on the news,' he says. 'I don't even know her.'

'Holly Frazier,' I say to him.

'Right. I don't know her. Did they – They didn't say she was stabbed multiple times, did they? They just said she was stabbed. So maybe it's not the same guy.'

'James,' I say, 'were you like Macaulay Culkin again last night?'

He lets out a loud, anxious breath, like he's about to swallow his phone. 'I was home by myself last night. But this time I went online and searched some news sites. And – and I called my mother from my landline. I – I'm doing this now, I'm making a record every time I'm home at night by myself. So I can prove I didn't go out and kill anybody. That's smart, right? It's freakin' crazy that I have to do that, but it's smart, isn't it?'

Outside my open window, a couple is pushing a stroller, enjoying a lazy Saturday morning. The air still has a hint of that morning cool, but it's going to be oven-hot today.

'That's smart, James. Very. Do you think you could supply me with that information?'

'Supply you with what?'

'That proof you were home last night. The phone call with your mother.'

'Why do you need that?'

'So I have it at the ready, in case the police start looking at you. While it's fresh in our minds.'

'How do I prove to you that I called my mother? You mean phone records?'

'Yes, that's what I mean. Or let me talk to your mother.'

'You want me to tell my mother that she needs to talk to a lawyer I hired so we can confirm that I didn't murder somebody? Are you *kidding* me? It would *kill* her. She's in a nursing home. It would *kill* her.'

'Well, then—'

'And why am I proving this to *you*, Jason? You're supposed to be the one on my side.'

'I am on your side. I am. But I need the information to protect you.'

'You don't *believe* me. You think I murdered that woman, don't you?'

The truth is, I'm not sure I *do* think that. People get stabbed all the time in this city. This could be a domestic incident with an obvious suspect, a boyfriend or something. Jesus, am I getting soft? Did my time off unscrew the part of my brain that reminds me that I'm a defense lawyer, that I'm this guy's warrior, that I'm the one person who holds steady against the tide of the full weight of the government and says, *I'll stand up for you*?

'Let's keep this simple, James, okay? You are telling me you called your mother. And you and I can agree that it would be a good idea for you to have that memorialized. In case the police ever come around. So, let's just do that. Get me that phone record. Call the phone company, or maybe they have your calls online, whatever – get me the information. Okay?'

Silence at the other end. It sounds like this guy might be sobbing. Muffled noises, too hard to tell.

'And if I don't?' he finally says.

I opt for avoidance. It's becoming my specialty.

'One step at a time,' I say.

13

Jason

Sunday, June 9

Late afternoon, I walk the four blocks to my favorite store on the near-north side to buy a new pair of running shoes. Yes, it's early for me. I know that. But it's symbolic. And anyway, I like to wear a new pair around for a few weeks before I start running in them. Just the smell of this place, the fresh rubber soles, brings something back to me that's been missing. I'll be training again within a few months.

It feels good just being inside the store, the signs for upcoming marathons and 10Ks, people going on about their PRs and training regimens. There are three employees working the store: a woman with blond dreadlocks tied loosely together in back; an older blond woman, closer to my age and more attractive; and a scruffy young guy.

I get the girl with the blond dreadlocks, the name *Minnie* on her name tag, dressed in running gear herself, an enthusiastic hard-core triathlete who is equally enthusiastic about my credit card. I buy a new pair of Brooks – I'm loyal – and new arch supports, two pairs of shorts, three tanks, two high-necks, nipple guards, gel packs, the works. I walk, not jog, around the store in the new treads. I've looked forward to this trip to Runner's High all week, the idea of reentering that part of my world, but by the time Minnie is ringing me up at the register – $342.74 later – I'm feeling wrong again, irritable, jumpy, my hands itchy, my tongue thick and pasty, my stomach mumbling nasty thoughts. Outside, it feels like during the hour I spent in the store, someone cranked the furnace way up, the air choking my breath, the sunlight stabbing my eyes.

What are you thinking? You're not going to be running anytime soon. You might as well have flushed that money down the toilet.

I get a bottle of water from the corner convenience store and take a couple of chugs. I pop an Altoid and chew it up, digging out every last granular morsel stuck in my teeth with my tongue. Head down, my eyes on the sun-bleached pavement, I cross the street to the west side, lean against a store window in the shade, and close my eyes.

A man passes me on the street and slows his pace, eyes on me, keeping them on me even when he has to crane his neck backward, a scowl on his face, a look of disgust, because he knows, it's all over me, I'm transparent.

This was a bad idea, I tell myself. *I can't do this.* This date with Alexa the court reporter. What the hell am I doing, thinking I'm in any kind of shape for a relationship with a woman?

Twenty minutes later, I'm seated at the outdoor café just a few blocks from my townhome, a place called Twist that I've wanted to check out since I moved into this neighborhood last winter. I arrived early and snagged a corner table outside, along the railing and looking out over the shopping district.

I see her first: Cleopatra in a blue summer dress. She has a sky-blue hair band, if that's the word, tucking her dark locks behind her ears and fashionable sunglasses, Audrey Hepburn–oversized.

This was a good idea, I tell myself.

She seems very pleased to see me when I raise my hand. She waves back, kind of a cute little gesture, and then comes over and drops across from me.

'*Hey* there,' she says. 'I've always wanted to come to this place.'

'Me, too. I'm glad we could do this.'

Ah, what a day, the full throes of summer (though it's still techni-cally spring), hot and humid but with a nice corner breeze – there's

53

no accounting for the wind patterns in our fair city – and a bustle of shoppers and people just wanting to be outside surrounding us.

Then she removes her sunglasses and the day gets better. Those liquid eyes, taking on the color of her sky-blue sundress. I love women's eyes that change color.

'So, Jason Kolarich,' she says. 'By the way, I never would have pronounced your name correctly if I hadn't heard it used in court.'

I get that all the time. It's a simple name, really. *Kola*, like the drink. *Rich*, like wealthy. 'Most people say *koh-LAR-ick*, which sounds more like a throat disease than a last name.'

She likes that, which is important, because I can't be with a woman who doesn't appreciate my sense of humor. Not that I'm already planning a future with this one. I'm not into the future right now. I'll settle for a decent present. It's pretty damn decent right now.

'You were impressive in court,' she says.

'Yeah? I wasn't sure you'd think so.'

She cocks her head. 'Why not?'

'Oh, the race card. A lot of people find that offensive.'

'But I thought that's why you did it,' she says. 'You wanted him to run away from that accusation. Which he did. And that left him with not much to say. His point was, suburban kids go down there to buy their drugs, and he looked like a suburban kid. But once you equated that with being white, you were making it look like *he* was playing the race card. And once he backed off that, he didn't have much to go on for why your client Billy was suspicious.'

Wow. That's exactly what I did.

She raises her eyebrows expectantly and leans into me. 'Pretty perceptive for a court reporter.'

'Pretty perceptive, period,' I say.

'But especially for a non-lawyer, right?' She leans back and smiles, like she zinged me. 'Lawyers think that nobody's as smart as they are.'

'That's not true.'

'In my experience, it is.'

I think about that for a second, my brain swimming. 'In mine, too, now that you mention it.'

She winks at me and something inside me reacts. Our drinks arrive. Normally, it would be straight vodka or a martini, but I can't handle much booze these days, so I go with a Tanqueray and tonic that is certain to be watered down. Alexa has something in a martini glass with fruit and chocolate in it. We snack on some truffled popcorn that is wicked good. Good times.

'We're not all bad,' I promise her.

She waves me off while she sips her whatever-martini. 'I didn't say that. But the whole system is set up so that we need lawyers. Everything's in code and so complicated that even a Rhodes Scholar wouldn't understand it without a lawyer who got all the secret passwords in law school. And then you guys waltz around the courtroom in your fancy suits and feel so superior to the clients and spectators, like you're Roman warriors in the Colosseum or something.'

I throw up my hands. 'It's a wonder you'd even date a lawyer.'

She drills a finger into the table. 'You call this a date? No. If you want to date me, I want flowers and a white linen tablecloth, and you pick me up and open the door for me. This isn't a date. This is just a drink.'

She winks at me again. A rosy flourish has gathered at her cheeks. The alcohol taking effect, that initial euphoric buzz. She can't be much over a hundred pounds soaking wet, so her tolerance is probably low. I sit back and look up at the clouds, take in the flurry of tourists and shoppers and partiers around me.

'I Googled you, y'know,' she says.

'You Googled me?'

She shrugs. 'A girl can't be too careful these days.'

True enough. I don't even want to ask what she found on the Internet.

'Football star with an attitude problem,' she says. 'Big-time defense lawyer. Some people think you were the undercover lawyer in the thing involving Governor Snow. Oh, sure.' She nods. 'I know all about you.'

'Did it mention I can juggle?'

'Nope.' She gives a grand shake of her head. 'You can juggle?'

'Nope.'

She claps her hands together and laughs. This is going well, and I've hardly spoken. Maybe there's a lesson there.

'Maybe I Googled you, too,' I say.

'Oh, wouldn't *that* be exciting?' she says. 'An only child, grew up in five different cities, went to three high schools, got an associate's degree from Tripton Community College – *Go, Trojans!* – and now I lead the glamorous life of a court reporter, where I transcribe what other people say and sell their words back to them.' Her smile lingers for a while, and then she looks at me sheepishly. 'I shouldn't say it like that. It's a good job. The hours are flexible, pay is decent, sometimes the stuff I transcribe is interesting. Your hearing was interesting, for example. You actually made me feel sorry for a rich suburban white kid.'

I finish my shitty drink. Alexa is still working on hers. Probably best I not get too far ahead of her on the drink count.

'Do you believe what you said in court?' she asks me.

I think about that. 'That's not a question I ask. I ask, can I sell it?'

'I know. But do you believe it?'

'I believe the cops saw this clean-cut white kid and thought he stuck out like a sore thumb in the Eagleton Housing Projects. They figured he had no business being there, except an illegal one. I'd have thought the same thing. I don't blame that cop at all for what he thought. But the law says you can't base probable cause solely on race, and the cop did. That's the loose thread in their case, and my job is to find that loose thread, wind my finger around it, and yank and tug on it as hard as I possibly can.'

'Does it bother you?' she asks. 'Getting guilty people off?'

I scrounge through the remnants of the truffled popcorn while I think that over. It's a simple question, after all. The simplest ones are often the hardest. I go with the stock answer.

'I'm part of a system. A system that would be very scary indeed if someone didn't stand up for the accused. If we just took the government's word that someone is a criminal . . .' I raise my hand. 'Someone's gotta stand post at the wall.'

She watches me, like she's waiting for more. But she doesn't push. She smiles, nods, sips her drink, enjoys the breeze across her face.

Sometimes, I do not say. *Sometimes it bothers me.*

'So you're an only child,' I say, changing the subject.

She nods. 'My parents married late. My mom was forty when she had me. Back then, forty was considered *ancient* to have kids. She said she didn't want to push her luck and try for more kids.' She looks down, runs her finger over the rim of her glass. 'They retired to Florida and died within a year of each other. Cancer, both of them.'

'I'm sorry.'

The waiter comes by and asks me if I'm having another. My eyes pass to Alexa's.

'Well, we've had our one non-date drink,' I say. 'Are you game for another?'

A pause. A momentary appraisal. I don't know if she's debating or if she's just feigning reluctance to keep me guessing. I used to watch a suspect react to a question during an interrogation and I knew, I *knew* whether he was lying before he even spoke. I can look a client or a witness in the eye today and, nine times out of ten, I can read everything he's thinking. But stick me at a table with a beautiful woman and it's like I'm trying to decipher hieroglyphics.

'Give us a second,' I say to the waiter. 'She's trying to decide if I'm worthy.'

She laughs. The waiter leaves.

'You're not trying to get me drunk,' she says. Part question, part flirtation. A certain part of my anatomy takes note. Jesus, how long since *that* happened?

'The thought never crossed my mind, Ms. Himmel.'

A smile appears and evaporates. 'I should warn you that I'm an old-fashioned girl.'

'Good,' I answer. 'Perfect. We'll shake hands good-bye. I'll let you in on the secret lawyer's handshake.'

The smile returns. Sincere, I think, not just polite. But again – like translating an ancient Chinese scroll. For all I know, she thinks I'm a complete asswipe.

'Seriously, no pressure either way,' I say. 'This has been fun. I'd love to keep hanging out, but either way, I'm good.'

I catch the waiter's eye. He returns, the question still lingering.

'I think we'll just take the check,' Alexa says.

'Please,' I say to the waiter, not skipping a beat, with as upbeat a tone as I can manage, like my chest isn't burning. Have I been rejected or is this a *See you again, take it slow* thing?

'This was fun,' I manage. 'Here.' I slide a business card across the table. 'You probably already have one of these, but here's another one, my cell is on it. I'd love to get together again sometime, but no pressure. The ball's in your court. Okay?'

'Okay. Thanks, Jason. You're a really interesting guy.'

Great. I'm interesting.

She's better off. She's making the smart move.

Run, Alexa, run.

The check comes. I already have my card out for him. Alexa digs into her purse and pulls out her cell phone. Already making arrangements for the rest of her evening? She's actually making a call, or checking her messages, right here in front of me?

Then my phone buzzes in my pocket. I look down, then back up at her. I reach for the phone and answer it. 'Hello?' I say, my voice playing back through Alexa's phone as well.

'Hello, Jason?' she says.

'Yes?'

'This is Alexa Himmel. You remember, from the drink?'

'Oh, sure. The non-date. I'm really interesting, and you're old-fashioned.'

'That's right. Hey, I was wondering what you're doing tonight for dinner?'

'Oh, I'd love to, Alexa. But unfortunately, you're not a lawyer, so you're probably not smart enough to hang out with me. I'd have to keep explaining things to you.'

'But I thought you'd like being the dominant person in the relationship. Smarter and more successful. Isn't that what all men want?'

I punch out my phone and make a face, mock injury. 'That's cold, woman. That is *arctic*.'

She bursts into laughter. 'You should have seen the look on your face when I asked for the check. You should have seen it. I'm sorry.' She puts a hand over her mouth but is still giggling. 'I'm so sorry, that was rude.'

I'm here to entertain.

'I mean, you're obviously this really nice guy and super impressive. I'll bet – I'll bet nobody's ever done that to you. Turned you down like that.'

I'm blushing, of all things. She got me.

'Jason Kolarich,' she says, clearing her throat and addressing me with mock formality, 'I would be very grateful if you'd join me for dinner tonight.'

I shrug my shoulders. 'I should warn you that I'm very old-fashioned.'

'Then I'll let you pay.'

This woman matches me jab for jab. That's probably going to be a problem for my ego. But she looks so casually elegant in her summer dress, and that edge to her, that sarcasm, that challenge, is much too much to resist.

'I'm powerless to say no,' I answer.

14

Jason

Wednesday, June 12

I handle a couple of court appearances in the morning, a bond hearing on a cannabis possession – the brother of a law school classmate whom I'm representing as a favor – and a status hearing on an armed robbery, a kid who was whacked out on meth who held up a strip club and got as far as the front door before the gun discharged into his foot.

Afterward, I return to the office and look at the stack of files in the corner that Shauna has given me for the *Arangold* trial. She identified a particular aspect of the trial – a fight over the flooring that was put in the civic auditorium – for me to handle. I need to read some depositions and go over some architectural drawings with the client, but my mind starts to wander on page one. I hate working on this case, and I haven't even started yet.

I light a match, hold it upright, and run through the words again:

I've got tar on my feet and I can't see.
All the birds look down and laugh at me.

Miss again – this time my index finger getting in on the fun with my thumb, the flesh near the knuckle. The match goes into the Styrofoam cup with the others.

I'm thinking about this meth-head client, whom I got through the public defender program – the PD outsources its overflow; the hourly rate sucks, but it keeps you busy and sharp. This kid has been in and out of rehab twice, done two stints inside, and is undoubtedly looking at a third stay in both. He'll fail rehab almost assuredly and find himself back under the spell of that drug, and next time he might shoot somebody else instead of his own foot. There are so many clients like that, especially in the drug world, for whom you have the feeling you're just a temporary stop on a merry-go-round that will end only when they're dead or sentenced to serious time.

Sometimes this job sucks. It doesn't help that I feel like shit, out of sorts, my head ringing like the old rotary phone hanging on the wall in my house growing up, plus I have the fucking dry mouth again. I chew an Altoid and chug half a bottle of water.

A half hour later, Joel Lightner waltzes in and I'm feeling better. At my request, Joel had drinks with one of the cops investigating the stabbings of those three women on the north side. He likes to do that anyway. It's good for business to keep his former colleagues on the police force happy. A private investigator needs lots of favors, and it's easier to call one in if you've bought the cop a steak and a night full of whiskey.

I already have printouts from the Internet, mostly *Herald* articles, on each of the three murders, but I've read enough media accounts over the years on things I've been involved with – the public corruption case against Senator Almundo, the gubernatorial scandal, my prosecution of six members of the Tenth Street Crew for the torture-murder of a witness – to know that reporters only rarely get the story right, and almost never complete. They pick and choose what is relevant and sensational, no different from writers of fiction.

Alicia Corey, age twenty-six, was a stripper who was last seen leaving her club at about two-thirty in the early morning of Wednesday, May 22. She was found dead the next morning in her apartment, the victim of 'six or seven' stab wounds. There was no sign of forced entry; police believe she was accosted outside her apartment and the assailant forced his way in, presumably at knifepoint.

Lauren Gibbs, twenty-eight, was a bank teller who also ran a website design business out of her home on the north side. She was found dead of 'multiple' stab wounds at her house on Friday, May 24. None of the articles on Lauren mentioned the number of wounds.

And then Holly Frazier, twenty-seven, a graduate student at St. Margaret's downtown and a barista at Starbucks, found dead of 'at least half a dozen' stab wounds near midnight on Friday, June 7.

I put down the papers I've printed out. Hard to discern a pattern when all you have is media reports. The police have not even confirmed that they believe these murders are related. But they haven't denied it, either.

Joel helps himself to a chair and uses my desk for a footrest. 'Turns out one of the main cops working this case is Chris Austin's nephew.'

I don't know who Chris Austin is. Probably a cop Joel worked with before he turned to the lucrative career of private investigation.

'Nice kid, the nephew. Vance is his name. Guys must give him shit for that. Anyway, I didn't get Vance, but I got one of the uniforms assisting on the task force who loved talking about the stuff. He spilled all he could for me and probably a little more. The kid can drink Scotch.'

I roll my hand for him to get to the punch line.

'What's with your hand?' he asks me. 'You smashing it with a hammer?'

'I don't have a hammer.'

He sniffs the air. 'You're lighting matches in here?'

'Keeps me awake,' I say. 'When I get bored.'

Joel shakes his head, like I'm not making any sense, but that it's not the first time he's felt that and it's not worth pursuing. He'd be right about all of that, especially the last part.

'Anyway,' he says, 'these three murders are definitely the same offender. All three women – Alicia Corey, Lauren Gibbs, Holly Frazier. Right?'

'Right.'

'He butchered them. Not just clean stabs. It was like he gutted them. Enjoyed it. Real violent. Angry guy, this offender.'

'Anything else connecting them? Any suspects?'

'None he mentioned. But there was one other thing,' he says. 'This guy has a signature.'

'A signature beyond gutting them like fish?'

'Yeah. Something else. Don't know what, though. That's where the lid came down. I mean, that's going to be real hush-hush, right?'

I nod. If the offender has some signature to his murders, the cops will usually keep that information out of the press. It makes it easier to distinguish real confessions from bogus ones, the crazies who want to take credit for crimes they didn't commit.

'He didn't give any hint? Anything at all about this signature?'

'No, and I didn't ask. I *wouldn't* ask. Guy could lose his badge over that.'

True enough. 'And what about the three women? Any pattern to them?'

He blinks his eyes no, a quiet shake of the head. 'All pretty young. "Nice-looking," he said, but not bombshells or anything. Well, the one was a stripper at Knockers. He said she was pretty hot. Nice figure, fake boobs.'

That was the one James Drinker said he dated. He got very defensive when I doubted that a stripper would be interested in him.

'Actually, what this uniform said was, she *used* to have fake boobs. Sounds like our offender was pretty vicious with that knife.'

I shudder. Did the freaky redheaded guy who sat in the same chair Lightner is sitting in do those things to those women? Lightner's eyes catch mine. We're thinking the same thing.

'You want me to look at your client now,' he says. 'James Drinker.'

I nod my head. 'At least check out that he's being straight with me. Name, address, work, that kind of thing. And obviously, you'll be happy to do this free of charge.'

'Obviously. All of a sudden, I'm a candy striper.' Lightner makes a face, but he knows I need this. I'm his best client, too.

I reach for the file that Marie opened for James Drinker. The informational sheet is always appended to the left side of the open file. I take a look at the sheet, and it looks weird immediately.

'This doesn't look like his handwriting,' I say. 'This looks like a woman's handwriting.'

I buzz my intercom. *'Yes, Your Highness?'* Marie squawks. She knows I don't have a client in here, thus the attitude.

'James Drinker,' I say. 'The weird redheaded guy? His info sheet looks like a woman's hand—'

'That's 'cause I wrote it for him. He said he sprained his hand or something and he couldn't write it himself. So he dictated the information to me.'

I stifle the easy smart-ass reply – *You take dictation?* – and hang up.

'Okay,' Joel says. 'James Drinker. Give me the sheet.'

'James Drinker, 3611 West Townsend. No phone number listed. No phone number?'

'That's Townsend and Kensington,' Joel says. 'Not a nice neighborhood. That's – I know that building. There's an apartment building at that intersection.'

Lightner knows every building in this city. It gets annoying.

'He says he's a mechanic at Higgins Auto Body,' I say. I give him the address, but he probably already knows it.

'Okay. Okay. Basic background?'

'Yeah, is he who he claims to be, criminal background, vitals.'

'Photos? A day in the life?'

'Oh, don't bother,' I say. 'I just want to make sure this guy's for real. I owe you one.'

'You owe me, like, fifty. Give me a day or two and you'll know whether he's for real. And get some sleep, wouldja?' he adds on his way out. 'You look like shit.'

15

Jason

I rise with my client, Billy Braden, as the Honorable Donald T. Goodson enters the courtroom, stumbles on a stair, and tries not to look embarrassed as he takes his seat at the bench.

Billy releases a heavy breath. This is the ruling that will decide his fate. He looks older than his nineteen years, genuinely terrified. I consider mumbling words of encouragement, but there's no point. We're going to know soon enough. And it may not be the worst thing for him to have sweated out this whole thing. When I first met him, he was a cocky kid with his hair hanging in his face and one of these rich-kid senses of entitlement, the trust-fund baby who was born on third base and thinks he hit a triple. But he buzzed his hair before the hearing a couple of weeks ago, at my insistence, and coupled with his nice blue suit and tie, he actually looks like somebody who could make something of himself if he put forth even minimal effort.

'State versus William Braden,' the clerk calls out, as if there were any other cases up on the call.

Judge Goodson looks out at the attorneys but doesn't greet us. That's probably one of the reasons lawyers always give him low marks on the confidential evaluations that the bar associations pass around. If he would just show basic courtesy to the bar, they'd probably give him halfway decent marks, and he could have his own felony court-room. But some people just can't get past themselves.

The nausea announces its arrival inside me, weaving through my stomach and drifting upward. I take a shallow breath.

His Honor raises his glass and reads from a prepared text. 'This matter comes before the Court on a motion to quash arrest and suppress evidence. The Court has heard testimony from the arresting officer, Detective Nicholas Forrest, and has considered written and oral arguments of counsel. The Court is now prepared to rule.'

Next to me, Billy Braden sucks in his breath and holds it.

'The Court finds that Detective Forrest lacked probable cause to arrest the defendant or to search him for the presence of illegal con-traband. Thus, the arrest of William Braden is hereby quashed, and any evidence of the illegal narcotics obtained incident to that arrest is suppressed in any future prosecution of this matter. The Court is filing a written opinion today consistent with this ruling.'

Billy exhales, his posture easing with the flood of relief.

'Mr Braden,' says the judge. Billy perks back up, back to military posture. 'There is not a single person in this courtroom who doesn't know that you had an eight-ball of crack cocaine on your person when you were arrested. You are free to go, Mr Braden, because our Consti-tution is concerned not with individual cases but with the rule of law. It's a crucial aspect of our system, but it is a technicality no less. You are a very, very lucky young man. I trust that I will not be seeing you back in this courtroom?'

Billy raises his hand as if he's about to give sworn testimony. 'I promise,' he says.

I wouldn't put money down on that promise. I wouldn't bet a used napkin. But for now, Billy has a new lease on life. His mother, Karen, gives me a big hug, and his father shakes my hand and covers it with the other. 'We can't thank you enough,' he says. 'Really, Jason.'

'My pleasure.'

Billy and I clasp hands, and he does that bump-hug thing against my shoulder. 'Hey, man,' he whispers, 'I owe you big. Seriously. Fuckin' *seriously*.'

'Glad to help, Billy,' I say.

He looks at me for a long moment, winks at me, smacks my arm, and leaves the courtroom with his parents.

16

Jason

Alexa and I step down from the promenade along the highway and into the small park near the beach. We sit at one of the stone benches and remove our shoes and socks. I angle away from her, slip out an Altoid, and pop it in my mouth as I get to my feet.

'You're sure this is okay?' she asks me.

'Why wouldn't it be?' I turn to her. She is in partial shadow, the overhead lighting catching one side of her face, the breeze off the lake playing with those straight bangs on her forehead. A beautiful sight. She even looks great in the dark. Better, actually – there is something about her that seems more at ease in the dark.

'Your knee,' she says. 'It's hard to walk in sand.'

'My knee's fine.' That's actually true. I can't run or anything like that, but there are actually pockets of time now when I don't even think about it in my daily routine, don't even recite the words of caution before I stand up or hustle through a crosswalk.

I'm tired of even thinking about it. I want to take in the moment. Dinner at Schaefer's, a bottle of Brunello di Montalcino – half a glass for me – and now a stroll along the lake.

As we walk down the sand to the shoreline, she takes my hand, ostensibly for support, but then she leaves it in that position as we walk. I'm not the most romantic guy in the world, I admit, but there's something sweet and intimate about holding hands. Talia and I used to always say that we wanted to grow old together and hold hands walking down the beach. That memory, casually breezing through my brain, freezes me for a beat, but it doesn't paralyze me like it did once upon a time. You just finally move on. You take steps: initial, gut-wrenching grief, then denial, then a dull ache that colors your world that will never, ever subside – and then one day it does; one day you look up and you realize it's actually possible to move on.

Our toes sink into the wet sand. The lake is endless, alternately blue, black, even purple. The air is thick and damp. Around us is the gentle harmony of waves crashing ashore and vehicles whisking by at high speeds on the highway twenty yards to the west; there is something special about feeling like there is nowhere else in the world right now that you can hear what I'm hearing.

'This lake is why I moved here,' Alexa says. 'For some reason, it makes me feel free.'

I know what she means. I live three blocks from the lake, a couple miles north of here. I always run along the water. My muscles are restless, yearning for the day when I can do it again, even as I'm unsure that day will ever come.

It's not my only yearning. Our first date last weekend ended at Alexa's door with a hug. Not even a kiss. She's an old-fashioned girl.

'Do you miss being married?' she asks me.

That isn't a question I expected. I spend my days being fast on my feet, ready for any challenge a witness or judge might hurl my way, but these simple personal questions always tie me in knots. But Mom always said, if you aren't sure what to say, go with the truth.

'I miss Talia,' I say. 'I never really cared about a marriage certificate, but she did, and I was fine with it. But yeah, I miss her.'

She looks up at me as we walk but doesn't respond. That probably wasn't a crowd-pleaser, but she asked.

'That was very honest of you,' she says.

I laugh. 'Brutally so.'

'There's nothing brutal about it. Would I be better off not asking and not knowing?'

'Maybe.'

'No.' She shakes her head firmly. 'A girl needs to know what she's getting into.'

Interesting choice of words. Am I hooking her in? Am I even trying to? Sometimes I feel like I'm just feeling through the dark, not knowing what I'll touch and unsure of what I'm even reaching for.

'I had my heart broken once,' she says. 'Not marriage, but I would've married him if he'd asked.'

'What happened?' There is a pause, longer than necessary. 'Brutal honesty,' I add.

'It turned out he was *already* married.'

'Ah. That would be a complication.'

'Yeah . . .' Her voice trails off. She looks out over the lake. 'Yeah, it pretty much sucked, I have to say.'

'How long ago did this happen?' I ask.

'A few weeks ago.'

I stop in my tracks. 'A few *weeks*—'

She bursts into a laugh. 'Sorry. Couldn't help myself.' She faces me and puts her hand on my chest. That simple touch flips a switch on inside me: *All systems go!* 'It was, like, three years ago,' she says. 'He was a jerk. And I don't miss him, to answer your next question.'

I move my face closer to hers. 'That wasn't my next question.'

'No?' Her mouth moves closer to mine, her head angling to the right. 'What,' she whispers, 'was your next question?'

I whisper back, 'I wish I had something clever to say, but I just want to kiss you.'

'That's clever enough for me.'

I don't care how many times you've done it, you don't forget a first kiss: the awkwardness and trepidation, each of you trying to find that fit, that rhythm. When it's good, it's like few things in this world. And this one is good. I taste red wine when we pull away.

She leans back and looks at me, her eyes searching me. As a rule, I don't like being searched. I never know what someone might find.

'Well, gee, Jason Kolarich. This is pret-ty romantic. You sure know how to sweep a girl off her feet.'

I don't have the foggiest idea how to do that.

'I still don't have anything clever to say,' I admit.

She rests her hands on my chest. 'Then how about you take me home?' she says.

We walk along the beach until we hit Ash Street, the closest principal artery, and walk up the stairs, wipe off our feet, put on our shoes, and hail a cab. Alexa lives outside the city in a small suburb to the south and west, Overton Ridge, so the cab takes a while with the traffic. We talk about all sorts of things: last fall's presidential election (she has opinions, I think the candidates are all full of shit); music (she can tolerate R.E.M., which is a relief because that could be a deal breaker); her childhood bouncing around from town to town while her father opened new Kmarts (I didn't even know that was a specialty, opening new stores). But as we pull off the highway and turn left down Wadsworth, the conversation starts to dissipate, replaced with tension. It seems to be a given what's going to happen next, and I sense it's meaningful to her, that she isn't casual about sex.

I don't want to be, either. I want to care about it. I want somebody, or at least some*thing*, to matter to me again.

She lives in a small brick bungalow, three from the corner. It hardly looks like we've left the city; in a way this block, with its low rooflines and tiny plots, resembles the neighborhood in the city where I grew up, Leland Park.

She uses her key and opens the door. I follow her in as if there were never a doubt. She takes me by the hand and leads me past a small room, a combination living room–dining room that is well kept, spotless. Her bedroom is also small – the whole place is – and also immaculate. Hardwood floors, wall closet, a single window with flowery drapes, a queen-size bed with about a hundred pillows and a teddy bear. The teddy bear is interesting.

Silently, she positions me by the bed and then faces me, taking my

71

face in her hands and kissing me differently than the first time, more assertive but still very soft. We remove each other's clothes methodically, gently. No tearing or ripping. We are taking it slowly, which works for me, savoring the moment, treating it like it's something unique and special. Finally, she backs up onto the bed, me hovering over her, and we touch each other everywhere, caressing surfaces, until her tongue is more urgent in my mouth, which I take as my cue, and then a switch is flipped and everything is more primitive, more aggressive, more needy, and we find a rhythm and I do better than I expected in terms of holding out, but when it happens I grunt so loudly I surprise myself.

We lie quietly panting, her hands drawing circles on my back, my face nestled in her hair, for a good ten minutes. I hear a car pass by outside. I hear a bunch of people, talking in that cheerful and familiar way, lubricated by alcohol and heading to their next destination, bed or another bar or late-night chow.

'Don't hurt me,' Alexa whispers.

For a second, I'm sure I heard her wrong. I raise my head. 'Did I – hurt you?'

She eases out from under me, my question unanswered, and heads to the bathroom. I ease off the condom, which was basically coming off anyway as my little man retreats into postcoital hibernation, and wrap it in a tissue. I put on my boxers and lie on the bed.

Nice night. As I stare at the ceiling, my mind drifts. To Talia, scrunching up her nose at one of my cornball jokes; to Emily Jane, our daughter, quietly breathing as she sleeps in the fold of my arm; to Shauna, watching over me while pretending she's not; to a serial killer butchering young women on the north side.

I sit up on the bed and wait for Alexa. I think of calling out to her. It's been, like, ten or fifteen minutes. But hey, maybe nature called, or it's some feminine thing that I don't understand.

It all comes back with a rush, the needle pricks inside my head and the stormy stomach, the bile in my throat, my mouth dry as sand. I steady myself and wait out the first wave.

Finally, Alexa walks back into the room. 'Sorry about that,' she says, casual in her tone. She crawls onto the bed and nestles into my arms.

'Are you good?' I ask.

'Oh, I'm great.' She adjusts herself to look at me. 'I'm great. That was – I really enjoyed that.'

That would be more believable had she not left the room for so long, but I see no reason to let my imagination run wild. It was great, and if there is sex a second time, it will be even better.

'Will you stay?' she asks.

I tell her I will. I suddenly realize how exhausted I am. We lie in silence, atop the covers, for how long I don't know, all energy draining from my body, thoughts beginning to mangle themselves together in dreams. As I fade off to twilight, my defenses down, it comes to me as naturally as the sound of my voice, as obvious as day following night: James Drinker killed those women.

17

Jason

Saturday, June 15

I wake with a start from a dream – dirt in my mouth, insects on my skin, my hands on the railing, trying to hold on but the gravitational pull is too strong – that quickly vaporizes into a mash of nonsense. I turn to Alexa, who has part of the bedspread pulled up over her. I am shivery, shaky, uneasy. I manage to make out the time on my watch: It's past two in the morning.

I climb out of bed gingerly and find my pants. I dig into the pockets, but I don't find them. That's where they were, I'm sure of it, but they're not there anymore. I try every pocket, patting them down, turning them inside out, but they aren't *there*.

I gently pat the nightstand by the bed, almost knocking over the alarm clock, touching a sticky note, then something circular that is probably makeup. No. Not here.

I get down on my hands and knees on the hardwood floor and feel around. I check everywhere, picking up lint along the way, particles of sand from our beach walk, various other minuscule items you find on a floor.

I tiptoe outside the bedroom, close the door, and flip the switch in the nearby kitchen, squinting in the urine-colored light, retracing my steps from the front door. Nothing.

My head is echoing a gong now, my limbs twitching. I ease back into the bedroom and drop to my hands and knees again, repeating the same steps and expecting different results. I reach far under the bed, and my hand finds something small, granular – a mint from the Jurassic era – but otherwise nothing. 'Shit,' I say, my hands moving wildly along the floor. 'Shit, shit, *shit*.'

I hear a soft moan from the bed. Alexa rolls back over toward me and says, in a sleepy mumble, 'Is everything okay?'

'Oh, yeah, sure,' I say quietly as I pull one leg through my pants. 'But I need to get going. Somewhere I need to be tomorrow morning. I totally forgot.'

Alexa pushes herself up slowly. In the darkness, as far as my eyes have adjusted to it, she looks like she's still climbing the ladder to wakefulness, peering at me with sleepy eyes. 'You're . . . leaving?'

'I have to. I'm sorry.'

She rubs her face. 'Is it your knee?'

'No, nothing like that.' I sit on the bed next to her. 'Let's do something tomorrow. Okay?'

She pauses. I don't know if she's considering it or if she's still half asleep.

'Call me tomorrow,' she says.

I press my lips to her forehead. 'See you tomorrow,' I say. I throw on my clothes and head for the door. I go to the corner and try to hail a cab on Wadsworth, but there's nothing here this time of night – I'm in a suburb, not the city – so I walk down a few more blocks to what passes for a downtown, a couple of banks and restaurants and a children's store, and give it another few minutes. Finally, I call information on my phone, and after a couple of tries locate a company that will send a cab my way. I stand on the sidewalk, hopping on the balls of my feet, my thoughts careening wildly to dark subjects. A homeless man has taken up residence within the cocoon of a travel agency doorstep, a dingy SpongeBob SquarePants blanket over him, a skanky black beard obscuring his face. I can't tell if he's asleep or watching me, motionless.

A police squad car rolls down the street. I consider skulking into shadows, but they've already seen me. I'm committing no crime, but I can't shake a feeling of something like guilt – but not guilt, not exactly, just a sense that I am wrong, that I am . . . not right. 'Waiting for a cab,' I tell them when they slow the patrol car and roll down the window before moving on, after a curt appraisal.

Guilty, but not guilty. Wrong, not right.

I am wrong. I am not right. I am falling.

The cab arrives. I show the driver a hundred-dollar bill and tell him it's his if we get home in twenty minutes. If there's no traffic, the highway makes that a possibility. My knees bob up and down inside the sticky taxi, the cheap torn seating and the inane interviews from some entertainment show on the small video screen.

James Drinker is gutting women like fish and hiding behind me, the guy who isn't supposed to say anything, isn't allowed to say anything, would be *punished* for saying anything at all to anybody at all. I put my head between my knees and grit my teeth. My tongue is like a piece of damp fur, my breath putrid, my forehead slimy with sweat.

I throw the driver the money and push myself out of the cab. I run up to my door, get in, give the door a push before I bound up the stairs two at a time, all the way to the third story, and rush to the bathroom. I open the cabinet under the sink and find the box for the allergy medicine, a white box with an orange stripe.

I pull out the silver-foiled sheet and pop one of the pills out, chew it up, and fall to my haunches. I wipe sweat from my eyes and fall back against the wall, finally finding a gentle, warm place on my bathroom floor.

Relax, I tell myself. *Everything's fine. Just because Drinker is a weirdo doesn't mean he's a killer. You don't have to do anything, and you can't, anyway. And this other thing you're dealing with – it's going to be fine. You need to do something, but you will, you always have; you overcame Talia's and Emily's deaths, you overcame poverty and a fucked-up childhood, you can do anything you want, anything at all.*

It'll be fine, I promise myself as warmth spreads through me. *It's all going to be fine.*

PEOPLE VS. JASON KOLARICH
TRIAL, DAY 1
Monday, December 9

18

Shauna

Roger Ogren completes his opening statement at two-thirty. His presentation is what Jason predicted it would be: efficient, to the point, not flashy or hyperbolic. He is, according to Jason, a lifer at the office, a guy who interned during law school, started in traffic court when he got his law degree, and has spent nearly a quarter-century handling major felonies. I've struggled to guess what the upshot will be on drawing a veteran prosecutor. Has he fallen into bad habits that I can manipulate? Will he be wise to any tactical maneuvers we dream up? The best I can get from Jason, other than thoroughly unhelpful comments like 'Roger is Roger,' is that Ogren puts on a straightforward case free of theatrics and imagination but may have the occasional blind spot for a creative defense attorney. (Now if I only knew a creative defense attorney – at least one who isn't my client.)

Age has robbed Ogren of most of his hair and left it heavily grayed; cancer took away a good thirty pounds. Tall and thin and weathered, experienced and street-smart, careful and humorless – this is my adversary. I try to make it a habit to get along with opposing counsel, but then again, nearly every case I've ever tried was in the civil courts, where the dispute is over money, and where few of the attorneys have any illusions about their clients and sometimes are willing to share as much in off-the-record, colorful commentary. Prosecutors, however, are different. Their client is the state, the people, and many of them bring a holier-than-thou approach to their jobs. Defendants are the bad guys, criminals who must be incarcerated, and thus their attorneys, who search for dust to kick up or technicalities on which to seize, are likewise unsavory.

Judge Judith Bialek – 'Judge Judy' behind her back – is a former prosecutor and a trial court judge going on eighteen years now. The bad news is she's inclined toward the prosecution, the good news that Jason always did well in her courtroom when he was prosecuting felonies. I've noted a crimp in her expression from time to time when she's looked over at Jason sitting in a chair that she probably never expected him to occupy.

'Ms. Tasker,' she booms to me, looking over her glasses, 'does the defense still wish to reserve its opening statement?'

It's been a debate between Jason and me all along. I want to deliver the opening statement now, to tell the jury, right now, right this second, before any impressions can cement in their minds, that Jason didn't kill anybody. I'm a believer that many jurors make up their minds after opening statements, and if I hold back now, Roger Ogren gets out his first impression without me giving mine. Strike that – the defense *is* giving a first impression, but not a favorable one: We have something up our sleeve, something perhaps too clever by half, not a straightforward, just-the-facts presentation like our adversary. Roger Ogren has the facts, the defense has snake oil.

'We will reserve, yes, Judge,' I say, standing at my seat.

Jason, who wanted us to hold back our defense, won our internal debate. He might be right. On these matters, he usually is. But the truth, which I prefer not to confront, is that I went along with his idea because I was afraid of overruling him and then being wrong. That is something they don't talk about in law school and something that attorneys in civil litigation rarely experience – the all-consuming fear that your mistake will land a client in prison.

The truth is that I'm absolutely terrified of making one of those mistakes.

19

Jason

'It was the right decision,' I say to Shauna after Judge Bialek calls a recess following Roger Ogren's opening statement. Over the last two weeks, she has argued fiercely for delivering the defense's opening statement at the start of the case, as is tradition – so much so that she actually wrote and presented her opening statement to me two nights ago in an effort to change my mind. It was a great opening, well couched and expertly delivered, but she was never going to change my mind about this. There's no way we're telling the jury what happened yet. I know this more than Shauna does.

Because I know things my lawyer doesn't.

Shauna looks at me, poker-faced. The jury hasn't filtered out yet, and she doesn't want to betray any reactions, any emotions, in front of them. Plus there is the gallery behind us, a plentiful group of reporters and onlookers, all of whom would be more than happy to send tweets or post online stories about a perceived 'disharmony among the defense team' or 'surprised reactions' from a lawyer or from me. I've been surprised at the media's interest in this case, which owes primarily to the fact that many people believe that I was the private attorney who played a central role in the scandal that embroiled our last governor, Carlton Snow. I was, and I did. But I've never acknowledged it publicly. Shauna wanted me to do so now in a blatant attempt to influence the jury pool, to trumpet the work that I did for the federal government, to display me to the public as a whistle-blower on corruption, a do-gooder who helped stop bad people from doing bad things. *From whistle-blower to accused murderer* was how one of the local papers blazed it in a feature story, even without my saying anything.

'You doing okay? I didn't think Ogren was that good. You doing okay?' This from Bradley John, the lone associate at our law firm, a young guy with a lot of talent and a terrific work ethic. If I could get him to cut his hair so he didn't look like the lead singer in some cheesy boy band, he might have a future in this profession.

'Ogren was good,' I say. 'He was what he needed to be.'

'There's water if you want it,' he says, nudging the bottle toward me.

'Okay, thanks, kid.' I stifle a snicker and catch eyes with Shauna. Among the other tasks she has delegated to young Bradley, Shauna presumably has given him the assignment of babysitting me, making sure I never get dry mouth, never come suddenly unglued in the middle of a long day of trial.

When it was bad for me, when I was scraping the bottom this past summer, I would use the dry mouth I was experiencing as an excuse to reach for my tin of Altoids. *My mouth is feeling kind of sticky and dry, better pop a mint!* I even used the excuse when I was alone, as if I were somehow fooling myself with the ruse. You know your life is going off the rails when you tell yourself the lie you've created for everyone else, and you believe it.

And the ruse was no casual thing. I did research. I bought a dozen different brands of breath mints, brought them home and opened each container, examining each mint individually to identify the one that bore the closest resemblance to a thirty-milligram tablet of OxyContin.

I ended up going with Altoids, even though they weren't the best replica, because when I've eaten mints in the past, it was usually that brand. Every morning, I replenished my Altoids tin with a half dozen new Oxy pills, enough for one every two hours of a workday and a couple extra in case I went straight from work to dinner. It became my top priority, ensuring a proper supply of OxyContin before I left the house.

Of course, I also needed to have real Altoids, in case someone saw me partaking and asked me for one. *Hey, could I bum one of those off you?* I couldn't very well drop a tablet of immediate-release oxycodone into their hands, which would have given them a lot more than minty breath. So I always carried around two of the mini-tins, the red peppermint tin for the painkillers and the blue tin of wintergreen mints for curiously strong breath freshening. I lived with the nagging fear of making a mistake and handing a friend or colleague the wrong tin.

More ridiculously still, I went through the same routine at home, sticking a sleeve of the Oxy tablets in a box of allergy medicine, even though I've never been allergic to anything in my entire life. But just in case, on the off chance that I might have a female visitor to my house, again I needed a ruse for my painkiller habit. I remember driving to the pharmacy, looking for a box of allergy medicine for my disguise, and not even knowing what to say to the pharmacist, finally settling on hay fever because my mother used to have that problem in the summer.

'I'm doing fine,' I say to Bradley, making sure Shauna hears it, too. I *am* fine. It's been over four months now, and I feel separation from the drugs. And I sure as hell am not going to come apart in front of my jury, who will scan me throughout the trial for any hint of emotional instability, among other things.

But the harshest truth I've ever had to accept is the one I swallowed a few months back: I lost control once, and I can't ever be one hundred percent sure I won't lose control again. I'm now an addict, and I'll be one for the rest of my life.

The judge reenters the room, and everyone rises. The jury filters back into their assigned seats. In response to Judge Bialek, Roger Ogren rises.

'The People call Officer Martin Garvin,' he says.

20

Shauna

Marty Garvin is a young cop, mid-twenties, with three years in uniform as a patrol officer. He looks more like an accountant, a bookish sort with a long nose that dominates his face. He is soft-spoken and careful with his words as he relates his background. It's clear that he is not a veteran witness; he pauses before each answer, measuring his words, probably a bit too much for the liking of the jury. But I have to concede that he comes off as earnest and straightforward.

They start with the 911 call, which started this whole affair. Technically, Officer Garvin is not the one to authenticate this recording, but we stipulated to its admissibility rather than force the prosecution to drag in the 911 dispatcher. Sequentially, this is the first step in the story, and I don't blame Roger Ogren for wanting to start with it.

The words echo through the silent courtroom, maybe the only words that the jury will ever hear directly from Jason's mouth:

'There's been a . . . death. Someone's been . . . There's been a murder. Please come . . . please come right away.'

On the tape, Jason's voice is ambiguous. Shaky, but not distraught – not as distraught as I would have liked him to sound, but not nonchalant, either. Sad, maybe. Disturbed, but not unhinged. If you knew Jason, you could believe that this is him sounding upset, the stoic warrior trying to keep it together. The problem is, the jurors don't know him. It is one of the many incongruities of the courtroom: People who are making a decision that could affect the rest of Jason's life know him less than anybody he's ever met.

The jurors listen with furrowed brows, some of their eyes closed, trying to envision the person delivering those words. The words of a distressed man? The words of a cold-blooded killer? My take is they could interpret this 911 call in whatever way necessary to suit their conclusions.

'I arrived just after midnight – I believe it was twelve-fifty A.M. – the first hour of July thirty-first,' says Garvin. 'The defendant met me at the front door of his town house.'

The defendant, not Jason. Depersonalizing the adversary. Officer Garvin has been coached well.

'Describe what happened next, if you would, Officer.'

'The defendant led me upstairs to the second floor of his town house. He made me immediately aware of a Glock handgun that was lying on the floor next to a dead body in the living room. He said the weapon might be loaded, but he wasn't sure.'

'Is this the weapon?' Ogren asks. From the evidence table behind the prosecution, Ogren removes the handgun. We have stipulated that this was the weapon Officer Garvin found at the scene. We have stipulated that it was the murder weapon.

And we have stipulated that, according to records filed with the state police, the owner of this handgun is Jason Kolarich.

Over the defense's objection, which Judge Bialek already over-ruled prior to trial, Roger Ogren shows the officer a series of photographs laying out the scene on the second floor of Jason's town house: the dead body with a single gunshot wound to the back of the neck, the handgun lying neatly nearby on the hardwood floor. Close-ups and faraway shots, angles capturing Jason's kitchen and shots showing his large window overlooking the street, dark at that time of night.

'Once you determined that the victim was, in fact, deceased, and after securing the handgun, what did you do next, Officer?'

'I asked the defendant if anyone else was in the town house. He said no. I told him I wanted to search his person for other weapons, and he allowed me to do so. I found no weapons on his person. I asked the defendant for permission to search the remainder of the house, and he gave me that verbal consent. My partner, Officer Middleton, stayed with the defendant while I searched the remainder of the town house. I determined that nobody else was present in the house.'

'What happened next?'

'I read the defendant his Miranda rights and asked him if he could tell me what had happened.'

'And what—'

'He said he wanted to call his lawyer.'

'What did you do in response?'

'I ceased any questioning. I told him he was not under arrest and that it wasn't the time for a phone call.'

That's right. It wasn't until nearly two hours later, at close to three in the morning, that Jason called me at my home. Three-oh-six in the morning, to be exact; I'll always remember the time on the bedside clock. *Shauna,* he said to me, his voice calm but with a slight tremble, *I'm being arrested for murder. Call Bradley John and have him meet me at Area Three.*

Shauna, I'm being arrested for murder.

SHAUNA, I'M BEING—

'I radioed for detectives and tried to keep the scene as pristine as possible,' Garvin continues. 'I directed the defendant to remain in the kitchen, where he sat in a chair while we waited for the police detectives. Detective Cromartie arrived about thirty, forty minutes later.'

Ogren pauses briefly for a segue. 'Officer, can you describe the defendant's demeanor during this encounter?'

Officer Garvin nods, ready for the question. 'He was very compliant. He was able to speak clearly and intelligently. He seemed calm. No outbursts.'

'Was he crying?'

'No, sir. I didn't see that.'

'Did he seem upset in any way?'

86

'Objection,' I say.

The judge allows the question. I scold myself for the objection. I've just highlighted the testimony, placed more importance on it. And since I did object, I should have at least done a speaking objection: *The officer couldn't possibly know if my client was upset, Judge.*

Shit. That was a mistake. An easy one I fumbled. *Get your head in the game, Tasker. This is the whole ball of wax.*

'The defendant showed no outward signs of any emotion,' says Garvin. 'He wasn't happy, but he wasn't crying or shouting or moving. He was calm and quiet.'

'Thank you, Officer.' Ogren nods to Judge Bialek. 'No further questions.'

21

Jason

After Shauna cross-examines Officer Garvin, Judge Bialek bangs a gavel and we are done for the day. Shauna didn't spend a lot of time on the cross. Garvin was just the first responder to the scene; his testimony didn't do much damage. Shauna only covered two topics. First, my demeanor, which Garvin had suggested was unreasonably calm – which would be translated by Roger Ogren in closing argument as 'icy' or 'cold-blooded.' 'In your three years on the beat, you've encountered a number of people in stressful, upsetting situations, haven't you?' Shauna asked the officer. 'And people show grief in different ways, do they not? Some cry, some scream, some remain quiet, some have *already* cried before you arrived and appear calm by the time you see them.' Yes, yes, and yes, the cop agreed.

And second, the fact that I lawyered up right away, invoking my right to counsel at the first question Officer Garvin posed. The law says that you are entitled to counsel before interrogation by the police. Every American who has watched one evening of television knows that. But many, and maybe most, of those same Americans would infer guilt from someone who immediately invoked. So Shauna couldn't let it go. 'My client, Jason Kolarich, is a criminal defense attorney, is he not? And a criminal defense attorney would be expected to be very much aware of his rights, wouldn't you agree? Does it seem unusual to you that a criminal defense attorney would follow the same advice that he gives to every single one of his clients, which is to confer with an attorney before talking to the police?' The last question drew an objection from Roger Ogren, which Judge Bialek sustained. That was fine by us. We just wanted the jury to hear the question.

'Meet you back at the Palace,' I say to my lawyers. 'Get some decent food first.'

'What would you like?' Bradley asks me.

'Whatever. I don't care.'

A sheriff's deputy named Floyd takes me by the elbow and walks me out of the courtroom. Once in the waiting area behind the court, he handcuffs me, hands in front, and perp-walks me to an elevator, then to a bus waiting underground. I'm joined by seven other men, also standing trial today and headed to the Palace for the night. I'm one of only two white guys; the others are African-American or Latino. I'm the only one in a suit. Most of them are wearing expressions that tell me they have a pretty good idea how their cases are going to turn out.

The Alejandro Morales Detention Center was named after a congressman who represented this area in the eighties, one of the first Latinos ever to serve in Congress. The 'Morales Palace,' less than a mile from the criminal courts, looks like an ordinary twenty-story concrete structure, save for the bars on the windows. It's used these days primarily as a youth detention facility, but with our state and county governments in their ever-present state of fiscal Armageddon, and real estate at a premium, the segregated prisoners sometimes overflow here from the county jail.

Segregation is typically reserved for gangbangers and either cops or prosecutors who run afoul of the law and, for various reasons, might not fare so well in general population. I'm a two-time winner because I've prosecuted and defended some of the people inside, thus my private cell. For this last week, when I'm expected to need lots of time to prepare for trial, I've been granted liberal privileges with the meeting rooms to confer with my attorneys. And because these meetings could interfere with the regimented timing for meals, they even let my lawyers bring me something to eat, as long as it's something the guards can open and inspect freely. Soup is out; sub sandwiches very much in. Every time I bite into a hoagie that Shauna brings me, I know that a correctional employee has already worked over every slice of turkey, lifted every tomato and pickle, searching for razors, needles, drug packets. I assume the guard is wearing a plastic glove while doing so. I prefer to imagine it that way, at least.

This evening, Shauna, Bradley, and I will go over the witnesses for tomorrow and finalize cross-examination questions. We will probably discuss, once again, whether I should testify, though I am certain I will.

Until then, I'm left alone in my deluxe penthouse, a ten-by-ten cell of concrete and bars, a stained and scuffed-up floor, a toilet with a broken seat, and a bed with a cushion an inch thick. Left alone with my thoughts, I'm taken these days to self-abuse. I don't kid myself. I have nobody to blame for my predicament but myself.

Dr Evans warned me about the dangers of taking OxyContin, and I assured him I was prepared for it. He asked me if there was a history of alcohol or chemical dependency in my family, and for some reason I lied and said no, said nothing about my father or my brother, Pete. He vigilantly monitored me over those first few months after the surgery, when the pain was sometimes teeth-gnashing, often searing needle-stabs, but again I assured him that I was sticking with the proper dosing regimen. 'Yes,' I told him, 'I'm taking them four hours apart. No,' I lied, 'I don't chew them up, I let them dissolve in my stomach.' I was cocky. I was a tough guy, and I could take as many pills as I wanted, as often as I wanted, without it becoming a problem.

Before I knew it, four pills a day was six, then eight, then a dozen. Even after the pain in my knee subsided – maybe mid-March, definitely by April – I gradually needed more and more to feel okay, whatever *okay* meant. Then I found myself in Dr Evans's office on April 1 – that's right, let's all say it together, April Fools' Day – with my crutches, even though I no longer needed them, even though I was essentially pain-free, lying to him, telling him the pain was excruciating. 'That's . . . odd,' he said. 'The healing has been remarkable. To still have this much pain . . .'

Then, wisely – and diplomatically, too, with that practiced bedside manner, never outright accusing me of lying – Dr Evans switched medication on me, moving from the immediate-release oxycodone tablets to the ones you can't chew up, the controlled-release tablets that dissolve into your bloodstream over hours, not minutes, before he took me off Oxy altogether a few weeks later. Suddenly, a guy who had never taken pain medication in his life before the knee surgery was scoring sheets of Oxy from a street merchant, a drug dealer named Billy Braden, one of my clients, no less. And still I needed more and more, building up a tolerance and never once considering stopping.

Funny, I can't even remember how or when it happened, when the dam broke, when I crossed that line from patient to addict. I can't identify a date or event or even a sensation, any moment when I said to myself, *You have a problem, these pills are controlling you, not the other way around*. But somehow it happened. In the blink of an eye, I went from taking OxyContin because it made my knee feel good to taking OxyContin because it made *me* feel good.

None of this would have happened otherwise. I would have handled differently that redheaded client who walked into my office and said he didn't kill two young women. I wouldn't have stayed with Alexa so long and allowed everything to happen. Shauna was right about her all along, but I was too high and too stubborn to listen. There were plenty of warning signs, not the least of which was the day that Alexa offered to be my alibi.

Well, it didn't quite work out that way, did it? I sure could use an alibi now. But I've never offered one. The murder happened in my house, with my gun, and with no sign of forced entry.

I shudder out of my funk. *Look forward, not backward,* they told me in rehab, the lanky brunette named Mara who smelled of cigarette smoke and made you look her in the eye. *Fix the problem.*

It's too late to fix most of the damage I caused. I hope it's not too late to keep myself out of prison.

SIX MONTHS BEFORE TRIAL
June

22

Jason

Saturday, June 15

I pop awake from a dream, some kind of a fairy-tale serpent with long fangs, loud hissing sounds, mortal danger, whatever. I am lying in the fetal position on my bathroom floor, and reality comes to me: sleeping at Alexa's last night, ditching out on her when I couldn't find my tin of Altoids, hailing a cab and racing back here. The crick in my neck causes a shiver of pain. My watch tells me it's just past six in the morning. I've been home maybe two, two and a half hours.

I push myself off the floor and find the box of allergy medicine next to me, the sheet of pills sticking out halfway. I pop out a pill and chew it up while I scratch my knuckles, my fingers, my palms, in vain.

I head downstairs, thinking about how I bolted on Alexa last night after saying I'd spend the night. She might not be too thrilled with me. Maybe we'll do something fun today.

I push a button to awaken my cell phone and notice, for the first time, a text message from Joel Lightner from sometime last night.

Your guy is for real, details if u want

Huh. So James Drinker checked out. Not what I'd call a shocker, but I really didn't know if he was being straight with me about much of anything.

'So our James is for real,' I say to Lightner when he answers his cell phone. By *answer*, I mean he moans and curses.

'What fucking . . . time is it?'

'Time for you to wake up, princess,' I say. I'm feeling much better now, happiness coursing through me, fifteen minutes after I popped the little white tablet. 'James Drinker is the real deal?'

It takes him a while. My guess is he was overserved last night. I hear yawning, grunting, throat-clearing, a sound like he's fiddling with glasses, and then a heavy sigh.

'He's for real, yeah. Weird, my guy says. Looks like that guy from *MAD* magazine on steroids, he says.'

'That's him. Big dude with goofy red hair flopping around.'

'Yeah, apparently. Anyway, he reports to work at Higgins Auto Body every morning. He lives in that shithole building on Townsend and Kensington.' Another morning sound, like he's stretching his sleepy muscles.

I'm on the floor now, doing my rehab. Ankle pumps, leg raises, knee bends. I'm supposed to do them for twenty to thirty minutes a day, three times a day, but I'm up to an hour each time. The knee is doing much better now. The knee is no longer the problem. I've graduated to bigger ones. Sometimes, like this moment, I actually admit it to myself, but it's only after I've had a happy pill, experienced the euphoria. Oh yeah, when I'm high, I can be exceptionally candid with myself, I can scold myself and promise big things to come, down the road, a new path, no more pills, a fresh start – just not right now. Later. Sometime soon. Definitely soon.

'It's six-thirty in the morning!' Lightner suddenly realizes. 'Who calls somebody at six-thirty in the morning? On a *Saturday*?'

'I do, Joel. You were saying about your report?'

'You're an asshole.'

'The report says I'm an asshole? I already knew that.'

Joel doesn't sound amused. I hear the sound of glasses unfolding and making their way onto his nose. 'He . . . fuck . . . I e-mailed this to you, but I wouldn't want to inconvenience you, so I'll just read it to you at six-fucking-thirty in the morning.' A loud sigh. Poor guy, he was sleeping. 'Right, address checks out, employment checks out, no criminal record with a full workup, credit cards, checking account, never married, no kids, one brother, went to Princeton High but doesn't look like he graduated, and he's been a grease monkey ever since.'

He makes yet another morning noise. A new one. He may have broken wind.

'Did our grease monkey look like a serial killer to your guy?' I ask. 'A butcher of women? A sociopath?'

'He didn't say. Can I go back to sleep now?'

So James checked out. He is who he said he is. So far, everything he's told me that I can confirm has been the truth. Maybe I was getting worked up for nothing.

'Sweet dreams, sugar pie,' I say, punching out the phone.

23

Jason

Saturday, June 15

'Hey there.' Alexa shows up at my door ready to go in an ice-blue running shirt that matches her eyes, black shorts, and Nikes. What's not to like about a sexy woman in athletic clothes?

I keep my tongue in my mouth and say, 'Hey. Want to come in?'

'Sure.'

I grab the new running shoes I purchased at Runner's High and lace them up. 'That was fun last night,' I say.

'Good. I thought so, too.'

I focus on my shoes and wait for a shoe of another kind to drop. But it doesn't. I look up at her. 'Hey, sorry I bolted like that last night.'

'No worries.' She waves me off. 'Nice house,' she says.

There's not much to see in the foyer. I live in a typical city town house, at least in this neighborhood: narrow and vertical, three stories. Other than a small back room, the only things on the ground level are the foyer and staircase. Which, for the record, was murder when I had one knee that didn't work.

'You want a tour, or do you want to hit it?'

'Let's hit it,' she says. 'I can have a tour later. If you play your cards right.'

Nice. Dangle a carrot in front of the man. Well played.

'Remember, all I can do is walk,' I remind her.

'I'll try to slow down for you.'

Nice again. This one is going to keep me on my toes.

We head east and then cut up north to Ash, which will take us to the lakefront. It's not quite as hot today, and the brisk lake winds provide even more relief. The sun is high, the birds are chirping, I'm getting a good sweat, the beach is filled with volleyball players, the promenade with runners and bikers and skateboarders, my knee doesn't hurt at all, and I'm walking with a woman who gives men whiplash. The world is in balance. For another ninety minutes, that is.

'You thought I'd be pissed off that you left last night,' she says to me between breaths. We're doing a decent pace for a walk.

'I wasn't sure. I said I'd stay and I didn't.'

'I don't smother people,' she says. 'That's not how I roll.'

'That's not how you roll, huh?'

'Not how I roll.' She's rolling along quite well right now, I have to say. I'm tempted to tell her to slow down, but then I'd be admitting I can't keep up, and that's not how *I* roll.

We stop about two miles down, close to where we started our walk along the beach last night. We sit for a moment on one of the steps down to the beach.

'Is this okay for you?' she asks.

'Sure, great.'

'Don't be a guy. You had knee surgery. It's okay to say it hurts or we need to slow down or whatever.'

Actually, it feels better than I expected, so I get up and start the walk back home. She hops back up and joins me again.

'You are *such* a guy,' she says.

I'd argue if I could. The hike back is just as enjoyable. I miss adrenaline and sweat as much as I miss mobility. It's nice to know I've turned a corner.

When we get back to my town house, we walk in silently and head up the stairs. The tour isn't much of one. We skip the second floor, a typical open-floor layout of kitchen and great room, and head straight up to the bedroom. She smells like sweat, and her moist, salty skin tastes like it. I ease her out of her running shirt and shorts, leaving only a running bra and undies. All good. She goes to work on me and we saddle up for round two.

It's better than the first time, as I expected, more familiar and decisive, less hesitant, and I let out a loud moan into her mouth, our teeth clacking, when it's over. We lie exhausted, panting like animals, for a long time before she suggests a shower is in order. At first, I take it as an insult, but then I realize she's talking about a shower for two.

When we have carefully ensured each other's cleanliness – and that would include round number three, thank you – we collapse on the bed. We lie there quietly for a time, Alexa's breathing dissolving into faint, rhythmic sighs. I ease my arm out from under her and walk to the bathroom. I open the cabinet beneath the sink, reach for the box of allergy medicine, and pop out a pill and chew it up. Then I cup some water out of the sink to swallow the granular remnants.

I rejoin her, trying to ease back into our position, but I awaken her. She adjusts herself so her head is on my chest, her fingers drawing on my abdomen. I close my eyes, and within minutes, the euphoria spreads through my veins.

'So you're an old-fashioned girl,' I say. I'm wondering in what era they did some of the things we did in that shower.

'I *am* old-fashioned,' she says into my chest. 'I want my man to be happy.'

'So I'm your man, am I?'

'If you're okay with that. But if you aren't, no problem. No pressure. Really.' She remains motionless, like she's holding her breath.

I run my fingers over her back. My eyes dance beneath my eyelids. I am swimming in goodness.

'Yeah,' I say. 'I'm more than okay.'

24

Shauna

Sunday, June 16

I fish around my desk looking for the transcript. 'Where's the Flynn dep?' I ask.

Bradley John is on the couch in my office reviewing another deposition. He's been with us over a year now, and is four-plus years removed from law school. He may look like a teenage rock star with that goofy hair, but he works as hard as anyone I know. He works as hard as me.

'I have it on the system,' he says, gesturing to the laptop computer resting beside him. He looks up at me. 'But you want a hard copy.'

He knows me well by now. Technology has created a sea change in the practice of law, but when I'm preparing for trial by reviewing deposition transcripts, I want them in my hand, with my notes scribbled in the margins and Post-it tabs sticking out everywhere.

'Jason would have a copy,' I say. I push myself out of my chair. My trial is about three weeks away, and I'm pretty much there in terms of the big-picture prep, but now we're getting down to the microscopic level, the nuance. 'And where is our Mr Kolarich, I wonder?' I say aloud. Jason hasn't been in the whole weekend. I know what he'd say: We have plenty of time. But I make mistakes when I rush things, and he probably does, too. We aren't flying by the seat of our pants in this trial. Rory Arangold's company is depending on it.

I walk down to his office, where the lights are off and Jason appears to be enjoying his weekend, unlike the rest of us. Now where would the *Arangold* files be? I dropped all of them in the corner by his fridge—

Oh. There it is. The entire stack of folders. Exactly as I placed them.

Jason hasn't reviewed a single page.

I dial him on my phone. No answer. 'Hey, tough guy,' I say to voice mail, 'don't know if you're coming in today, Sunday, but I need to schedule a meeting this week with you and Rory Arangold. So hopefully you'll be prepared by maybe Tuesday?' I think of ending the message there. But I don't. 'If you're not able to work on this file, if you're busy with other stuff or whatever, tell me now, Jase. Not the day before trial.'

I punch out and stare at those untouched files. He knows how important this is to me. He knows how nervous I am. Normally, he'd be right here with me, watching my back.

I let out a long sigh. He'll be there. He's just doing his typical procrastination. He'll waltz in and he'll decimate their expert.

'You okay?' Bradley is standing in the doorway.

'Oh, sure, sure,' I say. 'Let's get back to it.'

25

Shauna

Monday, June 17

I shake hands with my clients, new owners of a single-family home on the city's northwest side. They are beaming, excited about their new home and their family. He is an accountant and she's an elementary school teacher with a bun in the oven, their first child, who is scheduled to arrive in this world in about six weeks.

'Thanks for everything, Shauna. This was so easy.'

'Best of luck to you.' I walk them out of the title office, where the house closing took place. House closings are no fun, but once you learn how to do them, they're easy, and it's a steady stream of income in small bites that helps the firm keep motoring.

I put them in a cab, the husband in his suit, the wife in her maternity outfit, her stomach protruding, and watch them drive away. *Someday, maybe,* I think. *But,* as my mother always gently reminds me, *the window is closing.*

Our firm is just a few blocks away. I enjoy being outside, even for a brief walk, having lost most of my weekend at the office. When I get in, Marie hands me some messages and a couple of letters she's put on letterhead for me. Marie functions as our legal secretary and receptionist. Both Jason and I can type, so we can share a secretary, and Bradley John is more proficient on the computer than all of us combined.

'Is Jason in?' I ask.

'Just got in.'

It's mid-afternoon. He just got in? Maybe he had court. It's not my job to keep tabs on him. But it *is* my job to make sure he's pulling his weight on *Arangold*.

I walk down the hallway to his office and, just before I stick my head in, I hear Jason's voice. 'I've got tar on my feet and I can't see,' he says. 'All the birds look down and laugh at me.'

And then I smell smoke – or not smoke, but—

I poke my head in and see Jason shaking a lit match and tossing it into a styrofoam cup. He is startled when he sees me, but then he smiles at me.

'What the hell are you doing?' I say.

He chuckles and spins in his chair.

I've got tar on my feet and I can't see . . . All the birds look down and laugh at me.

'Just keeping myself awake,' he says.

'You're just keeping yourself awake by lighting a match until it burns your fingers? That's why your fingernails are black?'

'Relax, kid.'

'And what were you saying? Is that – Was that from "Let Me In"?'

He wags a finger at me. 'Good memory. I heard it on my way in,' he says. 'Stuck in my head.'

'That's not a happy song, Jase.'

He shrugs. 'Okay, next time I'll whistle something more upbeat. Would that please you? How about something from *Mary Poppins*?'

I raise my eyebrows.

'What?' he says. 'Don't look at me that way. Since when have we limited our R.E.M. repertoire to happy songs?'

I raise a hand. 'Okay, fine. Fine. It's perfectly natural that you're sitting here in the middle of the day in your office, setting your fingers on fire—'

'I'm not setting them—'

'– and singing a song about suicide.'

'– on fire, first of all. And second of all, you like the song, too. I listened to *Monster* on the way in to work, that's all. Jeez.'

Enough. Surrender. I look at my watch. 'I have to jump on a conference call with Rory Arangold,' I say. 'Did you get my voice mail?'

Jason seems to appreciate the segue, but not so much the new topic. 'I did, yeah. I did.'

'And? Are we a go on *Arangold*?'

'Yeah, sure.' He gives me a wide smile. 'I'm on it. I'll start on it today.'

I eye him with suspicion, not trying to hide it. But he doesn't seem to care. His eyes drift to the window and he smiles again, even chuckles to himself.

'Are you . . . *drunk*?' I ask.

He waves me off. 'Just high on life.'

Yeah, right. The day that Jason Kolarich is high on life is the day that gravity ceases to exist.

'Okay, sport. If you're sure. Want to get dinner tonight?'

He shakes his head. 'Can't do it, girl. Got plans.'

Jason and I have had our moments, so I'm entitled to a little ambivalence when a woman enters his life. And make no mistake, a woman has entered his life. Whenever he gets vague about his personal life – *Got plans,* he said – it means it's somebody he cares about.

'Do tell,' I say.

'That court reporter? Alexa? Nice girl, it turns out.'

I saw her briefly when she stopped in a couple of weeks ago. She was striking, as I recall. And Jason, the bastard, is tall, dark, and handsome, even if he doesn't realize it. And what court reporter personally delivers a transcript? So I guess it isn't a grand surprise that there were fireworks.

'That's nice to hear,' I say. I start to leave, but look back in at him. 'Seriously, you're – you're okay?'

'Sure. I'm fine. No worries.'

He's not fine. But I don't comment further. Anytime I get near the subject, he swats my hand away.

You're not his mother, I keep reminding myself. I've got a client and three lawyers holding on a conference call right now, waiting for me, so that will have to do for the time being.

26

Jason

Tuesday, June 18

My head pops off my pillow before my eyes even open. My heart is racing and I shake away the fading whispers of the dream, insects attacking my skin in swarms. I scratch my forearms and knuckles and palms, but it doesn't take away the itch. I look at the clock. It's half past four. I push myself out of bed as Alexa, lying next to me, releases a breath and moans softly. She was out with friends last night and came to my house afterward, about eleven. We had a nice hour of sex before we collapsed on the bed.

In my bathroom, I grab a pill from the box of allergy medicine. I'm getting low and will need to replenish soon.

I close my eyes and they dance beneath my eyelids. I let out a deep sigh as the warmth spreads through me . . .

It's going to be okay. I'll figure something out. Sleep is what I need.

I crawl back to bed, hoping not to wake Alexa, but she turns over as soon as she hears me. It's clear that she's been awake.

'Are you all right?' she asks.

'Sure, sure.'

'That's the second time you've gotten up.'

'Is it?'

'Yeah, it is. You got up at two and again just now, at four-thirty.'

'So you're keeping tabs on me?'

She puts her hand on my chest. 'Don't say it like that. I'm just wondering if you're in pain.'

'I'm fine.' I reach over and kiss her. 'Go back to sleep.'

She nestles into me and quickly drifts off. We fit together nicely in sleep. I breathe in the fruity scent of her shampoo and run my fingers over her back as she softly moans.

I jerk awake in that same cocoon, like I never slept at all save for the dream, birds feasting on the hair on my arms, grasping tiny hairs in their beaks and yanking them off. I squint at the clock. It's seven o'clock. I sit up in bed. My shoulders are tight. My hands are shaky and itchy. My stomach is considering a revolution. I get out of bed and walk to the bathroom for another pill.

'Morning.' Alexa walks into the bathroom rubbing her eyes, the back of her hair standing up. She is wearing a gray T-shirt of mine and silk underwear. If I were in the mood, I'd enjoy the view.

'Morning.' I put away the pills and close the cabinet.

She sits on the toilet to pee. 'Are you sure you're okay?'

'I'm sure.' I splash some water on my face and look into the mirror, but quickly avert my eyes. Not good. Ghoulish and mangy.

We lie around for a while and then go downstairs to the kitchen to scrounge up breakfast. I pretty much never cook anything that doesn't require a microwave, but I still have lots of cookware and utensils left over from when Talia was in charge of the cooking. What I lack, however, is ingredients for anything interesting like French toast or pancakes – not that I have the appetite for it, either.

'You should go back to the doctor and tell him your knee hurts,' Alexa says as she beats eggs in a pan. I do have eggs, and lots of meat, and really good coffee beans.

'My knee's fine.'

'Okay. Whatever.' She's doing something fancy with the eggs. I don't want to prolong this conversation and can't think of anything clever to say, so I walk through the great room – I actually hate that term, but that's what they called it when I bought the place, not a living room or family room but a 'great' room – and press my face against the window overlooking the street. People are walking their dogs or starting out runs. An old couple is slowly walking down the street, the man wearing a beret, the woman with her arm in a sling, casting their eyes upward at the sky, getting in their stroll before the temperatures reach sauna level.

'Okay, well, then, here,' Alexa says. I turn back. She is fiddling in her purse, which rests on the elongated breakfast bar. She produces a tin of Altoids and places it on the counter. 'You left these at my house the other night. Thought you might need them.'

Need them, she said. Not want them.

'What are those, mints?' I ask, a different kind of warmth passing through me.

'Sure. Fine. They're *mints*,' she hisses, turning her back to me again, going to work with a little more fury on those eggs. They aren't going to be scrambled; they're going to be annihilated.

Finally, after an awkward silence of I don't know how long, my chest burning, she spins back in my direction. 'Look, I like you, Jason. I really do. But I had a guy I really liked and he burned me really bad because he kept secrets. I don't need to know your life story, okay? But if there's something that really affects you, yeah, I'd like to know about it.

'Sooo . . . it seems to me, just sayin',' she says, waving her hands with exaggerated caution, 'that your knee still hurts you really badly, and for some reason I can't figure out, you don't want to admit that to me. So you're hiding pills in an Altoids container and you're getting out of bed every few hours at night, too.'

'So you're checking *up* on me.'

'Oh, for God's sake.' She throws down the large wooden spoon she was using. It actually lands on the corner of the counter and snaps back at her. 'I thought they were mints! I almost put one in my mouth! What are they? Vicodin? Something for pain.'

I look back at the window, at the treetops and the town houses across the street. I place my palm on the window and feel warmth.

'If something is hurting you that badly,' she says, 'then it's

108

affecting you. And if we have some kind of a relationship, then that means it's affecting me, too. And if we *don't* have a relationship, then that's fine, too, but then what the *hell* am I doing cooking you eggs?'

'Getting out your aggression, it looks like.' That's me, when shoved into a corner. Start with sarcasm. If that doesn't work, it can get uglier.

She leaves the kitchen without another word, heading upstairs. She is quiet up there, but I assume she's gathering her things to leave. This is what they call the moment of truth. Cue the dramatic organ music.

'Okay,' she says when she comes back down the stairs, fully dressed, her purse slung over her shoulder. 'You're a nice guy, Jason. Maybe if we'd—'

'My knee hurts,' I say. 'It hurts all the time. It should be better by now. It's June. It's been, like, six months. But it's not. It's not better.' The words just spill out, as if someone else were saying them. 'My doctor doesn't believe me so he stopped prescribing me OxyContin. So I have to buy these pills illegally.'

I'm looking out the window when I deliver this monologue. The fact that I ended with the truth seems, for some reason, to make the rest more palatable. There is a gentle but consistent ringing in my ears: *Wrong, not right.*

'He won't give you pain medication?' she asks, her tone gentler now. Her guard still up, but not quite as high.

'What did I just fucking say?'

She doesn't say anything. Neither of us does. Silence. The abrupt lurch of the fan, the air-conditioning kicking on. The smell of sweat on me, steamy and rancid. Then I hear her back at the stove, the wooden spoon on the pan, a cabinet closing, the freezer opening, bacon grease crackling in the pan.

Me, I don't move, staring out the window, watching the slow movement of the elderly couple down the street, grateful that I can't see my reflection.

27

Jason

I wake up alone on Wednesday morning, unless you consider the images possessing me throughout the night. Another shipwreck of a night, flipping all around my bed, retching into the toilet, thinking of serial murders, butcher knives, young women writhing in pain, their blood-soaked bangs stuck to their foreheads and cheeks.

Thinking of Alexa, too. How we left things yesterday morning after she made me breakfast, which we ate in relative silence, sticking to ridiculously safe topics like the weather and our schedules this week – depositions she's working, court appearances I have – ignoring the bomb I'd dropped about my 'Altoids' problem. Not that I exactly gave her the truth, the whole truth, and nothing but the truth. More like the partial truth with some lies mixed in. Doesn't roll off the tongue quite as fluidly.

We said good-bye after breakfast; she didn't even catch a ride with me downtown, walking to the train instead. A quick peck on the cheek, a curt 'Bye,' and that was it. Not that I blame her. If I were Alexa, I'd run away from me like I was qualifying for the Summer Olympics.

So now . . . Wednesday! I wipe the sweat off my forehead, make it to the bathroom, shower and shave and dress in my best monkey costume for court this morning. It's in one of the regional branches, not the criminal courts, so I decide to go straight from home to court.

I get there early and meet my client, who is worried beyond belief. I calm her down and gently prepare her before we enter the cattle call of a courtroom. I fill out an appearance and tell the clerk we want a trial, which means we'll go to the end of the pack. It's not until after ten o'clock that they call our case.

It's an attempted battery case that will be tried to a judge, not a jury. The husband says the wife tried to stab him during an argument over money. It's a common tactic in a child custody case, one side accusing the other of assault or battery, hoping to use it as leverage to get the kid in the divorce. Everyone in the criminal justice system knows it – the cops, the judges, the prosecutors – but nobody wants to acknowledge it openly. Prosecutors aren't allowed to drop the charges on a domestic battery, even if they suspect it's one of these bullshit cases, because it only takes one mistake – that one case out of a thousand where the husband ends up killing the wife, or vice versa – and then everyone traces it back and finds that the county attorney's office didn't pursue charges when it had the chance, and someone has to lose his job.

So these cases go to trial, but the prosecutors don't exactly put their best feet forward. They do their duty, putting on the allegedly aggrieved spouse, and rest. I have the additional advantage in this instance of representing the wife; most of these cases, it's the wife accusing the husband, but in this case the roles are reversed. I've never been in front of Judge Oliver, but I can see the look on his face while he listens to the husband, a big meat-eating guy, give his version of how his wife lunged at him with a kitchen knife, and I'm pretty sure I can get a 'not guilty' even if I don't cross-examine the husband. But cross him I do, tying him in knots until he's about to come out of his seat and do some lunging of his own.

The verdict isn't a surprise or an accomplishment, but I savor it nonetheless. This, I've come to realize, is truly my best medicine, the only thing I know, the only time I'm not thinking about those Altoids in my pocket – the competition. Every time I lose a case, it haunts me. Every time I win, I drink it in. And I keep track. As a prosecutor, I won all but three of my cases, with the proviso that a plea bargain is considered a victory because, regardless of the reduced offense the descendants plead to, they are convicted of something, and a conviction is a win. As a defense lawyer, I lose more than I win, in part for the same reason about plea bargains, and in part because it's not a fair fight. The prosecution gets to begin the lawsuit whenever they want, whenever they're sure they have a rock-solid case, and only then does the defense attorney enter the arena. They also have a considerable advantage in resources compared to most defendants, who can't afford fancy experts or investigators. I remind myself of all of that, but it still punches me in the gut every time a client goes to prison. I hate, hate, hate to lose, even more than I like to win.

My client, overcome with relief, kisses me on the cheek and takes my arm as we walk out of the courtroom. I pull out my phone, turn it on, and text 'NG' to the divorce lawyer who referred me the case. I have two divorce lawyers who routinely kick these cases my way. It's a decent stream of business to fill the gaps.

After wishing my client well, I look again at my phone and see that I have two missed calls from an unknown number and a voice mail.

'It's James, James Drinker,' the voice mail says. *'There was another murder last night. I didn't kill her, either.'*

28

Jason

Wednesday, June 19

Back in my office, I push away a half-eaten cheeseburger I had picked up on the way back and go online to the *Herald*'s website. It isn't hard to find, though by midday the story is no longer the headline. The victim is Nancy Minnows, age twenty-three, dead from multiple stab wounds. The police call it 'premature' to speculate as to whether there is a connection between this stabbing and the others.

The promised rain begins to fall in sheets outside, turning everything gray. It will douse the temperature a bit and funk up the air. But I like the post-rain smell. It makes me think that even nature is fallible.

On the roller coaster that is my opinion of James Drinker's culpability in these murders, I'm currently in a free fall, sure that he is the man who butchered four women. There is plenty of reason to believe otherwise, but this whole thing is starting to give me the heebie-jeebies. I grab my tin of Altoids for some midday happiness. As I chew up the tablet, it's not lost on me that I may not be in a superior position to be judging the guilt or innocence of anybody.

Ten minutes later, I have my phone to my ear, pinching the bridge of my nose with my free hand as I listen to the heavy breath of James Drinker on the other end of the connection.

'Her name is Nancy Minnows,' he says. 'And I don't know her.'

'Are you sure you don't know her?'

'What is that supposed to mean?'

'It means you might know a Nancy but not know her last name, or something like that. Or you might recognize her face but never knew her name.'

'Well, they showed a picture of her on the news this morning and I didn't recognize her.'

'It could be an old picture, something from a college yearbook or something that's dated. How old is this girl?' I ask, even though I already know the answer from the Internet.

'I don't know. She looked . . . young, I guess. Like the . . . like the others,' he adds with some hesitation.

'Well, if you're right that someone's trying to frame you, James, then they're not doing a very good job of it.'

'Yeah . . . yeah, I guess. But it's weird, right?'

Yes, it's weird. This whole thing is weird. Once again, this guy is giving me the creeps, but having a weird feeling about a guy isn't a very strong basis for breaking your sworn oath as a lawyer and turning in your client.

'I was home last night, alone,' he says. 'I didn't talk to anybody that I can remember. I was online for a while. Should I document all that?'

'Definitely. But James, you were going to get me those phone records,' I remind him. 'The ones that prove you were talking to your mother from your home phone on the night of the third woman's murder? The night that grad student, Holly Frazier, was murdered?'

'Oh, right. Yeah, I will. It'll be on my phone bill. When I get my bill this month, I'll send it to you.'

So he's not going out of his way to expedite the process, to ask the phone company for an early peek at his phone records or to set up an online account and do it that way. But this could explain his innocence as much as his guilt. If he really was on the phone with his mother that night, and he really didn't kill anybody, then he'd have no particular urgency to get me the data.

'Let's go to the police,' I suggest. 'I know you're concerned about handing yourself over to them, but you didn't kill those women, James, and the cops are going to come to you anyway, eventually. Between dating Alicia Corey and being friends with Lauren Gibbs, it's bound to happen sooner or later, so you look better getting out in front of it. And now you look far less suspicious, because there have been two more stabbings, and you're telling me you have no connection to these last two women.'

Silence, but he hasn't hung up.

'I said I don't *know* of any connection,' he says. 'It doesn't mean there isn't one. For all I know, one of them sold me clothes or served me coffee or cleaned my teeth or deposited my check at the bank.'

'That's not motive for murder,' I say.

'Maybe I liked them,' he says. 'Maybe I coveted them. Maybe I watched them, everywhere they went, obsessed over them, learned their habits, and then followed them home one night and killed them.'

I don't say anything. I feel a decided change in temperature.

'Maybe that's exactly why I chose them,' he goes on. 'Because my encounter with them was so casual and short that nobody would even remember it.'

I push myself out of my chair, my head dizzy, my heartbeat drumming. I breathe out. The warm rain still attacks my window. The remnants of my burger, the pink chewy flesh, bring a surge to my throat.

'I'm not going to the police, Jason,' he says.

I start to form words but can't find them. The call disconnects a moment later.

I call Joel Lightner right away. 'The mother,' I say. 'James Drinker's mother. He said she lives in a nursing home. I want you to find her.'

'What are you going to do with his mother?' Joel asks.

'I'm not sure,' I say. 'Find out where she is and then I'll decide.'

A pause. He's scribbling something down, presumably. 'Okay, princess, anything else?'

'One other thing,' I say. 'And this one isn't free of charge. Put this on my tab. Because it's going to be expensive.'

'Okay.'

'I want twenty-four-hour surveillance on James Drinker,' I say.

29

Jason

Thursday, June 20

Another night of fitful, interrupted sleep, the sensation of shadows looming large behind me, nightmares of serial killers removing bodily organs with steak knives. I avoid the bathroom mirror entirely and, on the drive to the office, actually look down to ensure that I am wearing pants.

My stomach is empty and grumpy this morning, a dull ringing in my ears as I sit in my office, rereading everything in the news reports on the four dead women. By eleven, I finish a first draft of a response brief to a *Santiago* proffer, a case in federal court where prosecutors are trying to link my client with a dozen other gang members in a drug conspiracy so they can use his statements in court without that pesky rule against hearsay. I have trouble focusing for any number of reasons. First, because I'm going to lose this argument; Judge Royster is going to declare this one gigantic conspiracy and throw the hearsay rule out his twentieth-story window. Second, because I can't get my redheaded client out of my mind. And third, even I can tell, in rare moments of clarity and self-confrontation, that I am not right in the head these days, that I am slipping.

'Knock, knock.' It's Joel Lightner, gently rapping on my office door.

'Hey.' I sigh. 'What's up?'

'In the neighborhood. Thought I'd stop by.'

'Did you put the tail on James?'

'Yeah, we did. Yesterday, he left work and went home. This morning, he got up and went to work. So far, nothing else.'

I sit up straight. He didn't come all this way to tell me that. 'You found James's mother?'

'Yep. Yep, yep.' He takes a seat across from me and grimaces. 'She's at the corner of Nicholas and Artisan Avenues, out west. Part of the Saint Augustine campus?'

I grab a notepad, stationery Shauna got for me, the name TASKER & KOLARICH in royal blue at the top, then JASON KOLARICH, ESQ., below it in a subdued font.

'Saint Augustine has a nursing home?' I ask.

'Saint Augustine has a cemetery,' Joel says. 'James Drinker's mother is dead.'

'Dead?' I drop my head into my hands, my elbows on my desk.

'She died this March. Just a few months ago. So your client lied to you,' he says. 'Is that the first time a client has lied to you?'

I shake my head with wonder. 'But – why even come to me, then? He comes and tells me all these scary murders are happening and then lies about his alibi? To *me*, his defense lawyer? It's not like he's been charged or anything. This whole thing is so . . .'

'Unsolicited?'

'Yeah,' I say. 'Exactly.'

'So he's a sick fuck.'

Right. That fits him. *A sick fuck.*

'Saw on the news there was a fourth murder on Tuesday night,' Lightner says. 'You've probably seen the papers. It's all over television, too. This thing is getting hot, Jason. They're calling him the North Side Slasher. The police superintendent is telling women to lock their doors, that kind of thing. We . . . have . . . a . . . serial killer. Nobody's denying it anymore.'

I'd seen some of the coverage, probably not as much as Joel. But he's right. The police are now openly warning that there is a *killer of women* in our fair city.

I look at Joel. He stares back. Down the hall, Marie is laughing at something Bradley said. Inside this office, there is silence, heavy and dark.

'Is he our offender?' Joel asks carefully.

'Yeah,' I say. 'Yeah, I think he is.' That was all it took, I guess, that one confirmed lie about his mother, to validate the notion that has swirled through me all along.

'You're sworn to secrecy, right?' he asks me, knowing the answer already.

'Of course I am. Unless I know for certain he's going to do it again.'

I scratch at my hand, searching in vain for that indefinable itch, until I draw blood.

Joel makes a face as he stands up. 'Heavy lies the crown, my friend,' he says.

30

Shauna

Thursday, June 20

I shake hands with Rory and Dylan Arangold at the end of a three-hour meeting. We're doing what you do as you near trial in a civil lawsuit: working on a dual track, considering an acceptable settlement while preparing for a trial if there isn't one. Yesterday, the lawyers for the city said they'd accept $5.5 million from us to 'make the case go away.' But $5.5 million will make Arangold Construction go away. It's above the surety bond they obtained, and they don't have that kind of money lying around, not in this economy.

The Arangolds are old-school males in the construction business, hotheaded at times but totally uncomfortable showing fear. Which is why it's so unsettling to watch them sweat so profusely as we cover every aspect of this case, as Rory taps at that calculator at the various permutations of damages a jury could award, as we consider the risks and rewards of the certainty of a settlement versus the likelihood of victory at trial.

'So you think Jason'll be at the next meeting?' Rory asks. 'Is that trial almost done?'

I've created an excuse for Jason, a major trial (the details vague) that has consumed him entirely. I won't deny that I find it a little insulting that they keep asking for my law partner, but then again, they probably wouldn't have handed me this case without him. I've handled some smaller matters for the Arangolds for years, transactional work and mechanic's liens and a few smaller contract matters, but I didn't really expect to get this case. I didn't expect two guys who still call waitresses *sweetheart* and who always compliment me on my appearance to hand over this bet-the-company case to someone with a vagina.

And so this lawyer and her vagina would really like to get these cavemen a good outcome.

After we say our good-byes, my associate, Bradley, goes to his office to check his messages. I walk down the hall to Jason's office and consider asking him to an early lunch. I catch Joel Lightner walking out the door, waving to Marie.

'Fuck!' Jason shouts out as I approach. I don't usually have that effect on him. 'Oh, hey,' he says when he sees me.

'What's up?' I ask.

'Nothing.' He sighs. 'Nothing.'

'You just like to yell "Fuck" at the top of your lungs every now and then?'

He shakes his head absently. 'Remember that weird guy, James Drinker?'

'The killer-who's-not-a-killer.'

He looks out the window, his hands on his hips. 'He lied to me. He claimed to have an alibi for one of the murders. His alibi was his mother. He said he was talking to her on his home phone. And now I come to learn that mommy is six feet underground.'

'Are you a cop now? It's your job to solve crimes?'

He gives me a sidelong glance, an evil eye. 'This is different,' he says. 'A guy comes into my office and says he committed this crime or that – fine, I represent him, I'd never tell his secrets. But four women have been murdered and there's no reason to believe there won't be a fifth, and a sixth, and meanwhile I'm holding my dick in my hands—'

'Jason, it sucks, but you can't turn in a client. You don't even know if he's guilty.'

Halfway through my lecture, he is shushing me with his hand, patting the air. 'This from the woman who doesn't practice criminal law because she doesn't want to help set criminals free. But it's okay to sit idly by and watch a serial killer run amok?'

That isn't fair. There isn't anyone who'd like to see this guy taken down more than me. But Jason, as always, is forgetting that he's a lawyer with rules to follow. If he disregards them whenever his conscience bothers him, they aren't rules at all.

'It isn't a question of "okay." It's a question of what you are ethically bound to do and not do. You can't just go with some gut feeling and throw away your law license.'

'My *law* license.' He makes a noise, something between a laugh and a grunt.

I raise my hands. 'I know this is tough, Jason. I do. It must be agonizing. I don't work in your area of the law, so this is new to me. But I have to tell you, it seems to me that the rules are pretty clear.'

'I know.' Jason shakes his head. 'I know you're right.'

My eyes drift to the corner of his office where I left the *Arangold* materials. They still haven't been touched, not one file.

'Listen,' I say, 'I know this is tearing your hair out, but speaking of hair being torn out – are you going to help me on *Arangold* or not? It's almost game time. Let's end the suspense.'

He squeezes his eyes shut and puts out a hand. 'I can't think about that right now. I gotta figure this shit out, Shauna.'

I take a deep breath. Beneath my anger and frustration is something more. Jason looks terrible. Strung out. Sleep-deprived. Skinny. For the first time, I begin to wonder if there is something seriously wrong with him, if something happened to him while I've had my back turned these last six or eight weeks.

'Are you okay?' I ask. Normally, this would be the wrong approach. Jason isn't your sensitive, sit-down-and-talk-about-your-feelings sort of guy. But I sense a dam about to burst.

He runs a hand through his hair. 'No, I'm not okay. I spend most of my time trying to get people off for things that they did, for which they are totally and completely guilty. I kick the search on Billy Braden's case so he can walk out of court and start selling drugs again right away. I'm just delaying the inevitable with these guys. I'm just making money. That's all I'm doing. And now I find a guy who I know is guilty – I *know* it. Maybe it's just my gut, but I know it. He's killed and he's going to kill again, Shauna, and he's making *me* a part of it. I feel like I'm a coconspirator. And I have to sit here and do nothing?'

He sweeps a desk full of papers to the floor, something out of a movie, the disgruntled employee with the asshole boss who's *just had it!* and quits.

'Fuck this,' he says, and he comes toward me, like he's heading out the door.

'Hey, come on,' I say.

He stops and takes my arm. 'I'm sorry about *Arangold*. I really am. But you're better off without me. Trust me.'

He releases my arm and leaves the office without another word.

31

Jason

Thursday, June 20

I look through the magazine rack and settle on the current issue of *Sports Illustrated*, the cover featuring two brothers, twins from South Korea, Hee-Jong and Seung-Hyun Lee, each of them seven-foot, three-inch centers, one a senior at Stanford, the other a senior at UConn. They are freaks of nature, the Lee twins, expected to go number one and two in the NBA draft next week. The headline beneath the two men: 'Is the NBA Ready for the Lee Twins?'

I drop the magazine in front of the clerk, along with a box of plain envelopes, multicolored construction paper, a pair of scissors, Scotch tape, and a pair of rubber gloves. I assume I look like a father buying art supplies for his kid, who also likes sports. The rubber gloves might stand out. Probably should have bought some dishwashing liquid or something.

I pull out my wallet for my debit card. I hardly ever use cash anymore. But then I catch myself, slip the debit card back in my wallet, and pay in cash.

When I was a kid, we used to steal the current edition of *Sports Illustrated* from the local library. Pete, the more handsome and charming of the Kolarich brothers, would chat up the librarian, divert her attention while I slipped the magazine into the back of my pants after ripping off the stamp sensor – or what I thought was a sensor.

When I was in high school playing football, I used to dream about seeing my name in that magazine, maybe a photo of me catching a pass in the Super Bowl. I would imagine some kid in a library just like me, stealing the magazine or ripping out my picture to put on his bedroom wall. *I want to be just like him. I want to be Jason Kolarich.*

Most of my fantasies, illusions of grandeur, used to involve sports, and almost always football. The acrobatic, impossible catch at a clutch moment, the crowd chanting my name, the announcer singing my praises over the roaring crowd. But as I've moved into my mid-thirties, it's sometimes more about coaching, inspiring a group of ragtag kids, given no chance to succeed, and impossibly winning the state championship or a national title. Occasionally it's a fantasy related to my profession, usually the innocent-man-on-death-row, a last-minute discovery that compels the governor to call the warden and halt the execution.

Lately, I'd be happy just to feel normal.

I check over my shoulder as I leave the convenience store. I've taken lately to suspecting that someone is following me. I can't place why, just a sensation that something is trailing behind me, stopping when I do, starting along with me, shadowing my every move.

I get into my SUV and drive. With the library on my mind and a local branch in sight, I pull into the parking lot and walk in. Over the main desk, there are signs welcoming me in multiple languages – *Bienvenidos, Mabuhay, Suswagatham* – and notices in vibrant colors for the 'Summer Book Club' and 'Rock and Read,' an advertisement for a children's author appearing next week, a program on 'The Secret Language of Peruvian Cuisine' that I would love to attend were it not for having to reorganize my sock drawer that night.

I'm not sure why I chose a library, other than the fact that it's not my home and not my office. Untraceable to me, in other words.

A young African-American woman behind the desk smiles at me. She seems pretty for a librarian, I think, but then I catch myself and realize I haven't been to a library since I was a punk kid, so what do I know about librarians? Plus, speaking of fantasies, the naughty

125

librarian look – hair pulled up tight, horn-rimmed glasses – was a staple of my adolescence.

I find a carrel in the back corner on the second floor and remove the items from my bag. I find the words I need in the magazine, cut them out with the scissors I bought, wearing the rubber gloves I bought, and tape them onto a piece of green construction paper. When it's done, the piece of paper says:

4 dead WOMEN James DrinkEr 3 6 11 WEst Townsend

It has the chaotic look of such notes, sometimes featuring entire words – *James* from a story on the NBA's LeBron, *WOMEN* from a headline about the WNBA's fiscal problems, *dead* from an article about a hockey player who overdosed on amphetamines, *Drink* from an advertisement for Dewar's – and sometimes partial words and individual letters and numbers of varying fonts and sizes.

I feel like I'm demanding ransom for some wealthy family's child or blackmailing a cheating spouse. It's not that bad, but it's bad. I'm betraying my oath. I've taken some liberties with the rules in the past, but this isn't a step over the line; this is taking a sledgehammer to a wall. But I'm done with sitting around like some do-nothing chump just because of some stupid rule. Four women are dead, and I'm not waiting for a fifth.

Getting the address is tougher, but just as important. They will print and analyze the envelope as meticulously as the note itself. *Detective* and *Vance* and *Austin* require a lot of cutting of various words, *police* is easy – the overdosing hockey player story – the street name, *Dunning*, a challenge, and the zip code a complete nightmare.

When I'm done, I find a mailbox downtown, north of the river, and drop the letter in. The last pickup is at two P.M., and I'm here ten minutes early. So with any luck, this should arrive on the desk of Detective Vance Austin tomorrow.

32

Jason

I overslept this morning, having not fully settled into sleep until about four in the morning, then awakening at six-thirty, then back down until nine. I desperately need some REM sleep, which makes me think of my favorite band and then my favorite person, Shauna. I ditched out on her yesterday, finally turning away the *Arangold* case, doing her a favor even if she doesn't realize it, and then ditched out on her literally by leaving the office to author my anonymous note. I noted, when I walked in this morning, a deep impression in the carpet, in the shape of a square, next to my refrigerator, a slightly lighter color on the fabric as well – Shauna had reclaimed the *Arangold* files that had been sitting there untouched for over a week. I can't imagine what Shauna is thinking about me right now.

'Nothing,' Lightner tells me over the phone. 'James spent the night at his apartment and went to work this morning. Will keep you posted.'

'Thanks, Joel.' At least we're keeping tabs on the man now.

My intercom squawks. I don't have any appointments this morning.

'Yes, my love?' I call out to Marie.

'Alexa Himmel to see you.'

Well, then. I figured her for gone after the Altoids incident. If she had an ounce of common sense, she would be.

She carts in her transcription machine behind her like a piece of luggage and leaves it in the corner of my office. She gives me a fleeting kiss, her lips full and wet, just the way I like them, and says, 'Sorry to barge in while you're working.'

'No problem,' I say, especially considering that I wasn't working at all. I don't have any trials coming up, and every other deadline I have isn't imminent, which is a good thing because I've been terribly inefficient, unable to focus, often rereading the same passage three or four times. My vision is starting to suffer, too, a shady border framing my eyes, as if everything were in a dream or flashback.

Alexa closes the door behind her. A big talk? I hope not. We've talked enough.

'Well, I have something for you,' she says. She is wearing a blouse with frills at the edge of her sleeves and a blue skirt. She cleans up good. She hands me a manila folder.

'Is this a subpoena?' I ask.

She smiles. 'Open it.'

I rip it open from the side and remove three, no, four sheets of foil, each containing thirty small pills.

She puts her hand on my cheek. 'Your knee will get better, but until it does, you shouldn't have to live in pain. Not my man.'

'Alexa . . . This is . . . How did . . .' I lower my voice. 'This is . . . *illegal.*'

She puts her hands on my chest. I like it when she puts her hands on my chest. She gives me a longer, softer kiss, a taste of strawberry on her tongue. I could learn to love this girl.

She puts her mouth next to my ear. 'Then maybe tonight,' she whispers, her breath tickling my ear, 'you can spank me for being a bad girl.'

33

Shauna

Friday, June 21

Bradley John, newly deputized as the second chair of the *Arangold* defense team, finishes arranging our lone conference room, which has now officially become the war room. He has set up the television and DVD player in one corner for the videos of the auditorium construction during its various phases; he has one end of the room devoted to the flooring issue, another to colonnades and shoring, a third to the various internal issues during Arangold's renovation of the civic auditorium.

'This case is bigger than two lawyers,' I say, as if I'm suddenly realizing it.

'Yeah, but you know enough about this stuff for *six*.' Bradley smiles at me. I like this kid. A solid mind and a good sense for how and when to say the right thing. This is one of those times.

And he's right. I've learned more about a major construction project than I ever wanted to know. I'll never walk into a football stadium or concert hall or government building without thinking of tuck-pointing and change orders, soil samples and pre-bid drawings.

'Hey, Shauna? Just out of curiosity – why the battlefield promotion? I'm not complaining, but Rory keeps asking about Jason, and now he's getting me. What's up with Jason?'

I let out a sigh while I organize the depositions in the order I want them. 'I was hoping you could tell me,' I say. Then I stop and look at him. 'Actually, that's a serious statement. Have you noticed anything unusual with Jason?'

Bradley gives a *Who knows?* shrug. 'I've been like you, boss. Buried in *Mariel* for the last two months and now into the fire with *Arangold*. I've barely talked to him.'

'I know.'

'But you know Jason,' he says, trying to appease me. 'If he's not on trial, he mopes around. He just had a tough stretch with the knee blowing out, he's missing the summer marathon season, he hasn't had a big trial lately—'

'But *this* is a big trial.' I drive my finger into the table. 'This is a bet-the-company case for the Arangolds.'

'He doesn't want to try this case? He turned it *down*? Oh.' Bradley pushes his lips out. 'Yeah, now *that's* unusual. Yeah, I don't know then.'

My eyes drift off in the direction of Jason's office, though I'd need X-ray vision to see it from the conference room.

'Be right back,' I say. I didn't like how Jason and I left things yesterday. He bolted on me and then disappeared for the entire afternoon. The lad is out of sorts, methinks, and needs a friend.

When I reach Jason's office, I see something I've never seen. His door is closed.

I knock weakly with the back of my hand. 'Anyone home?'

'Hey, Shauna, come in, come in.' Jason has a big enough office for a couch on the end opposite his desk, which is where I find him and his new lady friend.

'Shauna Tasker, Alexa Himmel.'

'Hi.' She gives me a quick once-over and waves at me from the couch. She could get up. It wouldn't kill her.

So I wave back. 'Nice to meet you.'

Yeah, she's Jason's type, all right. Exotic and mysterious, sexy.

'I didn't mean to intrude. Jason,' I say, feeling like a teacher or my mother, 'when you get a second, nothing urgent.'

'No problem. Alexa just stopped by for a minute. Shauna has a huge trial coming up,' Jason says. He's got that spacey grin on his face again, like he did when I caught him mumbling song lyrics and lighting matches the other day. On his lap is a manila envelope, opened, contents unknown.

'Oh? That's exciting,' Alexa says, in that way you say something and mean the exact opposite. I mean, surely it can't be as exciting as, say, spending your days transcribing what other people say. Seriously, trying a multimillion-dollar case with an entire family business on the line is *exciting*, but basically serving as a human tape recorder – that's the coolest!

She holds her stare on me, eyebrows raised, as if to say to me, *Was there anything else, sweetheart? Or should you be running along?*

I clap my hands together, heat rising to my face. 'Well, Alexa, nice meeting you,' I say, and for some reason I do a salute. I actually salute like I'm in the military. Why on earth did I do that?

'Aye, aye, Cap'n,' Jason says, saluting me back. He laughs. Alexa laughs. I make a decision right there: It's okay for Jason to laugh. Not okay for Alexa to laugh, not when she's basically laughing at me. Not okay for a little Kewpie doll court reporter to wiggle her sweet ass and be more welcome in Jason's office than his best friend and law partner. Not okay for a little low-rent typist who probably didn't make it past high school to talk down to someone who graduated law school at the top of her class and then built up her own law firm from scratch when nobody thought she would succeed, *nobody*—

Wow. Where did that come from?

'Okay, bye then.' I close the door to their continued amusement.

I return to the conference room and tell Bradley to shut up before he can even ask me. 'We don't need Jason,' I tell him. 'We'll win this case, just you and me.'

34

Jason

Wednesday, June 26

The next several days are like a blur. I ducked out early on Friday and spent the whole weekend with Alexa, most of the time naked, trying out new options sexually, the bad-girl thing she'd whispered in my ear being a particular highlight. I've never been into role-playing; the nurse and patient, the cop, the chambermaid, the prison guard, the flight attendant, the college professor – none of that has ever floated my boat. Nor does the rough stuff do anything for me. Aggressive, sure, but not abusive, not hitting or choking.

But every now and then, I like to talk. And so does Alexa. Most of it is merely suggestive, but when we get going, hot and sweaty, that old-fashioned girl gets pretty graphic.

But here's what we *don't* talk about: Never once this weekend did she ask me about my knee, never once about the pills. *I don't like to see you in pain* was the only thing she said, which worked for me.

The weekend became Monday, but I liked the weekend better so I adopted Monday as an unofficial holiday. I didn't have court, no meetings, no upcoming deadlines, and Alexa had the day off. Here's a summary: more sex.

I thought that worked pretty well, so Tuesday became a holiday, too, though I did have one meeting that I had to cancel.

In between these sexual escapades and Altoid chewing, I've

continually kept tabs on James Drinker. I've monitored the *Herald* online for any news of fresh murders by the North Side Slasher, but I didn't expect any, because Joel Lightner's team has kept Mr Drinker on a short leash. Lightner said his surveillance team was about to die from boredom, as our man tended to go straight to work, straight home, then back to work, then back home. On Saturday night, he worked all day, went to a movie at night – *Fast & Furious 6* – by himself, and then went home. On Sunday, he went to church – Saint Hedwig in his neighborhood – and then picked up some gyros on his way home. Once the week started, it was work and home, work and home.

At two o'clock on Wednesday, I'm reviewing the *Brady* material on a possession with intent that is up next week for a pretrial in federal court when Joel Lightner buzzes my cell phone. I received the morning report on James Drinker and didn't expect another call until he leaves work at five-thirty or six. So if Joel's calling, he must have news.

'Thought you'd want to know,' he says, 'that the police just paid our friend James a visit at his auto body shop. They took him to head-quarters twenty minutes ago.'

I release a week's worth of breath. It's about freakin' time; I sent that note to the police last week.

'Great,' I say. 'That's . . . great.'

'So that dilemma of yours? You never had to cross that bridge. They must have connected the dots on his relationship with the first two victims.'

Um, right. No reason to tell Joel that I already crossed that ethical bridge and found it wobbly and unsteady.

'Keep me posted, will you? And thanks, Joel.'

I keep my phone close by, cognizant of the fact that James Drinker might be calling any moment. That was the clear direction I gave him, what any lawyer would tell him: *Don't talk to the cops until you've called me.* But an hour passes and I haven't heard a thing. Maybe he got another lawyer. Maybe he's winging it in there. Maybe he's already given up the whole thing to them, one of those guys who can't keep his composure once the pressure's applied.

My spirits now fully revived, I pick up Alexa on the way home from work. We order in Thai food, but I don't feel like eating. My stomach has been reenacting the Civil War all day. I've barely touched any food. At seven o'clock, I get a text message from Joel:

Cops dropped JD back at work 6:40 pm he picked up car drove straight home

So the police let him go. Hmm. I wasn't sure how that would play out. I didn't put any details into the anonymous note about his connections to the first victims, Alicia Corey and Lauren Gibbs. I just said, he's your guy. Maybe that was a mistake. What did I think would happen – they'd sweat him and he'd spill the beans right there? Maybe I did. Wishful thinking.

But he's on their radar screen now. I've been around law enforcement long enough, both as a prosecutor and defense counsel, to know what deters these guys and what doesn't. And knowing that the police are watching you is usually enough to spook them.

So maybe I've stopped the bloodbath, at least. Maybe he's done. And if he starts getting thirsty again for the blood of young women, Lightner's team will be watching. The deal we struck was that if anything got to the point of looking imminent – if Drinker was sneaking around houses in the middle of the night, that kind of thing – Lightner's people would call 911 and expose him, if nothing else to stop anything from happening, even if Drinker got away.

So that's comforting, I guess.

At nine o'clock, I'm sitting on my bed, doing some online legal research for a suppression hearing I have next week. Alexa is arranging the clothes she's brought over to wear for tomorrow morning. She's been going back and forth, picking up items on a daily basis and bringing them to my place, which must be a pain in the ass for her. I've offered to stay at her house, but she prefers mine. It's more centrally located, I guess.

Alexa comes over to the bed, removes my laptop, and replaces it with herself, straddling me. Exploring the parameters of the Fourth Amendment case law on searches incident to arrest can be interesting, but exploring the parameters of Alexa's sexual appetite has proven more enticing still.

Life can be good. At least I can tell myself it's good.

Afterward, I'm lying on the bed while Alexa takes it upon herself to tidy up my room, which isn't necessary, but she does it without asking and says she doesn't mind. She cooks, she cleans, she satisfies my every sexual desire, she's cool about that tin of Altoids – what next? Does she like football and poker, too?

My phone buzzes on the nightstand. I pick it up and see an unknown caller. My heart skips a beat. Lately, that has only meant one person. I figured he would call.

'This is Jason,' I say.

'Well, well.' James Drinker breathes into the phone. 'You . . . prick.'

'Who is this?' I ask, because in all fairness, any number of people would like to say that to me.

'This is your *client*,' he says.

'Is this – James?'

'That's right, Jason. It's James. James Drinker. The client you just stabbed in the back.'

I won't deny I'm enjoying this, but the even keel to his voice is unsettling.

'I don't know what you mean, James.'

'No?'

'No.'

Silence. Alexa stops what she's doing and looks over at me.

'I just had a nice visit with the police,' he says. 'Detectives. They yanked me down to the police station and questioned me for . . . I don't know, two or three hours.'

'Where are you?' I ask, playing dumb. 'Are you at head-quarters?'

'Oh, no. They let me go, Jason.'

135

Yes, I should have been more explicit with my note. I should have cut out enough words from the *Sports Illustrated* to say *dated Alicia Corey* and *friends with Lauren Gibbs*. But they'll get there, eventually. He's in their sights now.

'Well, we knew they'd pay you a visit sooner or later,' I say. 'How did it go? You were supposed to call me, James.'

Dead air, save for his breathing, slow and steady.

'Did you call the cops on me, Jason?'

'No, I didn't.' Which is technically true.

'Are you sure, Jason? Because I think you did.' Still with that slow and steady tone, though I detect a slight tremble of anger.

I clear my throat. 'You have a connection to the first two victims. You dated Alicia and you were friends with Lauren. We always knew the police would talk to you.'

Silence. He is stewing. What I'm saying is correct, though. I told him, all along, that the cops would get to him sooner or later, and probably sooner.

'I never dated Alicia Corey,' he says. 'I didn't even know her or Lauren Gibbs.'

A burn spreads across my chest. Didn't see that one coming.

'You know what that means, Jason?'

It means the only reason the police would pay him a visit is because I tipped them off. He caught me. He got me. Was that his plan all along? Was he testing me?

And if so, why?

'It means you lied to me,' I say. 'You shouldn't do that.'

'True,' he concedes. 'But it also means that you told them about me. And you *really* shouldn't do that.'

'I wish I could help you, James. Even if you didn't know any of the victims, there's plenty of reasons why they might contact you. Who knows what evidence they followed that led to you.' *Like the fact that you killed those women, you maggot.*

'They didn't follow any evidence,' he says. 'They just asked me if I knew those women. They asked me twelve different ways, but in the end, that's all they asked me. They were fishing. They didn't have anything on me. Why would they pluck me out of the blue and bring me in? There's only one reason. That reason is you, Jason. You told them about me.'

'We're going in circles, James. Should I assume you no longer want to retain my services?'

'Do you think I killed those women, Jason? Do you think I'm a . . . psychopath?'

Sociopath, actually, but why split hairs?

'Do you?' A taunt to his voice, a dare. 'Do you think I like to cut women up with a knife? Do you think I like to torture them? Watch them suffer? Listen to them beg for their lives, smell their blood as the life drains from their eyes? Do you?'

The shadows framing my vision seem to darken and thicken, narrowing my sight line. My hand begins to itch. I'm not going to give this asshole the satisfaction of thinking he's getting inside my head – which, of course, is the first step in letting him do that very thing.

Silence, save for his labored breathing. Alexa is pretending not to listen, picking up clothes off the floor, but keeping one ear to my conversation.

'Because if that's what you think about me, Jason, I have one more question for you.'

'I'm all ears.'

'Am I really someone you want to piss off?'

I bounce off the bed, adrenaline surging through me. I may not be a hundred percent these days, but there are still a few things that can light my fire.

'You know where I work, James. Stop by anytime. I'll even give you my home address if you like.'

'Oh, I already have it, Jason, but thanks. It's a nice town house, by the way.'

'Are you threatening me, James? Because that's a bad idea.'

He clucks his tongue, *tsk-tsk*-ing me, scolding me.

'Relax, my friend,' he says. 'I didn't kill anybody and I'm not *going* to kill anybody. You believe me, don't you, Jason?'

'Whether you did or not,' I respond, 'you better watch yourself now. You're now officially on the cops' radar.'

'Boyyy, it sure didn't seem that way,' he hums. 'I have to tell you, by the end of the interview, they sure seemed like they felt this was a waste of their time. They even apologized to me for the trouble. No, I think I've been crossed off their list.'

'Oh, go ahead and believe that, James. You think the cops are going to tell you what they really think? They lie to suspects all the time. As easily as taking a breath.'

'Oh, *now* you tell me.'

I don't know what that means, but I do know this: He's probably right. If James Drinker has no obvious connection to these women, which apparently is the case, then my anonymous note will go into the loony-tune bin at Area Three headquarters. Now that a serial killer has been acknowledged, and even branded with a catchy name like the North Side Slasher, the crazies will be out in full force. The tip hotline is probably overflowing with calls identifying the real killer as Osama bin Laden, Donald Trump, Martha Stewart, or one of the Kardashian sisters, the one without talent.

So my note was enough to send some junior detectives over to Drinker's apartment, enough to haul him to headquarters for a brief inquiry, but then quickly dismissed as yet another frivolous tip.

Which means James Drinker is probably as free and clear as he says.

'I'm done with you,' I say, trying to regain the upper hand.

He laughs. Now he's the one enjoying this call. Needless to say, this conversation did not go the way I planned.

'I decide when you're done,' he says, and then the line goes dead.

35

Jason

Friday, June 28

I'm groggy and moody on Friday morning. I slept alone last night,
after spending the last six nights with Alexa. It was her idea that we
take a break – 'We wouldn't want to see each other seven whole days
in a row, now would we? I mean, that's practically marriage!' – and I
didn't disagree. That's become a pattern with her, making a serious
point – giving me space, not rushing things – but delivering it with
feather-soft sarcasm.

I couldn't sleep, the remnants of the conversation with James
Drinker in my head, texting Lightner at all hours to confirm with
his surveillance team that Drinker was still in his apartment. This
guy has officially invaded my brain. I don't have a lot of options or
recourse, but I have to figure out something. The problem is that my
brain isn't working at one hundred percent speed lately. The world is
moving in slow motion these days, my legs heavy, white noise
drowning out the cries around me.

I stop for Starbucks and make it into the office just past nine. Not
bad for me, on a non-court day like this one.

'So how was your big night alone?' Alexa asks me when she calls
me at the office, ten minutes after I hit my chair. 'Did you go to strip
clubs and eat steak burritos?'

That sounds a lot more fun than what I did. I stayed home by myself, reading some case law for a motion to suppress I'm filing next week, then giving up and watching half of season two of *Arrested Development* on DVD, popping Altoids every two hours along the way.

'Is that what you think guys do when women aren't around?' I ask.

'Yes, it is. What do they really do?'

'Masturbate, eat pizza, and watch sports.'

'All at the same time?'

'Sometimes,' I say. 'God didn't give us two hands for nothing.'

'Did you masturbate last night?'

'That's a very personal question, Ms. Himmel.'

'Did you?'

'Are you kidding me? After a week with you, I'm sore as hell, woman. I had an ice pack down my pants all night.'

She laughs hard at that comment, but I'm not kidding about the soreness. I've never met someone with this much energy in bed. This old-fashioned girl is going to break me in half.

'By the way, since we're being personal,' I say, 'I'm out of protection.'

'Condoms?' There is tapping in the background. Putting a transcript into final form, I assume. I don't really understand what court reporters do. I should probably ask her.

'Yeah. I'm out. Remind me to buy some more.'

'I told you, I'm covered,' she says. 'I have birth control.'

'You sure?'

'Either that or I'm planning on trapping you into marriage by getting pregnant.'

I give a good and awkward laugh, *heh-heh-heh.*

'Take a breath, for God's sake,' she says. 'I'm covered. You're not going to get me pregnant. But if it will make you feel better, by all means go buy some – oh – oh, no – oh, Jason—'

'What? What's wrong?'

'Oh, no.'

'What?'

And then, somehow, I realize it before she says it. She isn't working on a transcript. She's tapping her computer. She's on the Internet.

'Don't tell me,' I say, waking up my laptop and heading to the *Herald* website.

'Oh, Jason.'

And there it is, the garish headline:

NORTH SIDE SLASHER CLAIMS FIFTH VICTIM

A fifth woman, Samantha Drury, age twenty-five, was stabbed in her car as she was arriving home on the city's northwest side last night. Ambushed inside her garage, stabbed multiple times.

'Oh, baby, I'm so sorry,' Alexa says.

The bitter venom rushes to my throat. I grab my garbage can just in time as I retch liquids, my stomach in revolt. I take a couple of panting breaths and wait for my pulse to settle. This guy is just having fun now. Toying with me. Killing women as part of a game with me.

'What . . . what are you going to do?' Alexa asks.

Dim the lights, mute the sound: A calm sweeps over me, sudden and vivid, like I'd lost my breath but recovered it. Calm, not because I'm feeling peaceful or serene, but because finally I'm making a decision that, in the back of my mind, I always knew I might have to make.

I'm done with you, I told James on the phone two nights ago. I wasn't really sure what that comment meant; it was just my turn for a lob in the verbal tennis match, an attempt to regain some momentum in the conversation.

But now I'm ready to give those words some meaning. *I'm done with you, James Drinker.*

'I'm going to call the police,' I tell Alexa. 'I'm going to tell them everything. Even if it gets me disbarred.'

'Oh, Jason, really?'

No, as a matter of fact, *not* really, but that's what I need to tell her, that's what she needs to think. She can't be involved in what I'm going to do.

It's not that I would mind losing my law license over this. It would be well worth it. The reason I'm not going back to the cops is that it wouldn't work. There's nothing I can tell them that I haven't already told them. James Drinker probably has no more of a connection to Samantha Drury than he has to President Obama. And somehow I know that he has covered his tracks. I just know it.

No, the police aren't an option.

'I'll call you later,' I say. I punch out the call and dial up another one.

Joel Lightner answers his cell on the second ring.

'Jason – I was just about to call you. We just saw the news. I don't know what happened. Our people were on him. They swear he never left the apartment building after he got home from work. They swear it.'

'He snuck out somehow, Joel. He probably spotted the tail. He probably slipped out a fire escape or something.'

'My people are better than that.'

'Well, his *better* is better than their *better*, I guess.'

'Are we sure Drinker was the one who did it last night? I mean, maybe he isn't our offender.'

I realize I've been holding my breath, my head getting dizzy. 'It was him,' I say. 'There's no doubt.'

'Shit. I'm sorry, Jason. We fucked up. It won't happen again, I can prom—'

'Joel, I think we're done with the surveillance. I want your guys to stand down.'

'Stand down?'

'No more surveillance on James Drinker. Effective immediately.'

'We won't lose him again, Jason.'

'No. I want it over. As of right now. Stop the surveillance.'

'Why?'

'Tactical reasons,' I say. 'He's smart enough to know when we're tailing him. He'll be smart enough to know when we're not. Maybe he'll drop his guard and make a mistake.'

'That doesn't make any sense.'

'It's what I want,' I insist. 'I'm the client, you're my investigator. Do what I ask.'

Joel doesn't speak. He has a brain cell or two himself, and he knows me too well. He knows I'm not telling him to remove the surveillance detail for any *tactical* reason.

'My client sometimes has stupid ideas,' Joel says. 'Very stupid ones. What are you planning to do, Counselor? And why don't you want my people watching when you do it?'

'Just do it,' I say. I hang up before he can say anything else.

Because there's nothing left to say. I can't involve Joel any more than I can involve Alexa. I have to do this myself and let the chips fall where they may.

And I can tell myself that I tried. I tried to follow my lawyer's oath, giving my client the benefit of the doubt, hoping that if Drinker was the offender, the police would figure it out without his own attorney selling him out. When they didn't, I violated my oath and gave them a very large nudge, pointing them directly to Drinker, and still they've turned away from him. I don't have any other choice, as I see it.

For a reason all his own, James Drinker is intent on killing women in this city, and the only person who can stop him is me.

36

Jason

Saturday, June 29

The problem with summer in the Midwest is that it stays light outside for so long. Just my luck, we're only slightly over a week removed from the solstice, so today is the ninth-longest day of sunlight in the entire damn year.

Ideally, the best way to ambush somebody is to catch them outside their house – either inside their garage or on their walk up to their door – when it's dark. You have the element of surprise, you have the cover of darkness, and you don't have to hassle with details like house alarms, locked doors, or bolted windows.

But conditions have to be ideal, and for me, they are not. James Drinker doesn't live in a house with a garage; he lives in a high-rise. And he leaves Higgins Auto Body at half past five, six at the latest, according to the surveillance team that has followed him over the last week. So that's nowhere close to dusk, not this time of year.

All of which leaves me with only one option: walking up to his fourth-floor apartment, forcing my way in, and taking care of business.

When I was a kid, the intersection of Townsend and Kensington was a decent place to live, part of a middle-class Eastern European neighborhood called Power's Park, named after a steel company owner who built a plant here in the 1930s and hired Polish immigrants. There was a place not two blocks away from this intersection where my dad sometimes took us after Mass on Sunday called Magyar that served Hungarian food, my father's ancestry. We always knew it was coming after Mass when we piled into the beater station wagon and Dad would look at us in the rearview mirror and ask us if we were 'Hungary.' Laughed like hell at that joke, he did.

Dad would speak what little of the native tongue he knew with the owners and would order food like money was no object – which meant he probably had just scammed somebody out of something and he actually *had* some dough. He went nuts over the paprika stew and dumplings. Mom always ordered the same thing, veal crepes. Pete and I kept it safe with *debreceni* sausage with mustard and cabbage.

My dad was always happy there, probably because he only took us there after he'd scored in some way or another – the track or a card game or some grift he'd pulled. My dad's moods went up and down that way, depending on that week's income. He was a pretty good con artist, I assumed, but he was even better at conning himself into believing he was a winner on those rare occasions when his takings outgained his expenses. Would have been nice if he'd left a little of that money for Mom. But in the Kolarich household, it was all about Jack's mood. Would it be dinner at Irish Green and brunch at Magyar and flowers for Mom? Or would it be cold cuts and leftovers and Jack staggering home at two in the morning, half in the bag, looking for a boy to swat?

This neighborhood is no longer called Power's Park; now it's Old Power's Park. The steel plant moved out in the seventies, and Magyar is now a pawnshop, next to a payday loan center, next to a secondhand clothing store. The whites mostly fled this neighborhood when the mayor decided, twenty years ago, that this area would be an excellent location for subsidized housing projects – far, far better than, say, the available acreage on the near-north side close to all the affluent white neighborhoods.

So now it's a forgotten neighborhood, the streets littered with potholes and busted-up curbs, drug deals taking place in open view in dingy alleys or drive-ups at street corners. I can blend into this neighborhood if I wish – my hair's pretty long now, I have two days' growth on my face, and with an untucked T-shirt over blue jeans, I can basically play the part of the down-on-his-luck white guy.

I'm being overly cautious, but I don't have a surreptitious route into James Drinker's apartment, so the least I can do is make sure I'm in disguise while I case the neighborhood. I pass by his apartment building at 3611 West Townsend long enough to realize that there's a door controlled by a buzzer, but it seems to be broken and people are freely entering and exiting. I see an elevator, a necessity for an eleven-story building, but I don't plan on using it. I see mailboxes and a beat-up tile floor in the entryway.

The sun has fallen now, but I need to wait a little longer, because there's nothing to the west of this neighborhood that will offer any cover, so the beautiful sunset, with its fluorescent colors lighting up the sky, still provides illumination.

I walk around the place a couple of times and then head back toward my car, parked three blocks away in a lot secured by a high fence. I pay the fee to the guy at the gate and get my key. I leave the lot and park on a side street a half mile away.

I use my electric razor to shave. I squeeze out some hair gel that I bought at the store to grease back my hair. In the SUV's backseat, I use the extra legroom to change into a shirt and tie and suit.

When I was a prosecutor, I once lost my badge, which was a big no-no. Authentic law enforcement badges are a real treasure for the gangbangers; they trade them like currency. So I got docked some pay, but eventually they had to give me a replacement. Lo and behold, I found my original badge several weeks later, but I'd already paid the price for it, and I figured the odds of my getting through the paperwork to recoup my fine were about as good as my setting foot on Mars, so I kept the stupid thing. I wasn't supposed to do that. Sometimes I do things I'm not supposed to do. Tonight might be one of those times.

I make the decision to leave my SUV where it is on the side street. It's a small gamble. It's a pretty nice ride, but I shouldn't be too long, and I'd rather have my car at the ready without having to pay somebody cash to get my key. I don't know if I'm going to be walking or running when I leave James Drinker's apartment building tonight.

I'm wearing my trench coat, the shirt and tie showing through the nape, and the county attorney's office badge clipped to my coat. I walk with confidence. You don't do that, you're a sitting duck. But you keep your chin up, make eye contact with passersby, and look serious but disinterested, and with the trench coat and badge, nobody messes with you.

Unless they do.

I approach the building. There is really no turning back now. I've made the decision and I have to abide by it with full force. If I back down now, I could be in a world of shit. I don't know what James Drinker is capable of, but several people have underestimated him so far, me included, and I'm not going to do it tonight.

I take the stairs slowly, deliberately, not trying to conceal my steps but not going out of my way to be loud, either. I pass two people on their way down, both of them young men – late teens, early twenties – who show me some respect by keeping on their side of the staircase and then some. They could be badasses, for all I know, but why mess with law enforcement unnecessarily? They pick their spots like anyone else.

I get to the fourth floor and walk down to number 406, on the left side of the dimly lit hallway – dimly lit is good. The door is old, cheap wood, but probably on the thick side. There is no peephole, which is significant. I could work around it either way, but it's easier this way.

I rap my fist three times on the door and call out, in a voice not my own, 'James Drinker. County Attorney Special Investigators.'

Then I take one step back and hold up my badge.

'Who is it?' a voice calls through the door. It's a thick door, or he was sleeping and his voice is weak. Or he's wary, as he should be when

147

someone knocks on his door at ten o'clock at night, and the fear alters his voice.

'I'm a special investigator with the county attorney's office, Mr Drinker. We have a couple more questions to ask you. A couple things you told us on Wednesday.'

'What else do you want to know?'

'Do you want me to shout my questions to you in front of all your neighbors, or do you want to let me in? It's your choice.'

My heartbeat kicks into full throttle. There could be anything awaiting me behind that door. He could have made my voice. He could be expecting me. He could have that butcher knife or any other kind of a weapon.

Which is why I'm glad I brought my gun.

Two locks unbolt, a total of four clicks. Then the door pops open a couple of inches, straining the rusted chain lock, still attached. I make sure that the first thing he sees is the badge, front and center in his narrow line of vision.

And I make sure that the first thing he feels is a blast against the door, sending him backward as I charge into the room, the chain lock snapping away easily.

Not the most original of moves, but he clearly wasn't ready for it. He's in the midst of completing an ungraceful fall backward onto the hardwood floor, his body rocking backward, feet in the air, his shirt rising up to reveal the beer gut, his flaming red hair everywhere on the floor. Hands are free. No weapon that I can see.

'Hi, James,' I say.

Long, kinky red hair, check. Spare tire in the midsection, check. Horn-rimmed glasses, check. Muscular build, not as toned as I would have thought, but I never saw him in a short-sleeved T-shirt.

He checks all the boxes.

But the face is wrong. From a distance, sure, the prominent features all check out. But his nose is bigger. His teeth are straighter. His eyes are smaller, his cheeks rounder.

'James Drinker?' I say.

'Who the hell are you? Don't . . . What do you want to know? I didn't do anything. I already told your cops.'

The voice is all wrong, too.

He sits up, his arm over his body. He took a hard fall and he's scared out of his mind.

'I know you didn't,' I say. 'This is a misunderstanding. I'm sorry.' I fish a bunch of twenties out of my pocket. 'That's for the chain lock. And a few drinks, on me. I'm . . . I'm sorry.'

I turn for the door, my head buzzing. I played this out twenty different ways in my head, good outcomes and bad. I didn't plan for this.

Whoever this guy is who walked into my law firm, and who has killed five women in this city, he isn't James Drinker.

Who goes to an attorney's office to confess his sins wearing a disguise, and with an assumed identity? I never saw that one coming.

Not a fake name, either – a real person, with a real apartment, a real job, a clean criminal record. And with distinctive features like blazing red hair and thick black glasses and a beer belly, all of which he could easily mimic, that he would be remembered for, and that, from a distance, would make the real James Drinker indistinguishable from the fake one. So if I happened to send someone to look in on James, my people would have every reason to think that the person they were tailing was the same person who walked into my law office.

Whoever he is, he's smart. Smarter than I ever imagined.

I exit the building and start walking east on Townsend toward the big intersection, toward my car parked down the way.

He's been watching James Drinker, I now realize. When the cops showed up at Higgins Auto Body the other day and put the real James Drinker into the back of a car and drove him down to headquarters for questioning, he was watching. And he knew Drinker had absolutely no connection to the murders of five women. He knew that the only way the cops would have his name is from me.

He's probably watching me right now.

I stop and spin around on the sidewalk. I look in all directions.

There is street noise, partiers on a weekend, cars passing at the busy intersection. He could be anywhere. He's not going to be dumb enough to reveal himself to me right now.

He's been playing me all along.

I'm back at square one. I have no idea who he is. I have no idea why he's butchering young women. And I have no idea why he chose me.

But I have a feeling I'm about to find out.

PEOPLE VS. JASON KOLARICH
TRIAL, DAY 2
Tuesday, December 10

37

Shauna

'The People call Detective Raymond Cromartie,' says Roger Ogren.

Some people just look like cops. Ray Cromartie is one of them. The confident swagger, thick nose, wary eyes, and crooked smile. He is a bit overweight, with jowls and a ruddy drinker's complexion, a nick or two on his neck from shaving. His hair is wavy, the color of ash. He's the kind of man who could be charming at the right moment, comforting to a child, and intimidating as hell with a bad guy. His cologne lingers with me even as he's reached the witness stand and begun the introductory portion of his testimony.

Cromartie goes back over twenty years on the force, the last nine as a detective. Lightner, who knows all the cops, says he's 'good people,' which I've always thought was a stupid saying.

'I arrived about half past one in the morning, July thirty-first,' Cromartie says. 'I spoke with Officer Garvin and then took a look at the crime scene myself.'

'And what were your initial impressions?' Ogren asks.

'I saw no indication of forced entry,' he says, right out of a TV show. They teach prosecutors nowadays to be aware of all of the criminal trials people see on TV, to understand what assumptions they'll bring with them to the courtroom and what language they're comfortable with. *No sign of forced entry, Lieutenant!* 'I saw very little indication of a physical struggle, as you can see from the photographs. The second floor was relatively intact in terms of the furniture, things on top of the kitchen counters, that kind of thing.'

'What happened next, Detective?'

'I wanted to speak with the defendant. He was seated on the couch in the living room.'

'And did you speak with him?'

'I did. I made him aware of his Miranda rights. He indicated that he'd been given his warnings from Officer Garvin and that he was a defense attorney by trade and knew well his rights. I asked him if he was willing to speak with me. He said he was.'

'Describe the conversation.'

'I asked the defendant if he knew the victim. He said he did. He said her name was Alexa Himmel.'

Jason stirs, ever so slightly, at hearing Alexa's name.

'Please continue, Detective.'

'I asked him who Alexa Himmel was to him. He said, "We've been seeing each other for several months."'

He's quoting Jason verbatim there, or at least claiming to. He has his reasons.

'I asked him if Ms. Himmel lived with him. He said that she spent a lot of time at his house and spent the night often, but she had her own house in Overton Ridge.'

'Okay. And what happened next?'

'I asked the defendant what happened tonight. He said he came home from work and found Ms. Himmel dead on the living room floor. He said he called 911 upon finding her. He said the Glock handgun belonged to him, but he didn't kill her.'

'What did you say next, Detective?'

'I asked him if he knew of anyone who would want to kill her.'

'And what did the defendant say, Detective, when you asked him if he knew who would want to kill Alexa Himmel?'

Drawing out the question, highlighting the significance.

Cromartie pauses a beat for good measure. 'He said, "I have a pretty good idea, but I can't be sure."'

'And what did you say at that point?'

'I asked him who that person was that he had a "pretty good idea" killed her.'

'Did he tell you?'

'No, he did not. He said he wanted to talk to a lawyer and did not want to speak with me further.'

Roger Ogren pauses a beat, as if surprised. 'He said he thought he knew who killed Ms. Himmel, but he wouldn't *tell you*?'

'Objection,' I say, as if disgusted.

'Sustained.'

Ogren doesn't protest, having made his point with the question.

'What did you do after the defendant invoked his right to counsel?'

'I ceased any further questioning. An officer stayed with the defendant on the couch while we processed the crime scene. I went upstairs, first of all, to the third floor of the town house. The defendant's bedroom.'

Ogren admits into evidence photographs of Jason's bedroom, close-ups on the dresser of drawers and the contents of each drawer, and the bathroom, including shots of the medicine cabinet and the inside of the cabinet beneath the sink.

'What were you looking for in the defendant's bedroom and bathroom, Detective?'

'The defendant had told me that Ms. Himmel often spent the night. So I was looking for makeup, brushes, perfume, hair sprays or hair gels, tampons or maxi pads. I was looking for things in the shower like women's shampoo or soaps or loofahs. I was looking in the dresser for any women's clothing.'

'And *did* you find any evidence that a woman had been spending time routinely in that bathroom or bedroom? Any evidence that a woman appeared to be staying overnight on a regular basis?'

Roger Ogren is overstating what Jason said to Detective Cromartie. He knows better, but he's testing me. It's early in the trial, and he is trying to see how much he can get away with.

'Your Honor,' I say, standing, 'could the witness do the testifying instead of Mr Ogren?'

The judge admonishes Ogren, who nods with his eyes closed. 'Detective?'

'As you can see from the photographs, I did not find any of those things. I saw no evidence that a woman spent any time in that bathroom or in that bedroom. Nothing that would indicate that a woman was sleeping over every night.'

Now it's *every* night. I consider objecting again.

'I couldn't square what the defendant had said to me with what I saw upstairs,' he adds.

Jason pats my hand. I take his cue and stay silent, poker-faced. He doesn't like to object very much when he's the defense lawyer. Now I'm the defense lawyer, he the defendant, but I find myself following his advice. I shouldn't. It's my insecurity and fear getting the better of me. If it's Jason's idea and it turns out badly, it won't be my fault, it will be his.

'Well, what about an overnight bag?' Ogren asks. 'Anything that Ms. Himmel would have brought with her, just for that night? A bag with a change of clothes or toiletries, that kind of thing? Did you find anything like that, Detective?'

'No, I did not. I looked very pointedly for that kind of thing and didn't find it.'

Ogren walks Cromartie briefly through the remainder of his canvass of the house, which takes us to past two-thirty in the morning.

'I advised the defendant that I wanted to take him to headquarters for further questioning,' he says. 'I asked him if he would go with me voluntarily. He said that he would, but that he wanted to call his attorney, Ms. Tasker.' He nods to me. 'I told him that he could make that call before he left and she could meet us there.'

Shauna, I'm being arrested for murder, Jason had said to me over the phone, at 3:06 in the morning. Not, *They want to question me, Alexa's been murdered,* but *I'm being arrested.* He already knew it was coming. What did he reveal to Detective Cromartie in his mannerisms, his speech, his eye contact or lack thereof, his coolness or his sweat, the vibe he gave off? These are the kinds of things that rarely get revealed in a courtroom.

One of many things about that night, I realize, that I'll never know.

38

Shauna

Roger Ogren hits 'Play' on the remote. The television screen, facing the jury but angled so the defense may view it as well, comes to life in black-and-white. The fuzzy screen shows a nondescript room. Detective Ray Cromartie is in shirtsleeves, tie pulled down. Jason sits across a metal desk from him, his hair hanging into his eyes, in a button-down dress shirt open at the collar. To Jason's right is Bradley John, our associate, his hair slicked back, still wet from the thirty-second shower he must have taken when he got the call from me in the middle of the night.

Cromartie, on the witness stand, has already introduced the fact that Jason gave a recorded statement. The defense has stipulated to the admissibility of the videotaped statement, at least the portions that Roger Ogren plans to introduce. The whole thing wasn't very long, only about thirteen minutes – short enough that, if I were the prosecutor, I'd probably play the whole thing. But Ogren has decided to just pull out a couple of vignettes. One of the phrases Jason has always used to describe Ogren is *control freak*, and that fits. He just wants it exactly the way he wants it.

The screen shows Jason nearly front-on, only slightly angled so that a bit of Cromartie's profile is also apparent. I'm sure the detective isn't wild about the jury spending time with a close-up of the bald spot on the crown of his head or the fact that his tie is showing beneath his collar in the back, but presumably they're spending more time on Jason, staring into the table, his eyes narrowed as if in con-centration. To look at him, you wouldn't know that a woman was just found dead in his town house.

'I don't know what time Alexa got to my house,' Jason says on the tape. 'She said she was going to be there by six-thirty or seven, but I don't know. And I don't remember exactly when I got home. I wasn't checking that sort of thing. Just like I don't know what time I called 911. All I know is that I walked upstairs and I found her there. She was . . .' Jason waves a hand, like he's making a throwaway point. 'She was obviously dead. I . . . just stared at her at first. I couldn't believe it. She was . . . gone. Then I dialed 911.'

'You drove home tonight? That's how you got home?' Cromartie asks. His voice has more of an echo to it, the acoustics favoring Jason, the primary focus.

Jason nods. 'Yeah, I drove.'

'That's your SUV parked in the garage?'

Jason nods, his eyes rising to the ceiling over Cromartie's head. He scratches his hand.

'You came into the house through the garage?' Cromartie asks. 'The door to the garage?'

Jason nods absently. Still scratching his hand – the knuckles, the palm, searching for the itch. 'Right. I walked into the house and went upstairs,' he says.

'Was the front door locked, Jason? The front door, not the door that opens to the garage.'

The clock in the corner of the TV screen keeps time by the second: 4:12:06 . . . 4:12:07 . . . 4:12:08 . . .

'Jason—'

'I assume the front door was locked, yeah. I always lock the front door,' Jason says.

'And what about the back door, Jason? Was that locked?'

'Of course,' Jason says. 'I live in the city.'

Cromartie nods, that bald spot on the top of his head moving out of sight and then back in. 'And what about the door to the garage? Is that usually locked, Jason?'

Jason shrugs. *'Sometimes? Sometimes not, I guess.'*

'From outside, can you get into the garage without an opener?' asks Cromartie.

Jason shakes his head. *'No.'*

'No?' Cromartie presses.

'No. You need a . . . garage-door opener.'

'Did Alexa have a garage-door opener?'

'No,' Jason says. *'Just me.'*

'And you said Alexa was already there, dead, when you got home,' says Cromartie.

Jason looks at him like he is mentally impaired. *'Yeah. Of course.'*

'How did she get into the house, Jason? If she got there before you.'

Still scratching his hand. Now his forearm, too. Jason looks down in thought.

4:12:45 . . . 4:12:46 . . . 4:12:47 . . .

'Jason—'

'Front door, I guess.' Jason shrugs. *'She'd just use her key, I guess.'*

'Her key? Did Alexa Himmel have a key to your town house?'

4:12:55 . . . 4:12:56 . . . 4:12:57 . . .

At 4:13:04, Bradley John says, *'If he remembers. It's late, and it's been a difficult night, to say the least. Most people would be asleep right now.'*

'Understood, Counselor,' Cromartie replies with ice. *'If he remembers.'*

4:13:19 . . . 4:13:20 . . .

The jury is fixated on the tape, each of the jurors craned forward.

At 4:13:25, Jason looks up at Detective Cromartie and says, *'Yeah, Alexa had a key.'*

Stop tape.

Roger Ogren stands in front of the blank screen. 'Detective Cromartie, did you find a set of keys on the person of Alexa Himmel that night?'

'I did.'

'And what, if anything, did you do with those keys, Detective?'

'I personally tested each of the keys on each of the doors to the defendant's town house. The front door, the side door opening into the garage, and the back door.'

'And what did you find, Detective?'

'None of the keys on her key chain opened any of his doors. She had three keys. One was to her Prius. One we later determined was the key to her house, and the third was a key to her office at work. There was no key to the defendant's house on that chain.'

'Well, Detective.' Roger Ogren angles slightly toward the jury, his hands open in wonder. 'Maybe Ms. Himmel had such a key, but free of that key chain.'

'I considered that possibility, of course. We searched every inch of that town house and we searched the victim, Ms. Himmel. We combed the area outside the house. We turned every inch of the defendant's property inside out. There was no freestanding key to the defendant's house. The only keys to his house were on the defendant's key chain.'

'Well, as far as you could tell, was there *any* way that Ms. Himmel could have gotten into the defendant's locked house before he got home?'

'None.' The detective shakes his head. 'She had no key and no garage-door opener. I couldn't find any way that Ms. Himmel could have walked through a garage door or a locked front or back door. The windows didn't provide any access, either – they were not reachable from the ground. The defendant's statement didn't wash.'

'Objection,' I say. 'Move to strike.'

'The last comment is stricken,' says the judge, trying to unring the bell.

Ogren then moves back to the tape again, just at the point that he stopped.

'*Alexa didn't have a key, Jason,*' says Detective Cromartie, leaning forward now, on the attack. '*I checked. I checked every key on her key chain. She had no way of getting into your house without you letting her in.*'

Jason, running his nails up and down his arm, squirming a bit in his chair, shakes his head.

4:13:44 . . . 4:13:45 . . . 4:13:46 . . .

'*She didn't have a key, son,*' says Cromartie. '*If she did, tell me where it is. Or tell me how else she could have possibly gotten inside your house. I'm trying to help you, Jason, but you gotta help me. Tell me how in God's name she could have gotten into your house without you. Tell me how in the world she could have been in your home, dead or even alive, before you got home.*'

Jason sucks his lips into his mouth. His hands fidget. He shakes his head absently. He drums his hands on the metal table. '*We're done,*' he says to his lawyer, Bradley John.

'*We're done,*' Bradley says to the detective.

'*I have a lot more questions, Jason. A lot more. Like, where were you tonight that you didn't get home until after midnight? Can anyone vouch for you? How did Alexa—*'

'*I said we're done,*' Bradley says again. '*That means we're done.*'

Stop tape.

As Roger Ogren kills the DVD player, several of the jurors get *aha* looks on their faces, solemn nods, grim realizations. I imagine cartoon bubbles over their heads, displaying their thoughts, the words '**That's right, you *are* done**' in bold letters.

39

Jason

My lawyers, Shauna sitting next to me and Bradley John next to her, scribble notes as they listen to the examination of Detective Cromartie. He's done well on the witness stand. He's a strong, assertive type, but he isn't overplaying his hand, not coming on too strong. A good cop knows where to draw that line. Ray Cromartie, I've thought since that night, is a good cop. He was stringing me along pretty well before I abruptly terminated the interview. He scored one on the key for Alexa, with me shutting the interview down while I was on the ropes, and I'm sure he knew that, but he was clearly disappointed when I pulled the plug. He wanted what all of them want: a confession. He caught me in a couple of – ahem – inconsistencies, which is a nice consolation prize, but he didn't get what he came for.

Shauna is spending too much time on her notes. She's coping, I think. She's forcing herself to stay clinical, to focus on questions and answers and not on the reality of what is happening here, and what happened that night. This is tougher on her than I expected, hearing all this and bearing the burden of keeping me out of prison. She's one of the best lawyers I know, but she has almost no experience in a criminal courtroom. She mentioned more than once that we should consider some highbrow defense attorney, Gerry Salters or someone like that, but it had to be her. It had to be.

After some preliminary questions with the detective, Roger Ogren brings the television screen to life again, taking us back to the interrogation at a different point. Roger Ogren has decided to cherry-pick through this tape, playing various tidbits out of order, because some of the stuff on this tape will be shown to the jury through Cromartie and others through the Community Action Team squad officer. This part of the tape began around the sixth minute of conversation:

'You told me back at your house that you have a pretty good idea who killed Alexa,' Cromartie says. 'Can you help me out with that? Who killed her, Jason?'

I don't answer at first. Several seconds pass. I shake my head and wave a hand. 'His name is Jim.'

'Last name?' Cromartie asks.

'Just Jim,' I say.

'Well . . . what can you tell me about Jim?'

The way Cromartie says Jim, it's like he's dealing with a little kid who is obviously lying.

'He . . . he has red hair,' I say. 'He's big, muscular. He wears glasses. He has a paunch, like, a gut.'

'Why do you think Jim would kill Alexa?'

'To get to me,' I say. 'To get to me.'

'Why would Jim want to get to you, Jason?'

'I'm . . . I'm not sure. I just know that he's angry with me. I'm still trying to figure out why.'

'Did this . . . Jim tell you that he was going to hurt Alexa? Or you?'

I shake my head. 'Not in so many words. I wish he had. If he had, maybe I could have done something.'

'I don't understand what that means,' Cromartie says.

It wasn't a question, so I didn't answer it. A nice motto of mine, stolen from my mentor, and a nice tool for dominating a conversation. But probably not so nice when your audience is a jury trying to decide if you're a cold-blooded murderer.

After a lengthy delay, Cromartie opens his hand, visible to the camera. 'That's it? A guy whose last name you don't know, who might want to hurt you, but you don't know why?'

164

'I wish I knew more,' I say. 'I'd love to tell you more, but I haven't figured it out yet.'

Roger Ogren stops the tape. 'Detective Cromartie,' he says, 'since this interview with the defendant on the early morning of July thirty-first, has the defendant come back to tell you who "Jim" is?'

'No, sir, he hasn't.'

'Since this interview, which took place over four months ago, has the defendant come back to tell you why this "Jim" person wanted to hurt him?'

'No, sir.'

'During these four-plus months, has the defendant told you any-thing at all about this supposed murderer named . . . "Jim"?'

'He hasn't. Not a peep.'

Roger Ogren looks over his notes at the lectern one last time. Shauna takes a deep breath.

I lean into Shauna's personal space. 'You ready for him?'

'Is he ready for me?' she whispers back. False bravado, or I haven't known this woman half my life.

'Thank you, Detective,' says Ogren. 'No more questions for this witness.'

40

Shauna

Judge Bialek calls a recess before I cross-examine Ray Cromartie. I have my notes in front of me, drawing some arrows to move around some questions, but it's dangerous to get too wedded to notes. Once you write them down in detail, you tend to stay with them and stop listening to the witness. It becomes less of a fight and more of a conversation. You just have to let go and trust your preparation. You have to take off the training wheels and pedal that big bike down a dark, scary trail.

Jason is taking a bathroom break with an armed escort, so it's just Bradley John and me in the conference room adjacent to the courtroom. I don't like to stray too far during breaks. Elevators can break down, restaurants can take too long to bring the food. I can handle the stress of a trial, I'm used to it, but I could live my whole life and never get used to the stress of being late. So Jason's brother, Pete, who is in town for the trial, has brought us sandwiches from a deli.

I pick at a turkey and Swiss on wheat while I meditate. After a moment I push my notes away and breathe out. 'I can't look at this anymore. I just need to do it.'

Bradley is chewing on a pickle and staring at a transcript from the interrogation. 'I don't know why Jason *ever* agreed to that interview,' he says. 'He knows better than anybody not to do that.'

'Sometimes you can't take your own advice,' I offer.

'Yeah, but – I mean, it's one thing if you try to talk your way out of things. The perps I used to interrogate would do that all the time. They'd be full of stories. "Here's what happened, see, it went like this, see," and I'd let them just drone on and on and tangle themselves in knots. But Jason didn't argue a case for himself. He basically just let Cromartie beat him up.'

I scrap the sandwich and go for the good stuff, the salt-and-vinegar potato chips. 'You're forgetting that Jason was still under the spell of OxyContin,' I say. 'You saw him scratching his arms in there and smacking his lips. Classic withdrawal symptoms.'

'I know, I know. But all he had to do was take Five. Just assert his right to remain silent and shut the whole thing down. That's what I told him to do. I told him, before we went in—'

'I know you did, Bradley. I know you did.' I pat his arm. This interrogation has bothered Bradley as much as anything in this case, because it was the one thing that happened on his watch. He gave Jason sound counsel – to not make a statement – but he was overruled. Surprise! Jason didn't listen to advice. Truly, he wouldn't listen on his best day, and on top of everything else, there was the painkiller problem. It's hard to know Jason's frame of mind in that police station. I wish I knew. I wish I knew whether Jason knew what he was doing or screwed this whole thing up by talking to Cromartie.

'He looks guilty,' Bradley says. 'On that tape, he looks guilty.'

'I know he does.' Jason knows it, too.

I crinkle up the empty bag of chips and toss it toward the trash can. The bag unfolds midair and glides to the carpet, wide right. Golf was always my game.

'And the house key?' Bradley says. 'I mean, if Jason didn't say a word to the cops, they'd still be trying to piece together the sequence of events. But Jason told them he came home and found her there dead, and now we're stuck explaining how she got into a locked house without a damn house key and no sign of forced entry. I mean, am I missing something? Do we have an answer for that stupid house key?'

'I don't know of any answer,' I concede, feeling sweat dripping down my armpits.

'No. So that's all I mean. Jason did himself no favors.' He shakes his head. 'It was my job to stop him and I didn't, Shauna.'

'Let's not relitigate the past,' I say. Bradley has beaten himself up over this countless times. I thought I was done listening to it. It's the trial, I guess, the public unveiling of the interrogation for the jury, that has brought down a fresh rainfall of remorse on our associate.

'We have our case and we're going to make it,' I say. 'It may not be the greatest, but it's all we have, and we have to believe it with every fiber of our beings.'

'Right. That's right.' Bradley gives a presumptive nod and snaps back into trial mode. 'You're right. Jason didn't kill Alexa, right?' He gives me a playful push. For some reason, he likes to push me.

I busy myself with my notes, fitting them together sequentially and lining up the edges like a schoolgirl would.

'They can't prove that he did,' I say, more to the point.

41

Jason

'Good afternoon, Detective Cromartie. I'm Shauna Tasker. I represent Jason Kolarich.'

'Counsel.' Cromartie coughs into his fist and eyeballs Shauna.

'Detective, you are familiar with the concept of gunshot residue, or GSR?'

'I am,' he says. 'But it doesn't—'

'It was a simple question, Detective. Are you or aren't you?'

Cromartie frowns. He also pauses, wondering if either Roger Ogren or Judge Bialek will rise to his defense. But they won't. Judge Bialek usually likes to give witnesses a little freedom to elaborate on answers – especially because if they have something meaningful to say, they'll end up saying it, anyway, when the other side gets to ask questions – but Cromartie was going too far with a simple question.

'I am familiar with it,' he says, tucking in his lips, his attention enhanced now. He'll be more careful next time, a little more reticent to stray too far. Good for Shauna. Cromartie is probably an old-schooler; how he was going to react to questioning by a woman was anyone's guess. We're not guessing now.

'Gunshot residue, or GSR, is residue of the combustion components of a firearm after it discharges a bullet, correct?'

'Correct.'

'Basically, when a gun fires, the primer and powder combust and create an explosion.'

'That's right.'

'And GSR is the residue from that combustion. Residue, dust, particles might be found on the arm or wrist or hand of an individual after they've fired a gun. Is that correct?'

'Emphasis on the word *might*,' Cromartie says. 'It *might* leave residue. It might not.'

'Well, the reason you perform a GSR test is to determine whether an individual has fired a gun recently, correct? That's why you do the test?'

'Yes, it's a crude test, but that's the idea.'

Shauna properly ignores that remark. 'On the night of Ms. Himmel's death, you had Jason's hands swabbed for GSR at his house, isn't that true?'

'Yes, I believe we swabbed his hands at some point after we arrived. What Mr Kolarich did before we arrived is un—'

'You answered my question, Detective. And the results of the GSR test you performed on Jason were negative, correct? No gunshot residue was detected.'

Cromartie, realizing he's again getting no help from Roger Ogren, stops fighting. 'That's correct.'

'Very good.' Shauna, who hasn't looked down at her notes once, now reviews them, flips a page. More for a segue than anything else. I'm going to revise my assessment of Cromartie as a witness. He's fighting unnecessarily with Shauna. All the counterpoints he wanted to make – the GSR test isn't perfect; I might have washed up, even taken a shower before calling the police to remove any residue from my hands – he will make in redirect with Roger Ogren. To fight with Shauna here has diminished him and highlighted the strength of our position. I would expect more from a veteran cop, and more from Ogren, who probably figured he didn't need to tell Cromartie these basics, Testifying 101.

'We heard excerpts of your interrogation of my client following the death of Ms. Himmel, didn't we?'

'We did.'

'This interview took place at four in the morning, correct?'

'Yes.'

'My client hadn't had any sleep prior to the questioning, correct?'

'Any sleep? No, neither of us had slept.'

'And he was dealing with the loss of a woman with whom he'd shared a romantic history, isn't that true?'

I like how Shauna phrased that. When she was mock-crossing Cromartie in our office, with me playing Cromartie, I kept nailing her when she said *the loss of his girlfriend*. Saying it the way she did now – *a woman with whom he'd shared a romantic history* – sounded innocuous enough but was meaningfully different.

'Dealing with the loss? If killing someone means you're dealing with the loss, then yeah, I guess he was, y'know, dealing with the loss. It's kind of like killing your parents and then asking for mercy from the judge because you're an orphan.'

That line gets some snickers from the gallery, one person laughing outright. The answer jars Shauna to attention. She could object and move to strike the statement, but she doesn't.

'You don't know my client killed Alexa Himmel, do you, Detective?'

'It's what I believe.'

'But you don't know that for a fact, do you?' She approaches the witness.

'For a fact? I know the evidence strongly—'

'It's up to these good men and women of the jury to make that decision, isn't it, Detective?'

He gives an exaggerated sweep of his head. 'Of course it is.'

'You don't get to play accuser and *juror*, do you, Detective?'

He raises a hand, almost smiling. 'Luckily, I do not.'

'The evidence will decide this case, not you. Is that okay with you, Detective?'

'Objection,' Roger Ogren says. 'Argumentative.'

'Sustained.' The judge looks over her glasses at Shauna. 'We get the point, Ms. Tasker. Let's move on.'

Shauna, thankfully, doesn't miss a beat. 'My client was sleep-deprived, and a woman with whom he'd been romantically involved for several months had just been found dead in his house. Isn't that all true, Detective?'

Cromartie starts to answer but pauses, his eyes on the ceiling. 'I don't know about sleep-deprived. It was late, yes. All of us were probably tired.'

'And on top of that,' says Shauna, 'my client was under the cloud of a painkiller addiction at the time of the interview, wasn't he?'

'Oh, objection.' Roger Ogren springs to his feet. 'Sidebar, Judge?'

The judge waves him forward. She steps off the bench over to the corner of the courtroom, away from the jury box. The court reporter picks up her stenography machine and joins the attorneys and judge.

I can't hear them any more than the jury can, but I have a pretty good idea how this conversation is going to go. Shauna and I argued the point, with me playing Roger Ogren, several times over the past week.

Shauna is going to argue that the prosecution plans to use my OxyContin addiction against me, and thus my addiction is fair game. Roger is going to say that there's no actual proof of my addiction, certainly not at the time of the interrogation, unless I take the stand and testify to it. And Shauna will reply that I received treatment while in custody for my addiction, and she will call the counselors to the stand if necessary to lay the foundation, but she can't believe Ogren will make her go to that trouble.

I think we'll win the point, but just to be sure, we had Shauna ask the question first, so the jury would hear it either way.

Shauna makes eye contact with me as she leaves the conference, betraying no emotion but telling me it worked out for us. 'Let me restate the question,' she says, reclaiming her spot in the center of the courtroom. 'Detective, isn't it true that at the time my client was speaking with you, he was under the influence of an addiction to a painkiller called OxyContin?'

Cromartie, of course, has had a long time to consider his answer.

'I asked the defendant at the beginning of the interview if he was under the influence of any drugs at that time and if he was able to speak with a clear mind, and he said he was able to speak with a clear mind.'

A standard pre-interrogation question, to prevent exactly the type of cross-examination that Shauna is conducting now.

'You didn't answer my question, Detective.'

'I think I did, Counselor.'

'Then let me ask it again, and the judge can decide. Detective, isn't it true that at the time my client was speaking with you, he was under the cloud of an addiction to a painkiller called OxyContin?'

That's three times she's gotten to say it. And Ogren doesn't object, because she's not asking whether I admitted to being addicted at the interrogation – I didn't – but whether it was true, regardless.

'I don't know if he was or he wasn't,' Cromartie says. 'I asked him and he said no. That's all I knew at the time.'

'I'm talking about what you know *now*, Detective. Are you telling this jury that, as you sit here today, you don't believe that my client was suffering from an OxyContin addiction at the time you questioned my client? Is that really your testimony?'

'I didn't say that. We've come to believe that the defendant did have that addiction, yes. It's nice to hear you admit it. I didn't realize you would.'

Nice jab. The addiction is the third rail in this trial. It plays a significant role in the prosecution's narrative, a major piece of Roger Ogren's story that ends with my killing Alexa. Given our choice, Shauna and I would have liked to deny the whole thing. But the problem is that I've been treated in jail for the problem, so I can't really deny it. So instead, we're embracing it, trying to make the most of it. Shauna will argue to the jury that I was impaired when I submitted to the interview with the police. It can explain some of the – ahem – ambiguities in my statements.

But it cuts the other way, too. It gives the jury a vision of me that is not flattering – out of control, desperate, irrational, quite possibly dangerous, capable of doing things that, ordinarily, would be beyond a well-heeled attorney. Picture those old meth commercials – *This wasn't supposed to be your life!* – or the old egg-frying-in-a-pan, *This is your brain on drugs* ads.

Addiction freaks people out. It scares them.

And it makes it far, far more plausible to the jury that I killed Alexa Himmel.

FIVE MONTHS BEFORE TRIAL
July

42

Jason

Monday, July 1

My town house has shrunk in on me over the last thirty-six hours, since I paid the visit to James Drinker and found out I was chasing a ghost. I've kept Alexa away, ignored phone calls from Joel Lightner, secluded myself in my house to think.

Who is this guy? Who is this man who waltzed into my office in disguise, giving an alias, and telling me about dead women?

I think through every permutation and always come back to the same thing: I have history with this man. I prosecuted him. I prosecuted someone he cares about. Or I defended him, or someone he loves, with a result he didn't like, and now he wants to blame the lawyer.

I've tried to create a list of every case where I appeared as counsel, but it's impossible to get it anywhere close to complete. When you're a prosecutor in a major system like ours, you start with small stuff, traffic and misdemeanor and drug courts. Then you do a stint in juvenile courts, where the records are sealed. Then you're third-chairing bigger cases, and then after several years, you start handling your own major crimes.

I've prosecuted hundreds of people, probably thousands, each of whom has loved ones. The list of suspects is endless. And that's only the ones I can remember. The county attorney's office doesn't keep a list of such things. And with all the courtrooms I bounced around, all the different kinds of cases, it's impossible to come up with anything close to a complete list.

I need to talk to this guy. I need to search for clues. But I don't have a phone number for him. He never gave me one and he always calls from an unknown number, probably one of those throwaway cell phones, ten bucks at a convenience store, another ten for a hundred minutes.

He probably knows I went to 3611 West Townsend, apartment 406, and accosted the real James Drinker on Saturday night. He probably knows I'm twisting myself inside out trying to come up with something to make sense out of all of this.

I remove an Altoid and chew it up. I'm not keeping track. I've been good, if that's the word, about holding down these tablets to one every two hours. I think I'm off that now. I don't know. I'm not focused. I'm wide awake but half asleep at the same time. I'm buzzing with adrenaline while dozing off. All color is muted, tamped down with gray. All lines are blurry and shifting.

Alexa sends me a text message at two o'clock – I'M OUTSIDE YR DOOR, PLS LET ME IN! – so I go downstairs and open up. She puts her hands on my cheeks and peppers me with kisses like a child, wraps her arms around me, reassures me that everything will turn out fine, just fine. I've given her the highlights of what happened, so she recognizes as well as I the emptiness of her words.

When my cell phone buzzes at close to three o'clock in the afternoon, I nearly come out of my skin. I've received plenty of calls, and every time, my nerves rattle and my stomach revolts. I'm dreading the very thing I want – a call from the mystery man.

I approach the kitchen counter with trepidation, looking at the phone and mumbling something when I see that word on the face of the phone: *Unknown*.

What an appropriate word for him.

'Jason!' It's him. James Drinker, but not James Drinker.

I don't say anything. This guy does everything for a reason. He has a reason for this call, too.

He chuckles, makes sure I can hear his amusement. Part of the game. 'I guess we both know my name isn't James Drinker. What would you like to call me?'

Asshole? Lowlife? Dead man?

'Your call,' I say.

'Ooooh. Maybe I'll give something up, he thinks. Maybe I'll give a name that will tip him off, he thinks.'

'Tell me why this is happening,' I say. 'Tell me what you want. You want me to say I'm sorry for something I did? I'll say it. But don't take it out on innocent people. These women did nothing to you.'

'How do you know they did nothing to me, Jason? You don't know that.'

'You said you didn't know Alicia Corey or Lauren Gibbs.'

'That doesn't mean they didn't do something to me. People can be cruel to people they don't know. In my experience, crueler than they are to people they know.'

I don't respond to that. If I'm going to get anything out of this conversation at all, he has to do most of the talking. He knows that, of course. He knows I'm searching for a clue. It doesn't mean he won't give me one, though. He may not be able to resist.

'Come after me,' I say. 'Take it out on me, not them.'

'How do you know I'm not?'

My hands ball into fists. *One day,* I think to myself, *one day I will get my hands on this creep.*

'They're going to catch you,' I say. 'However good you may think you are, serial killers get caught.'

'Not all of them. The Zodiac Killer didn't. The BTK guy basically handed himself over. So did the Unabomber, unintentionally. It's amazing, isn't it? How easy it can be to kill people and get away with it?'

'You've made mistakes,' I say. 'You've left a trail, even if you don't know it.'

'Oh, I've left a trail, all right. But it won't lead to me. You haven't been paying attention, Jason.'

The line disconnects. I drop the phone and wipe sweat off my forehead. I look over at Alexa, who is watching me, eyebrows raised. I go upstairs to find my computer.

179

43

Jason

Monday, July 1

I go online and start with Google. I put in the name of the first victim, Alicia Corey, the stripper from Knockers.

'You're going to get a thousand hits because of the press coverage,' Alexa says, standing over my shoulder.

'I don't know how else to do it.'

She's right, though; the coverage was even more intense than I'd realized. There are dozens of articles from newspapers in the Midwest and even some in *The New York Times* and the *L.A. Times*, articles picked up from a wire service, no doubt, as the small string of words that accompany each hit are usually identical. There are also numerous entries from Facebook and Myspace, 'Alicia Corey' being a fairly common name. There's even a professional fighter by that name.

'Go there,' Alexa says, pointing to a link that says *Alicia Corey Reward*.

I click on it, a Facebook page, bearing the same title and a large photograph of Alicia Corey, an attractive blond woman who, in the picture, has her head slightly angled back while she lets out a large laugh. Underneath it, the heading contains a long note:

Our dear friend Alicia Corey – Lisha to those who knew her best – was taken from us on May 22 when she was tragically and brutally murdered in her home on the north side of the city by a killer now known as the North Side Slasher. Lisha was a ray of sunshine every day, a gentle woman with a terrific sense of humor and a giving soul. Dr Dennis Molitor, DDS, where Lisha worked as a dental hygienist for three years, is offering a $10,000 Cash Reward for any information leading to the arrest of the monster responsible for this senseless act of violence.

The note ends with an address and an e-mail where information may be sent. Underneath it, the page is filled with comments from well-wishers and grievers – *We love and miss you, Lisha! Our prayers are with your family. Please let me know how I can help. You're with God now, Lisha. Alicia was one of my finest students at Saddlebrook Middle School back in 2000 . . .*

'That's nice of him to do, the cash reward,' Alexa says. 'Don't you think?'

I bring a hand to my mouth, close my eyes. The initial news reports had just mentioned her nighttime job as a stripper. I guess that's more of a grabber, sexier than *dental hygienist.*

'Jason?' She nudges me with her elbow.

'Yes, it's very nice of him,' I say. 'Dr Molitor's a great guy.'

She puts her hand on my shoulder. 'You *know* him?'

'He's my dentist,' I say. 'I got a tooth filled in May.'

It doesn't take us long to find the rest of them, now that we know what we're looking for. Lauren Gibbs, the website designer and bank teller, worked at Citywide Bank in the Commercial District branch, where I banked. She was killed on May 24. I visited the bank to order some new checks, with my new address, in early May. Holly Frazier, the grad student who part-timed at Starbucks, was a barista at the location just down the street from our law firm, the place I buy coffee nearly every morning.

Nancy Minnows worked at my favorite store, Runner's High, as a salesperson. She was the blond dreadlocked girl, Minnie, who sold me shoes and running gear a couple of weeks before she was butchered like the others.

And Samantha Drury was the African-American librarian who was working when I stopped in to write my anonymous note to the police about James Drinker.

I think again of what 'James' said to me the other day on the phone, a conversation that sent ice down my spine, words I won't ever forget, when he discussed his connections to the victims. *For all I know, one of them sold me clothes or served me coffee or cleaned my teeth or deposited my check at the bank.* And now we can add to that, *waited on me at the library.*

Or close enough, at least. I don't recall Alicia Corey cleaning my teeth at Dr Molitor's – and to judge from her photo, I'd remember her – but James wouldn't have known that level of detail. He would have followed me, but not all the way into the dentist's inner office. I don't think Lauren Gibbs was the person who helped me order new checks at Citywide Bank, but the truth is, I don't remember one way or the other. Holly Frazier probably did serve me coffee at some point, but she's one of a thousand pretty young women you see in the city and doesn't stand out to me. Nancy Minnows, of course, was my salesperson at Runner's High, which James could have seen just by passing by the window. Just as easily, he could have seen me walk past the librarian at the front desk, hidden from absolutely nobody.

Either way, whether I directly contacted them or was nearby, I was close enough to have met them, to have laid eyes on them. *Maybe I coveted them,* 'James' had said to me, taunting me over the phone. *Maybe I watched them, everywhere they went, obsessed over them . . . Maybe that's exactly why I chose them. Because my encounter with them was so casual and short that nobody would even remember it.*

He was following me, identifying pretty young women with whom I came into contact, and murdering them. The story he hypothesized to me is exactly what the police will say, if they ever get around to discovering me.

'Those places would all have security cameras,' I say. 'A bank, a Starbucks, the library, the running store. The dentist office, maybe not, but it wouldn't be hard to pull a patient list.' I look over at Alexa. 'I'm on record in each of these places.'

'This can't . . . this can't be happening,' Alexa whispers.

'It's happening.' I blow out air. 'This asshole is setting me up.'

44

Jason

The next morning, Alexa goes with me to Joel Lightner's office. The sign outside his door on the seventh floor says JDL Partners, a suitably vague name for a company that serves customers who value discretion. He works from referrals, no print ads or fancy websites. He has a row of offices on the west side of the building, his own the largest, but decorated tastefully and simply. He doesn't want clients to think he's getting rich off their troubles, though he is.

Joel gives a warm greeting to Alexa, whom he's only seen once at a glance when she visited my office the first time. Normally he'd turn on the Lightner charm, crack wise, try to get the pretty girl to laugh, but current circumstances dictate otherwise.

When Alexa is taking a seat, Joel catches my eye and gestures at her with a question on his face. He's asking me if I'm sure I want her to be here for this sensitive conversation. But I do. Alexa knows my darkest secret; if she can be trusted with that, she can be trusted with anything.

Joel paces along his window, which gives us a view into a concrete skyscraper across the street. It is drizzling outside, teardrops on the glass.

'It's not much,' he says. 'Yes, if the cops are good, if they're looking that hard at security tapes, they might put you at each location.'

'They can easily put me at the dentist office,' I say. 'And I put down a credit card at Runner's High. Those two alone, right? I mean, that's what the police are doing right now. They're gathering data and cross-referencing. What do these women have in common?'

Joel makes a noise, his finger on his lips, pacing around. 'That's what I'd do.'

'And once they see where I work, it won't be hard to imagine I went to that Starbucks. Send a cop over there to show the employees my photograph, and they'll say, "Oh, yeah, he comes in all the time." The security cameras will just confirm it. And it will take them a grand total of five minutes to learn that I have bank accounts at Citywide, and that I was there recently at the district branch.'

'Okay, okay.' He holds out a calming hand. 'But – you have no motive. You're a successful lawyer. You've taken on some big cases, well-known cases. The Governor Snow thing. That thing with the terrorist attack, Jason. And now, suddenly, you're a psychotic serial killer who guts women with a knife?' He shakes his head. 'It doesn't fly. I might find some significance in your connection to these victims, but I wouldn't think you *killed* them.'

Now I'm pacing the office, too. One wall of Joel's office is devoted to old photographs from the Terry Burgos case. Sometime in the late 1980s, Burgos killed seven – I think it was seven – college students and prostitutes on a small college campus in a town just south of the city called Marion Park. Joel was the lead detective on the case, the one who arrested Burgos, who interrogated him and obtained a confession that helped defeat his insanity defense at trial. The case launched his career. It's the first thing any potential client knows about him, that he was the guy who once caught a serial killer.

'Do you . . . do you have alibis for the murders?' Joel asks with an embarrassed laugh, as if he can't believe he has to ask me that question.

'Yes, he does,' Alexa says. 'He was with me. Every one of those nights.'

I turn away from the wall and look at her. Joel has a look of relief on his face until he catches my eye.

A knock at Joel's door. Standing in the threshold is one of Joel's investigators, a young, attractive blond woman. As much of a pig as Joel is, he didn't hire her for her looks, or at least not in the way that would normally mean. He hired her because she can get people to do things she wants, a nice trait for a private eye who might need a peek at a sign-in sheet, the name of a hotel guest, or a particularly well-placed spot in a restaurant. Her name is Janet or Jennifer or Jessie or something.

'What's up, Linda?' Joel asks.

Right. Linda. That was my next guess. It occurs to me, as I look at her, that she's fantastic, a true head-turner, and that under ordinary circumstances I might experience at least, I don't know, a mild adrenaline rush or something. Like I remember what it was like to feel normal, something that's just across the room from me but might as well be on another planet.

'Need you for one second, Joel, when you can.'

'Go ahead,' I say to him. 'We can wait.'

Joel and Linda huddle briefly in the hallway outside. Alexa is still facing forward, toward Joel's chair, and I'm behind her across the room. I let the silence fill the air.

Finally, she turns her head back to see me and says, matter-of-factly, 'We were together each of those nights.'

'Sorry,' Lightner says, popping back in. 'Anyway. What were we – oh, the alibis,' he says, dropping into his chair.

'Alexa and I need to figure that out,' I say. 'Confirm those dates.'

Alexa shoots a glance my way but doesn't say anything.

'Okay, definitely do that.' Lightner nods, casting alternate looks at Alexa and me. 'Here's the thing, though,' he says. 'Just putting you at a location where you had the chance to come into contact with these people isn't enough. By itself? Not nearly enough, especially for a professional like you. If you had a criminal record or a history of mental illness or you had some dead-end job or something, maybe.

But you're too buttoned-up a guy, a successful professional. The fact that you happened to come into contact with each of them? It's just . . . not enough.'

'Well, that's good, then.' Alexa opens her hands. 'Right?'

'That's not what he's saying,' I interject. 'What he's saying is, if the asshole formerly known as James Drinker is any good at what he's doing, there's more than what we know so far.'

And Joel's absolutely right. There has to be more that he has on me. And I helped him with ideas, for God's sake. That scumbag sat in my office while I gave him a fucking tutorial on how to frame somebody for murder.

Joel points at me. 'We have to figure out what he has on you. Because whatever he has on you, he could use it any day.'

45

Jason

Tuesday, July 2

Alexa and I leave Joel's office and head to the elevator in silence. I don't like to talk on elevators, so I wait until we're clear of it, actually until we've walked out of the lobby. Joel has given me homework – figure out what it is that 'James' might have done to set me up, a smoking gun that will implicate me in these murders. Maybe we're giving James too much credit, but I don't think so. Underestimating him has become a hazardous exercise.

The sky continues to spit rain, enough for some people to don umbrellas, but neither Alexa nor I have one. We head into a coffee shop – not a Starbucks – grab some java, and find a table in the lounge, near the foggy window.

I lean in close to Alexa. 'I've given this a lot of thought since last night,' I say. 'About my whereabouts on the nights of the murders.'

I sound like someone in an old courtroom drama or *Dragnet. Can you account for your whereabouts on the night of the murder?* I think the word *whereabouts* exists in the English language purely for the purpose of establishing an alibi to a crime.

'You and I weren't together *any* of those nights,' I say. 'Not a single one.'

Alexa, stone-faced, raises her eyebrows, the look of a stubborn girl who's being told something she doesn't want to hear.

'Holly Frazier, the third victim, was killed on the night of Friday, June seventh,' I say. 'That was the day you came to my office with the court transcript. The day I asked you on a date for the first time. But we didn't get together again until Sunday.'

In fact, I recall with no shortage of dread, it was right after my trip to Runner's High, when I bought shoes and running gear from Nancy Minnows, that I first met Alexa at that outdoor café, Twist. It was definitely Sunday, June 9.

'And Nancy Minnows was murdered on Tuesday night, June eighteenth,' I continue. 'That morning, you and I had that . . . fight, or whatever you call it. The Altoids incident?'

She allows the smallest and briefest of smiles.

'You made us breakfast, then you left in a cab. I was home by myself that night. And the night after that, and the night after that. You and I didn't speak again until last Friday, Alexa. And the last girl, the librarian, Samantha Drury. She was killed last Thursday night, and we both know we weren't together. That was the night we did our own things. Remember? It was your idea. We'd spent, like, almost a whole week together, and you said, "Seven days in a row is practically marriage," or whatever you said.

'And the first two victims, Alicia Corey and Lauren Gibbs? They were murdered in early May, before you and I even *knew* each other.'

Throughout all of this, Alexa's expression remains tight, uncompromising.

'You and I were together every one of those nights,' she says. 'I would swear to that under oath.'

'You . . .' I take her hands in mine. 'Honey,' I say. I've never called her any kind of a pet nickname like that. I've never said anything but her name, Alexa. It jars me for some reason, like it means something.

'You can't do that, Alexa. You could get in serious, serious trouble.'

'But I won't.'

'You will, if it ever comes to that. If they set their sights on me and you give me an alibi, they'll scour the earth to prove it wrong.

188

They'll pull your home phone records, they'll ping your cell phone calls, they'll look at your computer, credit cards, movies you watched on pay-per-view, food you ordered in, whatever. They'll ask your friends. They'll have twenty ways of figuring out whether you were actually with me those nights.'

'I was home, by myself, each of those nights,' she says. 'Nobody will say that they were with me. Nobody knows where I was, any of those nights. So as far as I'm concerned, I was with *you*.'

Crazy. This is crazy.

'I've already thought about this, too,' she continues. 'When I'm alone, I read. Or I work. I don't make calls from a landline because I don't *have* a landline, just my cell phone. I don't even use my cell phone much. I don't go on the Internet, and even if I did, I have a laptop. I could have been with you when I was using it.' She looks up at me. 'I don't even know *how* to order a movie off the television. And I never, *ever* have food delivered. Except when I'm with you.'

'Seriously, Alexa—'

'Seriously, no one will be able to say I *wasn't* with you. Trust me, Jason.' She runs her hand up my arm, soothing me.

'Really?' I don't hide my skepticism. 'And how do we explain how we even knew each other before that court hearing on June fourth, when I was representing Billy Braden? What's your story there? How is it that we didn't meet until June fourth, but somehow we were dating in May when the first two murders occurred?'

'We met on April twenty-fifth,' she answers, not missing a beat. '*People versus Kerry Alexander.*'

I draw back. I remember the case, of course. My guy was charged with attempted criminal sexual assault. He was convicted on the lesser-included offense of battery, which meant he got nine months inside instead of nine years. That goes down as a loss, but he called it a win. Yeah, that was late April, that sounds right.

'You were there? Two months ago in court?'

'Yes, I was. I was the court reporter when the jury came back.' A sheepish smile crosses her face. 'I wanted to introduce myself to you then, but I didn't. You were pretty caught up with everything. Your client sure seemed happy with the verdict. You didn't, though. You seemed . . . troubled, I guess. Like something was bothering you.'

This is the first I've heard of a previous time we were together in court. She never mentioned this. She first knew of me in *April*?

'I never had a reason to bring it up before,' she says, reading my thoughts. 'But it's a matter of public record. Anyone can look it up. So,' she says with a shrug, 'we could point to that and say that we started seeing each other at that time. Late April, not early June.'

I shake my head. 'Even if we could theoretically pull this off—'

'We could. We easily could.'

'– but even so, I'm not making you lie for me, Alexa. That's not happening.'

She runs her hand up my arm, soothing me. 'You're not *making* me do anything. Last I checked, I'm a big girl.'

I pull away from her. 'No. It's very sweet, but no.'

'*Sweet?*' Now she objects, recoiling. 'This is no time for *sweet*. This is serious. And *I'm* serious. You didn't kill those girls, and I'm not going to let anybody say that you did. I appreciate your moral objection, but this will get us to the right result, which is that you're innocent.'

I don't have the energy to fight about this right now. It's not something we have to decide immediately, or hopefully ever.

She seems to understand how I'm feeling. She doesn't push the subject. She sits with me quietly, caressing my arm. 'Is your knee bothering you?' she asks. 'It seems like it is.'

I look down at my dress shoes, which I haven't polished for months. There was a time when I'd keep those things spit-shined, like mirrors. 'Actually,' I say, 'it's killing me.'

'You should take a pill, then.' Still running her hand up and down my arm.

So I do, removing the Altoids tin, popping in a tablet and chewing it up, letting out a long sigh.

'I hate that you're in so much pain,' she whispers. 'But I'm here.

I'm here for you, Jason. For anything. You know that, right?' She takes my hand and interlocks her fingers with mine.

We sit in silence. We don't check our e-mail on our phones. We don't sip coffee. We don't even look at each other. We just sit, heads together, holding hands, until relief finally comes, heat pouring through my body like warm syrup.

'We have to stay together,' she says. 'Every night. You see that, don't you? Any night that you're alone is a night that "James Drinker" can pull some stunt and try to frame you. We have to be together every night, Jason.'

I'm not even thinking about that right now. At this moment, I am weightless; my feet have left the ground.

'Okay,' I say.

'We have to go everywhere together.'

'Okay.'

'We have to do everything together.'

'Right.'

'Good,' she says. 'We'll get through this, honey. We'll get through this together.'

46

Jason

Tuesday, July 2

Under the new rule that I can't go anywhere alone, Alexa escorts me all the way to my office before leaving me. Inside, my law firm is a barren wasteland, with Shauna and Bradley John out on a trip to Arangold Construction as they prepare for trial. I walk into my office, poorly lit and overly air-conditioned, and pass the seat where the man who called himself James Drinker once sat and spewed all his bullshit to me.

I put my head back against the seat, thinking about everything that's happening, and for some reason I feel a little better about things. Surely, I can figure some way out of this mess. There's nothing that this asshole can do to me that would make the police believe that I'm a killer, right? What could he possibly have on me?

I almost jump out of my chair when my phone buzzes. I'm thinking *James Drinker* every time that phone goes off these days. When I check the caller ID, it reads *Unknown*.

Yep. It's him.

I answer the call but don't speak. I don't need to speak.

'Should I assume you're paying attention now, Jason?' he asks. He is speaking slowly, without inflection, but it's not hard to hear the satisfaction in his voice. A game to him. I just wish I knew what the game was.

'I'm paying attention. Why don't you stop by and we can talk about it?'

'Oh . . . I don't think I'm going to do that. I was just wondering when you plan to turn yourself in to the police. So you can tell them you're innocent, but somebody's framing you.'

I don't answer. He's reminding me that this is exactly what I told *him* to do, to go to the authorities and explain that he thought he was being set up.

'You're not going to the cops, are you?' he asks. 'You won't follow the same advice you gave me.'

'You had a reason for calling,' I say. 'Why don't you just get to it?'

'I just did,' he says. 'I want you to turn yourself in to the police and explain that this is all a misunderstanding, that you were set up. Framed! I'm sure they'll believe you, Jason.'

I don't say anything.

'Tell them that a guy came into your office wearing a disguise and giving a fake name. They'll believe that.'

I close my eyes.

'And tell them you violated your oath as a lawyer and gave up that guy to the cops. What was it you did, by the way? An anonymous phone call to the hotline, your voice concealed? An anonymous note like you see in the movies, with words cut out from a newspaper?'

I don't say anything.

Then I do: 'You better hope the police catch you before I do.'

'Oh, I *do* hope that,' he says. 'For me, it's the difference between exoneration and death. But it's the same result for you, Jason. Either way, you go down for five murders.'

'Do I?' My heartbeat kicks up. If he has something on me, I need to know what. But I can't seem too eager. I have to let him come to me.

'You're wondering what it is, aren't you? You've been scrambling your brain trying to figure out what's going on. Just play it out, Jason. I mean, you're the one who advised me on how to frame somebody, aren't you?'

I do a slow burn, thinking back to when we talked the first time, so ridiculous in hindsight, when he asked me how I would frame somebody and I laid out a list for him.

Motive, I told him. Close enough – I met all of the victims, or at least was in the same area with them; if I then became obsessed with them, which is what the theory would probably be, there's my motive. People have killed for less.

Opportunity, I recall saying. Check. I was home alone each of the five nights the women were murdered.

Means. The killer used a knife. I don't know what kind, but I'd be willing to bet it was something ordinary. Something anybody could easily purchase.

What else did I say to him? I'm not thinking clearly these days. I haven't been thinking clearly for months. I try to focus back to that conversation and come up with fuzz.

On the other end of the phone, it's dead air. 'James' is actually considering telling me, I think. That's more than I expected. More than *Go fuck yourself* or *Use your imagination*.

'What evidence do I have against you? Just some souvenirs I collected from you,' he says. 'Nothing you'd miss. Remember, Jason, you left me alone in your office for a few minutes.'

I move in my chair. The office around me comes alive, as if animated, no longer a place where I work but a crime scene of sorts. And now I remember another piece of advice I gave him during that conversation.

I told him that someone framing him would leave clues at the crime scene, things that belonged to James, or some trace evidence from his house or workplace.

He's right, too. I remember now, during our meeting, taking a trip to the men's room so I could pop an Altoid in private.

He stole things from my office and planted them at the crime scenes. Nothing too obvious, like a piece of my office stationery, or the police would already be at my door. But something effective. Something with my fingerprints, or better yet my DNA. Strands of

194

my hair off my couch in the corner. A water bottle I drank out of. A pen—

Oh, shit.

A pen cap I chewed. It comes back to me now, a white-hot blast up my spine. I'd been chewing on a cheap Bic pen while we talked. I refused to use that nice pen my brother had given me, refused to waste expensive ink on 'James Drinker,' so I went with the cheap Bic.

And I couldn't find that pen when I returned to the office.

He took my fucking pen. It would have bite marks and saliva. He could make good use of that. The story would be that it fell out of my pocket during a struggle. Nothing I would have noticed, while I was butchering poor Holly Frazier or Nancy Minnows or Samantha Drury. The cops would do a DNA search and come up empty, because my DNA isn't in the system. But if someone handed them the name Jason Kolarich, it would be a simple matter of obtaining a DNA swab from my cheek and pulling my dental records, and suddenly I have a lot of explaining to do.

And that's probably not all. I spend half my life in this office. I wipe my nose, I sleep on the couch, I have extra shoes and ties. Hell, he could have emptied my wastebasket into his bag while I was out of the office. There could be ten used tissues for him to strategically place. He could have ripped the label off one of my extra ties hanging on my door, something that wouldn't mean anything to the police – until they got my name, searched my office, and found a tie with a missing label.

It could be anything. Anything anything anything—

But I'll never know what he took. I'll never know.

'If the cops find me, I give them you,' he says. 'Maybe directly, or maybe anonymously. If you find me and kill me, I have a last will and testament that will direct the authorities to a safe-deposit box filled with all sorts of fun facts about you. It will be a step-by-step guide to the prosecution of Jason Kolarich.'

'I *will* find you,' I say. 'And I'm going to kill you.'

'You might. But I doubt it. But here's the thing, Jason. There's one very easy way to stop the murders of these poor women. Turn yourself in to the police. Pitch your story to them. It's totally up to you. Maybe you'll be able to talk your way out of it.'

Maybe so. But I'd bet everything I own that he's lined up enough evidence against me that I *couldn't* talk my way clear.

'So the ball's in your court,' he says. 'Are you willing to risk your ass to save innocent young women?'

47

Jason

Tuesday, July 2

I pick up Alexa on my way home. She has two suitcases and a bag with her, plus her stenography equipment. When we get to my house, she unpacks everything, hanging dresses and blouses and pants in the second bedroom's empty closet, lining the floor with shoes of all kinds. She puts lingerie and underwear in two of the drawers in the bedroom dresser. She puts makeup and toiletries in the master bathroom.

She's moving in with me. Neither of us has said so out loud, and even if we did, we'd recognize it more as an act of necessity than a progressive step in our relationship – I've begun joking that I should introduce Alexa not as my girlfriend but as my 'alibi' – but none of that changes the fact that she's moving in with me.

'You doing okay?' she asks as she rearranges some things in one of the dresser drawers while I sit on the bed. 'How do you feel physically?'

'I'm fine,' I say. Which is true, unless you count the dull pain over my eyes, or the incessant itching on my hands and forearms. Or the fact that I haven't had a full night's sleep in three months. Or my stomach, which is about as volatile as democracy in Egypt.

A clearheaded man might think that his body is telling him something. But clarity of thought is not something with which I have a lot of experience lately. I'm trying. Lord knows, I'm trying, because I need to get ahead of my murderous client, and I'm miles behind. I feel like I'm running in place. I feel like I woke up in a strange place, unsure of how I got there and not sure how to find my way back.

'You're thinking about him, aren't you?' Alexa asks me.

'Shit, I'm always thinking about him.' I've been checking the *Herald* online on an hourly basis, looking for any updates on the investigation or any word of another murder committed by the North Side Slasher.

'Did you get your list of old cases to Joel?'

'Yeah. This morning. For what it's worth.'

'It's not worth much?'

'I can't possibly go back and retrieve all the cases I worked on. We don't have a system like the PACER system in federal court, where cases can be sorted by attorneys' names. We don't have that.' I fall back on the bed. 'Do you have any idea how many cases I handled? From cattle-call courtrooms when I started, to juvenile and abuse-and-neglect cases that are now sealed? Arraignments and bond hearings I handled before turning the cases over to older prosecutors for trial? The major crimes I prosecuted, yeah, I can remember a decent number of them. But the rest? There's no record. And they all blur together for me. And here's the best part: He might not be *any* of those guys. He might be a friend of a guy I prosecuted, or a brother. I'd – I'd have better odds trying to guess the winning lottery ticket tonight.'

'Oh, it can't be that dire.' She closes up a drawer and looks over at me. 'Since he's such a violent person, it was probably a big-deal crime you caught him doing. Probably not a traffic violation, for example. Right?'

She's right, of course. And luckily for me, the really violent cases are the ones I remember best. 'But most of the time I spent prosecuting violent crimes was in the gangs unit,' I say. 'And this guy who came to visit me didn't look like a member of the Tenth Street Crew or the Insane African Warlords or the Columbus Street Cannibals.'

'Okay, well, still. Anything you can do to narrow it down. And you said it's likely to be someone who was recently released from prison?'

'That's where Joel's starting, with violent ex-cons released in the last year,' I say. 'It's the obvious place to start. But . . .'

'But what?'

'But this guy is intelligent. He'd know that. Somehow, I don't think it applies to him.'

Alexa finishes up, claps her hands, and sits next to me on the bed. 'Be optimistic,' she says. 'You're doing everything you can.'

'It's worth a shot,' I agree. 'I'll give Joel a week or two and see what comes of it.'

She looks at me, confused. 'What does that mean, you'll give him a week or two? What happens in a week or two if he can't find anybody?'

'I turn myself in,' I say.

Her hand, caressing my leg, suddenly stops. She grips my calf. 'You *can't* be serious.'

'I'm totally serious. I'll go to the police and tell them everything. Maybe he's bluffing about how he's framed me with physical evidence. And if he's not, if he really did plant chewed-up pens and whatever else at the crime scenes, then maybe I can still convince them I'm a patsy.'

'Maybe you *can't*. Then you go to prison for something he did.'

I shrug. 'I'm not going to let him kill anybody else. I'm not.'

She wags her finger at me, but decides not to argue the point. We still have a couple of weeks to battle out that issue. And as long as Alexa stays by my side night after night and provides me a rock-solid alibi, so our theory goes, 'James' will not kill anybody else.

So our theory goes.

'Okay, then, how about that present you promised me after I unpacked?'

'I probably built it up too much,' I say. 'It's not that exciting.'

'Whatever. What is it?'

I fish it out of my pocket. It can't be that much of a surprise.

199

It's a house key. A key that opens all three doors of my house – front, back, and side/garage.

She smiles at me, touches her nose to mine. 'Wow, my very own shiny silver house key.'

'It set me back four bucks,' I say. 'So if you don't like it, let me know and we'll exchange it for a nicer key.'

She kisses me and runs her fingers through my hair. She's always touching me, my hair, my neck, my arms.

'You sure know how to charm a girl,' she says, pulling me on top of her.

48

Shauna

Wednesday, July 3

No matter how much you prepare for a trial in advance, no matter how many boxes you check in the weeks before it begins, the final days are always a sprint. Bradley John and I, joined by Arangold Construction's in-house lawyer, the two Arangolds, father and son, and three paralegals, have been working around the clock the last few days. The trial starts next Tuesday, the ninth, and should last about three weeks. Bradley and I have divvied up the work – about two-thirds of the witnesses mine – and are now poring over the numerous pretrial motions our opponent, the city, has filed to tie us up in the closing hours.

Day has turned into night has turned into day, the movement of the hands on the clock nothing but a signal that we have less and less time to get ready. Some people, facing deadlines like this, just want it to be over. I'm the type who always wants more time.

We've taken a break to eat some sandwiches that Marie ordered for us, subs in paper wrapping with grease stains, their contents described in shorthand with black Magic Marker. A copy of today's *Herald* is strewn about, the headline about the scandal du jour, an investigative report that shows the mayor's administration has wasted millions of dollars on the city's new contractor to handle garbage disposal and waste hauling. Not the hugest deal in the world, but the *Herald* reporters are the ones who exposed it, so it *has* to be a big deal.

It's okay with me, however, because it's my theme for the trial. City employees who sleep on the job, unmanned hotlines where complaining callers can't get anyone to answer – the inefficient, incompetent city looking to blame my client, a hardworking father-son operation, for the mistakes that the city itself made.

I make a pit stop in the bathroom, and when I come out I see the light on in Jason's office. A Jason sighting has been rare these days. I haven't spent much time thinking about him, given the trial, unless you count the number of times I've cursed him under my breath for bailing on this case and leaving me with too much to do.

I venture into his office, not sure of much of anything when it comes to Jason anymore. I checked with Marie the other day on Jason's comings and goings, only to find that his appointment calendar seems to be shrinking.

'Hey,' I say without much enthusiasm, not a *Happy to see you* tone of voice.

He has his back to me, removing a bottle of water from his small refrigerator near his desk. When he turns to me, I draw a quick breath.

He is even skinnier than the last time I saw him, his face almost gaunt, the circles beneath his eyes prominent and dark. His hair is hanging in his face, the bangs curling around almost to his cheeks. He has two or three days' growth on his face, like sandpaper.

He is no longer the imposing jock-turned-lawyer, the high and tight haircut and formidable presence. He looks more like Kurt Cobain.

'How's it goin'?' Jason nods at me. 'Final sprint, right?'

'Um, yeah . . . yeah, final sprint.'

'Something wrong?' he asks. 'You look like you've just seen a ghost.'

That's because I have.

I invite myself into his office, stand by one of the chairs but don't sit. 'Thought maybe you were sick,' I say. 'Marie said you've referred some of your cases out.'

He sighs. 'A couple of dogs. Nothing worth keeping.'

I move my head up and down. 'You're not going into retirement?' I say, broaching the issue delicately.

'Spending more time on the yacht? Sailing the world? Not just yet. Everything okay on the trial?'

How nice of him to ask. 'You know how it is. You're sure you don't have enough time to get everything together. And then, somehow, it comes together.'

'Right, right.' He nods at me again. 'You're pissed off I bailed on you?'

Well, at least he noticed. He's seemed so caught up in his own little world, I didn't think he would take note of something like, oh, completely breaking his word to me and not helping with the trial, not being a good law partner. While we're at it, let's add *not being a good friend* to the list.

'We're managing,' I say, deflecting the question. There's a lot of deflecting going on in this exchange. 'What about you?' I ask. 'Are you okay?'

'Me? I'm all good.' *Deflect.*

'How are things with Alexa?'

'Oh, yeah, she's good. It's good. Spending a lot of time with her.'

The inanity of this conversation, catching up with each other like we're a couple of college classmates who bumped into each other years later, is enough to make my head explode. I want to grab him by the arms and shake him, but it takes two for a conversation like that, and only one of us is interested.

'Tell her to cook you some meat and potatoes,' I say. 'You're shrinking.'

'Right. Oh, hey.' He looks past me. I turn, too. Alexa comes waltzing in, carrying a shopping bag full of groceries.

Plans for the evening? I don't ask, but it's July 3. The fireworks are tonight. Maybe that's what they're doing. People who aren't about to start a trial go out and watch the fireworks. People with boyfriends snuggle up on a blanket and drink wine and watch the sky explode while they grope each other. I haven't been groped in a long time. I wouldn't mind being groped a little, or a lot.

'You remember Alexa,' says Jason.

How could I forget Alexa! How's it goin', girl?

'Sure. Hi,' I say.

'Hi,' she says, dropping her bag on the couch. She turns to me and salutes me in grandiose fashion, a reminder of my awkward gesture last time. If it were remotely amusing, I would smile. But it isn't, so I don't. It's so far from amusing that I couldn't see amusing with a telescope. This is bad. I don't know how else to say it, like the temperature changes when she walks in, the lights dim – something. This lady is bad news.

Not that she notices or cares what I think. She waltzes right past me and throws her arms around Jason. He seems a bit surprised by the public display of affection.

'Well, that's my cue,' I say.

'Good luck with the trial,' Jason calls out as I walk away. I don't bother with an answer.

49

Jason

Sunday, July 7

The Jason Kolarich Bizarro Tour continues onward. With July 4 falling on a Thursday, most people took off Friday and made it a four-day weekend. I guess I did, too, technically, by which I mean I didn't go in to work any of those days. But I barely left the house, afraid of encountering anybody that could end up being the next victim of 'James Drinker' simply because they spoke to me and happen to be female, young, and attractive.

So Alexa picks up my dry cleaning. She shops for groceries. She even took in my car for an oil change. And she spends the night, every night.

I have to credit Alexa for the suggestion that we spend each night together so that my friend the serial killer can't frame me for another murder. A nice chess move; we've blocked his king. If nothing else, it has bought me time while Joel Lightner and I try to figure out who the hell this guy is.

But tonight, I tell Alexa we're going out to a new Greek place that everyone's talking about. By *everyone*, I mean Joel Lightner, who mentioned it was popular. Alexa questions the wisdom of the decision, but doesn't put up a fight. She's probably feeling as cooped up as me.

So out we go, Alexa dolled up in one of her summer dresses and me looking like someone who badly needs a good meal, a haircut, and clothes that are a size smaller. The place is about as fancy as a Greek restaurant is going to get, which is to say not very fancy at all, but apparently they do some interesting things with the seafood and they have a dozen brands of ouzo and the lighting is a little darker.

We're in the bar area, doubling as the waiting area for the packed restaurant, and I do what I do whenever I leave the house now – I look for 'James.' Look without looking, trying for discretion, and not focusing too hard. Sometimes it's easier to find something when you're not actually looking for it, so I just try to keep my observation level as high as possible and wait to see if anything sticks out, lingering eye contact or, better yet, hastily broken eye contact, followed by defensive body language.

'James' could be here right now, in disguise or otherwise – but probably in disguise, given the security camera at the front door of the establishment. All I know for certain is he's muscular; I don't think he could have faked that. I don't know if he has a big gut or if he wore something to make himself look fat. I don't know his hair color, but assume it isn't red, or long and curly, either. I never got a great look at his face because he was wearing those thick glasses, but still – I think if we were face-to-face, I could make him.

There must be over a hundred people packed into the bar area and overflowing into the dining area. Nobody jumps out at me at first blush.

Nobody except Joel Lightner, sitting at the bar by himself.

Alexa excuses herself to the bathroom, so I'm loitering with a cocktail and waiting for someone to give us a seat. My phone buzzes and I check it, always wondering if it's going to be my lucky day and it's 'James' again. But it's not. It's Shauna, and I'm not particularly in the mood for hearing about how *different* I've become or registering the tinge of disappointment in her voice, so I let it go to voice mail.

The hostess standing behind the podium is a stunning blond woman, wearing a sleeveless black dress and wearing it very nicely. Nice tan. Nice cut to her arms. Nice smile. Nice cleavage.

'You come here often?' I ask.

She laughs. Nice laugh.

'Too often,' she says.

'What are the odds I can get moved up in line?' I ask.

'Not good.'

'What if I told you I was a lawyer?'

'Even worse, then.'

My turn to smile. 'I see you have good taste.'

'Which one are you?' She looks down at the list. 'Ko-LAHR-ick, right?'

'Right person, wrong pronunciation. KOH-la-rich,' I say. '*Kola* like the drink, *rich* like wealthy.'

'What kind of name is that?'

'A last name. My first is Jason.'

I pull out my wallet and remove a business card. As a rule, I hate it when people do that. I hand it over the podium to her. She takes it and reads from it. ' "Tasker and Kolarich." What kind of a lawyer are you?'

'A bored one.'

'Can I keep the card?' she asks, flashing a smile for the ages.

'If you didn't, I'd be insulted.'

'Oh, *there* you are.' Alexa grabs hold of my arm, throwing her weight into me. 'Sorry that took me so long!'

'Hey there,' I say, keeping my balance. 'Alexa, this is—'

'Our *hostess*! It's really super to meet you!' Her tone is less than sincere. And the look on her face is less than friendly.

The hostess isn't sure what to make of that. She looks at me.

'It was nice meeting you,' I say. I extend my hand to shake the hostess's. Then I steer Alexa back into the main crowd. 'What the hell was that?'

'I was going to ask you the same . . . *thing*,' she says, slapping my chest, part playfully and part not. 'Are you here with me or are you here with the hostess?' She is wearing an artificial smile, but her eyes are burning.

'Hey.' I step back from her. 'I was just talking to someone while you were in the bathroom. What's the big deal?'

'And what were you talking about? The stock market? Global warming? Or were you exchanging phone numbers?' She keeps that icy smile on her face, her eyes shooting lasers.

'If you must know,' I answer, 'we were discussing the proliferation of nuclear weapons in the Middle East.'

The smile turns into a frown.

'We decided we were against it,' I add.

Still frowning.

I throw up my hands. 'We were just talking.'

'I don't like it.'

'I noticed.'

'Ko-LAHR-ick for two?' the hostess calls out, needling me. 'Ko-LAIR-itch?'

'I don't like it,' Alexa repeats before she follows a waiter into the dining room.

50

Jason

Sunday, July 7

Once Alexa and I are seated, we order some shrimp on a sizzling plate with garlic and onions for an appetizer while we peruse the menu.

'Lawyers give out their business cards,' I say to Alexa. 'That's what they're for.'

'I see. You did it for *business*,' she says, looking at the menu, her expression as hard as stone. 'You think this hostess knows a bunch of criminals and she'll refer them to you.'

I pull out my phone and shoot a text message to Joel: ???

He texts back a minute later: SO FAR NOTHING. WHAT WAS THAT WITH ALEXA? SHE ALMOST SCREWED THE WHOLE THING UP. OR WAS THAT PART OF THE PLAN?

'You never know where business will come from,' I say.

NOT PART OF PLAN, SHE DOESN'T KNOW, I text back to Joel. JUST A JEALOUS GIRLFRIEND.

'You were flirting with her,' Alexa says to me. 'Just admit it.'

I look at her and cock my head. 'You're being ridiculous. Admit *that*.'

THE BUSINESS CARD WAS A NICE TOUCH, Lightner texts back. I thought so, too.

Alexa throws down her menu. 'Take me home,' she says. 'I don't want to be here.'

'What? We just got here.'

Her face is crimson, her mouth turned downward, a pouty scowl. 'My head hurts. I'm leaving. You can stay if you want. Maybe the *hostess* can join you for dinner. What's her name, anyway?'

Linda. Her name is Linda. She just started at this restaurant yesterday. She has another job, too: She's one of Joel Lightner's best investigators, the beautiful blond who interrupted our meeting the other day; apparently Alexa didn't turn around and see her that day, standing in the doorway. I probably should have discussed this whole scheme with Alexa, but I don't want her involved. She's involved enough, anyway, purely by her association with me.

'I don't know the hostess's name,' I lie.

'Well, now you can learn it.'

'Wow,' I say, opening my hands as Alexa gets up, not even waiting for me. 'You're going to walk out on me?'

'Sure looks that way.'

And she's gone. I throw down some cash to cover the appetizer and drinks we ordered and make my way out. Alexa has already left the restaurant. I'll catch up to her.

First, I take the opportunity for one more stop at the hostess station. I whisper something to Linda – 'You be careful now' – and she makes a point of laughing, like I just said something really charming. I shake her hand good-bye, my other hand covering our handshake. Affectionate but not too forward. I don't want to come on too strong here. I just want this beautiful young woman to stand out to whoever it is who may be watching. Joel has promised that they'll have her under the tightest of scrutiny, and that she is armed and well trained herself.

He'd better be right. Because if this has gone as planned, Linda Sparks has just become target number six.

51

Jason

Monday, July 8

A low growl, then thick sweaty gums, fangs dripping with saliva, black nose with nostrils flaring in anticipation; my movements are slow but steady, unsure of what will provoke it, and then its eyes come to life and it SPRINGS—

'Shit,' I whisper to myself. I catch my breath, wait for my pulse to even out, wipe sweat off my face. My dreams have graduated from serial killers and dead women and insects feasting on my skin to animals, mean and snarling, ready to pounce.

I roll over and Alexa is staring at me, wide awake, propped up on one elbow.

I blink twice and say, 'What . . . are you doing?'

'You had a bad dream,' she whispers. 'Are you in pain? I think the pain causes the nightmares.'

'I . . . yeah, maybe. Why are you up?'

'I heard you waking up,' she says, but she doesn't look like she just woke up. She looks like she's been watching me sleep.

She opens her hand. 'I got you a pill. There's water on the night-stand.'

'Oh. Yeah, okay. You don't have to . . . do that. I mean, I can do it myself.'

'I know you can. I'm just trying to help.'

I take the pill and chew it up. These dreams suck. It would be nice if I could sleep through the night just once, instead of lurching forward in terror every two hours.

'You're low on pills,' she says. 'You know that, right?'

Of course I know that. I monitor those things more closely than anything in my life. 'I've got it covered,' I say.

I put my head back on the pillow and stare at the ceiling. I should be feeling better soon.

'I'm sorry about what happened tonight,' she says. 'With that girl. I get jealous. I guess that's obvious.'

My breathing evens out. It's kicking in now, the euphoria, the giddiness. I look over at her, my eyes having adjusted to the darkness, her features becoming clearer now. Is she . . . Has she . . .

'Are you . . . crying?' I ask.

'No, no. No, no. I'm not sad. I'm happy. I'm happy when we're together. Are you?'

'I'm . . . happy,' I murmur.

'You'd tell me if you weren't, wouldn't you?'

'I'm happy. Go back to sleep.' I reach over and touch her arm.

'I don't like it when you talk to pretty girls,' she whispers to me. 'I don't want to share you. Is that so bad?'

'No . . . no . . .'

And then my thoughts turn into swirls, sideways and inside out, and then I'm falling, falling, falling onto something feathery and warm.

52

Shauna

Monday, July 8

Team Arangold – me and Bradley plus the client – leaves the court-house at two-thirty, having spent the last several hours arguing pre-trial motions in advance of jury selection tomorrow morning. We are counting time by the hours now, and the tension is showing in all of us. We had a decent afternoon in front of Judge Getty, so we're off to a good start, but you just never know with this stuff. Twelve people who know absolutely nothing about this case will hear from both sides and pick a winner. To call that prospect unsettling is an under-statement of the highest order. The future of a family construction business hangs in the balance.

And yet.

And yet, as Bradley and I walk across the courthouse plaza toward our law firm, all I can think about is my asshole law partner. And that little Barbie doll of his with the Cleopatra haircut and the cute figure and stunning blue eyes.

'What do you think of her?' I ask Bradley. We've spent so much time together, going into battle on the *Mariel* trial and now this one, that a relationship has formed beyond the formal employer-employee framework – not that we were ever that formal to begin with.

'She's hot,' he says.

'Okay, thanks, Bradley. That's hugely helpful.'

'Should I assume, because you're asking, that you don't like her?'

I consider denying the charge, but he's right – I wouldn't be asking otherwise. 'I'm just not sure that it's a good fit. And I'm not sure Jason's in a place right now where he can tell what's good for him and what's not.'

Bradley looks over at me, as if to comment, but doesn't. He just mumbles a *hmph* of agreement, or at least not disagreement.

'Spill it,' I say.

'You're very protective of him, is all.'

'So what if I am?'

'So nothing. I mean, he's like that with you, too. If he thought somebody was going to do you wrong, he'd break him in half. You're very important to him.'

'Not lately,' I say, surprising myself by the injection of self-pity, wishing I could snatch that embarrassing comment out of the air and shove it back into my big fat mouth.

We zigzag across an intersection, walking in shade now, a relief from the stifling heat.

'Let me ask you something,' says Bradley. 'What did you think of Tori?'

'Tori? Oh, their relationship was a train wreck.'

'A train wreck in hindsight. But before that. What did you think of her?'

I release a sigh. 'I didn't like her much.'

'Okay. And what about Jason's wife, Talia?'

'Talia was great.'

'Don't just say that because she's dead now. Forget the car crash, the whole tragic part. When she was alive and she and Jason were married – honestly, what did you think of her?'

The wound of that tragedy has scabbed over somewhat, but still hurts. Jason was in incredible pain, however he tried to conceal it, and therefore so was I. No matter what else. No matter how else I felt about that relationship.

The words come to me, but I bat them away, swat at them like a scary hornet.

I was jealous of her, I would answer if pressed.

'What's your point, Mr John?'

'You know what my point is. Nobody's good enough for your Jason.'

'Now he's *my* Jason? He's not my Jason.'

We stop at another intersection. I look over at Bradley, who is smiling widely.

'Okay, have it your way,' he says. The light changes, and we move forward, on to our building, on to the last stages of trial preparation, on to another damn topic.

53

Shauna

Monday, July 8

When I get back to the law firm, I take a look down the hall and find the door to Jason's office closed once again, but the office light on, spilling out under the doorway. That's the second time I've ever seen that door closed, the first being when he was in there with Alexa doing whatever it was they were doing. A closed door means privacy. A closed door means no visitors welcome. And the Arangolds will be here in an hour, so it's not like I have a lot of free time.

But I walk in that direction anyway, and I knock on his door anyway, and I poke my head in anyway, without getting an answer, because once upon a time Jason never closed the door, and once upon a time even if he did, there was one person in the world who could walk through it, and that person was me. And if Alexa doesn't like it, she can—

But Alexa isn't in the office.

There are two people in the office, Jason and a younger guy. Jason is behind his desk but standing, stuffing cash into his pocket. The younger man is on the other side of the desk, slouching in a chair with his feet up, his back to me when I pop in but now turning. He gives me a quick nod of acknowledgment, cool and confident. It takes me a moment, but only a moment, before I recognize him. He is much better at this than Jason, much better at pretending that he isn't doing what it looks like he's doing. He's had a lot more practice.

'Shauna,' says Jason, trying to act normal, still in recovery mode, a few bills sticking out of his pants pocket. 'You don't knock?'

I knocked. I just didn't wait for an answer. If I hadn't knocked, if I'd just walked right in without any advance warning, Jason wouldn't have had the nanosecond of time to try to hide the transaction that was taking place.

'You remember Billy Braden,' he says, gesturing to his client while shoving the money deeper into his pocket.

Sure, I do. Richie Rich. The son of wealthy doctors, the Highland Woods boy who deals drugs for fun, because it's cool to take a walk on the wild side, to play Candyman before Daddy gets him into Harvard and buys him his first condo.

'We were just discussing the appeal,' Jason says. 'The state's appealing the judge's ruling.'

I look away, close my eyes, wishing I could close my ears, too.

'Hey, man, gotta scatter,' Billy says.

'Yeah, okay. I'll keep you posted.'

'Cool. Nice seeing you,' Billy says, presumably to me, but I don't look at him.

And then he's gone. Then it's just Jason and me.

'Boy, that guy's a piece of work,' Jason says, still recovering. 'I mean, I've had clients who wanted to pay in cash before, but you'd think a guy with—'

'Jason.'

'—his bank account—'

'Jason.'

He stops talking. The silence sucks all of the oxygen from the room.

'Don't,' I say. 'Please don't lie to me. Tell me to fuck off. Tell me to get out of your office. But don't lie to me. Not *me*.'

I keep my gaze on the window, not having mustered the courage for eye contact just yet. My chest is burning, my limbs filled with electricity, my pulse racing so hard that it's difficult for me to stand still.

'It's painkillers, isn't it?' I say. 'You got hooked while you were recuper—'

'It's nothing,' he says. 'I'm not on anything. I'm fine, Shauna.'

My eyes close again. 'You're not fine. You're lying to me.'

'Shauna, I swear I'm fine.'

'I said don't *lie to me*!' Now I look at him, snapping my head around. 'Don't you dare lie to me, Jason. Anything but that.'

Jason falls into his chair, shaking his head, a hand over his mouth. 'I don't know how to prove a negative, Shauna. I'm not addicted to anything.'

'Swear on Talia's grave,' I say.

He makes a face, but his eyes still haven't met mine. 'What?'

'Look me in the eye, Jason Kolarich, and swear on Talia's grave that you aren't addicted to something.'

'Who . . . ?' Jason pops out of his chair. 'Who the hell do you think you are, demanding something like that? Fuck you, Shauna. *Fuck* you.' He points at the door. 'Now get out of my office.'

Now, finally, there is eye contact, now that he's refused to address the issue.

'I'll help you, Jason. I can help.'

'There's nothing to help.' He points toward the hallway. 'Now you were about to leave my office?'

I take a long breath. Something inside me breaks in half. I move toward the door but stop and turn before leaving.

'This isn't your office, not anymore,' I hear myself say. 'I want you and your drugs out of my law firm.'

54

Shauna

Six o'clock arrives before I've lifted my head. I've given my opening statement to the client and Bradley twice now. They've critiqued it, offered feedback, suggested a few tweaks, but overall people seem energized. Scared out of their minds, but energized, optimistic.

'You're ready,' Bradley says to me. 'You need some sleep. This is going to be a long fight. Don't start it exhausted.'

'I'm going to get sleep,' I promise.

'No, you're not. You're going to be up half the night practicing your opening. I'm trying to talk you out of it.'

'I'll take it under advisement,' I say, looking down the hall at Jason's office. I've blocked out our last exchange; the trial prep with the client has given me a cooling-off period. Did I really just kick him out of the firm? Did Tasker and Kolarich just become Tasker? It feels like a dream, something I remember but that didn't actually happen.

Leave it alone, I tell myself as I start walking down the hall. *Now's not the time,* I reason as I approach the door. *Opening statements are fifteen hours away,* I note.

I take a deep breath and walk in.

Jason isn't there. But his girlfriend, Alexa, is.

She's putting Jason's football into a box, along with a few other items from his desk. The rest of the office is intact, and there's just the one box. So he's packing up a few items but not moving out entirely. Not yet.

'He asked me to grab some things,' she says.

I nod. I consider turning and leaving, but I stand my ground.

'Alexa,' I say, 'I'm concerned about Jason.'

She braces herself. 'Jason's fine,' she says. Not *What do you mean? What's your concern?* Immediately defensive. As if she expected the question and had an answer at the ready.

'He's not fine,' I say. 'I think we both know he's not fine.'

'I don't know what you—'

'Alexa, I just walked in on him buying drugs from a drug dealer. Right here, in this office. And if I know he's doing it, then you must know, too.'

She raises her chin. 'He's in pain. He has chronic pain and a doctor who doesn't believe him.'

'He doesn't have chronic pain,' I say. 'He hasn't had pain in his knee for months. Do you see him hobbling around? Do you see him grimacing in pain?'

She sighs and shakes her head. 'I don't see those things because he's taking medication. The point is to *not* grimace in pain. That's why we have painkillers.'

'I think it's time you opened your eyes,' I say.

She cocks her head. 'And I think it's time you minded your own business.'

And there it is. A turf battle. This isn't about Jason at all, not for her. This is about possession, about *yours* and *mine*.

'Jason *is* my business,' I say, knowing that I'm playing her game, but playing it anyway.

Her face wrinkles up, mock confusion. 'Really? How many times have you two spoken in the last month? Because I'm with him every day, and I have to tell you, your name hardly ever comes up.'

My hands ball into fists as I move toward her. The kettle at boil. This woman, this woman is poison.

'I've seen your act, sweetheart,' I say. 'You like the ones who are broken, don't you? You've got a tiny radar that goes *beep-beep-beep* when you spot one. You could see from a mile away that Jason was struggling. That's why you were drawn to him, wasn't it? That's what you want. You want him broken so you can control him. I'll bet you're right there with a pill every time he needs one, aren't you? *Here you go, Jason. Take that pill. There, there, Jason.* Am I getting warm?'

She crosses her arms and glares at me. 'I'm with Jason because he's a great guy. If you can't see—'

'*I* know Jason's a great guy. Don't *you* tell *me* Jason's a great guy. I love Jason.'

Her lips part, then a small smile breaks out. Her eyes dance with some newfound inspiration. 'I think we're finally getting somewhere,' she says.

'Are we? Where are we getting, Alexa? Do tell.'

'You went a couple of rounds with him over the years, but somehow he never picked you, did he? This isn't about Jason. This is about you, Shauna.'

I'm speechless, like I've just taken a punch to the stomach, the breath whisked from me. I should have seen that coming. It's the default position for someone like her, a comeback so venomous and hateful and childish.

Is it also true?

I start to leave, pivot, end up walking in a circle, unable to decide on my next move. The air in this room is toxic. If I stay here, I don't know what will happen. My hands are visibly shaking. I open my mouth to speak, unsure if I'm capable.

Control it, Shauna. Keep control.

'If you have any true feeling for Jason at all,' I say, 'you will get him help.'

I leave the room and walk down the hall, numb, hollow. I walk past Bradley's office. He says something to me, but I don't respond, I don't even make out the words. I walk into my office and pick up my phone. I find the phone number in my contacts.

Joel Lightner answers on the third ring.

'Joel, it's Shauna,' I say. 'I need to talk to you.'

55

Jason

Monday, July 8

I empty the martini glass and place it carefully down on the table. It was a bad idea. My body can't handle the alcohol, and given the other things I'm putting in my body these days, I'm taking a risk even with one drink. For a moment, I think the vodka's going to come right back up. Across from me, Joel Lightner is watching me very carefully.

'She didn't kick you out,' he says to me.

'She did. She said the words.'

'She said the words, but she didn't mean them.'

'You're a freakin' mind reader now. A man of many talents.' I gesture to the waitress for another round out of instinct, knowing that I won't touch a drop of it.

'Shauna wouldn't kick you out of the firm because you refused to help her with a trial,' Lightner informs me.

The waitress is quick with the next martini. 'It doesn't matter,' I say. 'It's probably for the best. It's probably time, y'know?'

'Time for what? Time for you to run your own law firm? You have any idea how much of a pain in the ass it is to administer something like that? Until I hired an office manager, I was miserable having my own agency. The payroll and the books and the human resources bullshit. I know you, Kolarich. You don't want to run your own office.

You want to try cases and battle it out in court. You want someone else handling the rent payments and balancing the books.'

That isn't what I meant. I have no intention of having my own law firm, either.

'Let's talk about something else,' I say, my thoughts clouding up. 'Let's talk about how you can't figure out who "James Drinker" is and why the hell he's decided to single me out for the biggest mind-fucking of all time.'

'Hey, I'm not Superman. We ran the list of violent ex-cons released in the last year, I even went back eighteen months, and you didn't prosecute any of them. Maybe if you could give me a complete list of everyone you prosecuted, but you can't. The juvie stuff is sealed up, and there's all sorts of misdemeanor casework that you can't remember and I don't have records of. He could be anybody.'

He's right, of course. None of this is his fault. I'm just lashing out.

'Maybe this idea with Linda will work out,' says Lightner.

'I still don't like the idea.' I was never keen on using Linda as bait. But Joel talked me into it. He said it was Linda's idea. Linda Sparks is a former Marion Park cop, a martial arts expert with a license to carry a firearm, a firearm she knows how to use very well. And she has two of Lightner's other investigators tailing her night and day. If 'James' goes after her, he won't get very far.

But that assumes a lot of things I don't know. It assumes that 'James' even followed me to that Greek restaurant in the first place, and that he would take the bait if he was there. But we sure made Linda an inviting target. She fits the profile, and I flirted with her openly, even giving her my business card, which would be irresistible to 'James.' A dead woman with my business card in her purse? If 'James' was there, he's going to tail Linda, check out where she lives, scout out the whole thing. If he keeps to form, it will be a week or so before he makes a move. Could be longer than a week, could be shorter.

'Hey,' I say. 'What about this signature of his? Remember you said the cops told you he left a signature at every crime?'

Joel takes a sip of his drink and smacks his lips. 'I remember.'

'You can't get me any more information on that? If I knew what that was—'

'Jason, no cop investigating a serial killer is going to tell someone like me what the offender's signature is. That's their one chit. They hold it back so they can differentiate between bogus confessions and real ones, helpful information and unhelpful, and so they can separate copycat crimes from the real offender. Nobody's going to tell me that information, and I wouldn't ask them to.'

'Well, can you guess?'

'Can I guess? Sure, I can guess. Um, he leaves a rose at each scene. No, he writes a love letter to each of them and stuffs it in their mouths. Maybe he removes their front teeth. Wait, wait, here we go, he jerks off into a cup—'

'Okay, I get it. So why am I talking to you?'

'Why are you talking to me? Maybe because I'm the only person on the face of this earth who can tolerate you. Besides Shauna, whom you've managed somehow to alienate. Don't be an asshole. Call her up.'

I look at my martini, certain now that I won't touch the second drink. I miss vodka, though. I miss the buzz and the late nights, the give-and-take with Lightner and with Shauna, when we could get her out with us. 'Alexa tolerates me,' I say.

'Yeah, great. She must fuck you really well, kid, because you've disappeared since you met her. I mean, this has been a true honor tonight, just to have the pleasure of your company. And where *is* the lovely Alexa tonight? She let you off your leash. What's the occasion?'

I don't know why I put up with Lightner. 'She grabbed a few things from my office. I didn't feel like going back there and having it out with Shauna.'

'Well, she sure made friends with Linda,' he says. 'What was that? I thought she was going to slap Linda across the face. She looked like she wanted to.'

I shrug. 'She gets jealous. Wouldn't you, if you had a catch like me?'

Lightner gets a good laugh out of that. 'A catch like you? I believe this is not the first time I've mentioned that you look like shit, Kolarich. I mean, absolute dog shit. Comb your hair once in a while, guy. Eat a meal. Sleep a few hours. You know who you look like?'

'Brad Pitt?'

Joel's phone, resting on the table next to a bowl of nuts, starts to vibrate. On the face of the phone, it says *Shauna Tasker*.

'Don't answer it,' I say.

He answers it. 'Hey, girl. I've got your law partner here and he's brooding. No, that's okay, go ahead. You sure? It's no . . . Okay, I'll call you tomorrow. Hey, listen – you guys are going to work this out. Yes, you are. Yes, you are. Okay, tomorrow.' He clicks off the phone. 'You're an asshole,' he says to me. 'Shauna's a peach. Granted, she won't sleep with me, which is a major character flaw, but otherwise she's the best. Don't be an idiot. Kiss and make up with her.'

'I'll get right on that.' I fish out some peanuts, but think better of it.

'And just for my own curiosity,' says Joel, 'why *did* you bail on that trial with her? That's a heater of a case she's handling. I thought you lived for that shit. The high stakes and conflict. That's right up your alley. Why didn't you work on it?'

I throw some money on the table and scoot out of the booth. 'This has been a real treat,' I say. 'Let me know when you figure out who "James Drinker" is or if you get any leads on the surveillance. And definitely send me a bill for your services.'

'What are you doing? Don't leave. Let's get a steak.'

'I have to get home to paint my toenails,' I say.

'Jason.' Joel steps out of the booth, blocking my exit. 'Sit down.'

'I'm leaving.'

'No bullshit,' he says, raising a hand. 'What the hell's wrong with you? This whole new . . . I mean, everything. You look like you haven't slept in days and you're, what, thirty pounds lighter. Your clothes are *hanging* on you. You don't cut your hair or shave. You part ways with the best friend you've ever had and you act like you don't even want to be a lawyer anymore. Seriously, man. What's – Are you – are you sick?' He leans in for the last question, lowering his voice. 'Is there something I can—'

'I'm sick,' I say. 'I'm sick of helping criminals stay out of prison so they can hurt more people. I'm sick of people expecting everything from me and then being disappointed when I don't fit into their vision of how I'm supposed to act. Just – just leave me alone, okay? I appreciate the concern, but I'm totally fine and I don't need anything. Got it?'

Joel looks away, that whole *disappointed* thing I've managed to bring out in so many people, his tongue rolling around his cheek. 'Got it,' he says simply.

'You sure?'

'I'm sure, cowboy. You're totally fine and you don't need anybody. We're clear.'

'Good.' I nod at him and walk out of the restaurant.

56

Shauna

Monday, July 8

'This is a case about incompetency and inefficiency in our city government,' I say, standing at my desk in my office at close to midnight. 'This is a case about inefficient and incompetent bureaucrats who were given a job – to hire a construction company to renovate the civic auditorium – but who were totally unwilling and unable to properly prepare for the job. And when it turned out they *hadn't* adequately prepared, hadn't properly informed that construction company about all sorts of structural problems with the existing building and all sorts of problems below ground that affected the structure, it became a game of hear no evil, see no evil. It became anyone's fault but theirs. It became my client's fault, a father-and-son operation that's done business for over thirty years with hardly a blemish on their record.'

I close my eyes and let that sink in. The recent problems the city's had with the new garbage and waste-hauling contracts have grown more prominent by the day, soaking up the headlines in the *Herald*. Just today, in fact, Mayor Champion fired the head of Streets and San. So I'm hoping this theme finds a soft landing with my jury. If they live within the city limits, they'll immediately think about this scandal. If they live in the near suburbs, they're probably already inclined to think the worst of city employees.

I rub my eyes. I can't do this anymore. I can hardly concentrate anyway. Why did I pick today to have it out with Jason? And why the hell didn't he fight me when I told him to pack his stuff and get out? Why did he just accept it without a word? So now I'm alone at work, too? It's not enough that I'm alone in my personal life, I have to be alone in the professional world, too?

I drop into my chair. I'm tired. I'm so fucking tired of cold beds and pretending that I love my independence. I'm tired of telling myself how proud I am that I haven't settled for any of those nimrods who think I'm supposed to spread my legs for them because they went to Princeton undergrad or they wear hundred-dollar ties or once worked on the Hill. I'm tired of men who assume that they're smarter than me because they were born with a penis and me with a vagina, and the moment they realize the scale is tipped the other way, they lose interest.

I'm tired of assuming I'll have kids. I won't. It's time to see that, ma'am, because them are the facts. I'm thirty-five and a galaxy far, far away from a relationship with anyone even remotely—

The front door to our office pops open. Security checks in at night, but the security guy came through an hour ago. And they routinely announce themselves right away, so they won't send a thrill of terror up the spine of someone working late at night, like me.

'Hello?' I shout.

Footsteps coming my way. I get out of my chair.

'Hey.' Jason stands in the doorway, looking haggard and disheveled, his collar open and his tie missing altogether.

The *stranger danger* adrenaline subsides, replaced with the *Jason* adrenaline, a seesaw of emotion.

He didn't just pack his stuff and leave quietly. He came back.

'How's your opening coming along?'

'How's my opening coming along . . . how's my opening coming along.' I drop my head and make a noise. 'Is that what you came here to ask me?'

'No.' He looks down the hallway toward his office, like he's about to walk away. Since when have we been unable to communicate? When did that happen?

'Sometimes,' he says, still facing the hallway. 'Sometimes I wonder if I still want to do this. Be a lawyer. I'm not totally sure I do anymore.'

'Okay,' I say gently, soothingly, but inside it's like a dagger to my heart.

'But . . . I do know one thing.' He turns to me. 'As long as I practice law, I want to do it with you. I love you, girl.'

My eyes instantly well up. I come around the desk but stop short of him. 'Okay,' I say, choking out the word. I'm not going to cry. I'm not. Maybe I am.

His expression softens. 'Okay.'

'Okay,' I say.

His eyebrows curl in, serious-face. 'About this other thing—'

'Shut up. I don't want to talk about that now.'

He takes a deep breath and nods. 'Okay. Well, so . . .' He gestures to the hallway. 'I should probably—'

'Stay,' I say.

'Oh. You want some company?'

'I want you.'

To stay. Finish the sentence. I want you to stay. Not just, I want you.

'You . . . want me?'

'I want you,' I say again, and then my mouth is on his, my hand in his hair, and for an instant, for an insane, horrifying instant, I think that he's going to draw back, reject me, and if he does we'll never be the same, nothing will ever be the same, and then he kisses me hard and he lets out that moan, Jason's moan, and then he yanks my blouse out of my skirt and runs his hands underneath, and then we're tearing at our clothes and his rib cage is so prominent, skeletal, but he's still Jason, big and strong Jason, with Jason's soapy smell, Jason's big hands, and we fall to the ground, right there in the threshold between my office and the hallway, and he rolls me over and my head bangs against the door and we both laugh and then he's on top of me, running his hands everywhere, his tongue on my neck, then lower, then he's pumping hard and moaning, and I close my eyes and grip the back of his hair and cry out into his ear—

'Wow,' he says, falling over me when it's over, panting, his heart beating against my shoulder.

'Wow,' I agree.

He rises up and sits on the carpet, facing me, his hair all in his face, stuck with sweat. And there I am, up on my elbows on the office carpet, my skirt hiked up, panties curled around one ankle, semen dripping down my leg.

'Where did that . . .' He doesn't finish the sentence. He doesn't need to. But he could smile. He could look pleased. He could look moderately *happy.*

'I'm not sure,' I say. Then I say, 'Maybe I just needed to release some stress.' Playing defense, giving him an out, giving myself an out. Hating myself. Lobbing the ball gently onto his side of the court.

'Yeah, right.' He isn't smiling. He isn't saying, *I've always loved you, Shauna.* He isn't saying, *This feels right.*

Maybe Alexa was right. *He never picked you. You went a couple of rounds with him over the years, but somehow, he never picked you, did he?*

'It doesn't mean anything,' I say. Despising myself. When did I become such a coward?

'Yeah, no, I . . . I mean, it was great,' he says.

I scrunch up my face. *That was great,* the high school senior said to the other high school senior. See how far we've come! Maybe we can talk about R.E.M. music next.

'I should probably get back to my opening,' I say. 'And you should go home to Alexa.'

We put our clothes back on in silence, no eye contact. He gets himself together and isn't sure what to do. At this point, if he tries to give me the obligatory kiss, I'm going to vomit, so I walk back around my desk like I'm about to start reciting my opening again right away.

'Shauna,' he says.

I make a point of shuffling some papers before I look up, my eyebrows raised, holding back emotional responses that are aching to come out.

'Yes, Jason, what?'

'I just . . .' He thinks it over a moment, his jaw working but no words.

'Yes, Jason?'

His expression softens. He lifts his shoulders. 'Just wanted to say, good luck tomorrow. Which courtroom?'

'It's 2106.' As if either of us believes he's going to stop by to watch.

'Good, great. You want me to walk you to your car?'

'Security will. I'm fine. I'm going to stay a while longer.' I finger-comb my hair, try to compose myself.

He nods. 'Don't stay too late,' he says. 'You know when you're on trial, you always stay up too—'

'Jason, you should go,' I say, not interested in his attempt to recapture some intimacy. Even our associate, Bradley, knows I deprive myself of sleep while on trial. If that's the best he can do, he should hit the road. And that's clearly the best he's going to do tonight. Ever.

He didn't pick you.

'Okay. Good luck.' He taps the door and exits.

And just like that, our conversation went from *I love you, girl* to a Grand Canyon between us. I clean myself up with some tissues, feeling like a two-dollar whore. Well, I wanted him to fuck me, and he sure did fuck me.

I take a deep breath and steel myself. 'This is a case about incompetency and inefficiency in our city government,' I say, before my throat chokes closed.

PEOPLE VS. JASON KOLARICH
TRIAL, DAY 3
Wednesday, December 11

57

Jason

Katie O'Connor, the prosecutor playing second chair to Roger Ogren, rises from her seat. 'The People call Lieutenant Oswald Krueger,' she says.

She takes her position at the podium and adjusts her notes, tucks a strand of her orange hair behind her ear. She has the complete Irish look with the hair and the freckles. She is tall and thin and earnest, but somehow manages to give off the impression that she's a nice person at the same time. That's a hard thing to pull off, especially for a female lawyer – as Shauna has often reminded me over the years – being strong and firm but likable all at once. I have to stifle my instinct to root for her. I'll bet Shauna does, too.

Ozzie Krueger is also tall and thin, a balding man in his late fifties who wears a goatee and wire-rimmed glasses. He looks like my biology teacher at Bonaventure, except that Krueger doesn't reek of tobacco as he passes me and takes the witness stand.

'I'm a senior supervisor in the County Attorney Technical Unit,' says Krueger.

'Is that sometimes called the CAT Unit, Lieutenant?'

'CAT Unit, CAT squad, sure.'

'Lieutenant, can you describe in general terms what role you played in the investigation of Alexa Himmel's murder?'

Shauna could object to the use of the word *murder* as a legal conclusion, but she doesn't. I wouldn't, either. It's not like we're arguing suicide here. There had been some talk of arguing self-defense at trial – Bradley John and my brother, Pete, in particular, pushed for it – but I rejected it out of hand.

'Part of the CAT Unit's responsibility is to check computers and e-mails and the like,' says Krueger. 'I obtained Ms. Himmel's laptop computer and inspected it.' O'Connor spends a good amount of time establishing how Krueger went about obtaining the computer, how he preserved it, how he discovered she had an e-mail account with Intercast.

Now that she has set the table, the prosecutor is going to return to my interview with Detective Cromartie on the night of Alexa's death. The prosecution has already shown the jury snippets – my bravura performance in explaining the house key and my vague, shifty discussion about a guy named Jim who I suggested had killed Alexa – but now they want to go back to the beginning of the interview.

Cromartie, I thought, did a nice job during the interrogation. What I liked most – from a clinical perspective, certainly not a personal one – was how the interview began. Most cops, in my experience, lack imagination when they interview suspects. Most would start at the start, would get my name, rank, and serial number, all the essentials, and then the same for Alexa, and then work their way forward to the point where she ended up dead in my living room. When I used to interrogate suspects in Felony Review, I never followed that routine. Because every situation was different, every interviewee different. Sometimes I would start nice and easy, trying to establish a rapport. But I usually started at the pressure point, whatever that would be in the given situation. For a domestic, a situation like mine with a dead girlfriend in the boyfriend's house, I'd always start right there with the relationship. *Look, I can imagine what you're going through. You loved her, didn't you? Did she love you? Relationships can be tough, can't they?* I would even share some of my personal life, although it was made up. *I love my wife, but Jesus, sometimes – sometimes the ones you love are the ones that make you the craziest, right?* That sort of thing.

Cromartie did essentially the same thing with me. He went straight

236

for my relationship with Alexa, seeing what it would do to me. He couldn't really lose. If I was cold as ice about her, he would capture me on camera looking like a murderer. If I got weepy, my defenses might break down and the interrogation would be as easy as holding a bucket under a busted glass of water and catching the drips.

Katie O'Connor tells the courtroom that she's going to reference the video interrogation again. The jury, having already found some very interesting moments during this interview, is wide-eyed with anticipation.

On the basis of the time frozen in the corner of the video monitor, O'Connor wants to start the video at nearly the beginning of the interrogation, just after Cromartie had taken me through the preliminaries – date, time, the presence of counsel, et cetera. The screen comes to life and the jury and spectators are watching the interrogation. Me, I'd prefer not to watch, but that might send some kind of signal to the jurors, so I watch along with them.

Cromartie holds a copy of Alexa's driver's license in his hand, looking at it and then showing it to me. *'Wow, Alexa. Nice-looking lady,'* he says.

I don't answer.

'How long did you say you dated?'

'Several months,' I answer.

'She's a court reporter, huh?'

I don't answer.

'Was this a serious thing, you two?'

'We dated for several months, so, I guess so.'

'Were you engaged?'

'No.'

'Did you talk about that? Marriage?'

'No.'

'Did you love her?'

'It was a serious relationship,' I say. *'People throw that word around. But it was serious.'*

'Did she love you, do you think?'

I shrug, probably too casually in hindsight. I say, *'I think we both thought it was serious.'*

'Did she ever say she loved you, Jason?'

I pause. I'm not sure why. I shouldn't have been the least bit surprised by the question.

'She wasn't the type to say words like that a lot. Neither am I. Did she ever say it? I think she did, but not like a routine thing.'

That was stupid. I should have just said yes. You don't forget when your mate breaks through that barrier and says the *L* word. It's a memorable moment in any relationship. They either said it or they didn't, and you aren't unclear on that. If you are, then you're an asshole, which is exactly what I look like. An asshole, or a liar.

At this point in the interrogation, I was just an asshole. But I was about to be a liar, too.

'Did you two have any, uh, y'know, bumps in the road?' Cromartie asks me.

'No more than the next couple.'

'Did you fight, Jason?'

'No more than the next couple.'

'What about in the last few days? Any fights? Problems?'

'We had our ups and downs. We'd break up and get back together. It was like that sometimes.'

'But no recent fights?'

I shake my head. *'No. Nothing recent.'*

Katie O'Connor stops the tape. 'Lieutenant, you previously testified that you obtained Ms. Himmel's computer and her e-mail account?'

'That's correct.'

'Did you find any e-mails between Ms. Himmel and the defendant within the week or so preceding her murder?'

'We did.'

'I'm going to take you to the date of July twenty-seventh of this year. Did you find an e-mail on that date from Ms. Himmel to the defendant?'

'That's correct, yes.'

'People's Seven,' says O'Connor to the judge and Shauna. She pulls it up on a computer screen for the jury to read:

Saturday, July 27, 8:43 PM
Subj: Why??
From: 'Alexa M. Himmel' <AMHimmel@Intercast.com>
To: 'Jason Kolarich' <Kolarich@TaskerKolarich.com>

Why won't you return my calls? We can't even TALK now??? I want to know what's going on with you and why this is happening. Please call me.

'Is People's Seven a true and accurate copy of that e-mail?'

'It is,' Krueger confirms.

'Move for admission of People's Seven,' says O'Connor. Shauna doesn't object. She objected to all of the e-mails before trial, taking her best Hail Mary shot, throwing out every possible argument she could make with a straight face – lack of foundation, overly prejudicial – but lost. So it doesn't do us any good here to make a bigger deal about these e-mails than they already are.

'Running objection, Your Honor,' she says quietly, for the record.

'People's Seven will be admitted,' says Judge Judy.

'Just to refresh everyone's memory, Lieutenant, what was the date of Ms. Himmel's murder?'

'July thirtieth,' he says.

'So this e-mail was sent three days before she was murdered?'

'That's right.'

'Take you to July twenty-eighth,' says O'Connor. 'Did you recover an e-mail from that day that was sent by Ms. Himmel to the defendant?'

And then we are looking at another e-mail, technically the following day but really just sent about five hours after the first one they just read:

Sunday, July 28, 1:41 AM
Subj: Hey you
From: 'Alexa M. Himmel' <AMHimmel@Intercast.com>
To: 'Jason Kolarich' <Kolarich@TaskerKolarich.com>

Hey you, I'm trying to be patient and not push you. ☺ I always said I wouldn't rush you or push you into anything. But you owe me more of an explanation than you gave me, don'tcha think?

This is very hard for me, Jason. I don't deserve this. Don't you think I deserve better than this?????????????

And another, three hours later:

Sunday, July 28, 4:28 AM
Subj: Remember?
From: 'Alexa M. Himmel' <AMHimmel@Intercast.com>
To: 'Jason Kolarich' <Kolarich@TaskerKolarich.com>

Hi. I'm up and I'm pretty sure you are, too. I'm thinking about you and thinking about US and thinking that maybe we can just wipe the slate clean and start over. A first date? Remember the first date? When I 'called' you? That's when I knew we had the same sense of humor.

I'm sure you know this is killing me. I just want to hear your reasons. I promise, promise, PROMISE I won't bother you again if you just explain it. But if you keep ignoring me, I don't know what I'll do. Please don't do this to me.

And another, that afternoon:

Sunday, July 28, 3:59 PM
Subj: A lesson
From: 'Alexa M. Himmel' <AMHimmel@Intercast.com>
To: 'Jason Kolarich' <Kolarich@TaskerKolarich.com>

How To Hurt Alexa Himmel 101: Ignore her. Break her heart, but that's not enough. Also refuse to give her a good, honest explanation. Don't tell her you're a COWARD or why you LIED to her and led her to believe you were a GOOD AND DECENT person when you're not. Throw her in the trash after you've fucked her a bunch of times and had your jollies and leave her to die.

You'd probably like it if I died, wouldn't you? Well, just say the word, Jason, and I'll do it. I'm dead anyway.

And this one, completing a Sunday of e-mails:

Sunday, July 28, 7:12 PM
Subj: Seriously this is important
From: 'Alexa M. Himmel' <AMHimmel@Intercast.com>
To: 'Jason Kolarich' <Kolarich@TaskerKolarich.com>

I just had some GREEK food and thought you'd think that was funny. Are you laughing? You're probably laughing AT me not WITH me. Ha ha ha poor Alexa the fucked up girl.

Anyway, I just thought of something that could be seriously bad for you and I want to make sure you're protected so please call me just for that and nothing else, no more explanations or anything else but I'm not kidding.

The prosecutor takes a moment, allowing the jury to drink in everything they've seen so far, a portrait of a troubled woman, smarting desperately from a breakup.

'Take you to the following day, Monday, July twenty-ninth of this year,' says Katie O'Connor. 'The day before Ms. Himmel was murdered. Did you recover any e-mails from Ms. Himmel to the defendant on that day?'

He did, of course, an e-mail from Monday morning:

Monday, July 29, 9:13 AM
Subj: I wasn't kidding
From: 'Alexa M. Himmel' <AMHimmel@Intercast.com>
To: 'Jason Kolarich' <Kolarich@TaskerKolarich.com>

I know you're awake. I know you're reading this.

I wasn't kidding. If you don't get in touch with me your going to be seriously fucked.

'At this time, Your Honor, I'd like to return to the video interview,' says Katie O'Connor.

She starts off right where she stopped. Back to Detective Cromartie asking me about the state of my relationship with Alexa at the time she died:

'So just to be clear, Jason, just so there's no misunderstandings, you and Alexa were together as of today? You guys were still a couple?'

'Yeah, of course,' I say.

'Had you been together for, say, the past week?'

'Yeah.'

'The past two weeks?'

'Yeah. We'd been together.'

'Your relationship was fine. At the time she died, your relationship was good?'

'Our relationship was fine,' I say to Cromartie. *'Our relationship was good.'*

Katie O'Connor stops the tape. I maintain my *I'm innocent* expression, staring straight ahead, trying to show no emotion. It isn't easy. It isn't easy to be caught in a lie in front of a roomful of people. Especially when twelve of those people are deciding your fate.

I'm a liar. No one in this room has any doubt. And why lie? Because I'm guilty, right? That's how people think. As a prosecutor, I routinely relied on that bias. When I caught a defendant in a lie, I would harp on it in closing argument ad nauseam. But I never agreed with that presumption myself. There are many reasons that people lie. Why is telling a lie, in the heat of a criminal inquiry, limited to people who are guilty of the crime?

'Let's go back to the e-mails, Lieutenant,' says O'Connor.

She is working in chronological order. Logically, the right decision.

But tactically, as well. She is saving the best for last.

58

Shauna

'Lieutenant Krueger,' says Katie O'Connor, 'did you recover any e-mails from Ms. Himmel to the defendant on the date of Tuesday, July thirtieth? The day of her murder?'

'I did. I recovered an e-mail with content and with an attachment.'

The prosecutor puts that e-mail on the board for the jury:

Tuesday, July 30, 9:01 AM
Subj: I REALLY wasn't kidding
From: 'Alexa M. Himmel' <AMHimmel@Intercast.com>
To: 'Jason Kolarich' <Kolarich@TaskerKolarich.com>

Hi, there. Hope you're well. I'm really concerned about the
attached letter getting out. Maybe we can put our heads together
and figure out how to prevent it. But if you keep ignoring me then
I guess there's nothing i can do. . . . . .

< BAD.Letter.pdf >

'You said there was an attachment?'

'Yes,' says Krueger. 'You can see at the bottom of the printout of the e-mail. A document entitled "BAD Letter," in portable document format, or PDF as most people know it, was attached to this e-mail.'

'Did you print out a copy of that PDF document?'

'I did.'

'People's Fourteen,' says O'Connor. 'Is People's Fourteen a true and accurate copy of the document attached to that e-mail?'

'Yes, it is.'

The jury is now looking at the letter Alexa attached to that e-mail:

To: The Board of Attorney Discipline
Subject: Jason Kolarich, Attorney ID # 14719251

I am writing to report an attorney named Jason Kolarich, currently practicing at the law firm of Tasker and Kolarich. Jason has become addicted to a painkiller called oxycodone. It has hampered his ability to practice law, I fear to the detriment of his clients. He has lost a good deal of weight, and his behavior has become erratic. I am not a lawyer, so I don't know if the drugs have stopped him from defending his clients properly. I don't know if there are rules governing this, but I thought the state's board that regulates lawyers should know about this.

More than anything, I think a client, before they hire a lawyer, should know if that lawyer is a drug addict.

I am afraid to sign this letter, but I hope you will look into it.

'Lieutenant, do you know whether this letter was ever sent to the state's Board of Attorney Discipline?'

'I don't know one way or the other,' says Krueger. 'All I know is that, the following evening, Ms. Himmel was murdered.'

I could object, but I don't. The jurors wouldn't notice, anyway. Several of them, while stopping short of nodding enthusiastically or making throat-slashing gestures, indicate the impact this evidence has had on them. Eyebrows go up. Lips part. One of the guys in the front row, having craned forward throughout the showing of the e-mails, falls back in his chair, glances at his neighbor. I can imagine the bubble over his head: *Well, our deliberations won't take long, will they?*

I can hardly blame them. It doesn't get more damning than this. Alexa had become more than just an ex-girlfriend with separation anxiety. Now she was someone who was going to ruin Jason professionally if he didn't take her back. And roughly twelve hours later, she was shot in the back with Jason's gun, while standing in Jason's living room.

At the podium, O'Connor takes her time, flipping through her notes, pretending to locate her next line of questioning when, in fact, she just wants that letter to sit up on the screen for as long as possible.

'Lieutenant, sending an e-mail is one thing. It's another thing whether the intended recipient of that e-mail actually received it. Did you investigate whether the defendant had, in fact, received or opened these e-mails we've discussed?'

'I did. The defendant gave us permission to access his laptop. In addition, we issued subpoenas to review the e-mails sent to and by the defendant on his e-mail account.' Lieutenant Krueger takes the jury through that process. It was a thorny one, involving Judge Bialek, because an attorney's e-mails include many confidential communications with clients.

'We were able to determine the date and time that each e-mail was opened,' Krueger explains.

It gives Katie O'Connor the chance to put each of these e-mails back up on the screen. She pops up each e-mail and asks Lieutenant Krueger if and when Jason opened that e-mail. People's Exhibit Seven, the July 27 e-mail at 8:43 P.M., was opened at 9:35 that evening. People's Eight and Nine, in the early hours of Sunday, July 28, were opened on Jason's laptop within minutes of each other on Sunday morning. People's Ten, the How-to-Hurt-Alexa-101 e-mail, was opened an hour after it was sent, just after five P.M. on Sunday, July 28. Blow by blow, Lieutenant Krueger demonstrates that Jason was routinely opening these e-mails.

'People's Thirteen,' says O'Connor, referring to the final e-mail, the one with the attached letter. 'Sent at 9:01 A.M. on Tuesday, July thirtieth. When, if ever, was that document opened on the defendant's computer?'

'Three minutes after ten that same morning,' he says.

'And People's Fourteen, the letter to the Board of Attorney Discipline? When, if ever, was that document opened on the defendant's laptop?'

'Within the same sixty seconds,' he answers. 'Ten-oh-three in the morning. Just over an hour after the e-mail and attachment were sent, the defendant opened it up on his laptop.'

O'Connor nods. 'After that final e-mail with the attached letter, did you find any further e-mail communications between the defendant and Ms. Himmel, Lieutenant?'

'No, I didn't,' says Lieutenant Krueger. 'It was the last e-mail Ms. Himmel ever sent.'

59

Shauna

The judge calls a midmorning recess. Jason heads straight to the anteroom where he's able to confer with counsel. He doesn't even turn around to acknowledge his brother, Pete, who seems eager for my attention.

'He's . . . he's not in the frame of mind right now for you,' I apologize.

'That's fine, whatever.' Pete's tan has diminished since he's been in town for the trial. He owns a bar in the Cayman Islands, of all things, having received a healthy windfall of money under circumstances that are unclear – and therefore suspicious – to me. Where Jason inherited his mother's length and features, Pete is the spitting image of his father, Jack, a devilishly handsome face and a quick, easy smile, a guy who could charm a shark out of its chum. He inherited his father's penchant for substance abuse, too, though with Pete it was cocaine, not booze, and he promises that's way behind him now.

Pete was basically the fuckup of the family, the difference between Jason and him being athletic ability. Jason wasn't going anywhere good before the varsity football coach discovered him, but his prowess on the gridiron got him a scholarship to State, and even after he pissed that away by fighting with a teammate, he was away from home, away from some of the temptations and bad influences that had set him astray, and he ultimately thrived. Pete lived in Jason's shadow and got himself into plenty of trouble before, a couple years ago, Jason bailed him out of some serious problems and got him out of town with the previously referenced windfall of money, source unknown.

'I just don't get this, Shauna,' says Pete. 'We're getting crucified. Is it – is it too late for self-defense? I mean, this woman looks like a psycho, right? The idea that she came after him with a knife or even his own gun? I'd believe it in a heartbeat.'

'She was shot in the back, Pete, and she was unarmed,' I say, realizing I've made a misstep by joining the debate. It's not that I don't appreciate his point. I do.

Roger Ogren does, too. In fact, after discovering these e-mails, Roger expected us to plead self-defense. Whenever we'd talk to discuss details, he'd find a way to casually raise the point. *So we're still looking at a December trial?* he'd ask. *No continuances or affirmative defenses or anything like that?* He didn't think we'd stick to the speedy trial. He thought we'd come out with self-defense sooner or later. The fact that he was so worried about that defense, despite the fact that Alexa Himmel was shot in the back, from ten feet away, and unarmed, showed the power of those e-mails, not to mention the phone calls, which the jury hasn't heard about yet.

It was the interview, wasn't it? Roger asked me last week, when he finally confessed that he'd been expecting the self-defense argument all along. *He brought up that Jim guy in the interview and lied about how things were going with Alexa. Hard to walk that back to 'She came at me with my own gun and I had no choice.'*

'Pete, you know I can't talk to you about the case,' I say. 'What's done is done. This is what Jason wants. We're going to have to trust him.'

Pete knows all of this. We've been over it time and time again. He's come into town on and off since Jason was arrested, but he's been clearly instructed about not discussing the case with Jason. Jason, for his part, has been very protective of his little brother, demanding that he go back to the Caymans (Pete refused) and rarely speaking to him at all.

'Tell him . . . you know . . .' Pete's voice trails off.

'I'll tell him you love him.' I put a hand on his shoulder. Then I head into the anteroom to see my client.

60

Jason

When court reconvenes, the prosecution tells the judge that they'd like to read a stipulation to the jury about cause of death. There's no point in our denying that Alexa was shot through the back of the throat with a single bullet from my gun, and there's no doubt that this gunshot was the cause of her death. The jury has already seen the grisly crime scene photos, so there's little point, from Roger Ogren's perspective, in putting the medical examiner on the stand. This was the point made by Judge Bialek, who, like any judge, would rather that trials move more quickly than slowly and who is always happy to embrace a stipulation that spares her precious courtroom hours.

'Members of the jury,' says Judge Bialek, 'the prosecutor, Mr Ogren, is going to read a stipulation to you. A stipulation means that the parties have agreed that the facts stated to you are, in fact, true. You may accept these facts as true. You may consider them as evidence every bit as much as you consider any other information you receive in this matter. Mr Ogren, you may proceed.'

'Yes, Your Honor.' Roger Ogren stands before the jurors and reads from a piece of paper, as if he were unfurling a scroll and announcing first, *Hear ye, Hear ye.*

I take Shauna's hand in mine. We've agreed that, during this one portion of the evidence, it is best that we hold hands, given that the jury's eyes, not otherwise diverted by someone's testimony or an e-mail on a screen, might likely move to the defense table.

'The parties stipulate that on Tuesday, July thirtieth of this year, Alexa Marie Himmel suffered a gunshot wound to the throat while in the living room of the home belonging to the defendant, Jason Kolarich. That gunshot was fired from behind her, from a distance of approximately ten feet. The bullet severed Ms. Himmel's fourth cervical vertebra, and death was instantaneous. The county medical examiner has conducted an autopsy and routine toxicological examination and found no other evidence of any foul play, injury, or illness that would have caused Ms. Himmel's death.

'The parties therefore stipulate that this single gunshot wound was the proximate cause of Ms. Himmel's death, and that the manner of death was homicide.

'The parties stipulate that Ms. Himmel's time of death occurred between the hours of nine P.M. and midnight on Tuesday, July thirtieth of this year.'

The stipulation was my idea. We let Roger write the first draft, and I added a couple of facts before letting Roger take another turn at it. We could have scrapped the whole thing and allowed witness testimony to cover this, but we had the judge on our side wanting to circumvent hours of testimony, and a prosecutor is always happy to have stipulated evidence. Why not? Even with rock-solid witnesses, you never know what might happen. A cop or coroner might have a car accident. They might slip up on the stand somehow, in some way, and open a door for an ambitious defense attorney. Fear of the unknown is what keeps trial lawyers up at night.

But more than the prosecutor or judge, the person who wanted this evidence down in writing most of all was me. I want the jurors to be able to take this information back with them during deliberations.

Because it highlights the first mistake the government made.

61

Jason

Officer Janet Brannon, another member of the County Attorney Technical Unit, takes the stand at eleven. Her testimony will be short and sweet. Katie O'Connor is hoping to get her in before lunch so the government can get their next witness, an FBI agent, on and off before the end of the day. Judge Judy is hoping for the same thing.

'As part of the investigation,' says O'Connor, 'did you consider the possibility that someone other than the defendant shot and killed Ms. Himmel?'

'Yes, we did. We looked at many things.'

'Did that include fingerprinting the defendant's home?'

'Yes, it did. I oversaw the process. We took prints from every surface on the first floor, including the door and doorknobs on each side. We took prints from the garage. We printed everything on the second floor, not only the living room area where the murder occurred, but everywhere. And for good measure, we printed the third story of the town house, as well.'

'Is there anything you *didn't* print?' O'Connor asks.

'If there is, I can't think of it.'

'And whose prints did you find?'

'We found prints belonging to the defendant and prints belonging to Alexa Himmel.'

'Any others?'

'None that we could match.'

It doesn't hurt that I have a cleaning lady who comes once a week, a nice Polish girl named Dita, so presumably the place is fairly wiped down at any point in time.

'We checked for the presence of any shoe prints or markings and found nothing other than a shoe that matched the defendant's, a partial shoe print in the foyer by the garage-access door. Otherwise, no shoe prints.'

'And what about the handgun that fired the bullet that killed Ms. Himmel?'

'We examined the firearm and attempted to extract fingerprints.'

'What was the result, Officer?'

Officer Brannon says, 'There were no fingerprints found on that weapon.'

'Is that unusual, in your experience?'

'Not especially. Prints don't stick on firearms nearly as often as people think.'

'Did you find anything *else* while examining the firearm?'

'Yes,' she answers. 'We found traces of isopropyl alcohol and benzalkonium chloride on the firearm in several places. These are chemicals found, among other places, in your typical disinfectant wipes people keep in their homes.'

'Did you find any such disinfectant wipes in the defendant's home, Officer?'

'Yes, we found a canister of Clorox disinfectant wipes, fresh scent, on the counter.'

'Did you do any further follow-up?'

'Yes, we did,' says Brannon. 'In the garbage can in the defendant's kitchen, we found a used disinfectant wipe. It was still damp.'

'I see. And what did all of this lead you to conclude?'

Shauna could object. But she won't. The jury's thinking it already.

'Before the police recovered that gun, someone had wiped it down with a disinfectant cloth,' says the officer.

'Thank you, Officer. No further questions.'

'Someone . . . wiped down the gun . . . with a disinfectant cloth,' says Shauna. 'Well, let's talk about the gun, Detective.'

'Officer,' Brannon corrects.

'My mistake. *Officer*.' Only I know Shauna well enough to know that her *mistake* was intentional. 'Officer, this handgun was found by the police resting on the floor in my client's living room, wasn't it?'

'That's my understanding, yes.'

'So . . . it wasn't exactly hidden, was it?'

The prosecutor, Katie O'Connor, moves in her chair but doesn't object. She could. Roger Ogren would, if this were his witness. But O'Connor probably figures that we haven't been obnoxious with objections, so she won't be, either.

'Hidden? I wouldn't call it hidden, no.'

'It was in plain sight, for all to see.'

'That's my understanding.'

'In fact, the first thing Jason did when the police arrived was tell them about the gun. Isn't that true?'

'I don't know that for a fact, but I'd heard that, yes.'

'This was my client's gun, isn't that right, Officer?'

'Yes.'

'The serial number on the gun wasn't scraped off, was it?'

'No, it was not.'

'It was incredibly easy for you to type a number into a database and determine that this gun belonged to Jason.'

'It was, yes.'

'If Jason hadn't already said so himself.'

The witness doesn't answer. That's fine by Shauna.

'So Jason wasn't trying to hide the presence of the gun or the fact that it was his, was he?'

'As far as I know, no, he wasn't trying to do that.'

'Would it seem unusual to you that my client might handle his own weapon from time to time?'

Again, O'Connor considers objecting, but she probably thinks that Shauna's actually helping her, planting an image in the jury's mind of me holding that gun, being comfortable with it, maybe even playing pretend with it in the mirror, like Robert De Niro in *Taxi Driver*.

'Would it seem unusual that your client would handle his own weapon from time to time . . . No, that wouldn't be unusual,' the officer answers. 'It's his gun.'

'Exactly. So given that it wouldn't be suspicious *in the least* for Jason's fingerprints to be on a weapon that he's owned for over a decade, can you think of any possible reason why *Jason* would wipe down that gun?'

The witness has no answer for that.

It's a strong point, and the right place to end. If I was the one who shot Alexa, why would I wipe down the gun, when my prints being on the weapon wouldn't be suspicious in the slightest, and when I knew, as a longtime prosecutor and now defense lawyer, that trace evidence of the disinfectant would be found on the gun?

Why would I do that?

'Officer,' says Katie O'Connor on redirect, 'you've been on the police force for how long?'

'Six years, five months.'

'And in your experience, do even intelligent criminals sometimes do stupid things?'

'Objection,' says Shauna.

'Sustained.'

'In your experience, do criminals under incredible stress do stupid things?'

'Objection.'

'Sustained.'

'In your experience, would a criminal "under the cloud of addiction" to OxyContin do something stupid?' Using the same phrase Shauna used, mocking her.

'Objection.'

'Sustained. Ms. O'Connor, this line of inquiry is finished,' says Judge Bialek.

'So am I, Judge,' O'Connor says, sitting down with satisfaction.

The point of an adversarial criminal justice system is for each side to put forth their case, and somewhere in the middle, within that tug-and-pull of competing theories, emerges the truth. This is one of those times. They're both right. Shauna is right that it wouldn't make sense for me to clean off that gun with a Clorox disinfectant wipe.

And Katie O'Connor is right that I did, in fact, do that very thing.

62

Jason

Court reconvenes after lunch. Roger Ogren stands, flattens his tie, buttons his coat, and says, 'The People call Special Agent Dennis Jumer.'

The local cops still bring in the FBI a lot to assist with cell phone technology, most notably tracking the movements of suspects by their cell phone usage. We used this historical cell site analysis on occasion when I was working Gang Crimes at the county attorney, but nowadays they've taken this stuff to an art form. There are agents like Jumer who basically do nothing else but check cell phone records and put dots, or circles, on a map.

'I've been a special agent with the FBI for almost eleven years,' he tells Ogren. 'I've been assigned to our Narcotics and Firearms Task Force for the last five.'

'As part of your duties, do you analyze cell phone records?'

'Yes, that's the largest part of what I do these days. I typically do historical cell site analyses on cell phone records.'

'Why do you conduct historical cell site analyses, Agent Jumer?'

'The purpose is to determine the approximate locations of cell phones at the time the calls were placed that are detailed in the records.'

A cell phone is a radio, and when it's used it sends out radio frequencies in all directions. It will hit multiple towers belonging to that service provider, and that provider will have a switching channel that will pick which of its towers should provide service to the cell phone. Each tower has its own identifier, and the service provider records that particular tower in its call detail records.

So when you call somebody on a cell, the FBI can go back later and say, at this day and time, you initiated a phone call, and this was the tower that provided service to that phone. The tower providing service is *usually* the one that's closest to the cell phone's location, but not always, especially in an urban area with high call traffic. So it's not an exact science.

If this were an area of contention with us, we'd have some basis to go after this witness. In fact, as a defense lawyer, I once had Dennis Jumer on the stand for half a day, berating the FBI's methodology and criticizing them for not using triangulation or GPS, which are more accurate. I assume that Jumer remembers that day, and me.

Agent Jumer talks for a while about his credentials and experience; then he turns to the details of this case. He was brought in by the county attorney's office to analyze the cell phone records of Alexa Himmel and me for the week preceding her murder.

'We obtained the records, by subpoena, from Ms. Himmel's service provider and Mr Kolarich's service provider,' he says.

'People's Eighteen, Judge. There was a stip on this.' Roger Ogren displays on the screen a summary chart of phone calls made by Alexa's cell phone to my cell phone, or landline, or office, on the date of Friday, July 26.

Shauna nods to the judge. 'It will be admitted,' says Judge Judy.

'Did you prepare this chart summary?' Ogren asks Jumer.

'I did.'

'Please tell the jury what it shows.'

'This chart shows calls made from Ms. Himmel's cell phone to either Mr Kolarich's landline number, his cell phone number, or his direct line at his law firm, as well as the date and time of those calls, the length of time, and the cellular tower that originated the call. For privacy reasons, rather than using the actual phone numbers, we denoted Mr Kolarich's cell phone as "Kolarich Cell," his landline at home as "Kolarich Home," and his direct office line as "Kolarich Office."'

'And is this chart limited in time, Agent?'

'Oh, yes, I'm sorry. Yes. This chart covers phone calls made by Ms. Himmel's cell phone only for the date of Friday, July twenty-sixth of this year.'

'Just a one-day period?'

'Just a one-day period. Twenty-four hours. Just Friday, July twenty-sixth.'

The jury probably remembers the first e-mail from Alexa that was introduced into evidence, the *Why won't you return my calls?* e-mail that was dated Saturday, July 27. They are about to see all of the calls that I wasn't returning.

CALL DETAIL RECORDS FOR CELL PHONE OF ALEXA M. HIMMEL
Friday, July 26

Time	Destination	Length of Call (minutes)	Originating Cell Site
10:32 AM	Kolarich Cell	1	221529
2:47 PM	Kolarich Cell	1	221529
2:59 PM	Kolarich Cell	1	221529
3:12 PM	Kolarich Cell	1	221529
3:13 PM	Kolarich Office	1	221529
3:15 PM	Kolarich Cell	1	221529
3:58 PM	Kolarich Cell	1	221529
4:45 PM	Kolarich Cell	1	221529
5:22 PM	Kolarich Cell	1	221529
5:23 PM	Kolarich Cell	1	221529
7:02 PM	Kolarich Cell	1	221529
8:28 PM	Kolarich Cell	1	221529
8:29 PM	Kolarich Home	1	221529
8:31 PM	Kolarich Cell	1	221529
9:46 PM	Kolarich Cell	1	221529
10:37 PM	Kolarich Cell	1	221529
11:14 PM	Kolarich Cell	1	221529
11:17 PM	Kolarich Cell	1	221529

11:21 PM	Kolarich Cell	1	221529
11:25 PM	Kolarich Home	1	221529
11:27 PM	Kolarich Cell	1	221529
11:32 PM	Kolarich Home	1	221529
11:47 PM	Kolarich Cell	1	221529
11:49 PM	Kolarich Cell	1	221529

'That's twenty-four phone calls,' says Jumer, when asked. 'Twenty-four phone calls in a twenty-four-hour period. Really, a fourteen-hour period.'

'Agent,' says Roger Ogren, 'I see that each of these calls says that their duration was one minute. Does that mean that each call was precisely sixty seconds?'

'No, obviously not,' Jumer replies. 'This particular service provider – like all of them, I believe – charges you for a minute of time the moment a call is placed. So a ten-second call is charged as one minute. A fifty-nine-second call, charged as one minute. We are limited to what the service provider can give us, and they don't go lower than one minute.'

'So does this mean that every call made from Ms. Himmel's cell phone to one of Mr Kolarich's numbers was less than one minute?'

'Yes, it does. Sixty seconds or less.'

'Does the service provider differentiate, to your knowledge, between calls that are received by a live person and calls that are received by that person's voice mail?'

'No, there's no difference. All this computer knows is that the other line picked up.'

'So it's possible that some or all of these calls made by Ms. Himmel went to voice mail.'

'It's possible, sure. Common sense says it's likely. But it's impossible to know.'

'Fine, that's fine.' Ogren clears his throat. He's sounding a little nasal today, the onset of a cold. Trials can be murder on your health, though I usually didn't get sick until after it was over, like my immune system knew when it was okay to surrender.

'Agent, the farthest-right column refers to the "originating cell site."'

'Yes. That's the tower that provided service to her call.'

'And did you estimate the range of coverage of that cell tower?' Ogren puts up a chart of a map of the city and the near-south suburbs, including Overton Ridge, where Alexa lived.

'Yes. This map shows the estimated range of coverage of cell tower number 221529,' he says.

The map has a large red triangle at the location of that cell tower. From that red triangle, a large yellow-shaded area fans out to the east, about a third of a circle, showing the estimate of the range covered by that cell tower.

'This cell tower, like many in urban areas, is directional,' says Jumer.

'What does that mean?'

'Well, in some places, cell towers are omnidirectional, meaning they send radio frequencies in all directions. Imagine dropping a pebble in the water and watching the ripple. The ripple goes in all directions. That's omnidirectional. But many cell towers in high-population areas, like this one, are sectored. This tower has three sectors. So this area of coverage you see here in the highlighted area? That's about a hundred twenty degrees, or a third of the circle.'

Ogren uses his pen to point to a small x within the highlighted area of coverage. Popping off that x on the exhibit is a bubble containing the words *Alexa Himmel Residence*. 'Explain this x and this bubble next to it, Agent.'

'As you can see, Ms. Himmel's home residence is located within the highlighted area of coverage that this cell tower provides,' says Jumer.

'So these phone calls – how many phone calls were there?'

'Twenty-four phone calls,' says Jumer.

'Each of these twenty-four phone calls was made using the same cell tower's service.'

'Correct.'

'A cell tower that covers Ms. Himmel's home.'

'Correct. We can't say for certain that she made those calls from home. We *can* say for certain that the cell tower feeding her RF on each of those calls covered her home.'

Shauna catches my eye. I give a *Who cares?* shrug. We could argue with the agent on this point, but twenty-four calls pinging the same cell tower? Of course Alexa made those calls from home.

And that, of course, is one of the nice things about this evidence for the prosecution. They are using this evidence primarily to show Alexa's desperation, leading her to blackmail me with that letter to the Board of Attorney Discipline, leading *me* to kill her to cover up my addiction to painkillers. But this evidence also helps them show that, over the days that preceded her death, she was living at home, not with me – a nice reminder to the jury of one of the many things I lied about in the interrogation.

'Let's move to the next day, Saturday, July twenty-seventh,' says Ogren. 'Did you obtain a list of phone calls made from Ms. Himmel's cell to one of the defendant's numbers on that day?'

He did, and another summary chart is admitted into evidence. There were more calls for Saturday than for Friday, because it was a full day of calls, beginning at the dawn of the day – twenty minutes after midnight – and continuing all the way until the day's end, at 11:51 P.M.

'She made forty-seven phone calls to Mr Kolarich on that day,' Jumer summarizes. 'All of them for one minute or less.'

'And then, Sunday, July twenty-eighth, Agent.' They go through the same routine, producing a summary chart, admitting it into evidence.

'Sixty-three calls on that date,' says the agent.

'And Monday, July twenty-ninth, Agent Jumer. The day before Ms. Himmel's death,' he reminds the jury. Another chart, same basic result.

'Fifty-nine phone calls on that date to Mr Kolarich's cell phone,' Jumer says.

One of the jurors in the front row, a schoolteacher, is doing the math on his notepad: 24 calls on Friday + 47 on Saturday + 63 on Sunday + 59 on Monday = 193 phone calls she made to me in four days.

We've known this evidence was coming, of course, and I've always wondered how it would cut. On the one hand, it makes Alexa look wildly unstable, and I had a glimmer of hope that maybe the jury would start to turn on her – kind of a *Jesus, lady, get the hint and move on* sentiment – and feel some sympathy for me. Maybe some of the men on the jury, who've had messy breakups, might feel a kinship with me. Maybe some of the women, who usually are more critical of other women than are men, would lose patience with her.

That was a possibility, a hope. But it's one of those things that you can't predict, dependent on the circumstances, any number of factors; I knew I'd have to wait until the evidence was laid out and the jury reacted to know its impact.

Now it's been laid out. Now the jury has reacted. And I don't see anyone experiencing any pangs of sympathy for Jason Kolarich. Quite the opposite. They are seeing a desperately sad woman who, unbeknownst to her, is about to be murdered, and a cold, unfeeling man who broke her heart. And probably took her life, too.

63

Jason

The judge mulls over an afternoon break, but Roger Ogren says he is close to finishing, and the judge clearly wants this witness to wrap up early tonight.

'Proceed, Mr Ogren,' she says.

'Agent Jumer, let's talk about Tuesday, July thirtieth. The day of Ms. Himmel's murder.'

They do their thing, introducing another summary chart and displaying it on the screen for the jury, but this one isn't much of a chart.

CALL DETAIL RECORDS FOR CELL PHONE OF ALEXA M. HIMMEL
Tuesday, July 30

Time	Destination	Length of Call (minutes)	Originating Cell Site
6:14 PM	555-0150	1	221529
8:16 PM	Kolarich Home	2	221529

'There are two phone calls on here, is that correct, Agent?'

'Yes, sir.'

'For the moment, I'd ask you to focus only on calls made to the defendant.'

'Very good. Ms. Himmel only called Mr Kolarich once that day,' says Agent Jumer. 'As you can see, the phone call came at 8:16 P.M. to

Mr Kolarich's home phone, his landline. And the same cell tower, covering Ms. Himmel's house, provided service to that call.'

'This is the first time, on any of these summary charts you've shown us, that the length of call is different,' says Ogren. 'Instead of one, it says two.'

'That's correct. As I said, Ms. Himmel's service provider counts the first second of a new minute as a full minute in its billing. So anything from sixty-one seconds to one hundred twenty seconds would go down as a two in this box.'

'So we know from this chart that the cell phone call could have lasted as long as two full minutes,' says Ogren. 'But in no event less than one minute.'

'That's right.'

Too long for a voice mail, in other words, or so Ogren will argue to the jury in summation. It's hard to fill an entire minute of space on a voice mail; it's unnatural to talk that long. Sure, it's conceivable that Alexa would have droned on for more than a minute into a recording device; that's what Shauna will say in closing argument. She was clearly distraught and obsessive, so it's not completely out of the realm of possibility that this call made at 8:16 P.M. went into my home landline's voice mail and she prattled on for over sixty seconds. But, Roger Ogren will counter, none of the other myriad calls Alexa made to me over the preceding days took that long – why, the charts prove it!

The punch line being: *Jason was home* at 8:16 on the night of Alexa's murder. The call didn't go into Jason's landline voice mail. Jason was home, and he answered the phone, and he talked to Alexa for anywhere from sixty to a hundred twenty seconds. He didn't come home after midnight and find Alexa dead, like he claimed. No, no, no. He received a call from Alexa at 8:16 P.M., talked her into coming over to his house – a notion the jury would easily believe, given how desperate she was for his attention at that point – and then killed her with a single gunshot from behind so she wouldn't wreck his career by going to the Board of Attorney Discipline and ratting him out over his oxycodone addiction.

Then he cleaned up the place, wiped his prints off the gun with a Clorox wipe, probably took a shower and changed clothes to get the gunpowder residue off himself. And then he called 911 and tried to pass off a bullshit story to the cops about how his relationship with Alexa was terrific, peachy-keen, and she must have used a house key – a house key nobody can find – to get in, and some guy named Jim, no last name, yeah, he must have killed her. Yeah, go look for a guy named Jim, there's only half a million people in this city with that name.

Shauna will cross the FBI agent now, but there's not much she can do. About the only point she can score is that nobody knows if I received Alexa's call to my house at 8:16 P.M. or if it went into voice mail; the call detail records just show the call was picked up, not whether it was picked up by a computer or a person. And then she'll try to convince the jury in closing argument that I wasn't home, that I didn't come home until hours later, roughly midnight, like I told Detective Cromartie.

That 8:16 P.M. phone call will go under my list of regrets, my list of wish-I-could-do-it-overs.

I wish I *hadn't* been home for that call. And I really wish I hadn't answered it.

FIVE MONTHS BEFORE TRIAL
July

64

Jason

Tuesday, July 16

Ten minutes to midnight. I'm in my living room, looking out the picture window, a bottle of water and the tin of Altoids beside me. Alexa – my girlfriend, my alibi – is asleep upstairs, but sleep isn't for me right now. I'm waiting for a call. I'm always waiting for a call.

Nine days. Nine days since we set the Linda trap, when I flirted with Joel's investigator, posing as a hostess at the Greek restaurant, hoping to gain the attention of the man previously known as James Drinker. Nine days and nothing yet. Joel Lightner's team has followed Linda, who is continuing her undercover work at the restaurant, dutifully playing the part, showing up at the restaurant every night as hostess, coming home every night to the single-family house where she lives alone. She is everything 'James' would want – young, pretty, and with a clear connection to me now. And yet Joel's team has not had a sniff of him, no suspicious people following her, no cars driving slowly, no casual observer tracking her movements – nothing. Sometimes the North Side Slasher has moved quickly, sometimes he's taken weeks to make his move. We don't know when he'll strike. Or if. Maybe this is all a waste of time; maybe he never even followed me to the Greek restaurant.

It's been eight days since the night I spent with Shauna, fifteen of the strangest minutes of a strange period for me. She's out of sight now, having started her trial the day after our interlude, and taking Bradley John with her, leaving our office empty. They probably come back to the firm at night, but I'm not there to see them. I'm not working late these days. I'm not working at all. And I wouldn't know what to say to Shauna if I saw her, anyway. The last two times we talked didn't go so well – one where she accused me of being addicted to pills, the other where we ripped each other's clothes off and then departed about as awkwardly as could be.

And I'm drifting forward, deprived of a decent night's sleep going on four months now, popping awake more and more frequently, needing those Altoids more and more frequently. I am drugged and edgy, like someone given a sedative but then jolted periodically with electroshock, trying to focus on the real identity of 'James Drinker,' searching for anything he did or said that would narrow the field of candidates, always coming back to the same problem: When I'm chewing up these Altoids, I'm not thinking straight. I'm either foggy from the pills or I'm craving them, neither of which lends itself to good focus.

Name a client, I've told myself over these last months. *Name a client who didn't get my best effort.* And I want to believe that there is no such client. Kerry Alexander got a lesser-included battery conviction, nine months in the pen, when he could have gotten a decade behind bars. I got a not-guilty on the domestic battery case for that woman whose name, I'm embarrassed to admit, I've already forgotten. Billy Braden waltzed out of court altogether after I walked him on a Fourth Amendment argument. *Name a client.* I can't. I can't point to a client and say, *If my head had been more in the game, he would've gotten this result instead of that one.*

But then it comes full circle: I can only remember my conversations with the man who called himself James Drinker as well as I could see through fog: whispers of comments, stray words and phrases, but not the entirety of the conversations, or even full chunks of it. And here's what gets me: I didn't realize it at the time; I thought I was doing perfectly fine. So if I'm looking through a cloudy lens, who am I to judge how well I've handled *any* case?

That's why I've begun reassigning cases, referring all my cases out to other lawyers in the private sector, part of the cadre of defense lawyers who kick things to one another. I've become a lawyer with no clients. For now. For now, I say to myself. Until I clear things up. Until I get this thing with 'James Drinker' resolved, at which point I'll start cutting back on those happy pills and figure something out. No use trying to take on too much all at once, right? Right. Right, right, right.

My knees bounce up as my cell phone rings. Joel Lightner. I say a quiet prayer.

'Yeah, Joel?'

'I think we spotted him tonight,' he says, breathless. 'We were perched at Linda's house and we think we saw him across the street, between two houses. We saw somebody, at least. I tried with the camera, but I didn't get anything of value. Pretty much missed him. We tried to double back and catch him, Jason, or follow him, like we said—'

Right. Our best result was to spot him and tail him, follow him back to his home, get his address, then take our time with what we wanted to do. That was Plan A. Plan B, however, was just to snatch him.

'– but there's only so many of us. By the time we got there, he'd vanished.'

'Do you think he spotted you?' I ask, my pulse slowing, post-adrenaline. I was hoping for an A-plus. This isn't nothing, but it's more like a C.

'I don't . . . I don't know. By the time we doubled back over there, he was gone. Did he see us coming? God, man, we're pretty good at what we do. I really wouldn't think he'd see us. But all I can really say is, I don't know, and I sure as shit hope not. Fuck. Fuck, fuck, fuck.'

'Well, our plan worked, at least to a point,' I say. 'He must have followed me to the Greek restaurant. But if he knows we're on to him, then we're toast.'

'But if he didn't spot us,' says Joel, 'that means he's about to make a move. And we'll be ready for him.'

65

Shauna

I lean back in my chair and put my head against the wall, daring to close my eyes, knowing that I have hours of work ahead of me. The plaintiffs, the city, rested their case today and we start our defense tomorrow. The heart-pounding intensity that accompanies the birth of a trial has subsided. Now it's a war of attrition. Each side is soldiering on, trying to keep their wits about them, afraid that any particular moment on any particular day could be *the moment* that seizes the jury's attention, and wanting to make sure that when that happens, it's favorable to their side. Bradley and I are like each other's coaches, always propping each other up, giving pep talks, positive energy.

I'm alone. I sent Bradley home an hour ago. And Jason is obviously nowhere to be found. We haven't so much as laid eyes on each other since . . . since . . . that moment.

I call Joel Lightner, whom I gave an assignment over a week ago now, after that friendly encounter I had with Alexa in Jason's office, when she denied he was an addict, when she actually tried to claim that he still has pain in his knee, and when she accused me of feigning concern for Jason when, in fact, I was just trying to steal him back from her.

'Joel, what the hell, guy?' I say into his voice mail. 'Remember me? You were going to do that thing for me.'

I punch out the phone and do what I've done for the past week: Push Jason out of my mind and focus on the family business that is depending on me.

A moment later, my phone buzzes with a text message from Joel:

Sorry sorry busy with Jason tracking bad guy stretched thin tomorrow I promise

I sigh. Jason really got himself in a jam with that weird redheaded guy who might be a serial killer. What, exactly, Joel is doing to help Jason, I don't know.

And knowing those two cowboys, it's probably better I don't ask.

66

Jason

Wednesday, July 17

'You're sure about this,' Alexa says to me over the phone.

'I'm sure. I'll be with Joel, and as soon as I get home, I'll turn on some pay-per-view movie or something or I'll make a call from my landline. I'll be covered.'

This is the first time since we realized 'James' was framing me that Alexa and I have spent a night apart. She's been my alibi, kept me invulnerable from a frame-up. It's had the added effect, of course, of keeping young women in this city safe from a serial killer.

Tonight, Joel and I have decided, is the night to take a chance on 'James Drinker,' to give him an opportunity to attack Linda with us watching closely. So tonight, I'm going to stay home alone.

Or at least pretend to.

'Well, have fun, sailor,' she says to me. I haven't told her what I'm doing. There's no point in worrying her.

I head downstairs and make a big point of plopping down in a chair and watching a ball game on television. I never played baseball as a kid. Me and my friends, punks, idiots all of us, made fun of people who played baseball.

The game ends at nine-thirty. I stay in my chair until ten, then get up, stretch, and walk upstairs. I turn on the bathroom light and brush my teeth; then I turn off the light, turn off the light beside my bed, and crawl under the covers.

A half hour later, I slip out and crawl, in the darkness, to the staircase. I take dark stairs to the bottom level and sneak out the back door of my house. There is a small area there for barbecuing and not much more, then a high gate. I unlatch the gate and sneak into the alley, where a car is waiting for me. It's Joel Lightner.

I duck into the backseat and stay down. Joel navigates the interior alley system, making a couple of turns until we come out two blocks away from my house.

Unless this guy is magical, he didn't see me leave my house.

'Time to party,' Joel says, gunning the engine as we drive toward Linda's house.

67

Jason

Wednesday, July 17

Linda Sparks lives in a single-family bungalow on the northwest side that she inherited from her parents. It's the third house from the corner, on a quarter-acre lot that backs into an alley. She has a six-foot plywood fence around the back and sides of her property, making access from the rear difficult but not impossible. The front of her house, a small lawn and walk-up, has no restrictions on access. Her driveway leads into a two-car garage.

Across the street is pretty much the same story, bungalows backing into alleys, most with fences up in the back of varying degrees of difficulty. This is where Joel saw 'James' last night, on the side of the house across the street from Linda's place. He must have entered through the alley, jumped the fence, and walked along the side of the house. He would have to jump another fence to get to the front, but last night he wasn't interested in doing that, apparently. He just wanted to scope out the house.

Next door to the south, the house closest to Linda's garage door, the neighbors have extensive shrubbery circling around their front porch. A good place to hide for an ambush. The papers, and Joel's source at Area Three, have said that they believe the North Side Slasher likes to ambush women as they enter their houses. One of the women was jumped getting out of her car, presumably because the entryway to her home was too exposed, but the idea is the same. He likes to get them when their guards are down, where they feel safe, having arrived home. Too bad more people don't realize that this is when they're most vulnerable.

'If it were me, I'd sit in those bushes to the south, by her garage,' I say into my headphone. 'When she pulls into the garage, I rush inside before the door comes down.'

'Why don't you just announce your position, shoot a flare up or something,' Lightner whispers through my earbud, his tactful way of telling me to put a lid on it.

There are five of us covering Linda, which basically constitutes the entirety of Joel Lightner's operation. One guy is in the car with her, sitting low in the backseat; one is in her garage right now; one is in her house right now; Joel is watching the alley behind her house; and then there's me, across the street from Linda's house, lying flat behind a row of bushes that aren't very high but will do the trick as long as I stay horizontal.

'I'm five minutes away.' Linda's voice in my earbud. *'Any sign?'*

'No sign,' says one of the guys, probably the one inside the house, where it's safest to speak.

'You want me to keep coming?'

'Keep coming,' Joel whispers, his voice steely. We're all feeling that way, the butterflies, our senses heightened now. We all figured that 'James' would arrive early for the ambush, not being certain down to the minute of Linda's arrival. Linda's actually a little later than usual, by design, wanting to give 'James' all the time he needs.

The air is thick and moist. The street is quiet, calm, only a handful of cars passing, a residential street filled with blue-collar workers, midweek. Up the street, a gaggle of children, probably middle-school age, are shooting a basketball against a backboard over the garage door, but already parents are calling their children inside. The street lighting is minimal, casting only a very pale yellow interrupting the darkness that hovers like a fog over the house. Linda's house, in particular, lacks any lighting. The light over her garage and the

277

front-porch light are both off, again by design, making the target more inviting.

My skin is starting its familiar itch, my stomach swimming. I'm overdue on my happy pills, but I need to keep my wits about me. *I can feel it,* I'd say if I were in a movie. But that sums it up. If it's going to happen, it's going to be tonight. And if it's going to be tonight, it's going to be now.

'Two blocks away,' Linda says into my ear. *'Anybody see anything?'*

Nobody answers. I wiggle my toes, clench and release my calves, my thighs.

'Do you pull into the left side or the right side of the garage?' asks one of the guys, presumably the one in the garage.

'Left side,' she says.

'Well, pull into the right tonight. I'm in the left corner.'

'Roger that. Don't accidentally shoot me, Halston. I'm removing my headset.'

Linda's Grand Cherokee pulls up to her house, turns, and bounces onto the driveway as the garage door opens. Our guy Halston, in the left corner, is exposed, but only because I know to look for him. If someone's about to charge into the garage, Halston will see him before he sees Halston.

Linda gets out of the car as if nothing is unusual, doesn't rush but doesn't dawdle, either, fishing for something in her purse. My eyes dart left-right, left-right, looking for any movement, any signs of something wrong. Linda walks the long way around the car, toward the driveway, exposing herself as much as she possibly can, walking slowly but not breaking stride, not being obvious about it.

Left-right, left-right, something, anything.

And then she curls around the car and walks up to the interior door and disappears inside.

The garage door grinds back down. Only then, I assume, will the guy hiding in the back of her SUV get out, and the guy in the corner of the garage move.

'And here I was hoping this would be my last night sleeping on Linda's couch,' one of them says – the guy inside the house.

'*Stay in role,*' Lightner whispers harshly. He's right. This may not be over. If he's watching, he can't see a bunch of silhouettes in the house along with Linda.

Everything goes quiet again.

My mind races. Have we missed something? Didn't we think of everything? Has he outsmarted me again? I find myself ascribing superhero traits to our killer: *He's on the roof, rappelling down into her bedroom. He's hiding in the dirt and will pop out of the soil like Rambo. He managed to evade Linda's alarm and is hiding inside, beneath her bed.*

Five minutes. Ten minutes.

We were wrong, I think to myself. *He's not here.*

Then a red beater Toyota turns down the street, the car slowing, and pulls to a stop across from Linda's house. Kills the headlights. Kills the engine.

A boxy sign atop the car. Can't make out the name, but it's a pizza place.

The car's rear hatch pops open. The driver emerges, wearing a baseball cap. I can't make him out from my position. Decent-sized man, dark hair I think, best I can do.

'Heads up, heads up,' I whisper, later than I should have. 'Car stopped by me.'

'*This our guy?*' someone asks, breathless.

'I don't know,' I whisper. 'Did anyone order a pizza?'

The man pulls something out of the hatch. A pizza, it's gotta be, carried in one of those thick warming covers.

'*After we shoot this fucker, can we keep the pizza?*'

The man crosses the street, quick-stepping it toward Linda's driveway. His back to me, I rise and try for a better view. He looks big enough, I guess. I can't tell. It's dark, and I don't have his face.

'*Joel, I'm coming around the south side.*' Sounds like Halston's voice.

'*I've got the north, then,*' Joel says. '*Nobody answers the door.*'

The man waltzes up the driveway and turns for Linda's walk. He steps up on the porch and rings the doorbell. Halston, his gun drawn, shuffles along the south side of the house, approaching the front. The gate on the north side opens, Lightner with his gun facing upward.

'Count of three,' Joel says. 'One . . . two . . . THREE!'

At once, the front-porch light goes on and both Joel and Halston are within a few yards of the front door, guns poised on the man as they shout at him and into my ear, their words – 'Show me your hands!' 'Get the fuck down!' – echoing through my head in stereo.

The man, instantly shaken, drops the pizza and has a moment of What the fuck? before he drops to his knees, palms outward, head swiveling between the two armed men.

No, I instantly recognize.

My head shoots left-right, left-right, and then I stand, and then it happens, in my peripheral vision, movement to my right, we have startled each other simultaneously, just a quick flash of movement several houses down to my right, buried in the shadows.

A man turning and running?

I bolt from my position around the house and race to the fence leading to the backyard. I jump and climb it with some effort and don't stop running until I hit the fence to the alley. I climb it and land hard in the alley, looking north.

The alley is motionless, quiet save for my heavy breaths.

Then a figure crosses my line of vision, from a house through the alley in a flash and then out of sight.

I run with everything I have. It was always what I did best, even more than my hands, that speed, fastest white guy I ever saw, my teammates at State said, and I forget my knee and I motor like I never have before.

'The alley . . . across the street,' I shout into my headphone, far too late for anyone to assist me, the sounds of the ruckus in front of Linda's house still playing in my earpiece, as these guys finally begin to realize that they've been baited every bit as much as we tried to bait 'James.'

I reach the fork in the alley system where he crossed, eastbound, and start running again. I didn't bring my gun. Why didn't I bring my gun? I splash through a puddle, turning my ankle in a pothole, and then I hear a car's ignition, somewhere forward and to my right. I run to the next alley, running north-south, and see the car speeding away down the alley, headlights showing the way. I run toward it, losing ground badly, hoping for a partial license plate or a make and model, a smaller car, something like an Accord or Camry—

It passes under an alley light, and I – I can't make out a plate, the color is something light, white or silver, yes, it's an Accord—

And then it bounces into a left turn, tires squealing, and it's gone.

'Where are you, Jason?' Lightner calls out.

'He's . . . gone,' I say, my hands on my knees, panting. 'He's gone.'

68

Jason

Wednesday, July 17

We sit around Linda's kitchen table for a while, frustrated and spent, having just witnessed over a week's worth of preparation and stress, danger, and risk end without anything to show for it. The pizza's not half bad, the two bites I took before my stomach said stop, pepperoni and garlic. Doesn't go so well with the bottle of Scotch that is passed around freely, but no one's complaining.

'Not even a partial?' Linda asks me. 'Not even a single letter or number?'

I shake my head. 'Didn't see the license plate at all.'

'He's smart,' says the guy named Halston, a big Irish redhead. 'He played us well.'

'Screw him being *smart*,' Joel says. 'We were *dumb*. He tricked us with a prank we used to pull when we were kids.'

Maybe so, but Joel's being too hard on himself. Everyone was so hyped up, and it was believable, a good ruse for a killer. Everyone answers the door for the pizza man, even if only to say, *Sorry, wrong house.*

'We should have played it out,' Joel says. 'Answered the door, seen what he did. We had Linda covered six ways to Sunday. We should have given him a chance to make his move.'

Linda takes the Scotch and pours a few fingers into a glass. 'We won't get another chance like this,' she says.

Silence. Each of us believes what Linda just said. This was our chance, right here.

'On the bright side,' says Halston, 'the pizza guy has a great story now.'

That gets a hard laugh, a release of nerves and tension. It feels good to laugh. I can't remember the last time I laughed.

'The guy shows up to deliver a pie and suddenly he's got guns in his face and he's on his knees, begging for his life.' Lightner can hardly contain himself. 'He must have been like, "What the fuck is happening?"' He buckles over in laughter.

'The poor guy wet his pants,' Linda gets out, wiping her eyes. 'All he gets out of this is soiled underwear and a fifty-dollar tip. Is that how much you tipped him?' she asks Joel.

'I didn't tip him,' he says. 'I told you to tip him.'

'I thought you said you tipped him.'

'No, I said, "Tip him."'

'So nobody tipped him?' I laugh. 'We just sent him on his way? Did we at least pay for the pizza?'

Another round of laughter. Everyone at the table needs it. We let it linger, savor it, because the alternative is a lot more grim. Eventually it dies down, and we're back to moody and bitter.

'A silver or white Accord,' Lightner says, shaking his head. 'We'll just run that through the DMV and we can narrow our list of suspects down to about two million people.'

'It's something,' I say.

'It's nothing. This guy's a ghost. He's nobody.'

I'm nobody.

I stir at the memory, just like that, like the snap of a finger, bursting from the fog of a conversation some six weeks ago. Something 'James' said to me when he came to my office. A moment of self-pity, something like, *I don't matter to people*, and then: *I'm nobody to them.* An odd thing to say, I recall thinking.

'I guess we go back to looking at old case files,' Joel says. 'Anybody you prosecuted.'

I'm nobody to them.

And then, yes, I remember, clarity for once, finally, dark clouds parting ever so slightly and allowing in the sun: what he said to me when he left. He approached me, shook my hand good-bye, and said something odd again.

I hope I'm not nobody to you, Jason.

The last words he ever said to me, face-to-face.

I pop out of my chair.

I hope I'm not nobody to you, Jason.

You're nobody to me.

'What?' Lightner asks me.

'We've been looking in the wrong place,' I say. 'He's not someone I prosecuted.'

'No? Then who is he?'

'He's someone I *interrogated*.'

'Interr – You mean while you were on Felony Review?'

'Exactly.' I start pacing. Every assistant county attorney does a stint on Felony Review, where you're assigned to a police station to approve warrant applications and arrests and, at least back when I was there, to interrogate suspects. It was a wild ride, those eleven months, working three days on, three days off, if you were lucky, working day and night with the detectives and patrolmen, hearing their stories, high-fiving them when there was a solve, making friendships, feeling like part of their team. 'It was a line I used during interviews to intimidate suspects. I pulled it out when I needed it. "You're nothing to me." "You're nobody to me." Y'know, breaking them down.'

'Right? But . . .'

I shake out of my funk. 'This guy, "James" or whatever, when he came to my office, he repeated that phrase back to me. He said, "I hope I'm not nobody to *you*." It's probably something I once said to *him*.' I blow out air. 'He's someone I interrogated.'

Lightner nods. 'And you wouldn't be an attorney of record for something like that, right?'

'Right,' I say. 'I didn't prosecute this guy. I never filed an appearance because I never stood in a courtroom opposite him. I just handled him at the police station and then dished him off to people more senior than me.' I pin my hair back off my forehead, a show of exasperation handed down from my mother. 'How did I not think of this before?'

'Because it wouldn't occur to you,' Joel says. 'Because it's like a revolving door on Felony Review, suspects coming in and out and then you wash your hands of it. You probably spent no more than an hour with most of these guys, give or take. One hour, out of a one- or two-*year* process for them. You forget about them and you assume they forget about you.'

He's being charitable, cutting me some slack. He's not wrong, either, but still this should have occurred to me sooner. These suspects really were blips on the screen to me, and I to them, but that doesn't mean that something didn't stick in one of their craws.

'You must have gotten a confession,' Linda says. 'If you stand out to this guy that much, it means you made him talk.'

I wag my finger at Linda. 'You're right. And then, it's not necessarily a one- or two-year process. If I got a confession that stuck, his lawyer would probably tell him to take a plea. A confession could close down that case right away.'

'And then he'd have one and only one prosecutor to thank for his time in prison,' says Joel. 'That prosecutor might stick out to him.'

'I'll bet you used deception,' Linda says. 'That always pisses them off, like they forget about all the shit they really, truly did and focus on how unfair it was that you tricked them into admitting it.'

She's right. That's exactly how it works. And I was the master. I'll bet I somehow twisted him up and got him to cop to something he hadn't planned on admitting. There's more than one way to do that, and I mastered them all.

'So we forget about Gang Crimes and felony courtrooms, even the misdemeanors, and we focus on Felony Review,' I say. 'That's the good news. Wanna hear the bad news?'

Lightner already knows the bad news, I think. He gives a solemn nod.

285

'I don't remember any of those interviews,' I say. 'I mean, bits and pieces, some memorable moments, but names? No names. That was, what, eight years ago? And we were seventy-two on, seventy-two off back then.'

'I remember that,' Joel says. 'The prosecutors looked like hell by the third day. We'd let them shower in our bathroom and sleep on a roll-down mattress in one of the interview rooms. I don't know why they had you stay on for seventy-two hours straight.'

'You were *lucky* if it was seventy-two,' I remind him. 'If we caught a case that was ongoing, we stayed on it. I was once on for six days straight on a kidnapping.'

Lightner sighs. 'The point being, it's all a blur to you.'

'Pretty much, yeah. And that's just the bad news. Here's the *worse* news,' I say. 'Records. You think it's hard to track down cases where I filed an appearance and prosecuted someone? Try finding Felony Review records. Forget computers. Back then? We'd be lucky if my name was scribbled at the top of a sworn statement, which would be clipped to a pressboard and thrown into some box. Who knows if those paper records even exist anymore? For closed cases? The appeals exhausted? I'm not sure they exist at all.'

That takes the air out of the room. Everyone looks fried. I'm sure I do, too.

'Still, it's a start,' Joel says. 'We started with the most logical step, remember? We looked at violent ex-cons who were released in the last year. We thought we struck out because you didn't prosecute any of them. But now we can look at them again, right? Maybe you got a confession from one of them.'

He's right. We have a fresh start. We're in the game, at least.

'This guy has definitely pissed me off,' Joel says. 'I'm not letting this go. I'm seeing it through.'

'Me, too,' says Linda.

The others join in, too.

'We're going to catch this prick,' Linda says. 'Nobody sends pizza to my house I didn't ask for.'

69

Shauna

Friday, July 19

Bradley is doing redirect on one of the architects, talking about exciting things like soil samples, and my mind wanders. The jurors' minds are wandering, too. This is the ninth day of a trial about technicalities and specifications, and it's been a long week for them. Judge Getty has made noise about getting us out early today to get a start on the weekend, and the reaction was positively celebratory.

I've instructed Bradley that every witness on our side, other than our clients, can be no more than thirty minutes on direct examination. I don't want the jury to blame us for wasting their time, for being the stereotypical blowhard lawyers. Our evidence is concise, to the point, like our case.

Still, I am B-O-R-E-D and, knowing that this is the final witness of the day and I'm basically done, my mental machinery grinds to a halt. And my thoughts drift, as they have so often during this trial, to my law partner.

Under the table, I activate my cell phone, keeping the volume on silent. If Judge Getty saw me, he would string me up. I send a text message to Joel: WTF?

'WTF' stands for *Pardon me, but I'm slightly miffed and require an explanation.*

And I'm more than slightly miffed. Joel's late on his assignment for me. He promised me yesterday and didn't deliver. He comes back with a response right away: JUST FINISHED. YOU HAVE SOME FREE TIME? THIS REQUIRES FACE-TO-FACE.

'Hmph,' I mumble. That doesn't sound good. I text him back that I expect to be back at my office by four, and I'll make myself available anytime afterward. I consider asking for a hint, a little preview, but Joel, however boorish he may be, knows one thing, and that's when to be discreet. He's decided that this is one of those times.

Which is why I'm starting to worry.

70

Jason

I put the finishing touches on an appeal I'm writing for a guy named Taylor Prince, who was caught up in a large seizure of heroin by a joint county-federal task force sixteen months ago. It was a big headline for law enforcement, the arrest of over twenty people on the city's southwest side. Taylor wasn't one of the ringleaders – this guy would have trouble leading his own shadow – but he was part of the muscle in the operation.

Last December, Taylor was convicted and got fifteen years, stiffer than some of his cohorts who took a plea and got single digits. Taylor opted for a trial, but it was against my advice, because no matter how much judges will deny it, they still fiercely impose the 'trial tax' on those defendants who make them put twelve people in a box and clog up two or three days' worth of court time. So the guys actually selling the dope got between seven and nine years; Taylor, who was little more than a security guard, a guy with a gun standing outside on watch, was guilty of the selling, too – thank you, laws of accountability – but then additionally had a gun charge tacked on. So now I'm asking the appellate court to do something they'll never do – second-guess the trial judge on a sentence for convictions involving drugs *and* weapons.

Taylor is no genius and shouldn't bother applying for sainthood, but he isn't the worst guy who ever lived, either. He had an assault and battery conviction from three years ago, so he couldn't get a decent job, and someone came along and said, *Stand here all day with a gun and make sure nobody comes in, and we'll pay you fifty bucks a day*, and he took it. He took it because it seemed easy. He took it because fifty bucks a day was $350 a week, almost $18,000 a year, and because it put a roof over his wife and daughter's heads and food on their table.

Though ten years my junior, Taylor grew up three blocks from where I lived in Leland Park, went to all the same schools, and started down the same route I was traveling. But Taylor didn't have football to snatch him out of the quicksand like I did. I could have been that kid.

Sometimes I wonder if I'm still on my way to being that kid, if the last fifteen years of my life have just been an anomaly, an accident, I've been playing someone I'm not, and sooner than later I'll surrender to the gravitational pull down to what I really am at heart, the son of a grifter and alcoholic, a directionless loser.

A knock at my door. Joel Lightner walks in.

'Hey.'

Then Shauna walks in.

'Hey.'

This doesn't feel like a good thing. I smell a lecture. That's if I'm lucky. If I'm not, it's an intervention. *We love you, Jason. We're here for you. We want to be part of the solution, not part of the problem.*

Shauna closes the door, and I'm thinking, *Intervention, not lecture*.

'We're going to talk,' says Shauna, 'and you're going to sit there and listen. When we're done, you can tell us to go fuck off if that makes you happy. But you *are* going to listen.'

I swivel away from the computer and face them both. I don't say anything, don't accept her guidelines or reject them. Joel is fading back a bit, but is clearly with her on this.

'You know I've been concerned about you, and you know I think you have a painkiller addiction. We've sort of put that conversation on hold because I've been on trial. I don't feel very good about that – in fact, if you want to know the truth, it tears me up inside – but it is what it is. But I think part of the problem is your girlfriend, Alexa. I think she's enabling you. I think she's scary, since I'm being honest. And that's why I asked Joel to do me a personal favor and perform a background check on her.'

'You . . .' I look at her, then at Joel, with whom I recently spent a rather eventful evening, and yet I don't recall this subject coming up.

'Jason,' he says, unapologetic, 'last August, just eleven months ago, Alexa Himmel was the subject of an order of protection in Medina County in Ohio. A husband and wife,' he says, peeking at a piece of paper he's holding, 'Brian and Betsy Stermer sought an OP against her and got it. They said she was stalking Brian and demanding a sexual relationship from Brian and was physically threatening them and their children.'

'Sorry,' I say, 'I'm still at the part where the two of you are doing criminal backgrounds on my girlfriend behind my back.'

'Last October, she violated the OP,' he goes on, undaunted. 'She showed up on his front doorstep one day and she had a knife. She was arrested and convicted of contempt of court and, as far as I can tell, was damn lucky she didn't get charged with something a lot worse.'

'If it was as bad as you're saying,' I reply, 'she *would* have been convicted of something a lot worse.'

'In December, the Stermers went back to court to modify the restraining order, because it kept her one hundred feet from them, and they said she was standing just outside the hundred-foot boundary, on a public sidewalk down the street from their house, for hours at a time. She would wave to them. She had binoculars. Sometimes she would hold up signs. They said it was causing the entire family extreme emotional distress.'

'Sounds like legalese,' I say. 'Let me guess. They had a lot of money and fancy lawyers.'

'She was arrested again last February,' Joel says. 'She showed up at Dr Stermer's radiology office. She burst into his office and exposed herself to him. She was charged with criminal trespass, criminal contempt, stalking, and public indecency.'

I turn my head away, toward the window.

'She entered into a plea bargain. The Stermers agreed to drop the charges if she would leave the state. And she agreed. She left the state. And she moved here.'

'And met you,' says Shauna.

I stand up. 'Guys, it was really great of you to stop by. Thanks for the information, and I'll take it from here.'

'Jason,' says Shauna, 'if you'd lower your defenses for one minute, you'd see that this is serious. I take it you didn't know any of this? I mean, what do you even know about her?'

'What kind of a question is that?'

'C'mon, Jase.' Lightner drops his head a notch. 'You know it's a real question.'

'She was looking for you,' Shauna says. 'Not you, specifically, but someone like you. When did you meet? May? June? By then, you'd started dropping weight and not sleeping and looking like . . . like you look now. Like a drug addict in a nice suit. You were just what she was looking for, Jason, don't you see that? Someone who was struggling. The next person she could latch on to. But this time, someone who *needed* her. Someone who wouldn't reject her.'

'You know what?' I throw up my arms. 'I *wasn't* struggling, I'm *not* struggling, I don't "need" *anybody*, and by the way, fuck you, Shauna.'

'And you're protecting her because she makes you feel nice and warm and fuzzy all over about your drug addiction,' Shauna says, gaining steam now. 'She's manipulating the shit out of you, and you don't even know it. Or worse yet, you do, but you don't care.'

'Dr Freud over here.' I gesture toward her. 'A lawyer *and* a shrink.'

Shauna keeps her stare on me. I know that stare. I've seen that stare a thousand times. She knows she's right, regardless of whether she is or not.

'Listen, you don't know her like I do,' I say. 'If she's a little intense when it comes to me, it's probably because she doesn't have any family anymore. Her parents are deceased, and she doesn't have siblings. So yeah, she finds someone she cares about, she gets intense about it.'

Joel and Shauna look at each other.

'What are you talking about?' Joel says.

'She's an only child, and her parents passed away.'

'Oh, Jason,' Shauna says.

Joel pinches the bridge of his nose. 'She's not an only child, Jason. She has a brother. And he lives here in town.'

71

Jason

Sunday, July 21

It's near eleven in the morning. My eyes are heavy, my vision hazy; I fought the typical demon battles during the night, blood and fangs and cries of terror. Given the weekend, I kept up the broken-sleep pattern into the late morning, with a few doses of those yummy Altoids thrown in to lubricate the machinery.

I hate that I'm sleeping when there's so much to do, but the truth is that there's so *little* I can do. If running around the city would help me catch our killer, I'd do it. If standing on my head would do it, I'd be flipping upside down right now. I've racked my brain repeatedly to come up with names of suspects with whom I sat in a room and secured a confession, but if those names are out there somewhere in the netherworld of my brain, I haven't found them, and pushing myself toward them seems to have the effect of pushing them away, like reaching into the back of a cabinet and contacting the thing you want just enough to move it completely out of your reach. It's the worst kind of frustrating, this directionless angst.

I know I'm not well, and that a lot of what Shauna said is true. I know it the most when I'm in bed, either drifting to sleep or first awakening, when my guard is down, my justifications and rationalizations not fully engaged. Of *course* I'm not doing well. Of *course* I have to change things. But now's not the time. I can't spend time on pulling myself away from these pills while I'm trying to catch 'James Drinker.'

Now's not the time has become very good friends lately with *I don't have a problem*. They trade off hours, one of them always on call inside my brain.

Alexa's just getting out of the shower, wrapped in a bathrobe that is way too big for her, wiping a circle in the mirror out of the steam and brushing her hair. 'Are you okay?' she calls back.

'I'm fine,' I say. *I'm fine. I'm all good. I don't have a problem. And even if I did, now's not the time to deal with it.*

I've avoided a complicated conversation with Alexa. Haven't found the right time yet to ask her about the things Joel and Shauna disclosed to me. I've never been one for confrontation, which I fully realize is ironic given that the two things I've done best in my life – playing wide receiver on the gridiron and playing a lawyer in a courtroom – both involve conflict. But that's when you flip on a switch, when you're doing a job, when the people with whom you're butting heads aren't your friends and would just as surely knock you on your ass as you're trying to knock them on theirs.

But with one-to-one personal stuff, I've never enjoyed getting into people's faces. Probably something I got from Mom, who made it her duty to prevent 'Dad volcanoes,' as Pete and I used to call them when we were kids, who made conflict avoidance an art form. *A turned cheek will do you wonders, boy,* she used to always say.

'You sure?' She comes out of the bathroom, her hair combed back wet.

My cell phone buzzes. It's over on the dresser. Alexa takes a peek. 'It's Shauna,' she says. 'Wow, that's been a while.'

She looks at me for a reaction, but I don't give her one.

'Do you want to answer it?'

'No, I'll call her later.'

'Is she calling for any particular reason? I thought she was still on trial.'

'I have no idea why she's calling,' I say, which isn't really true.

'Shauna doesn't approve of me,' she says.

I don't answer. I'm probably supposed to say something.

'Has she told you that? Or said anything about me?'

'I think she's concerned about me,' I say.

'And she doesn't think I'm good for you,' Alexa finishes. 'I know. She told me that.'

'She did?'

'Yes. When I went to pick up a few things at your office, when you were going to leave the firm. She yelled at me. She said you and I shouldn't see each other. It was . . . unpleasant. If I may say so, I don't think Shauna's a very pleasant person.'

'Shauna's wonderful,' I say. 'Shauna saved me after my wife and daughter died.'

'Oh.' One word, but more than one syllable the way she says it, a bell curve of octaves, like she just discovered something meaningful. 'I think she likes being the only woman in your life.'

'That's not true.'

I'm adjusting my position in bed as I say this, not looking directly at her, but the ensuing silence brings my eyes to hers, and hers do not look amused. She looks, more than anything, like she wants to slap me.

'I'm sure you're right,' she says with mock sweetness.

She turns and walks back toward the bathroom.

'Alexa,' I say. 'You told me you're an only child.'

She stops in her tracks, her back to me. She turns around slowly, as if she's afraid of what she'll find behind her. 'What?'

'Is it true that you're an only child? Or do you have a brother, Aaron, in Glenwood Heights?'

She turns to face me again, her eyes narrowed, a look of discomfort. 'Why . . . would you ask me something like that?'

'You first,' I say.

'Me first . . . me first . . .' Her eyebrows rise. She lets out air. She crosses her arms. 'Aaron is my brother, yes. We aren't close. We never have been. He's not . . . he's not nice to me. He's not a good person. But technically, yes, I have a brother.'

296

'Technically.' I laugh. 'Why tell me this whole thing about how your mother had you when she was forty and didn't want any more kids?'

'Your turn,' she says, color coming to her face. 'How do you know about Aaron? Are you . . . Did you check *up* on me?' She's good at this. Regaining the moral outrage, or trying hard to.

'My friends did, yes,' I say.

'Shauna, you mean.'

'Shauna and others. They're concerned, that's all.'

'So they did, what, a background investigation on me?' Try as she might to resist, Alexa is losing composure, placing a hand on the dresser for stability as the earth moves beneath her, as the footing of this relationship shifts sideways without warning.

'Yes, they did. I didn't know about it. I was mad when they told me, actually.'

'Really? How mad? Did you stand up for me?'

'I did, in fact.'

'Well, go on.' She whips her arm about. 'Go on. Get it over with. They told you about Brian.'

'Brian Stermer,' I say. 'Yes.'

Alexa gives a bitter shake of the head, her eyes brimming with tears, red and swollen. 'Oh, God. I can't believe this.'

'They told me—'

'*I* told you!' she cries, slapping her chest. '*I* told you I'd been in a relationship that ended badly when I found out he was married. Did I leave out some details? Yes. Did I leave out the part where his wife found out about *me* at around the same time *I* found out about *her*? Did I leave out the part where Brian turned out to be a complete coward, who wouldn't admit to his wife that he was fucking somebody on the side, and so he had to turn me into a *stalker*? Did I leave out the part where his wife basically bullied him into telling lies about me to a judge, as if that would somehow make Brian's lies true? Or the part where *Doctor* Brian Stermer has more money than God and hired, like, ten lawyers to go after me, and I couldn't afford a single one?'

She is trembling now, her entire body, her face contorted, her voice getting deeper with emotion as she goes on.

I get out of bed. 'Listen—'

'Did I leave out the part where I didn't put up a fight when he wanted his stupid restraining order, because I was planning on staying away from him, anyway? So I just let the judge order whatever he ordered? I did, Jason. I left out those parts. This man screwed me over like nobody ever could, then when he got caught in his bullshit string of lies, he screwed me over even worse to cover up his new lies.'

I approach her, but she gives me a warning look: *Do not enter.*

She wipes at her cheeks with the fluffy arms of the robe and takes a gasping breath. 'Well, let's keep going, Jason. Let's get it over with. Why stop the laughs now?'

'I'm not laughing.'

More tears fall, little rivers angling along her cheeks. 'He said I showed up at his house with a knife, but I didn't. I can't *prove* I didn't. Apparently the judge felt like I was supposed to prove my innocence. I don't know how to prove a negative.'

I nod, but I'm not sure why.

'Let's see, what else? Oh, when they wanted to make the restraining order for a wider distance, because I was supposedly hanging out down the street, just beyond a hundred feet? Yeah, like anyone's just going to loiter around on a sidewalk for hours in the dead of December in northern Ohio. Do you have any idea how cold it was last December in Ohio? Yeah, but I'm standing out there for hours on end, holding up signs saying "Please take me back, Brian!" or whatever he said they said. I mean, really? Really, Jason?'

'Hey—'

'But you know what? I didn't fight that, either. I didn't fight him because I couldn't afford anyone to represent me and because I didn't care, anyway. I didn't care if the restraining order was a hundred feet or a hundred yards or a mile. I had no intention of going anywhere near him after what he did to me.'

'Okay,' I say. *'Okay.'*

'And now I finally meet a nice guy and he hears all this and he thinks . . . whatever you think . . .'

'I believe you,' I say. 'I do.'

She looks at me for a long time, her expression easing, her breathing slowing, the tears drying up. She takes a deep breath, runs her fingers through her wet hair.

'I believe you,' I say again.

72

Jason

Monday, July 22

'Hey.' Joel Lightner sticks his head in my office, cautious.

I wave him in. 'It's okay, Lightner. You're still doing a job for me, whatever else.'

'You're pissed at me,' he says when he walks in and helps himself to a seat.

'You're not at the top of my list right now,' I agree.

'I'd like to see that list. I'm pretty sure there's only one name on it: Alexa Himmel.'

I put down the court opinion I was reading. 'I take it you didn't come to apologize.'

'Apologize? Why would I apologize? For the background check? Shauna asked me for a favor, and she was doing it out of genuine concern for you. And she's right to be concerned.'

I raise my hands in surrender. 'Let's stick with business,' I say.

He holds his stare a moment, just to show his displeasure, before moving on. 'We're having a hard time digging up records, like you thought,' he says. 'We've found some in a warehouse. So far, no recently released ex-cons – by *recently*, I mean in the last eighteen months – were interrogated by you. We aren't done, but we're starting to run out of places to check. There are big gaps. You got moved around all the time when you were on Felony Review. It's not like you even stuck at one station house.'

None of this is a surprise, but it's a big blow nonetheless. We're running out of places to check. We're running out of ways to catch 'James.'

'Joel, this signature, the thing he does to all the victims. I need to know what it is.'

'We've already talked about this,' he says. 'They won't tell me. I won't ask.'

'It's the key to this, the more I think about it. Whatever it is he's doing to them, he'd probably want to tie it to me, right? If he's framing me, he'd want to make that signature tailored to me.'

'Yeah, you're probably right,' Joel agrees. 'If he's doing some strange, crazy thing to all the victims, he's probably doing it because it implicates you. But what?'

'I don't know,' I say. 'That's why you have to get it for me.'

Joel raises his hands. 'I can't help you. Even if I wanted to, they wouldn't tell me.'

There's got to be some way. I have to figure out that calling card he's leaving at every crime scene.

'Okay.' Joel starts to look uncomfortable, rubbing his hands, stalling. 'So . . . so listen.'

I look up at him.

'I'm just going to say this as your friend. I'm not sure about that lady, Jason. I got a bad feeling about her.'

'You don't know her.' I wave a hand. 'Leave it alone.'

'Jason—'

'She has a very sweet side, Joel. She does. Does she come on strong? Okay, maybe. But she'd do anything for me.'

'Yeah? That so?'

'Yeah.' I nod at him. 'The alibi, for example. She's willing to say I was with her at the time of each of the five murders. She's willing to be my alibi. Now, how many people would do that?'

Lightner doesn't seem as impressed as I am. 'I remember in my office, you guys said you were going to square up dates to confirm.'

'Yeah, we confirmed dates, and you know what? She wasn't with me on *any* of those nights. Not one, Joel. And yet she's willing to say she was. If the police walked in right now, she'd swear on a Bible that we spent those evenings together at my house.'

Joel thinks about that for a long time, seemingly unmoved, but thinking. 'That's a dangerous game, first of all. It could get you both in trouble.'

'I know. I told her that. I told her there were all kinds of ways you can attack an alibi. But she said she was home alone, just like me, on each of those nights, but she didn't do anything that would establish that. Didn't make any phone calls. Didn't order food to the house or order a movie off of TV or have any visitors over or anything that would tie her to her house.'

I don't even know how to order a movie off the television, she said.

And I never, ever have food delivered.

'It's still a bad idea,' Lightner says again.

'I know, Joel. I'm not going to let her do it. But the point is that she's *willing* to do it. Does that sound like someone who cares about me, or someone who doesn't?'

Joel makes a face. 'That's one way of looking at it,' he says.

'Is there another way?'

Joel lets out a bitter laugh and shakes his head again. 'Of course there's another way,' he says. 'And if you didn't have your head so far up your ass, you'd see it, too, Counselor.'

I wave a hand. 'Then enlighten me,' I say.

He leans forward and cups his hand over his mouth, like he's shouting across a canyon. 'She's not just giving *you* an alibi,' he says. 'She's giving *herself* one, too.'

PEOPLE VS. JASON KOLARICH
TRIAL, DAY 4
Thursday, December 12

73

Shauna

Judy Bialek hurries into her reception area, two work bags slung over her shoulder, looking just a bit disheveled as she nods to her receptionist and waves to the lawyers waiting for her. 'Sorry I'm late, everybody, crazy morning,' she sings as she brushes past us into her chambers. She is a divorced mother of three kids, all in high school. It is somehow comforting, in the midst of the angst and stress of this trial, to see the judge coping with some stress of her own.

Not that a judge is ever late. The meeting starts when the judge says it starts. Judges make you wait all the time – I remember once Judge DeCremer, in the civil division, scheduled no less than four pretrial conferences for the same time and made us all wait for him. I showed up with my client at one o'clock and left at a quarter to five.

The receptionist's phone buzzes. 'You can go on in,' he says to us.

Inside her chambers, the judge looks a bit more composed, sitting behind her long black desk, everything neatly in its place, her hair pulled up in back now, her black robe hanging to the side on a coatrack.

'I want to talk schedule,' she says. 'The government only has one more witness, is that correct, Mr Ogren?'

'That's correct, Judge. Her direct testimony won't take half an hour.'

'Okay. And then the government will rest?'

'Yes, we will.'

The judge nods. 'Ms. Tasker, I suppose the defense will move for a directed verdict.'

'Absolutely, Judge,' I say, but nobody in this room thinks the judge is going to toss the case for lack of evidence. This case is going to the jury.

'Assuming that your motion is denied, Ms. Tasker, can you give me an idea of whom you plan to call, and why, and how much time you need? Oh, and I forgot – you reserved your opening statement. How much time do you expect to use on your opening, too?'

I haven't told them anything yet. The defense is entitled to considerable leeway in withholding its game plan in a criminal case. Jason, of course, has the right to testify and the right not to testify, and that gives me the right to leave everyone guessing. Beyond whether Jason testifies, I haven't given a hint as to whom I may call in our defense, if anyone.

Don't tell them, no matter how hard the judge pushes, Jason advised me. *She'll push you, but she can't make you tell her. These aren't the civil courts you're used to. Don't let them know until it's time.*

I've followed that advice, to the chagrin of the judge, until now. Now it's time.

'Judge, we've decided to waive our opening statement.'

The judge is surprised. So is Ogren. His eyes have narrowed and he's blinking rapidly, thinking it through. First, we asked for the right to reserve our opening statement until the defense's case. Now we are forgoing it altogether. Why? He's probably narrowing the reasons down to two. One possibility is that our case is so incoherent that I don't have a story to tell. We'll drop a few bombs and try to muddy the picture, but we don't have a logical theory of what really happened, start to finish, so we won't bother trying to craft a narrative.

The other possibility is surprise. We've been holding back our argument and we're continuing to do so, because we want to spring it on the prosecution as late as possible.

I'm sure Ogren prefers the former theory to the latter.

'Very well,' says the judge. 'Do you plan on calling any witnesses?'

'We reserve the right to call everyone on our list for the moment,' I say. 'But we're going to start, today, with my client.'

Roger Ogren and Katie O'Connor each stir just a bit, casting glances at each other, Ogren taking a deep breath. They never knew for sure. They didn't know if, they didn't know when Jason would testify.

'I see.' The judge falls back in her chair. 'Would it be fair to assume that Mr Kolarich's testimony will take up the rest of this week, today and tomorrow?'

'I would assume so. At that point, Friday evening, I should have a good idea whether we're going to call anyone else.'

'Judge,' says Ogren, 'Ms. Tasker has named, as you said, the entire roster of Area Three detectives on her witness list. Including several detectives who didn't work on this case at all, by the way. First of all, we'd request that Ms. Tasker give us a good reason why they have to be called, and second, Judge, these men and women don't all work nine-to-five shifts. It's going to take some work to bring them in. We need as much notice as possible. And again, I'd hope that we could get a good explanation as to the relevance of—'

'I understand, Mr Ogren. It's not my first trial.' The judge holds him up. Ogren has the tendency to talk down to people, and judges are not fans of condescension.

'Okay, everyone. Let's put on your final witness, Mr Ogren. Then, Ms. Tasker, I'll give you fifteen minutes to argue for a directed verdict. I will tell you right now that you will face a tall climb, but of course I'll hear you. Assuming we go forward from there, Ms. Tasker, do you think Mr Kolarich's direct testimony can be completed today?'

'I would think so, Judge.'

'So that would give Mr Ogren tomorrow for cross-examination and then redirect and recross, and maybe we could get that done by then. Okay. Okay.' She nods. 'Ms. Tasker, tomorrow, you will give me a smaller list of witnesses you're going to call. It's not going to be the entire Area Three squad room. You understand that?'

'Yes, Judge. It won't be that long.'

'Very well. Let's get out there,' says the judge.

74

Jason

'We call Detective Molly Hilton,' says Katie O'Connor.

Molly Hilton is a short woman with frizzy blond hair and a hard look about her. I've never met her, but Lightner apparently knows her ex-husband from when he was a cop in Marion Park. These cops are a whole community unto themselves.

'My assignment,' Hilton says, 'was to piece together the sequence and timing of events on the day of Ms. Himmel's death, for both Ms. Himmel and Mr Kolarich.'

Oops, Katie forgot to tell her to call me *the defendant*.

'Anything else?' asks O'Connor.

'I also wanted to figure out where Ms. Himmel was staying at the time of her death, whether she was living at Mr Kolarich's house or her own.'

'In the course of undertaking this assignment, Detective, did you review phone records?'

'I did.'

Katie O'Connor refers again to Alexa's phone records on the day of her death, Tuesday, July 30, previously admitted into evidence:

CALL DETAIL RECORDS FOR CELL PHONE OF ALEXA M. HIMMEL
Tuesday, July 30

Time	Destination	Length of Call (minutes)	Originating Cell Site
6:14 PM	555-0150	1	221529
8:16 PM	Kolarich Home	2	221529

'Detective Hilton, do you see the first line on this chart, a phone call made from Ms. Himmel's cell phone at 6:14 P.M. on the day of her death?'

'I do.'

'Did you track down that phone number?'

'I did.'

'And whose phone number is that?'

She says, 'It's the phone number for Mario's Pizzeria in Overton Ridge.'

'I see. And did you investigate this phone call any further?'

'Yes, I did. We subpoenaed credit card records to review any transactions that might have taken place on that date,' she says.

'And did you find anything?'

'Yes,' she says. 'Ms. Himmel used her Visa card that evening to buy a small pizza and chef's salad from Mario's. We obtained from Mario's a copy of the delivery receipt.'

'Is this the receipt?' Katie O'Connor shows the witness a yellow receipt from Mario's Pizzeria, for a charge of $19.62, plus tip, with Alexa's signature on it.

'That's the receipt,' says the detective. O'Connor admits the receipt into evidence without objection.

'Does the receipt have a date and time indicated, Detective?'

'Yes, it does,' says Hilton. 'A small pizza and salad from Mario's Pizzeria were delivered to Ms. Himmel at 7:02 that evening.'

I have to stifle a smirk. I look down and control my expression.

'What other information did you pursue, Detective?'

'We looked at her cable television bill for the month of July,' says Hilton.

'Is People's Twenty-five a true and accurate copy of that bill?'

'Yes, it is.'

O'Connor admits that bill into evidence, too.

'As you can see,' says the detective, 'on the evening of her death, Tuesday, July thirtieth, Ms. Himmel ordered the movie *Doctor Zhivago* on pay-per-view television at 7:07 P.M.'

Just after the pizza arrived. A pizza and a movie – a three-hour classic at that, a film that would run past ten o'clock that evening. Not the behavior of someone living at my house. But more important, much more to the point, not the behavior of someone who was planning on dropping by my house, either. It's the behavior of someone who was kicking up her feet and settling in for a quiet night at home.

Or someone who very much wanted it to appear that way.

Oh, Alexa. How did I underestimate thee? Let me count the ways.

FIVE MONTHS BEFORE TRIAL
July

75

Jason

Tuesday, July 23

I drop Alexa off downtown and then head to work. I have a nine-thirty in federal court, a status on a weapons case, which is bad news for my client because a federal gun charge will get you triple what it would on the state side. Trial is scheduled for six weeks from now, if it goes. The government wants my guy to flip on people up the chain, and so far my client has refused. I come from a neighborhood where you don't narc on your buddies, so I understand my client's reluctance, but my loyalty is to him, not his pals, and he could shave five years off his sentence if he starts talking.

I get back to my office after ten and push around some paper, a few files I've kept, the ones I haven't referred out to other lawyers. I realize that it's not an optimal strategy for a lawyer, who makes his living representing people for a fee, to push away all his clients. It's not exactly a recipe for long-term success. But long-term success is not on my agenda right now.

The case files holding no interest for me, I return to the notes I've scribbled about my time interrogating suspects as a prosecutor, trying to relax my mind and come up with some breakthrough. It has to be somebody I put away, and it has to be someone who just got out of prison. This guy has way too much of a hard-on for me to have kept his powder dry for years. This is a guy who stewed in prison, every sit-up in his cell at night, every repetition of the bench press in the prison yard, every moldy piece of bologna he ate, every night staring at a cement ceiling, every morning in the shower, looking over his shoulder, blaming me for all of his troubles, plotting out what he'd do to me when he got released.

He'd want to get started on that plan right away. This is not a guy who's enjoyed years of freedom since. This is a guy who got out of prison and got right to work.

I drop my head, feeling helpless. My stomach is revolting against me and my body temperature is fluctuating wildly from sweat to chills and back. I don't want to take a pill. I didn't take one for several hours on the night we tried to trap 'James' at Linda Sparks's house, the adrenaline rush distracting me, and my mind was sharper than it has been for months. In fact, it was the night I realized that 'James' had been mimicking back to me one of my favorite lines during interrogations, the *you're nobody to me* comment.

So, no pills. No pills because they cloud my mind, and I need my brain to function right now, I have to think, I need to process information, I need to *think out of the box*, one of the things the corporate robots say, there has to be something, some way, but I'm so damn tired, my vision losing focus, maybe if I just sleep for a few minutes, a quick catnap . . .

'Who are you, James?' I mumble, and he's in my office, James in my office, James telling me he didn't kill anybody, James asking me how to frame somebody, James in my office when I leave to take a pill in the bathroom, James taking my Bic pen, James dumping out my trash for Kleenex or an empty bottle of water, anything with saliva or mucus for DNA, maybe fingerprints, *What evidence do I have against you?* he asks me, taunting me over the phone, *Just some souvenirs I collected from you*, just some souvenirs like a chewed-up pen, maybe some Kleenex from the trash, a water bottle, *just some souvenirs*, because That's How You Frame Somebody by Jason Kolarich, Chapter One, first you pick a time when I have no alibi, Chapter Two, next you pick victims connected to me, Chapter Three, then you take things from my office that implicate me, *souvenirs*, and you leave them at the crime scene, James in my office, taking souvenirs –

My head pops up off the desk, my eyes taking a moment to return to focus, my brain reorienting.

Chapter Four, you plant incriminating evidence at the patsy's house.

Or, failing that, the patsy's office.

I jump out of my chair. Did I say that to him? Did I give him that advice? I don't know. The fog is too thick. But it's what I'd do if I really wanted to lock somebody down; I'd leave some morsels at the crime scene, nothing obvious but enough for an inquiry, and then, for the cherry on top, I'd put something really incriminating at the patsy's house or office.

As far as I know, he's never been inside my house. But he's been here in my office.

There's something here, I realize. Right here, in this office. He planted something here, something subtle, something hidden, something the police will specifically search for. It would need to look hidden. It can't be dangling from the ceiling or plastered on the wall like a trophy. It has to look like I didn't want anyone to find it. But it's here.

Why didn't you think of this before? You know why. It's those little white round bundles of joy that turn your brain to mush. How much more proof do you need?

I go to the corner of my office and dig my fingers against the cheap carpeting, feeling for a hole, a place where he could have stuck something. I cover the entire perimeter of the room, pulling back case files, the refrigerator, the couch. Nothing. Nothing I can find, anyway. I don't even know what I'm looking for.

The couch. I search under it and run my hands under cushions, feel under the bottom. Nothing.

The fridge. That would be fiendishly clever of him, brilliant in its simplicity. But nothing there. No lock of hair tucked into the small freezer section, no bloody knife taped to the bottom.

I go through my desk drawers, removing everything, searching through my coffee cup full of pencils and pens, everything I can think of. I don't even know what I'm looking for. Bigger than a bread basket? Probably not. A woman's fingernail? Her blood?

I turn my attention to the case files strewn around my office. Sure, maybe. He could have dropped something inside them, into one of the accordion files or one of the manila folders shoved within them. It could be anything. It could be anywhere.

This is what he wants, I think to myself. *He wants to make me crazy, he wants me chasing my own shadow, my imagination scattering in all directions.*

I drop down on the carpet, woozy and nauseated. Over three hours now, and no pills. *Hold out. Hold out. You think better when you're not on those ridiculous things, those beautiful tablets, that horrible, soul-stealing medicine, those delicious, wonderful pills.*

I force myself up, my muscles seizing, my stomach twisting, my skin burning. I stand in the center of my office, only a few feet from my desk, five feet from each wall. The radiator, I should check the radiator, complete with peeling paint, below my long horizontal window.

Nope. Nothing underneath, nothing shoved inside. I remove the cover and can't put it back on.

I finally succumb to the itching and start on the backs of my hands, my knuckles, my forearms, scratching furiously, knowing that I'm only spreading it like wildfire across my skin.

'Where the hell is it?' I hiss.

Leave. Walk out of the room, get some fresh air, empty your mind and start fresh.

I try my desk again, pulling out the drawers, patting underneath. The chair. I check the chair for the first time, a burst of adrenaline for an original thought, some place I haven't already checked, but no, no murder weapon or DNA evidence that I can find, assuming I can find it at all because I DON'T KNOW WHAT IT IS I'M LOOKING FOR.

Then back to the knuckles, bloody now, and my beet-red forearms. And then my calves and thighs.

'Dammit,' I say to nobody, standing straight again.
I let out a long breath. I know it's here. I know it.
But I can't find it.

'Hey, stranger.'

I spin around. It's Alexa, standing in the doorway.

76

Jason

Tuesday, July 23

'What's going on?' Alexa asks.

'Nothing,' I say instinctively, as ridiculous a claim as that is. *Nothing, just thought I would empty out every file in the room, pull out every drawer, rip the front off my radiator, create an absolute tornado in my office, all in the name of a casual good time.*

Joel's words from yesterday echo between my ears, like something in a movie: *She's not just giving you an alibi. She's giving herself one, too.*

I got a bad feeling about her.

I don't like it when you talk to pretty girls.

My one-word answer to Alexa – *nothing* – crashes to the floor faster than Newton's apple. Things have been odd since I confronted her two days ago about the restraining order and her lie about being an only child, her brother living here in the suburbs. I accepted her explanation. I believed her explanation. But you don't just brush that whole thing off and pretend like it didn't happen. There was something accusatory in my bringing it up, there's no way around it, and it's hard to walk that back to normal. She's now been the object of suspicion, like a murder suspect who beats the rap, who is found *not guilty*, which is different from *innocent*, and you always wonder what really happened; the taint never fully diminishes.

It's so obvious that the chaos Alexa sees in my office is *something* – not *nothing* – that she can't bring herself to quarrel with me.

'Deposition got done early?' I ask.

She nods. 'I thought you might want to leave early. Looks like you don't.'

'Right.' I look around the room and shrug.

'You think he planted something in here for the police to find?' she asks.

I nod. I don't know why I didn't just admit that up front; it's pretty obvious what I'm doing. 'I could see him doing something like that,' I say.

'That would make sense.' She looks about the room. 'Do you want some help?'

A gut-check moment. Either I trust her or I don't. Do I really think she's capable of doing these things?

A better question: Am *I* capable of making that judgment?

'What happened to your hand?' she asks. 'Oh my God, your arms.'

'Oh, I'm fine, I'm fine.' Just a little scratching. Or a lot of scratching.

'Oh, Jason.' She takes my arm, then looks up at me. 'You're doing okay?'

'Sure, sure,' I say.

She pauses, chews on her lip. 'I'll leave if you want. If you want to do this by yourself. It's not a problem, really.'

'No, not at all,' I hear myself say. 'I could use the help. But I think I've looked pretty much everywhere.'

She surveys the room, nodding her head and humming to herself. 'You don't know what you're looking for, that's part of the problem.'

'That's the main problem, yeah.'

'Mmm-hmm.' She spins around the room. 'Did you pull up the carpet?'

'First thing I did.'

'The refrigerator,' she says.

'Check.' But I'm sure I'll recheck it.

She keeps looking around. 'Looks like you checked the heater.'

Check. But will recheck.

'The couch,' she says.

'Check.' But will recheck.

'We should go through your files again, probably.'

'Probably. I looked through them all.'

'Did you check every piece of paper?' she asks.

'Every piece – no. I was looking for things that didn't belong.'

'It could be a piece of paper,' she says. 'We don't know what it is.'

That's true. She's right.

'What about the diplomas and pictures on the walls?' she asks.

'The walls? No.' I shake my head, feeling a surge. Her words trigger a memory.

You played football at State, didn't you? 'James Drinker' asked me.

Yes. *Yes.* He was standing, admiring my ego wall when I returned from the bathroom after taking the Altoids. I remember now. What is wrong with my brain?

'Haven't gotten that far yet,' I say. Making it sound like I was just about to head there. I probably would've thought of that, eventually. I'd prefer to think so.

'Let's check those first,' she sings.

There are . . . ten frames on the walls. My college and law school diplomas. Certifications from various courts to practice before those tribunals. Certificates from the public defender and county attorney offices for my work there. A picture of me cross-examining a witness, drawn by a courtroom sketch artist when I was defending Senator Almundo from federal corruption charges. And my favorite, the photograph of me, taken by one of the university photographers, my body angled while airborne, my arms outstretched, my hands closing over the football. I don't remember if I caught the ball.

I start with that one, because that's the one 'James' specifically referenced. I lift it off its hook and look behind it. Nothing but a flat, smooth wooden frame. I balance it on my knee and twist off the levers that hold the backing in place, removing each piece of the frame, the matting, and the photo itself. He could have stuck something deep within it, after all.

Nothing. Alexa does the same thing with my college diploma.

I go next to the certificate from the county attorney's office, my name in a thick gothic font on gold paper. If I'm right about this guy, it was my time as an assistant county attorney that brought us together. If 'James' has any sense of irony, this is where it will be.

I gently lift the frame off its perch, a horizontal piece of wire resting on a nail, and turn it over.

'Well, lookee here,' I murmur.

Fastened to the back of this frame, with Scotch tape, is a hypodermic needle, the hollow tube with the syringe attached. And from what I can tell, some fluid still inside.

'He's injecting them with something,' I say to Alexa. 'That's his signature.' And I'd bet any money that this particular needle was used to inject the first two victims, the ones already dead when the man who called himself James Drinker paid a visit to this office.

77

Jason

'A needle,' Joel says. 'With fluid still inside?'

'Some, not a lot,' I say, perching my cell phone on my shoulder. I'm at my town house now with Alexa. The needle is inside a sandwich bag, resting on my bed. 'Maybe a quarter of the vial?'

'Well, that would be a signature, all right. Maybe it's some kind of incapacitating agent. Or, well, it could be anything. He could've injected it when they're half dead, or *all* dead, or he could have used it to subdue them in the first place.'

'It could be something meaningful,' I say.

'It's a milky, cloudy liquid?'

'Yep. Y'know, I'm wondering if I should just take it to the cops. What if there are fingerprints on it?'

'Is that what you think?' he asks. 'That this guy went to all this trouble to set you up, but he was dumb enough to put his greasy fingers all over it?'

He's right. I take this to the cops and I'm in no different position than I was before. I still can't identify the killer any more than a fake name he gave me. There's still some unknown evidence out there that 'James' has planted at the crime scenes. I'd be in just as helpless a position as before. Correction – worse: Now I happen to be in possession of one of the killer's weapons, complete with DNA on the needle tip, no doubt, of the skin and blood of Alicia Corey and Lauren Gibbs.

'How are we doing on that other topic? That thing we discussed yesterday?'

Alexa, he means. His suspicions about Alexa.

Alexa's in the master bathroom right now, the water running, but still I answer in a whisper. 'She helped me find this, Joel. I was chasing my tail looking for stuff. It was her idea to check the pictures on the wall.'

'That a fact? It was her idea, was it?' He sounds almost cheerful. He seems to think this proves something.

'You're delusional,' I say.

I hang up with Joel and get on my knees by the nightstand next to my bed. There is a small drawer and I pull it out completely, removing it from its hinges. I tape the sandwich bag containing the needle to the underside of the drawer and carefully replace it.

'That's not much of a hiding place,' Alexa says when she emerges from the bathroom.

'Well, hopefully, it won't need to stay hidden long,' I say. 'We're going to catch this guy. I can taste it now.'

78

Shauna

Wednesday, July 24

Two o'clock. Bradley and I look at each other with blank expressions. Rory Arangold puts an arm around my shoulder and whispers, 'Either way, you were amazing.'

The trial has ended. Closing arguments were completed a half hour ago, followed by instructions from the judge to the jury. The seven women and five men who will decide our fate have retired for deliberations. There is no chance they'll come back today. They'll get started today, will elect a foreperson and get organized, maybe will make some introductory comments. Tomorrow, Thursday, will be all day. And they won't want to carry this case over into next week. Friday, I'm almost positive. Friday, we'll get the verdict.

The adrenaline begins to drain from my limbs, from my neck and shoulders, my body turning to rubber. *Jason,* I think to myself. *I need to talk to Jason.* But I have to see this thing through. The jury shouldn't take more than two days. Wait for the verdict, be there for the client until then, stay on my game just another day or two, hold my freakin' breath, and then Jason.

Rory mentions dinner, Bradley says something about a stiff drink, but I tell them I have an appointment and I'll try to meet with them later. I have a feeling that I won't. I'll make up an excuse, a headache or something, and by then they'll be so drunk they won't care. A rain check, I'll say. We'll celebrate after the jury gives us the good news.

That should be my focus right now, the verdict, this case. I've kept my focus thus far. I've stayed on program. I haven't missed a single beat. We've done everything we wanted to do, from start to finish, for better or for worse. It's a good feeling, in itself, knowing that you have no regrets about your performance.

But I'm not in a place right now to feel good. I just want to get out of here, make my appointment, and go home.

The Arangolds aren't finished with me, hugging me and shaking my hand and filling me with praise. They are good people, and they deserve to keep their business. They deserve to win this case. I tell them all of that, knowing that they won't be hearing these words from me later tonight over wine or something stiffer.

Jason, I think to myself. *I need to talk to Jason.*

Two more days. It can wait two more days.

79

Jason

Friday, July 26

My office is a wasteland. Everything that Alexa helped me put back together I have taken apart again. I'm taking no chances. I'm going back over this entire office to make sure that the hypodermic needle I found behind my framed prosecutor's certificate is the *only* thing that my friend 'James' planted. I've tossed my car, as well, though there's never been a sign of anyone breaking into it. No chances. Taking no chances.

I'm drifting hard, trying to keep my spirits high, focusing on the fact that I've checked at least one move that 'James' has made, but realizing that there is a bad side to my discovery, too – it proves that my tiny glimmer of hope that 'James' was making this whole thing up about a frame-up was wasted prayers, that, in fact, he is doing that very thing. And that means that even if I discover who he is, and I turn him in to the police, I'm going to have some explaining to do of my own. Not an insurmountable climb, I hope, but the truth is, I don't know what lies ahead for me. I don't know what 'James' has planted at the crime scenes.

Which means that I could be sprinting toward my own execution squad.

My eyes pop open, and I realize I've drifted off – not an uncommon occurrence these days, during lulls of stress – when I hear the celebratory voice of my associate, Bradley John.

'Not guilty on all counts!' he shouts. 'Not guilty on all counts!'

Marie's voice now, whooping it up, too. I pop a pill from my Altoids tin and push myself out of my chair, glancing at the clock. It's just after ten o'clock. The jury must have announced first thing this morning.

'A complete and total defense verdict,' Bradley is saying to Marie. 'Four counts, all in our favor. And here she is,' he says, taking Shauna's hand as she appears in the hallway. 'Hey!' he says when he sees me. 'Defense verdict, all the way around!'

I give my congratulations, a high five to Bradley and a quick *friends* hug with Shauna. Defense verdicts in a plaintiff-happy forum like our civil courts is cause for mass celebration. There will be a long, liquid lunch that will turn into a long night. I'm hardly in the mood for this, but they deserve it. Shauna did it. She took on the city and knocked their teeth in.

'I need to talk to you,' Shauna whispers to me, but she allows for the merriment to continue for a while. There's no alternative. This is a major, major win for our law firm, one of the biggest.

It's early enough that lunch is premature, so everyone agrees to hold off on the heavy celebration for an hour or so, Shauna actually mentioning that her stomach is bothering her and she may want to postpone the festivities. That would be fine with me.

I walk back to my office, Shauna following me. Instinctively, I take a seat behind my desk, a bit more formal than the couch we'd usually share, without giving it any thought. Maybe that's saying something right there. Shauna, for her part, chooses not to sit at all. She is wearing a solid frown. Someone who just won a heater case, who just saw two years' worth of grueling work lead to a spectacular result, is frowning at me.

'Could I have one of those mints?' she says to me, nodding to the small tin of Altoids. Shit. I left them out. I was in too much of a hurry getting up to congratulate them.

'Sure.' As casually as I can, I bring out the other tin – the real Altoids – and open it up.

329

Shauna looks at me. 'No, I want one from the red tin,' she says. 'The peppermint.'

'What's the difference?' I shake the blue tin in my hand for emphasis.

'I want the peppermint kind,' she says again, her eyes growing hot.

'Shauna—'

'I'll give you a thousand dollars for one of the peppermint ones that you just slipped back in your pocket.'

'What the fuck, Shauna?'

'What the fuck, Jason? I'm serious.'

We stare at each other. This isn't going well. My cell phone buzzes – Alexa – but I let it go to voice mail. This is not the time for evasion. Shauna has busted me, and we both know it.

'That's what I thought,' she says, barely above a whisper. 'Now, listen to me, Jason. Are you listening? I mean, really listening?'

My face is hot, my eyes stinging. I don't answer.

'I'm not going to let you throw your life away. You are going to get off those pills, and I'm going to be there with you. We're going to do it together. But it doesn't work until you admit it.'

I laugh, like the whole thing is ridiculous, but nobody in this room is fooled. 'So this is, like, an intervention? Where's my brother, on the other side of the door? Where's Lightner? Where's Dr Phil?'

'It's just me,' she says. 'It's me. The person who cares about you more than anyone in this world. It's me, Jason.' She pats her chest for emphasis. 'I've got all the time in the world to help you. I'll do whatever you need.'

'There's nothing to do, kiddo, and this is getting redundant. We've been over this before. If this is going to be you hectoring me about a problem I don't have, then it's going to be a short conversation. Go out and celebrate, and leave me alone. I've got enough to deal with right now,' I say, and now the emotions are starting to build. 'I've got a damn *serial killer* who, as far as I know, is scouting out his next target right now, and who's apparently setting me up for the crime. And I can't find out who he is. I can't, Shauna. It's – well, it's taking up a bit of my time right now, okay? So please, take your touchy-feely intervention and conduct it on somebody else.'

Shauna watches me, almost clinically, like she's observing me for an objective evaluation. Then, without warning, her eyes begin to fill. Her expression doesn't change. If anything, it grows stonier. But those eyes always give her up.

'I'm pregnant,' she says.

80

Jason

Friday, July 26

I search Shauna's face, uncertain I heard the words correctly, but surer every second, as the tears roll down her face, as she picks at a fingernail, her eyes casting downward.

'I'm pregnant,' she says, 'and I'm terrified.'

'No. No.' I am out of my chair now, coming around my desk.

I approach her, and she weeps silently, the way she always does, her shoulders bobbing, and when she looks back up at me she has to blink away tears furiously, her mouth in a scowl.

Something clears inside me, not a sudden jolt but the slow rise of the sun, something long dormant waking up and rearing its head, stretching its limbs, clearing its throat, reasserting itself. *Now I remember,* I realize. *Now I remember.*

And it surges through me, shaking me so hard that the hand I raise to her cheek is trembling. I wipe at her tears with my thumb, pull her in close to me.

'I'm sorry,' she whispers.

'No. Don't ever—'

And then my throat chokes up, and I press against her, and everything is different, because it has to be different, I want it to be different, I've wanted it to be different for so long now that I've forgotten what it felt like, what it looked like.

'I'm addicted to OxyContin,' I say. 'I don't know how I let it happen, but I did. I thought I could take as much of it as I wanted, as often as I wanted, because I was strong. But I'm not strong. Not strong enough. I . . . I want to stop, Shauna. But I need help.'

'Then you will,' she whispers. 'I'll help you. We'll do it together.'

I press my lips into her hair, run a hand over her back. 'I promise you I'll beat it,' I say, my voice gaining strength again. 'I won't let you down. Ever, Shauna. I won't ever let you down again.'

She slowly draws back, puts her hands on each side of my face, looking at me. 'I know you won't,' she says.

81

Jason

Friday, July 26

Alexa opens the door to her home. Her smile disappears as soon as she sees the look on my face.

Things have been on a downward slide between us, a slow and steady decline. It's the kind of thing that neither party to a relationship openly acknowledges, but each one recognizes. This visit, this moment, can't be entirely a surprise to her. But there is so much that goes unsaid in a relationship that sometimes you don't know until you do it.

'Something's wrong,' she says to me, backing up, letting me into her home, but not taking her eyes off me, her facial expression telling me that she sees it coming.

'My *life* has been wrong for a while now,' I say. 'I have to turn it around. I'm *going* to turn it around. Right now.'

'You're . . . pale,' she says, reaching for me, but I recoil. 'Is it your knee?'

I resist the impulse to smile. 'I think we both know my knee is fine, Alexa. I've become a drug addict. And if I don't change that, I'm going to wind up in the gutter.'

'Okay, okay,' she says, coming to me again. 'Let me help.'

I take her by the wrists, blocking those hands that caressed me so often. 'You deserve better than this. I know that. But I have to start fresh. I have to end this between us right now. I'm very sorry, but that's the way it has to be.'

She doesn't take it well. She pulls back from me, shaking her head, breathless, wagging a finger like she's warning me, *no no no*. She doesn't speak. It's as if the wind has been stolen from her. Like a child gearing up for a loud cry.

'Are you going to be okay?' I ask, trying to strike the proper balance between concern and dispassion. I need to keep some distance now. It won't make it any easier for her if I touch her, soothe her, take her in my arms one last time.

'Am I . . . going . . . am I . . .' She staggers into the living room, bracing herself against the love seat.

I consider all sorts of platitudes. *It's for the best. I think you're great. You're going to find someone special. It's just not the right time.* Empty words, all of them. Words to ease the discomfort of the deliverer of the bad news more than the recipient. She is suffering now, and my feelings for her were genuine, too, at least on some level. But I can't separate our relationship from the pills. I'm not sure there *was* a relationship without those pills. So I'm not going to coddle her with some mouth candy that I think I'm supposed to utter. I'm not going to pretend that this is going to feel better for her tomorrow.

She has made it to the couch, where she sits. I fetch a glass of water, not that she requested it, and place it on the table next to her. She is trying to breathe.

'Alexa, I'm worried about your safety,' I say. 'With this killer out here who has a hard-on for me. Can I . . . Would you let me buy you a plane ticket somewhere? Anywhere. You name it. I can put you up in a hotel somewhere where you're far away—'

'Oh, wouldn't *that* be convenient,' she spits. 'You dump me, then ship me off to another state.'

'I'm serious, Alexa. When we were together all the time, I didn't worry about you. But now . . .'

She raises her eyebrows.

'I don't want anything to happen to you, and I can't protect you

335

except to get you out of town for a while. Just until we figure out who this guy—'

'I'm not a charity case. I don't want a plane ticket. I want *you*.' She looks up at me.

I open my hands. 'I can't give you that. I have to start over. I'm sorry.'

'I thought you *loved* me,' she whispers.

I squat down. 'Alexa, I haven't been right in the head. It's not fair to you, but it's true. Of course I have feelings for you, but when you're addicted to drugs, that becomes your love affair. I know it's hard to understand.'

Actually, I think she understands it quite well. Shauna, I think, had it right about her. She liked that I needed help, that I was struggling, that I needed *her*. Amazing, really, what a wake-up call can do for your sense of reality. The truth is that Alexa was a part of my spiral, she was enabling the spiral.

'I'm going to get help,' I say. 'And I'm going to move on. And I hope you can move on, too.'

She hiccups a laugh. Something has risen inside her and reached her eyes, turning them hard. 'You'll be back. I'm the best thing that ever happened to you.'

I draw back, surprised at the abrupt change. But there's no handbook for this kind of thing.

'I have to leave,' I say. 'I'm going to leave now. Take care of yourself, Alexa.'

I stand and try to think of something appropriate to do or say. Failing that, I head for the door.

'Who's going to be your alibi?' she says, regaining some composure now, standing at the couch. 'Who's going to keep you out of prison?'

I flap my arms. 'You were never my alibi,' I say. Then I turn and leave.

82

Shauna

Friday, July 26

The Arangold victory party starts at lunch on Friday and continues onward. I couldn't deny them or Bradley this moment, however little I feel like doing it myself. I manage to stay with the crew until a little before three o'clock, when I duck away. I catch a lot of grief for leaving, but at the end of the day everyone's feeling very happy, and there's only so much they'll complain.

I come back to the office, which has been officially closed for the rest of the day, and find Jason in his office, looking out his window. His hands are in constant motion, clench and release, clench and release, his foot tapping to the beat of some silent rhythm. He turns when he hears me.

'You're supposed to be at a party celebrating,' he says.

Somewhere in there, fighting to get out, is my Jason. But he's been traveling incognito these days, messy long hair and stubble on his cheeks, maybe thirty pounds lighter, sunken, bloodshot eyes. *If you hadn't had back-to-back trials,* I tell myself, not for the first time, *this never would have happened.*

'I don't want to be anywhere but here,' I say. 'So? How did it go with Alexa?'

He makes a face. 'Hard. Brutal. But it's done.'

'It's *done* done?' I ask. There's some reason, after all, to believe that Alexa Himmel has a hard time letting go.

337

'I told her it was over and that was that. I wasn't going to change my mind.' He raises his hands. He doesn't know if the breakup will stick with Alexa, if she'll accept it or resist. He – no, *we*, we will have to be prepared to deal with it either way.

His cell phone, resting on the window ledge next to him, buzzes. The screen lights up with the word *Alexa*. He looks at me and shrugs.

'How many times is that?' I ask.

'Third call since I left her about an hour ago,' he says.

The phone stops buzzing and goes dark. A moment later, a small robotic noise comes from the phone, and it lights up again. *3 new voice mails*, it says.

His office phone rings, his direct line that he doesn't give out to almost anyone. There was a time when only Joel Lightner and I had that number. Alexa became the third one.

'So this is tough for her,' Jason says, an understatement of the patently obvious.

Made more obvious still when the office phone stops ringing, and his cell phone buzzes and lights up again: *Alexa*. Then: *4 new voice mails*.

'It'll take her some time,' he says. He comes over and takes me in his arms. It's what I've wanted him to do since I walked in. But I don't want to push. We're together, whatever that means, whatever that entails. That's all we are right now. I'm having his baby. Will there be more? Neither of us is ready to ask that question, much less answer it.

'Now for the even harder part,' he says. 'My return to normalcy.'

Fortunately for Jason, I've been doing research, a little at a time every night when I needed a mental break from trial preparation, about addiction and recovery.

'I haven't looked closely at which rehab clinics are the best,' I tell him. 'But I do know that there are some that special—'

'Shauna,' he says, 'I can't go into rehab right now. Not right now. Joel and I are trying to hunt this guy down. I have to keep mobile until then.'

I'm sure my facial expression says it all.

'Don't look at me like that,' he says. 'I'm ready to do this. I'm going to do it. Starting right now. But not in a clinic. I'm not making an excuse—'

'You are, actually. That's *exactly* what you're doing. This has to be your number one priority—'

'It will be tied at number one with stopping this guy. Look, Joel's people are doing most of the grunt work, anyway. I can focus on rehab. But I can't be hidden in some clinic somewhere without phones or a computer. I have to be reachable and ready to act, whatever "ready to act" means.'

I don't like this. This isn't how you dive into detox. This is dipping a toe. Is he as ready as he thinks he is to start his recovery?

'I've thought about this.' He pulls me to the couch and we sit. 'If I tried to go cold turkey right now without help, it would be murder. It would be a losing battle. But there's a middle ground here, between nothing and what I was doing.'

'You want to wean yourself off.' The Internet tells me that some people do it that way, ramp down the medication, spread out the doses, slowly rebuild their defenses. But that's under the care of a physician.

'I'll wean myself off. I'll cut down to – I was thinking a pill every six hours. And without crushing them between my teeth first. It will be a huge change for me, believe me. It will get me started on the process, but not take me completely out of the box while that asshole is out there killing women.'

As much as I don't like it, I can't deny his reasoning. He can't very well turn his back on a serial killer roaming the north side. And just as important, I have to understand that this isn't my decision. I can't force Jason to do anything. He has to want to do this. I really have no choice but to accept his terms or walk away.

'Every six hours,' I say. 'Not one minute earlier.'

'You hold the pills. You're the key-master.'

He hands me the vaunted tin of Altoids. We look at each other. It's a real moment for him, I realize. A torch has been passed.

'And you're going to be intense and focused on what?' I ask. 'If you just stew in your juices, sitting around thinking about "James Drinker" all the time, you're going to be reaching for those pills a lot sooner than every six hours.'

He looks off a moment, then smiles, really smiles, not a polite grin but a happy smile. I haven't seen that expression on his face in ages.

'Exercise,' he says. 'I'm not going to have much strength, but I'll exercise myself to exhaustion.' He shrugs his shoulders. 'Go for long walks. And I'll go for long rides in the car. Read books. I don't know. I'll think of something.'

'It's going to be really hard,' I tell him. 'The hardest thing you've ever done.'

He nods, turns back to the window. 'I know,' he says. 'Just . . . hang in there with me, okay?'

83

Shauna

I peek my head into the bathroom. My bathroom, my condo, two blocks away from Jason's town house. A thousand square feet in all, one bedroom, one bathroom, a decent kitchen, and a great room with a spectacular view of the high-rises in the commercial district to the south. The condo of a successful single woman.

For Jason, it must feel like prison. We made a decision that he should leave his house and stay with me during this interval of time. Change everything, completely alter the landscape, remove any associations that enabled his problem.

'Hey,' I say.

The toilet is in mid-flush. You can hear everything from everywhere in this place, so it wasn't hard to hear the guttural sounds from his throat, his stomach lurching, his dry retching, the gasps of breath in between. Jason looks better in the sense that he seems more lucid, more self-aware. He looks worse by any other criterion. He hasn't slept more than two hours at a time, always waking with a cry of some sort, ready for the fix that isn't going to come. His eyes are dark and cloudy. His skin has a greenish pallor, the permanent look of someone who's about to vomit. He moves fluidly at times, with a halting, hesitant gait at others. Every six-hour interval between pills is its own adventure, from contentment to discomfort to agony.

But he has stayed true to his plan to exercise his way out of this, to let the adrenaline be his drug. He's speed-walked outside (I never thought the day would come that Jason, jock extraordinaire and marathon enthusiast, would do any exercise that included the word *walk*) and jogged on my fold-up treadmill inside the apartment. Not wanting to completely trash his knee all over again, he's gone to aerobics, too. He has hit the indoor pool in my condo building no less than five times in the three nights he's been here. He does push-ups and sit-ups and leg lifts on the floor, anything he can do to tire himself out and churn the adrenaline. He has little energy and no stamina, and what little reserve he does possess, after months without exercise, is easily spent. That's the point, to continually tire himself out and occupy himself with the physical exertion.

Realizing that all of this exercise is just making him drop more weight – not that this is his primary concern – he's tried to eat. He does the cooking, anything to keep himself occupied, but he hasn't held down a single meal yet. In between the episodes of vomiting, I've seen him double over in pain from the cramps, mostly in the abdomen and thighs. Not that he realizes I've seen it. He tries to hide it from me, the pain, the struggle. That's as much a sign as any that Jason is back, the heroically stoic routine. So instead of saying, *Shauna, my legs are cramping so much I'm going to scream*, he just asks for a hot bath – the preferred short-term remedy for cramps. I've drawn more hot baths in the last few days than I've taken all year.

Sitting on the bathroom tile, his back against the vanity, wearing only boxers, he raises his tired eyes to mine. 'Sorry for the sound effects,' he says.

'Don't ever say you're sorry,' I tell him. Then, my eyebrows raised, I say, 'The Candyman is here.'

He shakes his head out of his funk. 'Six hours already?'

'Six hours already. Your OxyContin, sir.' A sentence I was pretty sure I'd never utter in my lifetime. I hold out my hand.

He shakes his head, waves me off. 'No. I'm going to hold out.'

'That's noble of you,' I say. 'But let's stick with our program. You've done great.'

'No. No. One more hour.' He unfolds himself and stands up, facing me.

(I must make this statement: As terrible as I feel for this man, as much as his every moan and quiet grimace turns something sour inside me, I do have eyes, and they work pretty well. Jason was always a cut, muscular guy at six-three, two hundred twenty pounds, a real battleship. Thirty pounds lighter? Six-three, one ninety? His face is drawn, his eyes sunken, an unhealthy color to his skin. All of that, yes. But his body? He looks like he stepped out of an underwear ad for Calvin Klein. I couldn't pinch fat on him with a pair of tweezers. His stomach is a sheet of thin skin raked over rock. His chest and shoulders are a tad smaller than at his fighting weight, but they are more pronounced, every tiny muscle rippling with his every movement. He's like something Michelangelo carved out of stone.)

'What?' he says to me.

'Nothing,' I say. 'Can I get you anything?'

'A loaded pistol?' he suggests.

His cell phone rings. He switched from a buzzer to ringtones, so if Lightner calls with news, he won't miss the call. Lightner has been given his own ringtone, the theme song from *Dragnet* (DUNNN-*duh*-DUN-*dun* . . . DUNNN-*duh*-DUN-*dun*-DUNNNNN).

But Lightner hasn't called yet. Guess who has?

Twenty times, I think it was, on Friday alone, just to his cell phone. Saturday? Forty-seven calls. Forty-seven. Sunday? I lost track, but we think it was sixty-two or sixty-three times she called him.

And today – well, today isn't over yet. There's still two hours left in Monday, but we're closing in on sixty phone calls again.

Jason always looks at me when the phone rings, as if I have any input. I always say the same thing: *It's your decision. Answer it if you want.* I'm not going to tell him how to handle this. Look, Alexa was bad news, poison, the worst possible person for Jason at the worst possible time. But I've had my heart broken, too. It sucks. It just sucks.

343

Some of us handle it differently. I don't enjoy witnessing her suffering.

But I'm not focused on her. It's Jason who has my complete attention. Anything that will set back his recovery is bad; anything that doesn't, I'm agnostic. A simple test, in theory. So if he can interact with her, help talk her down, so to speak, I'm all for it. What I'm *not* for? Alexa sucking him back into that life, because I'll bet it was a mighty comfortable one, full of guilt-free sex and drugs. (Who knows, maybe they played rock and roll to go for the trifecta.)

So he's answered a few of her calls – one on Friday afternoon, one last night, and one this afternoon, his comments to her clipped, succinct. *I need to be alone to get through this. I can't see you or talk to you. I'm really sorry, but I'm not changing my mind.* Some version of that, with my moving as far away from the phone as I can, knowing that on the other end of that call, a stricken woman was pleading with him to take her back.

Oh, yeah, it sucks, no way around it.

And that's just the phone calls. Saturday, the e-mails started, too, beginning with something basic, the *Why won't you call me back?* variety, then something safe but heartfelt (*I'm trying not to push you,* complete with smiley-face emoticon, but also *This is very hard for me*), followed in the early morning hours of Sunday with something a little more disturbing (*Maybe we can just wipe the slate clean,* and *This is killing me,* and *If you keep ignoring me, I don't know what I'll do*).

Yesterday afternoon, as Jason was cooking dinner and actually hopping in place to calm himself, he pulled up an e-mail she sent called 'A lesson' that complained that Jason hadn't given her an adequate explanation (he had, I thought), that he lied to her and used her (he didn't; it was the other way around, actually), and ended with this: *You'd probably like it if I died, wouldn't you? Well, just say the word, Jason, and I'll do it. I'm dead anyway.*

'Jason,' I say, 'we really should call the police.'

He runs some water in the bathroom and splashes it on his face. 'Shauna, please. I can't keep having this argument.'

'But the situation keeps getting worse.'

He knows I'm right. Around seven last night, another e-mail arrived in his inbox, with a more ominous tone, calling herself *poor Alexa the fucked up girl* and then this: *I just thought of something that could be seriously bad for you and I want to make sure you're protected so please call me just for that and nothing else.* And then this beauty, from this morning: *If you don't get in touch with me your going to be seriously fucked,* complete with the grammar mistake (rare for her, Jason insists) and the apocalyptic conclusion.

Jason dries his face with a towel. 'I know,' he says. 'But it would kill her. The police show up at her door? Or a restraining order? I already hurt her badly. That would devastate her.'

'This is venturing into *Fatal Attraction* territory,' I say. 'What about you? What about me? Aren't you the least bit worried? I mean, what about that doctor in Ohio?'

He shakes his head slowly. Alexa, not surprisingly, had an answer for the background research Joel pulled up on her. Jason accepted her side of the story. I can't deny that a cheating husband, lying to hide his affair, would not be a first. But every phone call Alexa makes to Jason's cell phone draws me closer to believing the worst about her.

'I'm not letting you out of my sight,' he says, looking at me with a half smile, because he's giving back to me the very thing I said to him. That was the deal. If Jason needed fresh air, or a drive, or laps in a swimming pool, I'd be there with him. It is turning into a mutual-protection arrangement. 'Alexa would never do anything like you're thinking,' he says. 'And if she tried to hurt you, she'd have to get through me first.'

'That's what I'm afraid of.'

He moans as he leaves the bathroom. 'She wouldn't do that. She's in pain, but she wouldn't do something like that. She doesn't even know we're together right now. I told her I was alone and outside the city.'

He drops onto my bed with another moan.

345

'She just needs to get it out of her system,' he says. 'Nothing's going to happen to us.'

Jason's cell phone rings again. That just brings another moan from his throat.

I walk over to check it – Jason insists one of us check every call to his phone, because even though it's probably Alexa, it might be—

'Jason,' I say. 'It's an unknown number.'

84

Jason

Monday, July 29

I snatch the phone from Shauna before it goes into voice mail and answer the phone.

'Long time, no see, Jason,' says the man who calls himself James Drinker. 'Where you been hiding out?'

'Let's call it an undisclosed location,' I say.

'I get you, I get you. Hey, you're probably thinking, as long as I don't know where you are, I won't do anything else. Is that what you're thinking?'

I don't answer. This guy is always a step ahead, always inside my brain.

'Tell me something. How was that pizza? You seem like a garlic kind of guy.'

'Is that right?' *Let him talk. Maybe he'll give something up.*

'I'll give you credit, my man. That was a close one, over there at Linda's house. Maybe if your knee was feeling better, you'd have caught me.'

'How do you know I'm not watching you right now?' I ask.

He breathes out of his nose, blurring the connection. 'No, I don't think so. Listen, I just want you to know, your plan isn't going to work. I don't care where you are. I'm still going to do whatever I want to do.'

'But how do you frame me, then?' I ask. 'How do you know I'm not in Hawaii right now? Or with five people who can verify my alibi?'

He gets a good laugh out of that one. 'You really don't get it,' he says. 'That's okay. You'll know soon enough, Jason Kolarich. I just want you to know: This next one? This next one is going to be my favorite.'

THE DAY OF ALEXA
HIMMEL'S DEATH
Tuesday, July 30

85

Shauna

I open my eyes and roll my head over to my bedside clock and begin with panic – *it's ten!* – my brain hardwired for work after two consecutive trials, month after month of seven-day workweeks. It's a moment before it all returns to me: I'm off today, will probably be off for days, maybe the whole week, maybe the entire time that Jason needs before he goes to some professional clinic.

I rub my eyes and listen. The television is on in the living room, *SportsCenter*, I think, some animated guy talk. The scent of strong coffee.

It was a long night, like all of them have been since Jason started his recovery. Jason popping awake every couple of hours, hitting the floor for push-ups and sit-ups to combat the nervous energy, the itch, the cravings. Jason at six this morning, fists pumped in the air, *Seven hours again! Seven!*, celebrating his newfound tolerance, *Seven is the new six!* I watched him with my eyes half shut, dancing around like Rocky, knowing that in one hour he was going to be doubled over, grimacing from cramps and nausea.

I poke my head out of the bedroom. Jason is back to his exercise, push-ups on the floor. I take a quick shower, towel-dry my hair, and throw on a robe. It feels like a lazy Sunday morning.

When I get back to the living room, Jason is in a T-shirt and shorts, his laptop open on the floor. His eyes meet mine. 'Not good,' he says.

'What? Another e-mail?'

He nods, pushes the laptop toward me. I sit down on the floor and read what's on the screen. It's a new e-mail from Alexa, sent an hour ago:

Tuesday, July 30, 9:01 AM
Subj: I REALLY wasn't kidding
From: 'Alexa M. Himmel' <AMHimmel@Intercast.com>
To: 'Jason Kolarich' <Kolarich@TaskerKolarich.com>

Hi, there. Hope you're well. I'm really concerned about the attached letter getting out. Maybe we can put our heads together and figure out how to prevent it. But if you keep ignoring me then I guess there's nothing i can do. . . . . .

< BAD.Letter.pdf >

'There's an attachment,' I say, my stomach swimming now.

'There sure is,' he says.

BAD Letter, I think. *BAD, in all caps.* A special meaning to a lawyer.

The document pops up on the screen:

To: The Board of Attorney Discipline
Subject: Jason Kolarich, Attorney ID # 14719251

I am writing to report an attorney named Jason Kolarich, currently practicing at the law firm of Tasker and Kolarich. Jason has become addicted to a painkiller called oxycodone. It has hampered his ability to practice law, I fear to the detriment of his clients. He has lost a good deal of weight, and his behavior has become erratic. I am not a lawyer, so I don't know if the drugs have stopped him from defending his clients properly. I don't know if there are rules governing this, but I thought the state's board that regulates lawyers should know about this.

More than anything, I think a client, before they hire a lawyer, should know if that lawyer is a drug addict.

I am afraid to sign this letter, but I hope you will look into it.

I look at Jason, who is staring passively at the ceiling.

'Isn't she a peach?' I say.

'She's hurting,' he says. 'She's hurting so much.'

I close up the laptop. 'Do you think she'd do it? Send it?'

Jason gets up, stretches his arms. 'Everything she said in that letter is true, Shauna. I hope I didn't let any clients down. I don't think I did. God as my witness, I don't think I did. But I can't know for sure. I'll never know for sure.'

'Jason, this isn't the time for self-reflection. This is the time for self-preservation.'

He scratches his hand and looks out the window. 'I need to talk to her,' he says. 'I need to go see her.'

'That's what she wants,' I say. 'Just call her.'

'No, I need to see her.' He shakes his head. 'This has to be face-to-face.'

86

Jason

I ring Alexa's doorbell and take a couple of steps back. A flutter of nerves passes through me, but my whole body is so screwed up right now, it's hard to tell what's causing which problem inside me. My skin is tingling, my abdominal muscles are churning, a dull ringing has taken up nearly permanent residence between my ears.

I hear footsteps approaching the front door and steel myself. The curtain over the small side window moves, and then the lock on the door clicks.

'Hi,' she says. She is wearing a long football jersey and torn jeans, no shoes or socks. Her hair is matted and messy. Her eyes are red and puffy but, it seems, hopeful.

Hopeful, that is, until her eyes move to the suitcases next to me.

'I brought your things,' I say.

'I don't want them. Keep them.'

'Alexa, c'mon.'

She leaves the door open and walks into her living room. I'd rather have this conversation on the front porch, but this will do. I carry in the suitcases and set them down by the door.

'Do you . . . want something?' She sits on her leg on the couch.

'I'm fine.' I sit next to her. It's an old, beat-up leather couch. 'I just want to talk to you for a few minutes. Is that okay?'

Her eyes narrow. '*Now* you want to talk.'

'You got my attention, yes,' I say. 'I got your e-mail and that letter. If you feel like you want to send that, go ahead and send it. I won't deny what you wrote. Maybe I deserve to be reprimanded. I'm sure I do, actually—'

'Forget about the letter,' she says, her expression switching in a finger-snap. 'You know I could never hurt you.' She touches my arm. Somehow it would feel cruel to recoil, to move my arm away, to deny her that small gesture.

My phone rings, giving me an excuse to reach into my pocket, thereby breaking free of her and altering my body position. 'Just need to make sure it isn't Joel,' I say, by way of apology. Actually, I know it's not Lightner calling because we programmed the *Dragnet* theme as a ringtone for his calls, but Alexa doesn't know that. I look at the face of the phone and don't recognize the number, then set it down on the couch between us.

The other ringing, the one taking place inside my head, grows shriller. My temples begin to throb. Skin on fire, bitterness on my tongue, a stomach ready to rock-and-roll at any time.

'Alexa,' I say, 'our favorite serial killer called again last night. He said he's going to kill again, and the next one is going to be his "favorite." I'm really concerned he might go after someone I care about.'

She scoffs and makes a face. 'Well, that rules out me, doesn't it?'

'No, it doesn't. Listen, please – *please* get out of town. Drive somewhere. Fly somewhere. Please.'

'I'm not going anywhere. What's he going to do to me that you haven't already?'

'Oh, c'mon, Alexa. You'll get past this. You know you will. Sometime soon, you're going to look back and realize that . . . this is for the best.'

'How can you say that?' She leans toward me, her hand moving toward my face.

How can I say that? Because we both knew I was drugged up,

and getting worse, and making more and more excuses as time wore on. The oddest part is that whenever Alexa invoked the excuse of my bad knee, whenever she had a pill at the ready for me when I awoke at night, I viewed her as an ally, the only one who understood me.

The addiction was my fault. But she feasted on my weakness. If I was the captain of my personal *Titanic*, she was my first mate, whispering sweet nothings, telling me what a good job I was doing steering the wheel, and don't worry about those glaciers. I can't forget that. If I do, I'll lose everything.

But now is not the time to get into all of that. This moment calls for a defter touch.

'I have to focus on "James Drinker" or whatever his name is,' I say. 'He has to be my singular focus.'

She watches me with those wide deer eyes, wounded, fighting tears again.

'You're doing this because of this man?' she says. 'Or because of the drugs?'

She recalls, of course, that I mentioned the addiction when I broke up with her. And now I'm talking about a serial killer.

'It's both things,' I say. 'But this man – he's dangerous. And he's not done. I need to catch him, and I need you to be far away so you're out of harm's way.'

She grabs my forearm. 'Just give me one more chance. I'll do whatever you want me to do. I'll be whoever you want me to be. Please, just one. What can it hurt?'

I gently peel her fingers off my arm and pull away, get to my feet. 'I'm afraid it's over, Alexa. That's not going to change. So please accept that.'

'I don't. I don't accept that.'

I start for the door.

'I gave you everything!' she cries. 'I gave you every part of me. I opened myself up to you in every way because I *trusted* you.'

'I'm . . . I'm sorry how this turned out,' I say. 'You deserve better.

But it's over and it's not going to change. You need to understand that.'

She breaks eye contact, tears flowing freely, her jaw steeled.

I reach the door and open it.

'Shauna turned you, didn't she?' she says. 'She's been trying to break us up all along. She's staying with you right now, isn't she? She's being super-helpful about your "recovery," I'll bet. Yeah, I'll bet she is.'

'This has nothing to do with Shauna,' I say.

'That's bullshit.' She laughs with bitterness.

'Good-bye, Alexa. Please take care of yourself.'

Her eyes are suddenly ablaze with fury, her mouth tangled, her hands balled in fists. My stomach clenches up, stealing my breath. I turn away so she can't see me.

'This is not over,' she says. 'You think this is over?'

I catch my breath, squeeze my eyes shut. 'It's over, Alexa.'

'One phone call to the police hotline,' she says. 'That's all it would take.'

I pause, gritting my teeth, my abdominal muscles twisting into knots, my stomach in upheaval, black spots dancing before my eyes. I need to get home. I have to get home.

'Yup, that's all it would take,' I say before I pull open the door and leave.

87

Jason

I stagger through my door and collapse onto the cold tile of my town house foyer. My stomach unleashes its contents, but there aren't any contents, only bitter, sticky liquid in my mouth. I put my face down on the tile and try to catch my breath. The floor spins and jukes beneath me.

Something they don't tell you: The first days of withdrawal are not the hardest. It's the time after those first few days, when your mind and body are settling in on a new reality – that the fun candy isn't coming in like it used to – that the mind and body decide to tell you what they think of that decision.

Shauna comes rushing down the stairs. She came with me this morning to my house to help pack Alexa's clothes and toiletries, and we decided to stay at my place for the rest of the day. A change of scenery, mix things up, keep me out of a funk – amateur psychology, but we're doing the best we can.

'Take this,' she says, handing me a pill. I'm past seven hours now. I did a shit job of planning this thing. 'Don't chew it, Jason, no matter how much you want to.'

I do what she says. I swallow it and wash it down with water she gives me. It will work the way it's supposed to – slowly releasing pain suppression, albeit over a short time window – instead of the way I typically took it, crushing it between my teeth to get the entire impact all at once. Every time I've taken one of these over the last several days with Shauna's oversight, I've had to fight the instinct to bite down, to release all of the glorious love instantaneously. This process would probably be easier if I had the kind of OxyContin that is typically marketed these days, time-release pills that are crush-proof so addicts can't do exactly what I used to do and go for the instant home run. But someone would have to prescribe that for me, and nobody will, certainly not Dr Evans, whom I haven't seen in a month. So I'm left with the ones I purchased from Billy Braden, the crushable boys.

Shauna helps me up the stairs, which isn't easy given our size differential, but somehow I make it to the couch in my living room. I curl up on my side in the fetal position while she examines me. I am shivering and sweating. My head is screaming, the high-pitched whine that televisions make when they're doing a test: *This is a test, this is a test of the emergency broadcast system, this is only a test,* BRRRRRRRRRRRR—

'This is too hard for us alone,' she says. 'I was beginning to think we could do this. You were doing so well. But Jason, this is—'

'I'm not . . . not checking into a . . . not yet . . . not yet . . .'

She buries her face between my neck and shoulder. 'Keep fighting, Jase,' she whispers. 'Will you keep fighting?'

'I'll keep . . . fighting,' I say, as I lurch forward again, more dry-heaving. 'Shit, Shauna,' I say between halting breaths, 'how did I . . . ever let this . . . happen?'

'It happens to the best of people,' she says, wiping my wet hair off my face, stroking my cheek. 'It's poison. It ruins people. But it didn't ruin you, Jason. You stopped in time. You're going to break free of this. You have to believe that.'

'This isn't . . . this isn't going to end well . . . you know that . . .'

'It *is* going to end well, Jason. You're going to beat this.'

'No,' I say, squeezing my eyes shut, my hands clutching my stomach. 'I mean Alexa . . . Something bad's go – going to happen . . .'

359

88

Shauna

4:30 P.M.

Jason begins to stir, making wake-up noises on the couch, where he's been since he came home a few hours ago. Something really turned him sideways today. None of these days has been good, but these last few hours have been the worst by far. It's unnerving, to put it gently, seeing him like this. He was taking this on bravely, using exercise and activity to keep his mind off things, even extending his withdrawal interval from six hours to seven. It was bad, sure. He threw up and cramped up and couldn't sleep. It wasn't a picnic. But he had a game plan and he was sticking to it. He seemed to be succeeding. I was beginning to think I'd overplayed this whole recovery thing in my mind, that this was going to be easier than I thought.

I don't think that anymore. The hour that Jason endured when he first stumbled into the house was his worst hour, twenty times over, constantly retching and seizing up, sweating profusely and trembling at the same time. I almost dialed 911 for an ambulance, but he wouldn't let me, he said he was okay. After some amount of OxyContin infiltrated his system, he began to calm, but still not as much as I'd hoped. It wasn't until he fell asleep an hour ago that I felt safe even leaving his side on the couch.

He sits up now, moaning. I'm behind him, by the breakfast bar in his kitchen, looking at my laptop online at detox clinics. 'Hey,

360

sunshine,' I say, coming over to him, sitting next to him on the couch. 'Rough ride you had there.'

His hair is matted from sleep and sweat. 'Yeah, it wasn't too fun. I got too cute with the time intervals. I need—'

'You need to get professional help,' I interrupt. 'You need to quit trying to self-administer your recovery. I don't care about "James Drinker" or Alexa or anybody else. That will all sort itself out. I only care about one thing right now, and that's getting you clean. You need to go in now, Jason. Tomorrow. Let's do it the right way.'

'Okay.'

'I know how much you – What? Did you say . . . *okay*?'

'Okay,' he says. 'You're right. If I don't beat this, nothing else will matter. I'll check in somewhere tomorrow.'

'Oh, Jason.' I put my face against his. It's not like Jason to give in so easily on something like this. He must realize it now, too, the climb he's facing, how hard this really is.

'This thing is kicking my ass,' he says. 'I took way too much of this crap for way too long.'

A bit of color has returned to his face. Out of the woods, for the moment. Some awful moments, followed by some not-so-awful moments. That's what this is going to be like, I realize, this roller-coaster recovery.

'You want to eat?' I ask. The only thing he's been able to tolerate is peanut butter toast.

'No . . . not now.'

'You have to try.'

'Later. Don't make me eat right now.'

At five o'clock, his highness finally dines on peanut butter toast and a bottle of water. At five-thirty, he throws up. At six o'clock, he does push-ups to failure (that's how jocks talk about weight lifting, doing reps 'to failure'), which in this case is seventeen push-ups, not bad by most people's standards but low for Jason. At seven o'clock, it's time for another pill – back to six-hour intervals – and he forces himself to swallow it; at first I think the pill must be hard to swallow, but then I realize that's not it, that he's really fighting the urge to chew it up and get a surge of the good stuff all at once.

At eight o'clock, he's feeling pretty good. He has good color. His eyes are clear. He has enough energy for thirty-five push-ups.

At a quarter past eight – actually 8:16, to be precise – his telephone rings, the landline, a portable phone collecting dust on a rechargeable cradle in the corner of the room.

'Hey, my cell phone,' he says, patting his pockets as he stands up. 'Where's my cell? Oh, shit – I left it at Alexa's. I left my cell at Alexa's.' He walks over to the portable phone and checks the caller ID. 'Speak of the devil,' he says.

'Don't answer it. Or answer it, if you want to,' I quickly add.

He lets out a long sigh and picks up the phone. 'Hello? What? I can't under— Okay, slow down . . . slow down, *what*? Where— where are you? Where are you?' Jason goes quiet for a long time.

'Jason, what's going on?' I holler.

He puts a finger to his lips to shush me – right, he doesn't want Alexa to know I'm here with him, and there I go shouting to him.

Jason turns his back to me, resting a hand on the top of his head as he listens. 'What now? It's hard to hear you – we're talking over— go ahead. I said go— what? Say that— say that again.'

Jason's posture goes ramrod straight.

'I'm coming over,' he says. 'Sit tight. I'll be right over.'

'*What?*' I say, when Jason punches out the phone.

He turns to me. 'I have to go,' he says. 'I— I have to go.'

89

Jason

8:50 P.M.

I find a parking space on Wadsworth, a few houses down from Alexa's bungalow, and race up the steps to her door. I knock on the door and it falls open.

I step in. 'Alexa? Alexa.'

She is sitting in her living room, the lights off, the curtains pulled, the room dark, save for the illumination from the television, an old movie, *Doctor Zhivago*, I think, with the sound on mute.

'Are you okay?' I ask.

'Am I . . . okay. *Huh*,' she hiccups without humor. She is motionless, the dancing light from the TV playing shadows across her body, her face.

Something makes me stay where I am, halfway between the front door and the living room where Alexa is sitting, her back to the wall, facing me. The flickering light is messing with my vision, playing with her facial features, masking them, exaggerating them.

'Did you hurt yourself, Alexa?'

She doesn't answer at first. The smell of food – pizza? pizza – wafts past me. She doesn't even like piz—

'You have no idea what I'm capable of,' she says. 'You never did.'

'Tell me.' I raise my hands. 'Tell me what's going on. I couldn't even understand you on the phone. I thought you said that you were going to kill yourself.'

She makes a noise in her mouth, like a giggle, something fleeting.

'No, Jason, that's not what I said.'

She raises her hand, holding something, showing it to me in the dark.

'You left your iPhone here,' she says slowly, as if she's saying something of paramount significance. 'There's a voice mail you should hear from this afternoon.'

She lowers her hand and plays with my phone. A moment later, blaring out from the speakerphone is Joel Lightner's voice:

'Get ready to be happy, sport. I found him. I found our fucking guy! We were looking for cons recently released from a state penitentiary. This guy came out of a federal facility in January. You got him to confess to a gun charge, like, eight years ago, but you handed him over to the feds and they prosecuted him. We were looking in the wrong damn place! His name is Marshall Rivers. He's got a history of violence against women and, since he got out, he's been working at a dry cleaner's two doors down from Higgins Auto Body! He probably saw James Drinker every day! Anyway, Marshall Rivers, does that ring—'

The recording stops abruptly, mid-sentence. I steady myself with a hand to the wall, squeeze my eyes shut, lower my head, then slowly raise it. *Marshall Rivers.* Marshall—

Okay.

I remember him. I remember Marshall Rivers.

I remember a bad guy. Pure evil.

I remember a scared witness, a young woman.

I remember what I did to him.

And when he got out, he came back to pay me his respects. He came to my office in disguise, assumed a different name, and watched me sit helplessly while he carved up five women on the north side of the city.

Marshall Rivers is 'James Drinker.' Marshall Rivers is the North Side Slasher.

'Finally,' I mumble. Then I look at Alexa, remembering the truncated nature of the voice mail. 'Did you pause the message or did it just stop there?' I ask. 'Is there more?'

From her dark corner, Alexa stands slowly and inches toward me, crossing the line of the television light, blocking it out, leaving us in darkness, her features changing with each step—

– the face of a ghost, a haunted figure, piercing eyes, a wry grin, a scowl, terror and rage and panic and fear—

'There's more,' she says to me. 'There's a lot more.'

EIGHT YEARS AGO

90

Jason Kolarich
Assistant County Attorney

The shower water scalded his skin, the way he liked it. The heat would stay on him for hours, keep him refreshed. It was little things like that – small meals, lots of coffee, catnaps when you could get them, and hot showers – that kept him on his game.

Whoever it was who decided to put Felony Review prosecutors on seventy-two-hour shifts had a sadistic streak. He had until tomorrow morning at ten before his shift ended and he could really sleep – unless, of course, he caught a case and had to see that one through post-shift.

He dried off, dressed in the same underwear and the same clothes, knotted his tie and finger-combed his hair. The door in the police locker room popped open, and cool air hit his skin.

'Counselor, we need you.'

'Coming, dear,' said Assistant County Attorney Jason Kolarich.

He was upstairs five minutes later, his shirt still wet from beads of water, his brain foggy. He walked into the detective squad room's small kitchen, which served as Kolarich's makeshift office. He put his hand out, and Officer Richard Nova dropped the report in it. Kolarich read it over quickly and then looked up at Nova, looking for any facial expression, finding none.

Kolarich read the report again. 'We have the gun.'

'Right.'

'And eyes.'

'Right.'

'Whose eyes? Yours?' Kolarich looked up at Nova. Richie Nova was stocky and fit, young and sometimes too eager, but one of the by-the-book guys, one of the good ones. Most cops were good ones. Some of them were not. It made a difference to Kolarich.

'Mine *and* Gina's. Happened right in front of us, the gun toss.'

Kolarich flipped past the officer's report to the suspect's priors. Something similar in the past, five years ago – an aggravated assault pleaded down to simple; he'd accosted a woman with a firearm. With the plea, he avoided prison. Six months later, he was arrested for the rape of a teenage girl in an alley off Marquette; the witness had a change of heart and he was released when she refused to testify. In another six months, a gun charge and possession of cocaine that got him three years, give or take. He'd been out just about a year, and now he was back to his first crime, abducting women at gunpoint.

That made three women, including this one tonight, that he'd attacked.

'Marshall Rivers,' said Kolarich. 'He sounds like an aristocrat.'

'He's no aristocrat, this one.'

'Okay. Where's the witness?'

'She's in Two,' said Nova.

Kolarich grabbed a notepad, stuck a Bic pen in his front shirt pocket. In Interview Room Two, a young woman was standing over a small wooden crib, where an infant slept with blankets wrapped tightly over her. Kolarich didn't know where the crib had come from, but they must have kept it around for situations just like this.

It was almost ten o'clock at night. The attack had happened around six, as dusk had settled over the city in early spring.

The woman, the mother, was really just a girl, all of eighteen years, with dark, kinky hair pulled back with a rubber band, a thin face, and large brown eyes. She was wearing a pink cotton long-sleeved shirt and jean shorts, denim cut off a respectable length down her thigh.

Kolarich trod lightly, lifting the wooden chair off the hardwood floor to avoid scraping. 'Miss Flores?' he said.

'Yes,' she said with some effort, a hint of *j* on top of the *y*. English was not her first language. It might not be her language at all. She sat in the chair opposite Kolarich and laced her hands together, as if in prayer.

'*Hablas inglés?*'

'*Un poquito,*' she answered with apology. 'Lee-tle.'

'*Bueno.*' Where the hell was Witness Services? Why didn't Nova bring up a translator? Gina Alvarez, Nova's partner, spoke Spanish, but he needed the official translator. It was a union thing. Pass over the certified translator and someone would file a grievance. It took another half hour before Lisa from WitServ showed up.

'Tell her I'm a prosecutor, and would she please tell me what happened?' said Kolarich, which Lisa translated to Caridad Flores.

She felt more at ease with the translator in the room. The story came out in short bites, because each sentence had to be translated, even when Kolarich thought he understood it, so it had an odd quality to it, not simply a freewheeling, natural conversation. Caridad Flores spoke in a soft, restrained voice, fear shaking her words. Fear from what happened, Kolarich thought, or maybe fear of him, of law enforcement.

She was walking on the sidewalk on the 7100 block of South Briar Way with her baby in one of those travel pouches you wear over your shoulders and drop your baby in, so the baby's back is against your chest, facing forward, that kind of thing. A nice walk in the fresh air before she put her baby daughter, Gracelia, down for a nap.

But then a car pulled up to the curb. A man got out. He had a gun. He blocked her forward progress and motioned toward the car. She may not have spoken English, but a gun to your infant's head requires no translation.

Then she did something that the offender probably didn't expect. She did something smart. She realized that if she got into that car, she and her baby would never get out.

So she ran. And she flagged down a patrol car, around the corner and a block away.

Kolarich knew the rest from the police report. Patrol Officers Nova and Alvarez did a drive-around, found the vehicle that fit the description and the partial plate, and lit their overheads. The offender sped forward. Two blocks into the chase, a gun flew out the driver's side window and bounced against the curb. Nova jumped out of the car and retrieved it while the driver, Officer Alvarez, continued the chase and cut off the offender with the help of a second patrol unit two blocks farther down. Marshall Rivers was taken into custody without incident. A search of his person and vehicle revealed a crowbar, switchblade, and rope.

Caridad had described the man who confronted her as muscular, bald with a goatee, a white T-shirt, and a tattoo on his right forearm of a knife and snake.

'Okay,' he said. He nodded to Lisa. 'Explain the lineup to her.'

Officer Nova and the detective assigned to the case, Lou Carnellis, had been putting together a lineup for identification. They used Interview Room One to do it, because it was the only room with the one-way mirror and observation booth.

Kolarich stood with Nova and Carnellis on the opposite side of the plate glass. 'He hasn't requested counsel?' he asked Carnellis.

'Nope.' Carnellis had lost most of his hair and sucked on lollipops ever since he quit smoking, so most people called him Kojak or Telly, the name of the actor who played the TV cop. Kolarich called him Carnellis. Kolarich was friendly with the police officers, but didn't want to get *too* friendly. He wasn't their pal. Sometimes he had to be the heavy. Easier to do that if you aren't drinking buddies.

Five men entered the room, each of them holding a card with a number. Kolarich knew that two of them had come from county lockup, and two worked here in the station but had dressed down to civilian clothes. And the man holding the placard that said 2 was Marshall Rivers. Rivers was muscular and bald, with a thick goatee that emphasized his scowl. Kolarich would have identified him even if he hadn't known already. The guy was bad. Those eyes, something menacing just radiating off him, like he'd never known good, he only had one direction and it was through you. A shudder crossed Kolarich's shoulders.

The lineup wasn't bad. Two others were completely bald and two had receding hairlines. All of them were stocky enough. One of them, a weight-lifting rookie officer, was bigger than Rivers, the rest of them comparable but probably not as big as the suspect. Three of them had facial hair, and two did not. The key was to make sure that Rivers wasn't the *only* anything – not the only big guy, not the only bald guy, not the only goatee. He had to fall somewhere in the middle, or the lineup wouldn't hold. It was like a game of Goldilocks.

Rivers, he noticed, had his arms behind his back. He was covering up the tattoo on his right forearm, which Caridad Flores had described.

'Tell everyone to put their hands behind their backs,' said Kolarich.

Carnellis did so, operating a microphone on the console.

'We're good to go,' he said.

Caridad Flores came in with Officer Alvarez, Nova's partner, and Lisa the translator. Kolarich explained the drill to the witness, though she probably already knew it. When she turned toward the plate glass, her face tight with fear, a small gasp escaped her and she choked up. Kolarich smelled something, then heard the sound of tiny droplets, then saw it for himself: a small pool at the feet of Caridad Flores. She had wet herself.

'*Número dos,*' she whispered through her hand. She turned away, and Gina Alvarez put an arm around her.

'Now, arms at their sides,' Kolarich instructed. Carnellis gave the command, and Marshall's tattoo came into view. Caridad looked again and let out a large cry.

'*Número dos!*' she repeated.

Kolarich nodded. Officer Alvarez hustled her out of the room.

Caridad Flores was hovering over her baby when Kolarich returned to Interview Room Two with Lisa the translator. They all sat down.

'I'd like you to sign a written statement,' said Kolarich.

The witness listened to the translation, then said something back so quickly that it failed Kolarich's four years of Spanish at Bonaventure. She was upset, that was clear enough. Her eyes filled, and she pressed her hands against her chest.

'She wants to know if that's necessary,' said Lisa.

'Tell her yes.' Kolarich looked at Caridad Flores. '*Sí, por favor.*'

The witness and Lisa talked back and forth a moment in animated terms. Kolarich gave up trying to follow them.

'She says,' Lisa started, then let out a sigh. 'She said she may not be positive about everything that happened.'

Jason gave a grim smile. It was how he expressed frustration when it was inappropriate to throw something or shout an obscenity.

'Tell her that with his criminal record, he'll go away for a very long time,' he said, hoping it was true.

After another lengthy exchange, Lisa shook her head, while Caridad Flores stared at a wall, refusing to look at him.

'Ask her where she's from,' he said to Lisa.

She did. Kolarich heard the answer: Sixty-fifth and Roseland.

'That's not what I meant,' he said.

Lisa knew that. So did the witness.

'Ask her,' said Kolarich.

'Ask her what? I already did.'

'Lisa,' said Kolarich, scolding her. 'Ask her if she's here legally.'

He could have added a few things, like *I can keep her here all night and find out*, but he wanted to start with a light touch.

When the question was translated, Caridad Flores broke into a sob, then a number of *por favors* spilled out of her mouth.

Shit. She was undocumented. She wanted nothing to do with law enforcement. She wasn't going to sign a statement. It probably had something to do with a fear of Marshall Rivers, but her bigger fear was being deported.

'Okay,' said Kolarich. 'It's okay.' He patted the air. Caridad Flores looked at him, unsure of what was happening, what was going to happen.

Kolarich said, 'Give me a few minutes,' and left the room.

Kolarich quickly found Detective Carnellis. 'Put him in Three,' he said.

'Three? Why Three?'

Kolarich gave him a look. The question between them was obvious, as was the answer. Interview Room Three didn't have one-way glass. Nobody would be able to observe the interrogation.

'Put him in Three,' Kolarich repeated.

Kolarich found a phone at one of the detectives' desks. He balanced it between his ear and shoulder and fished the card out of his wallet.

Lisa the translator came up behind him. 'You're going to call Immigration on her?'

Kolarich dialed the phone.

'Jason,' she said. 'You're going to get this poor girl deported? Or locked up until trial? She has a *baby*.'

Kolarich looked at her. 'Tell me honestly, Lisa. You think there's a snowball's chance in hell that this woman will show up and testify against the offender?'

Lisa blinked twice. 'No,' she conceded.

'So without her, I have no case on the attack. She's all I've got, Lisa. She's it. So if she's unwilling to testify, I need another avenue. Just . . .' He waved at her. 'Tell Caridad it will all be fine.'

He finished dialing and the phone rang.

'*You* tell her,' Lisa spat. 'I'm not going to lie to her.' She stormed off.

'*Patrick Romer*,' the voice answered, in that crisp, federal-law-enforcement tone.

'Romie, it's Jason Kolarich.'

When his call was over, Kolarich went to Interview Room Three, where the suspect was sitting with his left hand cuffed to the metal table. Kolarich tended to trust his first vibe, which had been negative, but now he was seeing him up close, and he let it wash over him as he walked in and introduced himself to Marshall Rivers. Rivers was wearing a plain white T-shirt, torn and straining against his muscular upper body. His head was freshly shaved, and he wore a goatee. He had a bad complexion and eyes that screamed out at Kolarich. *Menacing* – that word stayed with him. This man was bad. Trouble. He wore a dull expression, but those predatory eyes gave him away. The kind of guy who could part a sidewalk of pedestrians just by walking in a straight line.

Three women, Kolarich thought to himself. The first one, the case was pleaded out; the second time, the woman was scared off.

He didn't want to miss the third time.

'You need anything, Marshall?' he asked. 'Take a piss, cup of water, cigarette?'

He hoped that Marshall smoked, or chewed tobacco, something that Kolarich would do, too, if so. It formed a bond, a small thing, but meaningful.

Rivers shook his head but didn't speak. A smirk played on his face. A tough guy. Not afraid of nothin'.

Kolarich eyed the tattoo on Marshall's forearm. It ran all the way from elbow to wrist, a bloodred dagger with a black snake curled around it, a multipronged tongue hissing out of the viper's mouth. His mother must be so proud.

'I was disappointed to learn you went to Annunzio for school,' said Kolarich. He pointed to himself. 'Bonaventure.'

Rivers watched him a moment, then showed his teeth. 'Bon-Bons, huh? Too bad for you.'

Rival south-side high schools. It was time to play south-side geography: Which parish did you attend, which place did you go for kraut dogs, which bar was your favorite, Lucky Joe's or the Green Castle? It loosened Marshall's tongue. Gotta get that tongue loose first.

'You don't live near Annunzio anymore,' Kolarich noted.

'Nah. Not the same place no more. I like burgers more than tacos, know what I mean?'

'Tell me fuckin' about it.' Kolarich rolled his eyes and spoke out of the side of his mouth. 'You been by Leland Park anytime lately? I think English is the second language down there now.'

Rivers liked that. He liked that a lot. It seemed to Kolarich like the right way to break through with this guy. People who didn't amount to a whole lot, like Rivers, tended to blame other things for their troubles, principal among them the shifting demographics. There were lots of good, decent people on the city's south side, but it was just like any other neighborhood – there were plenty of assholes, too. Marshall Rivers was one of them.

And Kolarich was a chameleon. When his goal was to connect with a suspect – and it usually was – he could flip a switch inside himself. He had actually fallen pretty hard for a Mexican girl at Bonaventure, a sophomore named Tina who never gave him the time of day, but at this moment, Kolarich forgot all about her.

'Anyway.' Kolarich jabbed a thumb at the door. 'This *mexicana*? I'm sorry, this *Latina* girl, excuse me.' He shook his head. 'Seems like a nice girl, but I swear to God, she doesn't speak two words of English.' He chuckled. He put out his hands. 'Best I can understand her, she says you confronted her and tried to get her into a car. Is that true?'

Rivers froze up. 'Nah, man, that ain't what happened at all. That chick, she waves at me for directions, see, so I pull over the car, and then she asks me if I want a little sucky-sucky. I said no fuckin' thanks.'

Kolarich expelled a short breath, a small laugh, and covered his eyes with his hand in bemusement. It was about what he expected from Rivers, who'd had several hours to come up with that tale. *Yeah,* he thought to himself, *that's why an illegal immigrant would run to the cops, the last people in the world she ever wants to see. Because a potential john turned down her offer of a blow job while she was carrying her baby in a pouch.*

'That's about what I figured.' Kolarich put his hands flat on the table. 'For Christ's sake. Why am I not surprised?'

Rivers, still a bit wary but loosening up, showed his teeth again, a shark baring his fangs.

Kolarich threw up his arms as if agitated. 'You know what? Fuck this,' he said. 'I'm not going to screw up your life based on the word of some *chiquita* who probably doesn't have her green card and can't even bother to learn our language. I'm not going to do it. I don't care. I'm not. So forget that, Marshall. I'm not pursuing that.'

Rivers watched him, his eyes intense, cautiously appraising the prosecutor. 'You're serious?'

'Yeah, I'm serious. I'm not charging you on that.' Kolarich flicked his wrist, a straight line in the air. 'That's done.'

Rivers nodded, sitting back in his chair, still cautious but getting looser and looser by the minute. *This guy's all right,* he must have been thinking. 'I appreciate that, man.'

'The gun, though.' Kolarich knifed a hand onto the table. 'Coppers saw you toss the gun. That's not on the immigrant girl. That's got nothing to do with her.'

'I didn't toss no gun.'

Kolarich raised a hand. 'Here's *my* problem. I have to clear this case, right? This is a case, with a number assigned to it, that needs a resolution, or someone's going to be all over me asking why the fuck there's no "solve" next to it.'

Rivers didn't speak. Kolarich fell back against his chair, his eyes on the ceiling. Then he made a face, tilted his head back and forth, all like he was pondering how to get around this thing.

He came forward again, elbows on the table. 'Let me ask you, off the record. Not quoting you, nobody but you and me. It is your gun?'

'Nah, man. Not my gun.' Rivers closed his arms in on himself. He was tightening up, becoming defensive. Kolarich would lose him if he wasn't careful.

'Okay.' He clapped his hands together. 'This is going to turn into a case, then. Because I got two coppers who say you tossed it from the car.' He jabbed his thumb at the door. 'You get that? I can shit-can this part about the Mexican girl, because the coppers, they didn't see that with their own eyes. I'll tell them that I don't believe the girl, and that's that. But the gun? If I go out there and say, no, he denies it, they're going to insist that you be charged, because you're calling them *liars*. They can't have that. They can't have a file that says they lied. Know what I mean?'

He thought that Rivers could follow that. It all made sense.

'So then you go to trial, Marshall. You go to trial, and it's you against two decorated police officers.'

Rivers ran his tongue over the inside of his cheek. His foot tapped the floor like a drummer on too much caffeine.

'S'posin' it was my gun,' he said. 'Just . . . s'posin'.'

'Well.' Kolarich put out his hands. 'If you tell me it's your gun, if you put that in writing, I can agree not to charge you. The cops, they don't give a fuck about what happens to you after the arrest. They just want their arrest to be righteous. They don't want anyone saying they fucked up. So, yeah – you admit it was yours, and you agree to give up the gun – can you do that, surrender the gun?'

'Fuck.' Rivers flipped a hand. If it got him a pass, he'd hand that pistol over to God Himself.

'Okay, so nobody's calling the cops liars, I make the decision not to prosecute you, and we get another gun off the street.'

Rivers pointed at him, animated now, seeing real hope for the first time. 'And *you* put it in writing, too.'

Kolarich smiled. 'You're a smart man. Yeah, of course I will. In fact, I'll write it first, so you know I'm being straight.'

Kolarich slid the notepad over in front of him and removed the Bic pen from his pocket.

In exchange for the statement below, the county attorney's office agrees not to prosecute Marshall Rivers in state court for unlawful use of a weapon or for any other firearms charge and will transfer this matter in accordance with Operation Safe Streets. Mr Rivers acknowledges that he's been made aware of his rights pursuant to Miranda v. Arizona.

Kolarich signed his name below the words and drew a signature line for Marshall Rivers, too. 'There,' he said, sliding the notepad across to Rivers.

Rivers read it over, then looked up at Kolarich. 'What's that mean, a "transfer"?'

'It means I'm going to close the file,' said Kolarich. 'I "transfer" it from an "active" case to a "closed" case.'

Rivers looked down at the paper again. 'And what's this Oper—'

'Operation Safe Streets is our program for getting guns off the street. If you bring in a gun, we take it, no questions asked. That's why I can do this, Marshall. That's why I can give you a pass. Because you're giving up the gun.'

The best lies, in Kolarich's experience, had some truth interwoven. There had, truly, been programs like that in the past, sponsored by the city police department. Most people had heard of them, presumably Marshall included. *Bring in your gun, we'll take it off your hands, you walk away, no hassle.*

But it wasn't called Operation Safe Streets.

Rivers scratched at his face. 'Should I get a lawyer?'

'That's absolutely your right,' said Kolarich. 'Might not be a bad idea. You want a lawyer to look at it, no problem.' He checked his watch. 'Shit,' he said.

'What?'

Kolarich tapped his watch. There was a clock on the wall as well. 'This time of night, there isn't a public defender around. You can sleep in a cell downstairs and they'll have one for you, maybe, noon tomorrow. Another twelve, thirteen hours. It's absolutely your right,' he repeated. 'Plus . . . well . . .' Kolarich grimaced.

'What?'

'Well, the coppers again.' Kolarich leaned his head on a hand. 'Can I just say this? Cops are a pain in the ass.'

'What about 'em?'

Kolarich sighed. 'The two cops that pinched you, they have to stay here until this is closed. They'll have to stay here all night. I'm just worried that, if I make them wait, they're going to say to me, *Why not just charge Marshall so we can all go home?* For them, that's the easiest outcome. They just want me to sign off on a charge of unlawful use of a weapon so they can go home.' Kolarich sighed again. 'Which, I suppose, is the easier thing to do, now that I'm thinking—'

'No, no.' Rivers waved his hands. 'I wanna go home, too, right?'

Kolarich shrugged. 'Yeah, we all do. But you definitely have the right to a lawyer—'

'Nah, nah. I get what this says. I get it.'

Rivers picked up his pen and started writing. He signed it in both places, next to Kolarich's signature on the prefatory language and at the bottom after his written statement.

'Great,' said Kolarich after reading the statement. 'You'll be out of here in ten minutes, Marshall.' He extended a hand, and Rivers shook it.

'Appreciate that, man. Y'know, all of this.'

'No worries.'

Kolarich left the room with the piece of paper and walked into the squad room. Walking out of the kitchen was Steve Glockner, the assistant public defender assigned to the station house, holding a cup of coffee.

'Hey, Jason,' he said. 'What's up?'

'Not much. You?'

Glockner sighed. 'Busy night. Sometimes I wish some of these mutts wouldn't invoke.'

Glockner was prone to the occasional off-color remark about his clientele, but deep down he was a true believer in the Bill of Rights. Working inside this station house on a crazy multiple-day shift like Kolarich, but on the other side of the equation, he mainly wanted to make sure suspects didn't confess without speaking to him first. But first they had to invoke, they had to utter those magical words: *I want a lawyer.* Until then, a public defender had no role in the process.

Kolarich put a hand on his shoulder. 'The right to an attorney is inviolate,' he said. 'Sacred. Cherished.'

Glockner gestured absently toward the interrogation rooms. 'I heard someone came in on an attempted kidnapping?'

Kolarich made a face. 'Didn't pan out. Dropping that charge.'

Glockner put his face in the steam of the coffee. He was just as tired as Kolarich. 'Score one for the bad guys,' he said.

When Glockner left, Kolarich looked around the squad room and had no difficulty finding his man. He looked like a bank manager in his suit.

'Mr Kolarich?'

'Agent Drew?'

Special Agent Frank Drew was working the late-duty shift tonight for the FBI. He extended a hand to Kolarich. 'Romie says you're good people.'

Kolarich shook it. 'What did he *really* say?'

Drew laughed. 'He said he owes you.'

Patrick Romer was an assistant United States attorney who had worked with Kolarich on a joint state-federal drug operation last year. Kolarich had helped him beyond what was necessary, including helping a recalcitrant witness modify his attitude.

'This guy, Rivers, has one prior gun violation,' said Drew. 'We usually want more than that for Safe Streets.'

Operation Safe Streets was a program launched by the U.S. Attorney's Office that scooped eligible firearms cases from local law enforcement so that the cases could be prosecuted in federal court, where the penalties for repeat gun offenses could reach the double digits in years. Typically, they found offenders with multiple gun violations on their records and put them away for ten to fifteen years in federal prison.

'This is his third time using a gun,' said Kolarich. 'He pleaded down the first one, so he only shows one gun violation. But it's really two. Tonight is his third.'

'Only counts as two. You know that.'

'He's a bad guy, Agent Drew.'

'Still.'

'Still, what? He attacks women. He's evil, this guy. And anyway, is this your call?'

Drew smiled. 'You know it's not.'

'Romie authorized this,' said Kolarich. 'He said if I got a confession, he'd authorize it. Well, I got a confession.'

Gun-toss cases could be tricky, Patrick Romer had told Kolarich over the phone. It's one thing to find the gun on his person, another to find it on the street and say that you saw him toss it. *A gun toss and only one prior gun conviction?* he'd said. But Kolarich pushed the matter hard, and Romer finally got tired of listening to him. *Get me a confession,* Romer had said. *You get me a confession, and we'll prosecute.*

'Romie authorized it,' Drew agreed. 'I'm just saying, you won't get fifteen years for this. Maybe ten, more like six or seven if he pleads—'

'Yeah, and we prosecute him in state court, it'll be, like, two or three, probably. This guy attacks women, Agent Drew. This is his third victim. I'll take six years over two any day.'

Drew wagged the file in his hand. 'Speaking of women. What about this witness? Caridad . . . Flores?'

Kolarich shook his head. 'Dead end.'

'Dead end? Let me talk to her. She saw the gun.'

'No,' said Kolarich. 'The *cops* saw the gun.'

'It says in this report she saw the gun. It says he stuck it in her baby's face.'

'The report's wrong. She didn't.'

Drew didn't look satisfied.

'You have two cops that saw the gun toss, Agent. And now you have a signed statement. That's more than enough.'

'Where is Caridad Flores?' asked Agent Drew.

She was about twenty yards away from them.

'She's in the wind,' said Kolarich. 'She's worthless. Isn't really sure what she saw. You don't need her, anyway.'

Drew's lips bunched up. He read the statement and looked up at Kolarich. 'By any chance would you know the immigration status of Ms. Flores?'

'Didn't ask,' said Kolarich. 'But I'll tell you this, Agent Drew: If she's undocumented, then she was pretty damn brave to run to the cops, wasn't she? I'd call that heroic, wouldn't you?'

Agent Drew studied him, maintaining that poker face they teach at Quantico, before releasing a sigh. 'Fine,' he said. He removed a pair of handcuffs from his belt. 'So where's our guest of honor?'

'Better he hears it from me,' said Kolarich. 'Give me one minute, then come in.'

Kolarich unlocked the interview room and found Marshall Rivers with his elbows on the table, his feet tapping a beat. He used the key to unlock the handcuff that tied Rivers's wrist to the table.

'So I get to leave?' Marshall asked.

'You get to leave *here*. But you're not going home, Marshall. You're being taken into federal custody for unlawful possession of a weapon.'

Kolarich stood back. Marshall Rivers got to his feet and rubbed his unshackled wrist. 'What?'

'You're going to be prosecuted in federal court. You'll receive four or five times the sentence you would've gotten in state court. How does that sound?'

'You *lied* to me?' Marshall's chest rose and fell, the venomous hatred returning to his eyes. He lunged for Kolarich, his hands aiming for his throat. Kolarich brought his hands underneath Marshall's arms, divided them, and stood Rivers up with a double forearm shiver. Then he drove Rivers backward, feeling the crunch of his body against drywall, the clacking of his teeth, the air escaping Rivers like a cushion. Kolarich grabbed his shirt, propping him up.

'Now you know how it feels to pick on someone your own size,' Kolarich whispered, 'instead of a teenage girl.'

'I'll . . . remember this,' Rivers managed through gritted teeth. 'You don't know me.'

Kolarich flipped him around so Rivers's face was planted in the wall, twisting one arm behind his back. 'I know all I need to know,' he said. 'You're nobody to me, Marshall. You get that? You're a fucking stain on the bottom of my shoe. I'll forget you as soon as you're gone.'

That last part was probably true. There was little original about Marshall Rivers. There were plenty of guys like him, and there'd be more to come. And this little stunt Kolarich pulled, yes, was probably over the line, but he was planning on losing absolutely zero sleep over it.

The door to the interview room opened. 'Jesus!' Agent Drew shouted. He rushed over to the corner, where Kolarich had Marshall Rivers pinned to the wall. Drew cuffed him quickly and placed a hand between his shoulder blades. 'There's a protocol for a prisoner transfer,' he said to Kolarich. 'You're not supposed to uncuff him while I'm outside the room, for Christ's sake.'

'That's why I like this job,' Kolarich answered, straightening his tie. 'You learn something new every day.'

Kolarich left the room and walked back down the hall to the squad room. Marshall Rivers bellowed behind him, his protests slowly fading as he was escorted down the stairs and out to the FBI car waiting for him.

Lisa the translator caught up with Kolarich as he entered the squad room. 'What do I tell Caridad?' she asked.

'Tell her to go home and forget she ever met us. Tell her the bad guy's going away for a long time and we won't be needing her.'

He felt Lisa's hand on his shoulder. 'You're a good egg, Charlie Brown.'

'Counselor.' The lieutenant stuck his head out his office door and nodded at Kolarich. 'We have a double homicide in Cowan Park. Rosen will take you.'

Probably a gang shooting. It would consume the next twenty-four hours of his life, at a minimum. Kolarich rolled his neck, took a breath, and nodded.

'I'm on it,' he said.

PEOPLE VS. JASON KOLARICH
TRIAL, DAY 4
Thursday, December 12

91

Shauna

Judge Bialek denies my motion for a directed verdict after the close of the prosecution's case, refusing to throw out the charges against Jason for lack of evidence. She gave me more than my allotted fifteen minutes to argue the motion, which was charitable of her, because she was no more likely to toss this case than she was to sprout wings and fly out of the courtroom. After breaking the bad news to me, the judge summons the jury.

'Is the defense prepared to call its first witness?'

For the first time in the trial, Bradley John rises to address the court.

'The defense calls Jason Kolarich,' he says.

Everyone takes note of Bradley's sudden participation – the judge with a double blink of her eyes, Roger Ogren with a rifle-quick jerk of the head, the jurors with more casual looks of surprise, not having any firsthand investment in the case.

The biggest witness in the case, and the second-chair attorney, who has yet to speak before the jury, handling him? It was a mutual decision made between Jason and me. His idea, primarily, but I went along with it. A lawyer cannot knowingly suborn perjury, cannot question a witness on the stand if she knows he's lying. Bradley, on the other hand, does not know everything I know, and in fact does not know with any certainty, one way or the other, whether the testimony Jason is about to give will be the truth, the whole truth, and nothing but the truth.

But I'd be lying to myself if I said this was all about ethics. As artificial and staged and thoroughly rehearsed as this conversation he and Bradley are about to have may be, it is a conversation nonetheless. Jason doesn't want to have to answer these questions from me. He is afraid of how I will react. And maybe how he'll react, too.

Bradley organizes his notes while Jason takes the witness stand and is sworn in. After giving his name for the record, Bradley cuts to it.

'Jason,' he says, 'did you murder Alexa Himmel?'

'No, I did not.'

'Did you have anything to do with her murder?'

'No, I did not.'

Jason likes to say he is the son of a con artist, which is true, and he likes to say he can bullshit with the best of them, also true. But there is an earnestness to the way he answers these questions, no flash or sizzle, no overwrought emotional appeal, not even a puppy-dog face for the jury, that works. I think it works. I'm doing my best to retain a clinical perspective, a lawyer's objectivity, to view this through the eyes of the jury and not from my own memories.

'You watched segments of your interrogation with Detective Cromartie?'

'Yes, I did.'

'You heard the testimony about your handgun, the prints being wiped off?'

'Yes.'

'You heard the testimony about the e-mails Ms. Himmel sent you and the many phone calls she made to you in the days leading up to her death?'

'I heard it all. And I have to say, if all I knew about the case was the evidence the prosecution has shown the jury, I'd probably think I was guilty, too. But I'm not guilty. I didn't kill her.'

'Will you address this evidence with me today?'

'I've been waiting all week.'

'Do you know who *did* kill Ms. Himmel?'

'I believe I do, yes. I didn't, when the police questioned me, but I do now.'

Roger Ogren stiffens in his chair.

'Will you discuss that with me today, as well?'

'Yes, I will.'

The jury is at full attention. This is Jason's one chance. The evidence against him has been pretty solid. The jury has to be leaning toward conviction, if they aren't all the way in, hip-deep, by now.

Bradley peeks at his notes. 'Okay, then, let's get to it,' he says.

92

Shauna

Bradley John begins the substance of his direct examination with the videotaped interrogation, Jason's lies to Detective Cromartie about his relationship with Alexa.

'It was stupid of me to lie about that,' Jason says. 'But I was trying to protect her. It was – obviously, from everything we've seen here – a very difficult time for Alexa after our breakup. I would think she'd find it embarrassing, humiliating, really, for others to know how she behaved afterward. I felt like that was between Alexa and me, and nobody else needed to know. I felt bad enough about our breakup already and I thought I owed her some respect.'

'But Jason, this was a murder investigation.'

'I know. I understand. But I knew I didn't kill her, so I didn't see how the status of our relationship really mattered in terms of catching the killer. I mean, what I did was wrong, but I only did it out of respect for Alexa. I certainly wasn't covering *up* anything.'

'Jason, you worked as a prosecutor here in this county, did you not?'

'Over eight years,' he says. 'And then I've been in private practice for about three years.'

'In that time, on either side of the criminal justice system, have you seen occasions when phone records, like the ones we've seen in this case, were used by law enforcement to help solve crimes?'

'Of course. So many times, I've lost count.'

'And what about searching Internet servers for e-mail correspondence?'

'It's a routine part of investigations, especially more recently, as Internet usage and e-mail have skyrocketed.'

'Is there any reason why this case would be any different in that regard?'

'No, not at all. And I guess that's the point I'm trying to make. If I killed Alexa and was trying to cover it up, why would I lie about something that I *knew* the police would discover? Why would I say our relationship was just fine when I knew that she'd called me hundreds of times after the breakup, phone calls that I knew were on some provider's records ready to be subpoenaed? When I knew there were e-mails out there that showed that our relationship had ended, and ended badly? I mean, if I'm a diabolical killer who carried out this crime and tried to cover it up, I'm the dumbest diabolical criminal who ever lived.' Jason opens his hands. 'But I wasn't thinking of any of that, because I wasn't covering up any crime. I was just trying to show Alexa some respect.'

Good. That was almost verbatim how Bradley and Jason practiced it. I think it sounds reasonable, convincing. And if *I* find it convincing – knowing, as I do, that Jason had an ulterior motive for what he told Detective Cromartie in that interrogation – the jury might buy it, too.

Roger Ogren stands as Jason nears the end of his speech. 'Your Honor, I'm trying to be patient, but I have to object to this speech and move to strike. This has moved from a direct examination to a summation, a monologue.'

The judge nods. 'I'm going to overrule, Mr Ogren. I understand your point, but this is the defendant testifying.'

That's what Jason predicted the judge would say. Criminal defendants get more leeway when testifying in their own defense, with their liberty at stake and the Bill of Rights waving like the Stars and Stripes at its most magisterial.

'However, Mr John,' the judge adds, 'let's resume the Q-and-A, please.'

'Thank you, Your Honor.' Bradley comes from a school where you thank the judge for everything she says to you, even if she just called you an idiot and held you in contempt.

'Next, Jason, let's talk about one of your least favorite subjects: OxyContin.'

Jason smiles and grimaces at the same time. He takes the jury through the highlights, the knee surgery, the recuperation, ultimately the addiction. 'You don't admit it to yourself,' Jason says. 'It's happening right in front of your eyes, and a part of you knows it, but you make excuses to everyone around you and suddenly you're believing those same excuses.'

Bradley nods. 'Jason, did there come a time when you finally admitted the addiction to yourself?'

'Yes. It was the Friday before Alexa died.'

'Friday, July twenty-sixth.'

'Correct.'

'And how is it that you remember that date so clearly?'

'Because, for one thing, it was the day that Alexa and I broke up.'

'Can you explain how the one has anything to do with the other?'

Oh, does Roger Ogren want to object. He knows, I think, what Jason's going to say, and he doesn't want his victim getting trashed, an age-old tactic of the defense bar. But he's also built his entire case around this relationship, this catastrophic breakup, and if he jumps up and keeps the jury from hearing something directly germane to that topic, he looks like he's hiding something, like he's afraid of some fact. That's how I'd feel, at least, if it were me.

'I think, by the time it had reached that point, it was obvious to everyone close to me that I had a problem,' Jason says. 'I'd lost a lot of weight, I was losing focus, I was moody all the time, I was really a completely different person. I think it was obvious to Alexa, too. It *had* to be. But she made excuses for me as much as I was making them for myself. In rehab, they call that person an enabler. And if I was going to beat this addiction, I couldn't be with an enabler. I needed to break free of the drugs and break free of her. I needed people surrounding me who would say to me, *Don't take drugs*, not, *Here, honey, have some more.*'

'You're not blaming Alexa for your addiction?'

'God, no. The blame for my addiction falls on me and only me. All I'm saying is, I had to get out from under that spell. I had to win that fight or I'd lose my life. It really came down to that for me. It was going to kill me, sooner or later. And I needed people around me who would help me fight it. Alexa, for whatever reason, and she had a good heart deep down, but . . .' Jason shakes his head, like he's reliving a sad memory. 'She always told me it was okay to take the pills, it was okay to want to feel good. I needed someone yelling "Stop!" at the top of their lungs.'

Bradley allows for an appropriate pause before he moves on.

'In any event, Jason, you and Alexa did break up in the days preceding her death.'

'Yes, we did. The previous Friday.'

'Friday, July twenty-sixth?'

'I guess that's the date,' says Jason.

'I'd like to refer you to People's Eighteen, Jason.' Bradley references the chart on the screen, previously set up. 'This is a summary chart of Call Detail Records from that date, is that correct?'

'Yes,' he says. 'You can see that on the CDR for that Friday, the phone calls begin happening in earnest at 2:47 in the afternoon. You can work back from that time. I went to her house at some time around one or so, give or take. I told her our relationship had to end, that I was going to get clean, and I wasn't going to change my mind. She started calling me within the hour, and as you can see . . . she didn't stop.'

'Did these calls go into voice mail, Jason? Or did you answer them and speak with her?'

'Mostly voice mail. I talked to her a couple of times. Not on Friday, I don't think. But Saturday, I believe I answered one of the calls in the afternoon. I can't be sure of which one.'

Bradley references the Call Detail Records for that Saturday. Like

Friday, every call was less than a minute in duration, thus receiving the rounded-up 1 in the duration column.

'A short conversation, I take it? Less than a minute?'

'Very short,' Jason says. 'I don't know if you've ever had a bad breakup,' he says, ostensibly to Bradley but really to the jurors. 'Whether you're the one who breaks up or the one who got dumped, it's an awful thing. So . . . on the one hand, I had to be firm, I had to let her know that we wouldn't be getting back together. My life depended on that, I thought. But on the other hand, I'm human. I felt terrible about how things went with us. I knew she was hurting. So I just wanted to answer a call or two, not to give her false hope, but to let her know that I was sorry. Maybe give her a tiny pep talk, for lack of a better word. You know, "It will all work out, it will take some time but you'll be fine," that kind of thing.'

'I see,' says Bradley. 'Now, Jason, that Friday, and the next day, Saturday, and all of those days, what were *you* doing?'

'I was trying to wean myself off the painkillers,' he says. 'I was trying to quit. It was . . . it was hell, actually. It's physically painful, it's mentally tortuous – I vomited, I cramped up badly, my skin burned – but I was dealing with it.'

'And were you dealing with this alone, or did you have any help?'

'Alone,' Jason answers. His eyes remain fixed on Bradley, deliberately avoiding mine. This was the subject of a heated debate, to say the least, Jason wanting to remove me entirely from the equation, pretending that I wasn't with him during those initial days of his withdrawal, not wanting to risk the possibility that I might become a witness. *You can't be my lawyer and a witness,* he said to me, stating the obvious. *I need you as my lawyer.*

That was his stated reason, anyway. We both knew, I think, that his reasoning ran deeper. He didn't want to put me in the position to have to testify under oath. He didn't want to put me in a position where I would have to lie.

Or where I would tell the truth.

93

Shauna

'Jason,' says Bradley John, 'I'd like to talk about another exhibit the prosecution admitted into evidence.'

Bradley puts on the screen the e-mail that Alexa sent, with the attached letter to the Board of Attorney Discipline. 'Did you open and read this e-mail, Jason?'

'I did. Something like ten o'clock on Tuesday morning.'

'This is Tuesday, the thirtieth of July? The day Alexa died?'

'Correct,' Jason says.

Bradley puts the letter itself on the screen. 'Did you read the letter?'

'I did, yes.' That's already been established by the prosecution, anyway.

'What was your reaction, Jason?'

'More than anything, I was sad,' he answers. 'It was spiteful. It wasn't like Alexa to do something like that.'

Roger Ogren is maintaining appropriate courtroom demeanor, the stone face, but I see his lips twist up just a little. This is one of those times when you realize a trial is just a show, a performance, a competition, not the reflection of the truth it's supposed to be. Roger Ogren knows about Alexa's history, the doctor in Ohio and the restraining order. He fought like hell, successfully in the end, to keep any reference to it away from the jury. So the jury will never hear it. But Ogren himself, he knows all about it. And he knows we know, of course. And so Jason telling this jury that it 'wasn't like Alexa to do something like that' is, to the lawyers in the room, pure bullshit. An untrue statement taken from an artifice constructed by Roger Ogren and, ultimately, the judge, who agreed with his argument and kept Alexa's past off-limits.

It is the first time during Jason's testimony that Roger Ogren is certain that Jason is lying. And it has changed how he views him. Whether that will make a difference to us is anyone's guess.

'Beyond that,' Jason goes on, 'what she wrote was basically true. I'm not aware of any case I handled during that time period where a client of mine suffered as a result of my problem. But it's no doubt true that I had that problem.'

'What did you do, Jason, after reading that e-mail and the attachment?'

'I went to see Alexa,' he says.

Roger Ogren, in spite of himself, rifles to attention. This would be news to him.

'When did that happen?' asks Bradley.

'Not long after I read the e-mail,' Jason says. 'I packed up Alexa's clothes and toiletries, whatever belonged to Alexa that was in my house, and then I drove them over to her house. I needed to return those things, anyway. And I wanted to talk to her.'

'Did you? Talk to her, I mean?'

'Yes. I drove to her house. I brought in the suitcases. We sat in her living room and talked. I told her that she could send that letter if she wanted to, that it was basically true and that I wouldn't deny the charges.'

'What happened next?'

'She told me she'd never send that letter, that she'd never do anything to hurt me.'

'Objection, hearsay,' says Roger Ogren.

Bradley says to the judge, 'It's not offered for the truth of the matter asserted, Your Honor. Only to show the effect on Mr Kolarich's state of mind. This is all about motive, from the prosecution's standpoint. They want to paint this picture of a man threatened, and we are offering this to show that he didn't feel that way at all.'

'This is offered *precisely* for the truth of the matter asserted, made by someone who isn't here to contradict this so-called truth,' Ogren snaps back.

The judge holds up her hand. 'The objection is overruled.'

'Your Honor,' Ogren says, 'I'd request this testimony be held *in camera* first so we can address these hearsay problems before they are simply tossed out in open court—'

'What hearsay problem? That objection was overruled,' Bradley says, his competitive juices flowing. He'd be better off shutting up. When you're ahead, shut up. A young lawyer's mistake. Some of the best decisions an attorney makes are when she keeps her mouth closed.

'We're not hearing this testimony twice, Mr Ogren,' the judge says. 'And the two of you, I'm going to say this once: You do not talk over each other and you don't talk at all unless I indicate that I want to hear from you. Is that clear?'

'Yes, Your Honor,' says Ogren, defeated, and says Bradley, satisfied.

'Jason,' says Bradley, 'when Alexa told you she was never going to send that letter, and that she'd never do anything to hurt you, did you believe her?'

Borrowing a page from Ogren's playbook, earlier in the trial, repeating helpful testimony in the form of a question. Ogren can hardly object.

'Of course I did. I was surprised she even sent that e-mail in the first place. Like I said, it really wasn't like her to do something mean-spirited like that. So, I'm sorry – the answer to your question is, yes. I believed she would never send that letter to the disciplinary board.'

'And what happened next, Jason?'

He lets out a breath, a small courtroom victory accomplished. 'Then I went back home, and I continued my recovery. I remember Tuesday as being a rough day, but honestly they all were.'

'You were home all day?'

This is a question the police and prosecutors have wanted answered since July thirtieth, when they found Alexa Himmel's body. Where was Jason until sometime just after midnight, when he claims that he first returned home and found Alexa dead?

'No, I didn't stay home the whole day. I went to the beach later that day. Can't be sure when. Maybe – maybe mid-afternoon? It was a nice day. I sat on the beach and watched the waves. I did some power-walking, too. The adrenaline helped. It was kind of like a substitute for the drug.'

It's a bit unsettling how well Jason can lie. He never went to the beach that day. He was lying on the couch, alternating between suffering and sleep, the entire afternoon and evening. He couldn't even hold down the peanut butter toast I made him.

'You stayed at the beach for how long, Jason?'

'I can't be sure. Until it got dark.'

'Do you recall, during that time in late July, when it got dark?'

'Oh, around eight.'

Getting close to that 8:16 P.M. phone call to his house. The call from Alexa, that sent him scurrying over to her place. If he'd never answered the phone, if he'd refused her pleas, if he'd just stayed home with me—

'And I stayed there in the dark for a while, too,' Jason goes on. 'Sometimes that's the best time to be by the lake. So maybe eight-thirty, maybe nine. I mean, it could have been nine-thirty, too.'

'And then what did you do?'

'I drove around,' he says. 'All over, I guess. Everywhere and nowhere. I wasn't traveling to a destination.'

'That sounds . . . unusual,' Bradley says, faux confusion.

'Not if you consider why I was doing it,' he says. 'I wasn't going anywhere. I just needed time to pass. You have to understand, what you're doing when you're in withdrawal, when you get down to it, is simply killing time. Every minute you're clean is a victory, another minute closer to not needing pills anymore. They're horrible minutes, but necessary. So I was doing anything to distract myself, trying to ignore the cravings, trying to hold out. If watching a children's cartoon would pass the time effectively, I'd do it. If suspending myself upside down would help, I'd do that. All I was trying to do was get my body and my mind accustomed to not having OxyContin.'

'But the car?'

'Sure, the car. I never once took Oxy while in my car. I'd take it at home or in my office at work. That's where the maximum temptation was. I was better when I was places I didn't associate with the drug. Like the beach. Or driving, concentrating on the rules of the road and the speed limit and staying in my lane and playing music really loud and all of those things. The more I had to focus on that, the less I was focusing on Oxy.'

Good, I say to myself. *He handled that well.*

'When did you get home?' Bradley asks.

'It was sometime after midnight.'

'And what happened when you got home?'

'When I got home,' Jason says, 'I went upstairs. And there was Alexa. Lying on my living room floor.'

94

Jason

'I don't remember exactly when I called the police,' I say in response to a question from Bradley. 'But it would have been very shortly after I found Alexa dead.'

Bradley takes a drink of water, maybe for dramatic effect, but I think because his nerves are giving him dry mouth. Funny, I never had that problem myself – my mind and body seem to function best in situations like this, under pressure – but it was a problem that plagued me through my addiction.

He's done a nice job with me. I'll have to remember to tell him so. If this thing goes south for me, he'll take it hard. Not as hard as Shauna, but hard.

'Jason, did you call 911 on your cell phone or on your landline?'

'Landline telephone,' I say.

'How is it that this detail sticks in your mind?'

'Because I remember the light was blinking on my machine. I had a voice mail. After I called 911, I sort of sat there, numb. And I pushed a button and listened to the voice mail.'

'Was this a voice mail from 8:16 that evening?'

'I don't remember. I mean, I didn't check the time. I just pressed the button to retrieve the message and I listened to it.'

Since I'm making up this entire business about the voice mail, it is tempting to say, *Yeah! I remember very clearly that the voice mail had come at 8:16 P.M., and the message was more than one minute but less than two!* But who remembers shit like that? So I don't want to overplay my hand here. If you're going to lie, lie about stuff that really matters, and play it safe on less important details, so it doesn't *look* like you're lying.

I am, after all, the son of a con artist.

'And what was the message?'

'It was from Alexa,' I say. 'It was a long message. She was talking about wanting to get back together, she was watching a love story on television about star-crossed lovers and she wondered if maybe there was a chance for us, and she was going to come by my house if that was okay.' I pinch the bridge of my nose and pause. Respectful silence. Pained silence. I look back up at Bradley and let out air. 'Obviously . . . she decided to come by.'

Bradley puts on the screen the Call Detail Records for that day, showing the 8:16 P.M. phone call with the number 2 in the column for duration.

'Was the voice mail more than one minute but less than two?'

'Oh, God.' I sigh. 'Bradley, the truth is, I have no idea how long it was. I mean, I had just found Alexa . . .' I swallow hard and pause, summoning emotion. I can't fake-cry. I hardly cry for real, so the concept of faking it is foreign to me. But I bring my fist to my mouth and bow my head and pause.

'I'd just found Alexa . . . lying there,' I go on, 'and now I'm hearing her voice on the phone. It was . . . I mean, it was crazy, it was . . . like a dream or something.' I take a long, hard breath. 'If you told me it was ninety seconds, I'd believe you. If you told me it was ninety *minutes*, I might believe you, to be honest.'

'And did you keep that message on the phone, Jason?'

'I wish I had,' I say.

'But you didn't?'

Everyone knows I didn't. The police checked my voice mail and it was empty. My phone company has no retention policy on voice mails. If the user deletes the voice mail, it's gone with the wind. They don't even know if I *had* a voice mail at 8:16 that evening. All the phone company knows is that something – my voice mail or a human being – answered Alexa's call, initiated the connection with her cell phone, at 8:16 P.M.

'Bradley – sorry, Mr John,' I say, 'I honestly don't remember deleting that phone message, but I'm sure I did. It's like – I do it by rote. I hear a message on my home phone and then I delete it. It's automatic for me.'

It's automatic for most people, which is why, again, I'm not over-playing my hand here and claiming that I specifically recall pressing 7 and erasing her message. My ex-girlfriend is dead, I've just called 911, but I remember deleting a *voice mail*?

It's little things that separate good lies from bad. Maybe I should teach a class, or write a how-to manual. *Lessons from My Father.*

'Jason, let's talk about whether Alexa had a key to your house. Do you recall portions of the videotaped police interview where that subject was discussed?'

'I do.'

We're going here next because Shauna considers this subject a low point for us. She decided it was best to sandwich this topic between more favorable matters.

'*Did* Alexa Himmel have a key to your house?'

'Yes, she did. Of course she did. Until we broke up, she practically lived with me.'

'The testimony we've heard,' says Bradley, 'is that the police could find no such key on Alexa or anywhere else in your house.'

'I heard that, too. I don't know what to tell you. I really don't. I never got the key back from her. She still had it.'

'Did she typically keep it on her key chain?'

'Oh, boy.' I blow out air. 'I really can't say for sure whether she had it on her regular key chain or separate. I'm sorry. I really don't know. Whenever we were together, I'd open the door. It was only when she was there by herself that she'd have to use the key. So I'm not sure I ever even saw where she kept the key or what she put it on.'

That sounds pretty good, I think. Better to do what I just

did – throw up your hands, chalk it up to one of those things that probably has an obvious explanation, but you can't think of it – than to have some elaborate explanation that checks every box. Again, if I'm a devious liar, why wouldn't I come up with some carefully crafted explanation?

'Now, Jason, I'd like to turn to our final subject,' says Bradley. 'I'd like to talk about this person you mentioned to Detective Cromartie as the possible killer. I'd like to talk about the person you called Jim.'

95

Jason

'I'm going to replay a small portion of the police interview, Jason.'

Bradley hits 'Play' on the computer. The projection screen comes alive. The jury gets to hear this snippet of the interview for a second time:

'You told me back at your house that you have a pretty good idea who killed Alexa,' Cromartie says. *'Can you help me out with that? Who killed her, Jason?'*

I don't answer at first. Several seconds pass. I shake my head and wave a hand. *'His name is Jim.'*

'Last name?' Cromartie asks.

'Just Jim,' I say.

'Well . . . what can you tell me about Jim?'

The way Cromartie says *Jim,* it's like he's dealing with a little kid who is obviously lying.

'He . . . he has red hair,' I say. *'He's big, muscular. He wears glasses. He has a paunch, like, a gut.'*

Bradley stops the recording. 'Jason, who did you mean by "Jim"?'

'He was someone who came to my office. It would have been very early this summer. I want to say the first full week of June.'

'What was his name?'

'He gave the name James Drinker. He said his name was James Drinker, that he worked at Higgins Auto Body here in the city, and that he lived in an apartment building at the intersection of Townsend and Kensington in Old Power's Park.'

Roger Ogren and Katie O'Connor are scribbling feverishly, trying to keep up.

'Can you describe this individual from a physical standpoint?'

'He was a very odd-looking person. He had long, kind of curly red hair. Thick black glasses. He was very muscular, like a weight lifter. And he had a big protruding stomach, a beer gut, I guess. Just like I told Detective Cromartie.'

'What did you two discuss?'

'I can't answer that,' I say. 'When a client comes in and tells me something, I'm sworn to confidentiality under the attorney-client privilege.'

'What if you, as an attorney, think this client is kind of shady? Up to no good?'

'That makes no difference. The privilege sticks.'

'What if it turns out he's lying to you about his true identity?'

I shake my head. 'It doesn't matter. If the attorney-client privilege were broken every time a client lied to his lawyer, very few clients would have the privilege. Plenty of clients have lied to me over the years, Bradley, on big things and small things. It doesn't eviscerate the privilege.'

'Does the privilege always apply, no matter what?'

'Basically, yes. The only exception is if the client tells me – I mean, literally *tells* me – that he or she is going to commit a crime. If I hear them say that, I have a duty to report them.'

'Did that happen here?'

'No, it did not. I may have had my suspicions – well, I *did* have my suspicions. I can't give you the details of what we discussed, but he never said he was a killer, much less that he was planning to kill again. So I had to keep it all confidential.'

'Let me jump forward in the police interview, Jason.'

Bradley, who knows computers better than I ever will, dials up the next passage, skipping a handful of questions.

'*Did this . . . Jim tell you that he was going to hurt Alexa?*' Cromartie asks. '*Or you?*'

I shake my head. *'Not in so many words. I wish he had. If he had, maybe I could have done something.'*

'I don't understand what that means,' Cromartie says.

Stop tape.

'Detective Cromartie said he didn't understand what you meant by that, Jason. Can you tell us what you meant?'

'Well, it's just what I explained. He was my client, for the purposes of the privilege, the moment he entered my office. If this individual had told me that he was going to hurt Alexa, or me, or anyone else, for that matter, I could have done something. I could have reported him. That's why I said, "I wish he had" told me that. I didn't know he was going to hurt Alexa. It never occurred to me.'

'Objection,' says Ogren. 'We're assuming facts not in evidence, and there's no foundation for that statement. There's absolutely no evidence in the record that this unknown man of mystery did anything at all to Alexa Himmel.'

'I'll sustain that objection,' says the judge, 'but let's limit the speeches, Mr Ogren.' The judge has the court reporter read back my answer and strikes the last two sentences.

'Well, Jason, regardless of what this man calling himself James Drinker may have done, did he ever give you any indication that he was going to hurt Alexa?'

'No, he didn't.'

'Very good. This man, "James Drinker." Did you confirm that there was, in fact, a man named James Drinker who worked at Higgins Auto Body and who lived at 3611 West Townsend, here in the city?'

'I did confirm that, yes. So I assumed he was on the up-and-up.'

'How many times did you speak with this man?'

'Twice at my office, in early June.'

'Any other time?'

'Well, in a manner of speaking, yes.'

'Explain that.'

'In very late June, let's say that . . . well, a crime had been committed that concerned me. By that, I mean, I was concerned that my client had committed that crime. And I wanted to discuss it with him.'

'Did you call him?'

'I *couldn't* call him. He left no home phone and no cell phone. On rare occasions, I would speak with him by phone, but it was always him calling me, and it was always on one of those disposable phones you buy at the convenience store with a blocked phone number. So I had no way of calling him.'

'So what did you do?'

'I went to his house. I believe it was a Saturday. The last Saturday in June. His apartment at 3611 West Townsend, in Old Power's Park. I think his apartment number was 406.'

'Did James Drinker answer the door?'

'Yes, he did.'

'Describe his appearance.'

'The same general characteristics. Long curly red hair, big muscles, black glasses, a big gut. Still funny-looking. But it wasn't the same person.'

'Can you explain that?'

'The person living at that apartment, James Drinker, had all the same general features as the man who came to my office. But it was clearly a different person. Different eyes, without the glasses on. Different nose. Different voice. I apologized to the guy and I left.'

'So, Jason. What did this mean?'

'The man who came to my office gave me a bogus name and wore a disguise.'

Roger Ogren actually chuckles a bit, then raises his hand in apology.

'That's okay, I thought it was crazy, too,' I say. 'Why would a client come to you, for a confidential discussion, and wear a disguise and give a fake name?'

'And did you come to discover an answer to that question?' Bradley asks me.

'Yes,' I say. 'Because he was afraid I would recognize him. And because he wanted to mess with me.'

'Objection,' says Roger Ogren. 'Foundation.'

'Sustained.'

'Okay, you need to explain that,' Bradley says, as if he's just as curious as the jury, and the prosecution, and my brother, Pete, sitting in the gallery, must be. 'Did you come to learn this person's true identity?'

'I did. This person's name was Marshall Rivers.'

Roger Ogren looks like he's about to drop his pen.

Annnnd *there*, he drops it.

'And who was Marshall Rivers to you?'

'About eight, nine years ago, when I was a prosecutor, I took a confession from Marshall Rivers on a gun charge. Possession of a firearm. We were also looking at him for trying to forcibly abduct a woman and her child.'

'And you said you took his confession?'

'Yes, I was the prosecutor assigned to the police station where he was brought in after his arrest.'

I begin to provide the details from that night, as best as I can remember them. I recall the big picture, but not the small details. The whole thing doesn't particularly stand out in my mind, because I dealt with dangerous criminals like him every day, and because the mind games I used on Marshall were the kinds of methods I employed on a daily basis during Felony Review.

Before I get too far, Roger Ogren objects and asks for a sidebar with the judge. I'm not privy to the conversation between the judge and the lawyers in the far corner of the courtroom, but I know Bradley is arguing that the details of my interrogation of Marshall Rivers are very relevant.

The judge overrules the objection. Bradley walks me through that entire sequence of events. I wish I didn't have to emphasize what I did to Marshall, because it shows the jury a side of me that is less than forthcoming, even devious. But the details show why Marshall was pissed off at me. It shows his motive to do what he did to those women and, in his mind, to me.

'Ultimately, Marshall got around six years in federal prison, because he was a repeat offender,' I say. 'He ended up getting into some trouble while in prison and received additional time. But the initial six years, they came from the confession we took. From the confession I took.'

'And when did he leave prison, if you know?'

'He left in January of this year. He moved back to the city. And according to the police, he was responsible for the murder of five women in this city this past summer.'

'The murder of five women?' Bradley asks.

'That's right,' I say. 'Marshall Rivers was the man the media has called the North Side Slasher.'

96

Shauna

Some of the spectators didn't immediately place the name Marshall Rivers, but all of them have heard of the North Side Slasher. The judge gavels loudly, but it takes her a couple of times to establish order. These are small courtrooms, and when it gets loud, it gets loud. The criminal courts, I've come to learn, are a lot rowdier than the civil courtrooms where I typically roam.

The north side murders were officially 'solved' – if that's the right word – one week after Alexa was killed. I remember seeing the Wednesday, August 7, edition of the *Herald* in a grocery store, the headline 'We Got Our Guy' above a photograph of the mayor, the police superintendent, and several police detectives gathered at a news conference. Word had leaked over the previous weekend that the police believed they had broken the case, but it wasn't until the following week that the rumors were made official.

'He was your client, Jason?' asks Bradley John.

Jason lets out a chuckle of bemusement. 'Yes. I mean, under an assumed name, and wearing a disguise. He never told me he was going to kill anybody, nor did he outright admit he *had* killed anybody. And he never gave me his real name or showed me his real face.'

Technically, explaining what a client *didn't* tell you isn't a breach of the attorney-client privilege. But Jason's getting in the vicinity of being too cute.

'So yes, he was my client, but he was also a mystery to me. I think

412

he blamed me for his time inside and he wanted me to know that he was killing people, and there was nothing I could do about it, because of the privilege. He wanted to torture me. And it worked.'

'Jason, are you certain that the man who came to your office was Marshall Rivers, wearing a disguise?'

'I am,' says Jason. 'I've seen many photos of him in the newspaper since he was found dead. Put a red wig on him and one of those fake fat suits for a belly and it works.'

Roger Ogren is not having a good half hour. He would have the typical anxiety of any prosecutor when the defendant takes the stand, having no idea what he'll say and expecting to have to audible a cross-examination. Roger's done that many times. And I assume he would regard Jason, his former colleague, as something other than your ordinary defendant, so he knew this might be a rough one for him. But surely he didn't expect this.

He probably assumes we have a lot more evidence to put in, more witnesses to call, additional facts to bolster our theory. So this final question-and-answer may be a pleasant surprise to him.

'Jason,' Bradley asks, 'do you know for a fact that Marshall Rivers killed Alexa Himmel?'

'No,' he answers. 'I would have no way of knowing for certain. I was arrested only hours after Alexa was murdered, and I've been locked up since then.'

Bradley John looks over at Roger Ogren, then at the judge.

'No further questions,' he says.

97

Shauna

'So when did you discover all this information about Marshall Rivers?' Roger Ogren says to me as we head into chambers after the completion of Jason's direct examination. 'Before the arraignment? Before the prelim? Six goddamn months ago?'

'Children, children.' Judge Bialek makes a calming gesture with her hands.

'Mr Ogren's upset, Your Honor,' I tell her. 'His case is falling apart.'

The judge, already out of the black robe she detests, looks over her glasses at me with disapproval. And maybe disagreement, too. There was some sizzle this afternoon with the cameo appearance of the North Side Slasher, but no steak: At the end of the day, we have put on no concrete proof that Marshall Rivers played the part of James Drinker in Jason's office, and we have absolutely no proof whatsoever that Marshall Rivers killed Alexa Himmel.

'Mr Ogren,' she says, taking a seat and folding her hands. 'I think the answer is probably that the defense *did* have this information long ago, but Ms. Tasker wanted to surprise you with it. She didn't want you to have time with it, to play with it, to investigate it, to refute it. She wanted to spring it on you so you'd be caught flat-footed in the middle of trial without any time to respond.'

'I think you're absolutely right, Judge,' Ogren agrees.

'The problem for you, as you well know, is that she's perfectly entitled to do that very thing. She hasn't violated any discovery rule that I'm aware of. She's not trying to introduce a piece of evidence that she didn't disclose. And there's no affirmative defense for *Someone else killed her, not me,* so she didn't have to disclose that, either. And I'm going to guess that there's a reason that Ms. Tasker put the entire roster of Area Three detectives on her witness list. I'm going to guess that Area Three handled both Ms. Himmel's case and the north side murders?'

'Indeed, they did,' I say, without a smirk.

'Mr Ogren, I think you've had your pocket picked fair and square.'

He shakes his head, bemused. 'I need a continuance, Judge.'

'Well, I'm not going to give you one. I have Mr Kolarich's cross-examination scheduled for completion tomorrow.'

'I need more time.' Ogren's tone is defiant, not pleading. 'In the interests of justice, I need more time.'

The judge pauses, purses her lips, thinks about it. 'Ms. Tasker, who else are you planning on calling?'

'Our next witness will be Detective Vance Austin, the lead investigator on the north side murders.'

The judge nods. 'Is that all?'

'It depends on what he knows, Judge. But that's my current plan.'

'All right. Good enough. Mr Ogren, when the defense rests, which could be . . . Monday or Tuesday?' She looks at me for confirmation; I shrug. 'Whenever that happens, I'll hear any request you may have on a continuance before you put on your rebuttal case. But Mr Ogren, hear me and hear me well: Don't be optimistic. I would strongly advise you to put your Area Three detectives to good use between now and Monday.'

'I understand, Judge.'

'Cross-examination tomorrow morning at nine,' the judge says. 'That's all.'

PEOPLE VS. JASON KOLARICH
TRIAL, DAY 5
Friday, December 13

98

Jason

Roger Ogren didn't get a lot of sleep, but he appears eager nonetheless as he looks me over before he begins his cross-examination. Maybe it's the packed room. The trial has typically been well attended, but now it's standing room only, people lining the walls, talk of a second room being set up to accommodate the overflow. My mention of Marshall Rivers yesterday has turned the media into a pack of howling canines – with all necessary apologies to howling canines.

'Good morning, Mr Kolarich.'

'Mr Ogren.'

'Very exciting testimony yesterday,' he says. 'The North Side Slasher.' He makes a *wow* gesture with his hands, a look of wonderment. He pulls it off better than I might have expected. Roger's kind of a fuddy-duddy, but he's pissed off, and the electricity animates him. It doesn't bode well for me that he's got some game today.

'So let's just be clear up front. You can't say for a fact that Marshall Rivers killed Alexa Himmel, can you?'

'For a fact? No. I wasn't there when it happened.'

'You can't place Marshall Rivers at the scene of the murder, at the time of the murder, can you, Mr Kolarich?'

'I can't say one way or another where he was, no.'

'The murders attributed to Marshall Rivers on the north side this summer – those were stabbings, were they not? Multiple stab wounds on each victim?'

'That's my understanding, yes.'

'Alexa Himmel wasn't stabbed, was she?'

'No.'

'She was shot just below the neck.'

'That's correct.'

'You can't even prove that Marshall Rivers ever set foot in your law office, can you?'

'Prove it? I'm saying it was him.'

'You're saying it was him . . . based on seeing his picture in a newspaper?'

'That's right.'

'Marshall Rivers didn't have red hair, did he?'

'No.'

'Marshall Rivers did not have a large, protruding stomach, did he?'

'I am not sure I know that answer, Mr Ogren. Most of the newspaper photos were head shots.'

'So you don't know if Marshall Rivers's midsection was . . . fat, pudgy, what have you. You don't know.'

'Correct, I don't know. But Marshall Rivers was very muscular in the chest and shoulders, just like the man who came to my office. That's the part you can't fake, Mr Ogren. You can put on a wig. You can give yourself a fake belly. But muscles in the chest and shoulders? You can't fake that.'

Ogren pauses a beat, frowns. He could object to my unsolicited statement, but he's going to have to deal with it sooner or later, so he lets it slide.

'You're describing for us the build of Marshall Rivers's chest and shoulders, as you observed them from a *head shot*. In a *newspaper photo*.'

'Best I could do, Mr Ogren. They weren't all head shots. Some were wider angles. And I also interrogated him, remember. I took his confession. He was very stocky then.'

'*Then* being over eight years ago, true?'

'True. Yes.'

'And the build of his upper body, you say, resembled that of the man who came to your office.'

'Correct.'

'And this man who came to your office – you haven't shown the jury any photographs of this person, have you?'

'Photographs? I'm a criminal defense lawyer, Mr Ogren. People come to me to share their secrets. Most clients wouldn't take too kindly to my snapping a photo of them when they walk in the door.'

Ogren's eyes narrow at my jab. A couple of the jurors find it slightly amusing, but this isn't the time to be glib. I need to watch myself.

'So when you say that Marshall Rivers's build resembled that of the man who came to your office – we only have your word for that.'

'I guess that's true, yes.'

I could give them Marie, who spent some time with my redheaded client and who could describe him as well as I could. But I'm not making Marie take the stand. I don't need to.

'Okay. Let's talk about your police interview.' Ogren reviews his notes on the podium. He uses them for guideposts, nothing more. 'You admit that you lied to Detective Cromartie in the police interview several times?'

'I did lie, yes.'

'You lied about the status of your relationship with Ms. Himmel.'

'Yes. As I said, I was trying to be—'

'Respectful of her,' Ogren finishes. 'Yes. Having been a prosecutor for eight or nine years, you understood the importance of getting accurate and complete information from witnesses, didn't you?'

'Yes, of course.'

'Witnesses who think they can decide for themselves what information is important and what information is not – they can really hinder an investigation, can't they?'

'Yes, that's true.'

'And you knew that back on July thirty-first, when you were giving your interview.'

'Yes, I knew that.'

'But you repeatedly lied, anyway.'

'I lied about my relationship with Alexa, yes.'

'When you were being interviewed by the police, you didn't say anything about a serial killer, did you?'

'What could I say, Mr Ogren? First of all, I didn't know for a fact he *was* a serial killer. And second, even if I did, I didn't know his name. I knew his fake name, but how was *that* going to help?'

'So instead, you gave *half* a fake name. You gave the name Jim, but no last name.'

'That's right. I sort of caught myself mid-sentence and just left it at "Jim."'

That, of course, was not an accident.

'Nothing was stopping you from saying "James Drinker" or "Jim Drinker," was there, Mr Kolarich?'

'Stopping me? I wasn't totally sure whether I could even give out his first name, given the privilege.'

'I see. That attorney-client privilege, that worked out pretty well for you, didn't it, Mr Kolarich? You could drop a name, or half a name, and then hide behind it, isn't that right?'

'Objection, argumentative,' says Bradley John.

'That's okay, I'll answer that,' I say. 'I'm willing to answer that, Judge.'

'Your Honor, I'll withdraw my objection,' Bradley says. 'I apologize.'

The judge isn't too thrilled with this whole exchange, but waves me on.

'There's nothing convenient for me about this attorney-client privilege. If it weren't for that privilege, Mr Ogren, I would have called the police the first time I met with this man who identified himself as James Drinker. I didn't have direct, concrete proof that he was a killer, but I certainly had my suspicions. And I would have been more than happy to tell Detective Cromartie all about him. But at the time of that police interview, I didn't know the name Marshall Rivers. All

I knew at that time was this guy came to my office twice, gave the name James Drinker, and it was a fake name. That's *all* I knew. I didn't know his true identity.'

I glance at Shauna, whose eyes break from mine. She suspects I'm lying, but doesn't know for certain. She doesn't know what happened when I went over to Alexa's house that evening after the 8:16 P.M. phone call to my house. She doesn't know that I heard Joel Lightner telling me, via voice mail, that Marshall Rivers was the north side killer.

She doesn't know what happened afterward, either.

'Then let's talk about Alexa Himmel,' Ogren says, moving away from a bad moment. He goes to the prosecution exhibit showing Alexa's letter to the Board of Attorney Discipline. 'You testified that you went to see Ms. Himmel, and she told you that she wasn't really going to send that letter.'

'That's right. She was trying to get my attention. But she wasn't going to send it.'

'Were you *alone* when you went to see Ms. Himmel?'

'Yes, I was alone.'

'Can anyone verify that you went to see her?'

Shauna can.

'Not that I know of,' I say.

'No one else was there, besides you and Ms. Himmel?'

'No.'

'Other than your word, do we have any proof at all that this conversation even happened?'

'Other than my word? No.'

'But we *do* have independent proof that Alexa Himmel was saying things to you like . . . oh, let's see.' Ogren finds one of the e-mails and puts it up on the screen. 'That "your going to be seriously fucked." We have proof she said *that* to you, in an e-mail, don't we?'

'Yes, we do.'

'And that she called you a "coward" and said you "lied to her" and you left her to die. We have proof she said *that* to you, don't we?'

423

'We do.'

'And we have proof that she had gone to the trouble of preparing an entire letter to the disciplinary board that oversees lawyers, accusing you of misconduct. We have proof she did *that*, don't we?'

'We do.'

'But this one conversation where, apparently, Alexa Himmel said to you, "Don't worry, Jason, I'd never hurt you," that conversation, we only have your word.'

'You only have my word, yes.'

'And we have proof – in fact, you've admitted – that in the past, when it comes to Ms. Himmel, you've been willing to lie.'

'I did lie at the police interview, yes.'

He's doing a pretty good job of kicking me in the balls here.

'The night of the murder, Mr Kolarich. Can anyone verify that you were at the beach from mid-afternoon until sometime after sundown?'

'Not that I know of.'

'Can anyone verify that you went for a three- or four-hour drive around town afterward?'

'No. Just me.'

'You didn't make a single phone call on your cell phone during that entire interval of time, did you?'

'I don't remember making any. I'm not entirely sure from my own memory, but the CDRs you pulled of my cell phone for that night say I didn't, and I have no reason to quarrel with that.'

'You didn't stop for gas.'

'No.'

'You didn't even eat food, did you?'

'I – no, I don't think – well, I brought some granola bars with me. I remember I ate granola bars on the beach. There wasn't much food I could hold down when I was going through withdrawal. But those granola bars I could eat.'

'What kind of granola bars, by the way?'

'Oh, they come in a green box. They're hard, not soft. Oats and honey flavor, I think it is.'

'What brand?'

'I don't know the name of the brand. Green box.'

'The call to your home phone at 8:16 P.M. on Tuesday, July thirtieth,' he says, jumping quickly, having taken a shot with the granola thing, trying to catch me in a lie but not scoring. 'You say it was a voice mail.'

'Correct.'

'You listened to it after you called 911, you said.'

'Right.'

'You never mentioned it to Detective Cromartie, did you?'

'The voice mail? No, I'm sure I didn't.'

'Or to the patrol officer who first responded.'

'I'm sure I didn't.'

'So we have to take your word for *that*, too. The fact that there was a voice mail.'

'You do.'

Ogren flips around his notes. He's probably close to done. He should be, anyway. Quit while you're ahead. And he's definitely ahead.

'One final topic,' says Ogren. 'The matter of Alexa Himmel's supposed house key.'

'It's not a *supposed* house key. I gave her a key to my house.'

'When did that happen, Mr Kolarich?'

My eyes drift to the ceiling. 'Oh, the beginning of July. About the time she moved in with me.'

'Where did you get it made?'

'Witley's Hardware down the way from my house, about three blocks.'

'Did you pay for it with a credit or debit card?'

'A credit card? It was, like, four or five dollars. No, I believe I paid in cash.'

'You've never paid for something that was four or five dollars with a debit card? You've never swiped your debit card at a McDonald's or a Walgreens?'

Knowing Ogren, he's memorized my credit card bills and will point to examples where I did that very thing. So I have to tread lightly. 'I imagine I have, yes,' I say.

'But not for *this* purchase. For *this* purchase, it was cash.'

'That's right. But I did buy it. She did have a house key.'

'But you have no corroboration for that.'

'I don't.'

'And you can't tell us what happened to this . . . this key.'

'No.'

'Nor can you explain to us how Alexa Himmel got into your house before you were home, if she didn't have a house key.'

'But she *did* have a house key, Mr Ogren, and that's how she got in. I just don't know what happened to it.'

'But we're taking your word, and your word alone, for that, as well.'

I sigh. 'I guess you are, Mr Ogren.'

Roger has done a valiant job of showing that every piece of our defense, thus far, has been built on my testimony and mine alone. *The word of an admitted liar! A man who would say anything to stay out of prison! Do not believe that man!*

'Your Honor, we reserve the right for further questioning during rebuttal,' Ogren says. 'But for the time being, I have nothing further.' He only had last night to prepare for this cross-examination, after I threw out all sorts of things yesterday I'd never said publicly. He did well, very well with the time he had. But he's not done with me by a long shot. The prosecution gets a rebuttal case, and he surely has already mobilized his considerable resources to proving that the things I've said on the witness stand are lies.

Many of them are, of course. Some of them are not. We'll see what his cops can come up with over the next few days.

99

Shauna

'Let's take ten minutes,' says the judge after Roger Ogren completes his cross-examination of Jason.

I nod to Jason's brother, Pete, give him one of those grim half smiles, and then walk straight to the anteroom. Jason goes to talk to Pete for a minute, so it's just Bradley and me inside the room.

'Redirect,' Bradley says. 'I was thinking—'

'I wouldn't do redirect, personally,' I say. 'We got our points out, he got his out. He did a nice job.'

'It was okay.'

'No, it was better than okay. It was very good. He shaved down our entire case to resting on the credibility of Jason's testimony. That's not a good place for us.'

'Then let me do some redirect.'

I shake my head. 'Bradley, nothing that Jason can say will change the fact that it's Jason saying it. The guy standing trial for his life. The guy they've already seen lie repeatedly to a police detective in that interview. They have to take his word for everything he says, because there's no corroboration. No one saw him on the beach or driving around the night of the murder. No one heard his conversation with Alexa where she assured him she wouldn't send that letter.'

I shake my head again, for no apparent reason other than it seems appropriate.

'So . . . what? What now?' Bradley asks. 'We call Detective Austin,

427

the lead on the north side murders, and pump him for information?'

I shrug. 'Not much else we can do.'

'We're fishing, in other words,' he says.

'Totally.'

'Because what Roger Ogren said in there was right, Shauna,' Bradley goes on. 'Marshall Rivers was the North Side Slasher, not the North Side *Shooter*. If Rivers killed Alexa, then he switched MOs from butchering women to shooting them in the head.'

And here I didn't think I could feel any worse. I know all of this, of course, but hearing it in such a tidy, withering summary, from my own cocounsel no less, lights a tiny bomb in my stomach.

'That's going to be a pretty hard thing to sell to the jury,' says Bradley. 'Don't you think?'

'Maybe so,' I say.

Or maybe not. I know more than Bradley about what happened that night, but far, far less than Jason. To varying degrees, our client has kept us both in the dark.

We're all going to find out together.

PEOPLE VS. JASON KOLARICH
TRIAL, DAY 6
Tuesday, December 17

100

Jason

Standing room only in the courtroom again today, the gallery seats full and people jammed all along the walls. The press requests for this trial, previously modest, tripled over the weekend, including now correspondents from national media outlets. The media's favorite story of the summer, the North Side Slasher, has returned for an encore.

They all showed up yesterday, Monday, and formed a line that snaked up and down the hallway outside the courtroom, only to learn that Judge Bialek had decided to delay the resumption of trial for another day. She didn't say why. In the typically mystical ways in which judges often operate, she simply instructed the court clerk to notify everyone outside that there would be no trial testimony today. The spectators all left, disappointed and disgruntled. The reporters, of course, stayed, wondering what this all meant, smelling something big. It wasn't long before Twitter feeds and Internet blogs were full of speculation, and Shauna and Bradley were ambushed with feverish questions when they came to court this morning.

'What did the detectives find this weekend?' 'Why did the police visit Jason Kolarich's house yesterday?' 'Why was Alexa Himmel's body transferred back to the medical examiner's office?'

Shauna's face is drawn. Her movements are a beat slower than usual. She has hardly slept the last four nights since my cross-examination on Friday. She has a habit of doing that, anyway, when she's on trial, and with everything that's happened in this case since Friday, I can hardly blame her.

'Ms. Tasker,' says the judge, 'is the defense prepared to call its next witness?'

'Yes, Your Honor. The defense calls Detective Vance Austin.'

Vance Austin strides to the witness box in a decent gray suit and black tie. He is a rugged, cop-handsome guy who, according to Joel Lightner, comes from good stock. He looks like an alpha male, a guy to whom others turn. He smooths his tie as he takes his seat in the witness chair after swearing his oath.

'Vance Austin,' he says to Shauna, spelling his last name, as if anyone wasn't sure how to spell it. 'I'm a detective, first grade, here in the city.'

'Detective, at some point this year, approximately in May of this year, did you become involved in the investigation of the murder of a woman named Alicia Corey?'

'That's correct.'

'Her murder took place within your jurisdiction at Area Three headquarters?'

'That's correct.'

'Did you subsequently become the lead investigator in a series of homicides involving young women on the north side of the city?'

'That's correct. I led the task force.'

'And the killer was known in the media as the North Side Slasher?'

'Some reporters called him that. I didn't.'

Shauna pauses. 'What did you call him?'

'I'm too much of a gentleman to repeat it here.'

That gets an unusually hearty laugh from the spectators, all of them hyped up, eager.

Shauna smiles. 'Right. But – five women were murdered on the city's north side within approximately a one-month period this past summer, correct?'

'Five *confirmed* women,' says Detective Austin.

'Yes, thank you. Five confirmed women. Alicia Corey, Lauren

Gibbs, Holly Frazier, Nancy Minnows, and Samantha Drury. Are those the women?'

'Yes.'

'And those murders have now been solved, is that right, Detective?'

'Those five have been, that's correct.'

'Who killed those women, Detective?'

'A man named Marshall Rivers.'

Shauna nods. 'When did you solve this case?' she asks.

His head inclines from side to side. 'Well, we confirmed it on that Tuesday . . . it would have been the first full week of August of this year.'

Seven days after Alexa was murdered.

'Would Tuesday, August sixth, sound right?' asks Shauna.

'Yes, that sounds right. It took us a couple of days with some lab work to make it official, to confirm things. We probably knew we had our guy the previous Friday, but I think we went public on the following Tuesday afternoon.'

I would have loved to have watched that press conference. But by then, I'd been in county lockup for a full week for Alexa's murder. Shauna, who visited me as often as she could as my attorney of record, had given me tidbits for several days, rumors that the police thought they had solved the case, the killer was believed to be named Marshall Rivers, there were a lot of details that had to be confirmed, et cetera.

'Do you have any doubt whatsoever that Marshall Rivers was the man who killed those five women this past summer?'

'None,' Austin answers, his jaw high. 'Zero.'

'Without going into too much detail,' Shauna says, 'can you give us an idea about the evidence you built against him?'

'Well, we – we found the murder weapon in his apartment, first of all. He used the same knife on each victim, a folding lockback knife with a partially serrated blade. The blood and DNA of each of the five victims was intermingled on that knife's blade and handle. We had an eyewitness description, a decent one, from one of the murders that matched Marshall Rivers. We brought the witness in and showed her a photo array that included a recent photo of Rivers, and she picked him. We have Rivers on a security camera at Citywide Bank in the Commercial District branch, where one of the victims, Lauren Gibbs, worked, on two different days, never doing any business in the bank whatsoever, just looking in the direction of Ms. Gibbs, who was a bank teller. And we reviewed his Internet searches. He had done extensive research on most of the victims. He'd looked at their Facebook pages, he'd found their home addresses in some cases – things like that.' Austin nods at Shauna. 'Then, there's something that we've kept confidential that I think you're planning on asking me about . . .'

'That's fine, Detective, we can stop there,' says Shauna. 'I'd like to talk a bit more about Marshall Rivers, specifically.'

101

Jason

'Detective Austin,' says Shauna, 'Marshall Rivers had a criminal record, did he not?'

'He did. Three felony convictions.'

'Do you have those committed to memory, Detective? Or would you like me to take you through them?'

'Oh, I know them,' he says, sporting a wry grin. 'By now, I know Marshall Rivers pretty darn well.'

I'm reminded of Joel Lightner here. For him, it was Terry Burgos, the college janitor who killed a half dozen women and stowed them in an auditorium basement. Joel worked that case so hard, from start to finish, that he developed some sort of bizarre connection with the guy, some nostalgic affinity as time passed. That's how Vance Austin is feeling toward Marshall Rivers. Not that Vance Austin can credit outstanding police work to his solving of the murders, but human beings are remarkably adept at cherry-picking the facts most favorable to their egos.

'His first conviction,' says Austin, 'was about thirteen years ago, when he was twenty. He tried to coerce a woman into an alley at gunpoint. He pleaded the case down to simple assault in state court. With the plea, he avoided prison. He was arrested on a sexual assault nearly six months later, but the charges were dropped when the victim refused to testify. Another six months later, he was convicted of possession of a firearm and possession of a Schedule One controlled substance, and he served just over three years. Most recently, he was convicted in federal court of possession of a firearm under similar circumstances as his first conviction; he tried to force a woman and her child into his car by threat of a firearm. He got seventy-five months on the weapons charge, or about six and a half years in federal prison. He attacked a prison psychiatrist, a woman, while inside and got another eighteen months added to his sentence. Prison psychiatrists said he was capable of violent and impulsive behavior, that he had no sense of remorse or right versus wrong – so he was pretty high up on our list.'

The way that information rolls off Austin's tongue, you get the feeling he's said these things many times – like, for example, to these young female reporters with the movie-star looks, who are just doing their job, sure, but who also can't help being just a little bit attracted to this strong, powerful man who caught the bad guy and helps them sleep safely at night.

'When was Marshall Rivers released from federal custody?' Shauna asks.

'This past January. January . . . the sixteenth, I believe it was.'

'And that most recent conviction, in federal court,' says Shauna. 'He was initially arrested by city police officers. That case started here locally, with the county attorney's office, not with federal agents, isn't that correct?'

'That's correct.'

'And in fact, Mr Rivers gave a statement – a confession – to an assistant county attorney, didn't he?'

'He did, yes.'

'And that assistant county attorney was Jason Kolarich, was it not?'

'So I've come to learn,' he says. 'That wasn't easy information to come by, because Rivers took a plea in federal court. He didn't go to trial, so there wasn't much of a record. But yes, over the weekend we were able to track down that information and confirm it.'

He's sounding a little defensive here, because it's something he didn't know until recently, and he wants to be the guy who knows *everything* about Marshall Rivers. Some people, in the coming days and weeks, might say Austin should have known that fact, should have tracked it down at the time when the north side murders were solved. But I'm not one of those people. My name barely crept into that case at all. It was a federal prosecution having nothing to do with a state prosecutor like me, and the case didn't even go to trial. Rivers pleaded out to avoid a possible ten-year sentence. The police would have no reason to dig any deeper into that file. They had no inkling that Rivers was acting out of revenge – they thought he was a garden-variety sociopath who preyed on young women – so they had no reason to look for objects of his revenge.

'And wouldn't you agree, Detective, that the reason that Mr Rivers took a plea in federal court, instead of fighting the charge, is because he had no chance after Jason secured his confession?'

'Objection,' says Roger Ogren. 'Foundation.'

'Sustained.'

'Isn't it fair to say that he had Jason Kolarich, and *only* Jason Kolarich, to blame for being sent away for over six years?'

'Objection.'

'Sustained. Move on, Ms. Tasker.'

Fair enough. Shauna made the point, anyway.

Shauna nods, waits a beat or two, sneaks a peek at the jury. 'Detective, how did Marshall Rivers subdue his victims?'

'In each case, he assaulted the victim as she was returning to her home. In most cases, he gained entry to the victim's dwelling, and in one instance the attack took place within the victim's automobile. But generally, he would lie in wait and ambush the victim.'

Just like he ambushed Alexa Himmel as she walked into Jason's town house, Shauna will argue in her final summation to the jury. She won't have every single answer. She won't be able to explain why this particular ambush-murder didn't go according to script, how it was that he ended up shooting her in the back on the second floor of my town house instead of carving her up with a knife on the ground floor. But it's not the defense's job to dot every *i* and cross every *t*. We just have to kick up enough dust to get reasonable doubt.

'Detective, was there anything else that connected these murders? Anything in particular that Marshall Rivers did to his victims that would serve as some kind of trademark or calling card or . . . signature?'

'There was,' says the detective.

'And before you tell us about that signature, let me ask you: Has this information ever been publicly revealed?'

'No, it hasn't.'

'Is that common, when you have a string of murders that appear to have the same trademark or signature – is it common to keep that signature out of the press, away from the public?'

I assume most people already know that the answer is yes, based on what they've seen on television.

'That's correct,' says Austin. 'Particularly when the string of murders has received significant media attention. When that happens, we tend to get a lot of bogus confessions, people just looking for attention. You can tell real from fake confessions when you hold back information, so only the real killer would know it.'

'I see. It also helps you distinguish between crimes committed by that killer versus crimes committed by a copycat.'

'That's also true. You can't be a copycat if you don't know the killer's signature in the first place.'

'So, Detective, what was Marshall Rivers's signature, his calling card, never before made public?'

Shauna laid that on pretty thick. Detective Austin doesn't seem impressed with the melodrama. Or maybe he's just pissed off he has to make this information public. Maybe he wanted to save it for the book he's going to write.

He says, 'The offender injected a drug called fentanyl into each victim.'

'Can you tell us what fentanyl is?' Shauna asks.

'I'm not a chemist or a coroner, but, generally, yes. It's a very

438

powerful narcotic, kind of like morphine or heroin, but typically much more potent. It mostly comes here illegally from Mexico. We see it a lot here in the city as "China white" or "AMF." It's not the biggest drug problem we have, but it's definitely out there.'

'Isn't it true that fentanyl can also be used as an incapacitating agent?'

'Yes, it can be.'

'Meaning it can be used to knock out or paralyze a victim.'

'That's correct.'

'And it's powerful, isn't it? It's more powerful as an incapacitating agent than, say, GHB, the date-rape drug.'

Detective Austin hedges, his head moving side to side. 'You may be going past my knowledge base. I've heard people say what you just said, but I don't know it to be true. It's powerful, I'd agree with that.'

Shauna can live with that. 'And in fact, Detective, didn't you come to believe that Marshall Rivers used the fentanyl injection to incapacitate his victims?'

Austin bows his head, a curt nod. 'That's correct. Now, whether he incapacitated them immediately with the fentanyl injection or whether he first subdued them and then used it to prevent them from fighting back – that's a difficult thing to know.'

'And it's also possible that he wasn't using it to subdue them at all. That he was just injecting them as some kind of branding, to put his personal stamp on the murders. Isn't that also possible?'

'You can never rule that out,' says Austin. 'Sometimes with these sociopaths, they do strange things like that. They want ownership over the murders.'

Good. Well done, Shauna.

'Now, Detective, fentanyl doesn't show up on a routine toxicological screen performed on someone during an autopsy, does it?'

Austin grimaces, chuckles to himself. 'No, it surely does not.'

'You know that from firsthand experience, don't you, Detective? From your investigation into the north side murders?'

'That's correct. Our medical examiner performed a routine tox screen on these victims, and that test doesn't check for fentanyl.' He makes a face, indicating his opinion of that routine drug screen. 'We only came upon this because we found a broken hypodermic needle at one of the crime scenes. I think it was Holly Frazier, the third victim . . . Yeah, it was, it was Holly's. So we had the needle tested, and it contained traces of fentanyl. Then we sent the medical examiner back to specifically test the other victims for the presence of fentanyl. Those tests came back positive every time, going back to the first two victims and going forward to the next two. All five victims tested positive for fairly high doses of fentanyl.'

'Judge,' Shauna says, 'at this time, I'd like to refer the jury to the stipulation previously entered into between the parties and read to the jury, in which it is stipulated that the autopsy of Alexa Himmel included a routine toxicological screen.'

Which made sense, to be fair to the government, especially when the cause of death in Alexa's case was a bullet to the head or neck region. It's not like they had any reason to think this was connected to the knife murders committed by Marshall Rivers, not back then in late July.

'Very good,' says the judge.

'Detective Austin, were you aware of additional testing performed by the county medical examiner this weekend on the blood and body of the victim in this case, Alexa Himmel?'

'Yes. I oversaw it. Dr Agarwal performed the tests.'

'Dr Mitra Agarwal is the chief deputy medical examiner?'

'Yes.'

'A very competent pathologist?'

'The best.'

'And was it your understanding that Dr Agarwal's charge was to search for the presence of fentanyl in Alexa Himmel's blood?'

'Yes, that was the reason for the additional testing.'

'And was it, Detective? Was the drug fentanyl found in Alexa Himmel's body?'

'Yes, it was,' he says.

The jury reacts. Everyone reacts. The same chemical injected into the other five victims was injected into Alexa, too. It's the first piece of hard evidence tying Alexa Himmel's death to Marshall Rivers. We just got back the ME's report yesterday. Shauna said that she was waiting over at the county attorney's offices when Roger Ogren came storming out of his office and passed her without saying a word, his face flushed – *like he'd just swallowed a bug,* Shauna said. Katie O'Connor, the second chair in the trial, was actually the one who broke the good news to Shauna. Roger Ogren, no doubt, had been sure that the test would come up negative. But when it didn't, he was obligated to tell us so.

Now he's probably kicking himself, thinking he shouldn't have ordered the additional test. But it wouldn't have mattered. Shauna, in her closing argument, would have blistered the prosecution and police so hard for not doing the additional testing – *What are they hiding? If the government is so sure that Marshall Rivers didn't kill Alexa, here's their chance to prove it! Ladies and gentlemen of the jury, if the government doesn't have that level of confidence in their case, how can you?* – that Ogren probably would have been shamed into doing it, anyway. This way, at least, he's wearing the white hat, ordering the test voluntarily.

'Dr Agarwal found traces of fentanyl, injected postmortem, in Ms. Himmel's jugular vein,' Austin says.

That is a point Austin has added, no doubt, at the request of Roger Ogren. The other victims were injected antemortem – prior to death – while their blood continued to circulate, carrying that drug into the far reaches of their bodies, easily detectable as long as your toxicology test was looking for it. A drug injected postmortem, as it was with Alexa, obviously does not travel; the blood has stopped circulating. Instead, the drug tends to pool in the vein or muscle where it was injected, in this case the jugular vein in Alexa's neck. So Roger Ogren will try to drive a truck through this distinction: *The others were injected while alive, but Alexa Himmel was injected after death.*

102

Jason

'Detective Austin,' says Shauna, 'we've discussed that Marshall Rivers's use of the fentanyl injection on his victims was information that was withheld from the public, correct?'

'That's correct.'

'Why is that? I mean, you solved the five murders, didn't you?'

'Yes.'

'So isn't the Marshall Rivers investigation closed?'

'No, it is not closed.'

'And why not?' she asks.

Austin doesn't hesitate in his response. I thought he might. I thought that Roger Ogren might get to him, make him tone down a few things. But in the end, the north side murders were a huge deal and they belong to Austin; he doesn't care much at all about my case.

He says, 'Because we've always suspected there was a sixth victim.'

Another wave of murmurs ripples through the gallery. *A sixth victim! The North Side Slasher lives on!*

'Detective, I'd like to show you a document marked as Defense Exhibit One. I'm going to put it up on the screen here and ask you if you recognize this.'

The jurors, fully consumed with this testimony, turn their heads in unison, like spectators at a tennis match, to the projection screen.

Now u finaly know who I am
Now u will never forgit
Number six was difrent
But she was my favorit

'Detective,' says Shauna, 'do you recognize this document?'

'Yes, I do. When we searched Marshall Rivers's apartment on August second, we found these words typed on his computer. This is a printout of those words.'

Shauna moves for admission of the document, which is granted without objection. She pauses, giving the jurors some time to read it, and reread it, and process it.

'This document, taken from the computer of Marshall Rivers, has never been made public, either, has it?' Shauna asks.

'No, it has not.'

'It was only yesterday that this document was turned over to the defense. Is that your understanding?'

'Yes.'

'Detective, this note led you to investigate the possibility that Marshall Rivers had killed a sixth person, correct?'

'It was a possibility.'

'Did you ever find that sixth victim, Detective?'

'No, we did not.'

Shauna is quiet a moment. She looks over at the jurors, who are reading the words on the projection screen with great interest, trying to make them jibe with things that I said during my testimony.

'Detective, the third line of this note says that "number six was different," with the last word misspelled. Do you read it the same way?'

'Yes, I do.'

'Marshall Rivers's first five murders were relatively . . . similar, weren't they? They involved an ambush, they involved injections of fentanyl and, ultimately, brutal cutting and slashing with a folding lockback knife with a partially serrated blade. Isn't that correct?'

'It is, yes.'

'Wouldn't an attack that ultimately ended up as a shooting in the back with a handgun qualify as "different"?'

'Ob-jection,' Ogren says, more as a whine. Shauna's question is clearly out of line.

'Sustained.'

'Well, Detective,' says Shauna, 'as the lead investigator on the north side murders and on Marshall Rivers himself, do you now believe that this note was written specifically for Jason Kolarich?'

'Objection!' Roger Ogren calls out. He's right again, but it still sounds like a gripe, a grumpy complaint.

'Sustained,' says the judge.

'Okay,' says Shauna, nodding. 'Well, didn't you take from this note that this sixth murder, his "favorite," held a unique, personal significance to Marshall Rivers?'

'Judge!' Ogren calls out.

'Because the last victim was *Jason Kolarich's girlfriend*?'

'Ms. Tasker, stop right there,' says Judge Bialek. 'The objection is sustained. These questions are inappropriate for this witness and you know it. Now *move on*.'

Shauna knows they're inappropriate. A courtroom tactician ordinarily wouldn't even ask these questions of a witness. She would save them for closing argument, identifying each line of the note found on Marshall's computer and tying it to his obsession with me. *Now you finally know who I am, now you will never forget* – corroborating my testimony that Marshall came to me in disguise and under an assumed name. *Number six was different*, as Shauna said, because it turned from a knife attack to a shooting. *She was my favorite*, because it wasn't just some random woman, but rather a woman very special to me.

Typically, the lawyer would save these arguments for closing, when she is free to argue anything she wants from the evidence. She wouldn't ask them of a witness who could fight her. But Shauna has a couple of reasons for doing it now. One, she wants the reporters to hear it. She wants them to take this information and publish stories and call for an end to this prosecution, to build public pressure.

And second, she knew Roger Ogren would object. She *hoped* he would object. Because now the prosecution looks like it's hiding the truth. The white hat Roger Ogren is wearing has just received a stain or two.

103

Jason

'Since we're on the topic of the inventory of Mr Rivers's apartment in early August,' says Shauna, 'did you or your colleagues look at any keys or key chains recovered from his apartment?'

'Yes, we did,' says Austin. 'He had a key ring that held six keys. I remember when we first searched his apartment on August second, they were hanging on a hook by his front door. Anyway, yes, this weekend we took a look at the keys on that key ring.'

'Detective, did you visit Mr Kolarich's house yesterday?'

'I did.'

'And who was with you when that happened?'

'I was accompanied by Detective Raymond Cromartie, Katie O'Connor from the county attorney, and you, Counselor.'

'What was the purpose of the visit?'

'To see if any of the keys on Marshall Rivers's key chain opened Mr Kolarich's door.'

'And *did* any of the keys from Marshall Rivers's key chain fit into the lock on Mr Kolarich's front door?'

He nods. 'Yes, one of them did.'

That juror in the front row, the one who tends to visibly react – the one who leaned back in his chair and looked around at his colleagues when he watched me lie in the police interview – now repeats that gesture, making faces at the woman next to him, only this time I daresay his allegiance has switched to the defense.

'May I approach the witness?' Shauna asks.

'Yes.'

'Defense Exhibit Four,' she says, holding up a clear bag containing a single, rather shiny silver key. 'Is this the key that you found on Mr Rivers's key chain that opened Jason Kolarich's front door?'

'That's it,' Austin says.

Shauna holds up the bag for the jury to see. No need to formally publish it, to actually hand it to the jurors. It's just a basic house key. But it will mean everything to Shauna in closing argument. *Marshall Rivers jumped Alexa as she entered Jason's house, and he kept her key as a souvenir. He wanted Jason to know he'd killed her.*

The mystery of Alexa's missing house key is no longer a mystery.

104

Jason

'Detective,' says Shauna, 'just one final area of inquiry. We talked previously this morning about the fact that Marshall Rivers injected fentanyl in his victims. Did you find evidence at his apartment that he was doing this?'

'Yes. When we searched his apartment, we found over a dozen fentanyl patches, which can be broken down and cooked and then used for injection. We found a pack of unopened hypodermic needles. And we found three used hypodermic needles in a plastic sandwich bag.'

'And back on August second, when you discovered these three used hypodermic needles, did you test them for the presence of fentanyl?'

'We did. All three tested positive for fentanyl.'

'Did you find anything else on those hypodermic needles?'

Austin raises a fist to his mouth and clears his throat. 'One of them contained trace DNA of the first two victims in this case, Alicia Corey and Lauren Gibbs,' he says. 'The second hypodermic needle contained trace DNA belonging to the fourth victim, Nancy Minnows. And the third needle showed trace DNA of the fifth victim, Samantha Drury.'

'So . . . one needle had the first two victims' DNA, another had the fourth, and another had the fifth.'

Austin nods. 'Correct. And as I said before, the third victim, Holly

Frazier – the needle used to inject her had broken off and was left at the crime scene. That's how we learned about the fentanyl in the first place.'

'Sure.'

That was no accident, the needle breaking off at the third crime scene. Marshall Rivers wanted the cops to know all about the fentanyl.

'As for why Rivers used the same needle for the first two victims,' says Austin, 'it's anybody's guess.'

Except mine. I don't have to guess. That's the needle Marshall Rivers stuck behind my framed prosecutor's certificate on my office wall. At that point, he had only killed the first two women. He needed their DNA on that needle so it would implicate me.

'Now, Detective, did you recently submit those three hypodermic needles for additional DNA testing?'

'Yes, we did. Last Friday, following the testimony of Mr Kolarich, we decided to have those three needles checked for the presence of Alexa Himmel's DNA.'

'Did you expedite that testing?'

'We did. Yeah, I think our county lab set a new record. We got the results back last night, Monday night.'

'And?' Shauna turns toward the jurors.

Detective Austin says, 'The hypodermic needle that contained trace DNA of the first two victims, Alicia Corey and Lauren Gibbs, also contained trace DNA belonging to Alexa Himmel.'

Check, please.

The judge immediately bangs her gavel, and the additional sheriff's deputies manning the courtroom rush to silence the roar from the spectators. It takes them a while. This is too splashy for the reporters to resist. Especially when taken with everything else that has come out today – the note on Marshall's computer that jibes with my story, my house key on Marshall's key ring. With the possible exception of Roger Ogren and Katie O'Connor, there is not a single person in this courtroom who thinks I killed Alexa Himmel.

That was one busy needle. First, it was injected into Alicia Corey. Then it was sunk into the skin of Lauren Gibbs. Then it was hidden behind a certificate on my wall. Then it was tucked safely away in my bedroom.

Then it was sunk into Alexa's jugular vein.

But ultimately, it made its way back to the apartment of Marshall Rivers.

It's kind of ironic, when you think about it. Marshall was using that needle to implicate me for murder. And it ends up being used as evidence that *exonerates* me of a different murder.

'Ms. Tasker,' says the judge, flushed, after she finally brings the courtroom back to silence. 'Do you have any further questions?'

Shauna glances at her notes, then at me. I write something on a piece of paper and show it to her. She looks at it and walks over to me. There is such a looseness to her stride, such a relaxed look on her face, that I almost don't recognize her.

'You never said what happened to Marshall,' I whisper.

'I didn't? I guess I didn't,' she acknowledges. 'But everyone knows what happened. Everyone knows all about him.'

We look at each other for a long time. Then she leans in and whispers into my ear.

'He killed himself,' she says. 'Right, Jason?'

Shauna draws back, looks me over with a poker face. But she doesn't wait for an answer. She returns to the podium to address the judge.

Marshall Rivers was found dead in his apartment on the evening of Friday, August 2, nearly three full days after Alexa was found dead in my town house. And two days after his rent was due. His landlord let himself in and found Marshall lying in a pool of blood. The police responded, and it wasn't long before the search of that apartment led them to conclude that Marshall Rivers was the infamous North Side Slasher. The bloody knife, the hypodermic needles, the packets of fentanyl, all told the story. The suicide note on his computer didn't hurt, either.

The timing of Marshall's death was a difficult one for the medical examiner to pin down. The circumstantial evidence helped somewhat. Marshall hadn't been scheduled to work at the dry cleaner's on Wednesday, July 31, but he did miss work the next day, Thursday, August 1, so it looked like he died before the morning of August 1. The medical evidence? Rigor mortis had long come and gone by the time he was found that Friday night, so sometime before August 1 made sense to the coroner. The best estimate, from the larvae present, was that Marshall Rivers had been dead approximately seventy-two hours when he was found.

Marshall Rivers, in other words, died within relatively the same window of time that Alexa Himmel died.

'I have no further questions,' says Shauna. 'And the defense rests.'

THE DAY OF ALEXA HIMMEL'S DEATH
Tuesday, July 30

105

Shauna

9:05 P.M.

I sit upstairs on Jason's bed with my iPad, doing research on addiction recovery centers around here. They certainly aren't hard to find. But finding the right one could be a chore. So I'm looking for reviews, as well. Some of these clinics specialize in painkiller addiction, which is probably a better fit, but how the heck do *I* know?

I check my watch and do the math. Jason got the call from Alexa at a quarter past eight. Even with bad traffic – and I doubt traffic is bad this time of night – Jason would have reached Alexa's house by now.

What's going on there? It didn't feel right, the way Jason popped up and left. Alexa calls in a breathless panic and he goes running.

She could have told him anything. Jason wouldn't tell me, but it's not hard to imagine. *I'm going to kill myself, I swear I will!* Or: *'James Drinker' just tried to kill me.* Anything.

I should have gone with him. He said no. *That will make it worse*, he said to me, undoubtedly true, but still – I should have gone.

And his ultimate rationale: *I have to get my cell phone, anyway.* He'd left it at Alexa's house earlier today, after reading that threatening e-mail from Alexa about telling the Board of Attorney Discipline about his drug problem. *I need to get it sooner or later.*

True. And maybe that's all it was. Sure, she'll beg him to take her back. But he won't. He knows better.

455

Maybe he's hoping that this one last time with her will do the trick, will finally calm her down and make her go away. Fat chance, but I could see Jason thinking that, giving her the benefit of the doubt.

And I can't discount the level of guilt he's feeling, however misplaced it may be. No matter how much she manipulated him, he assumes responsibility for her broken heart.

Is she capable of something more? *She wouldn't hurt him,* I tell myself. Would she? No. No?

But if I really didn't see Alexa as a threat, then why did I run upstairs to Jason's closet to retrieve his gun, hidden in the old pair of wingtips in the back of his closet? Even though I despise guns, can't stand the sight of them, detest the very idea of them, I carried down the gun, the Glock handgun, the creepy black instrument of death, and put it in Jason's hands.

Take your gun and be careful, I said to him.

I let out a long, nervous sigh, my stomach stirring. Then I continue my search of rehab clinics.

106

Jason

9:10 P.M.

Blaring out from the speakerphone on my phone, held in Alexa's hand, is Joel Lightner's voice:

'Get ready to be happy, sport. I found him. I found our fucking guy! We were looking for cons recently released from a state penitentiary. This guy came out of a federal facility in January. You got him to confess to a gun charge, like, eight years ago, but you handed him over to the feds and they prosecuted him. We were looking in the wrong damn place! His name is Marshall Rivers. He's got a history of violence against women and, since he got out, he's been working at a dry cleaner's two doors down from Higgins Auto Body! He probably saw James Drinker every day! Anyway, Marshall Rivers, does that ring—'

The recording stops abruptly, mid-sentence. I steady myself with a hand to the wall, squeeze my eyes shut, lower my head, then slowly raise it. *Marshall Rivers.* Marshall—

And then I remember him. I remember what happened. I remember what I did to him.

Marshall Rivers is 'James Drinker.' Marshall Rivers is the North Side Slasher.

'Finally,' I mumble. Then I look at Alexa, remembering the truncated nature of the voice mail. 'Did you pause the message or did it just stop there?' I ask. 'Is there more?'

From her dark corner, Alexa stands slowly and inches toward me, crossing the line of the television light, blocking it out, leaving us in darkness, her features changing with each step—

– the face of a ghost, a haunted figure, piercing eyes, a wry grin, a scowl, terror and rage and panic and fear—

'There's more,' she says to me. 'There's a lot more.'

She pushes a button, and the recording continues.

'– a bell with you? Anyway, it's him, Jason, I know it! He lives here in the city. He's on Hampton, 2538 Hampton, Apartment 1. Call me back, man. We fucking got him!'

I stare at Alexa's hand, at my phone. My eyes adjusted to the darkness, I make out her face better, almost cartoonish, dark and eerie.

'You've been crying,' I say.

I walk over to the wall and flip on a switch. Alexa winces, her eyes squinting in the light.

'I have to call Joel,' I say. 'Then you and I have to—'

'No, don't do that.' She shakes her head slowly, something in her eyes, in the certainty of her tone, revealing herself to me. She approaches me slowly. She is freshly showered, her hair still wet, dressed in baggy, kick-around sweats.

I put my hands on her shoulders. 'Alexa,' I say, 'what did you do?'

She touches my cheek, her hand trembling furiously. Only then, up close, do I see that her whole body is quivering. Her legs buckle, and I catch her, helping her to the couch. I stand over her.

'Tell me,' I say.

Her eyes search me, her nostrils flaring, her mouth moving without sound. 'I fixed it,' she says. 'I fixed everything for you.'

'Did you—'

'He can't hurt you anymore,' she whispers. 'He can't hurt *us*.'

I take the phone from her hand and check the voice mail we just heard. The call came from Lightner today at 2:04 P.M. She listened to this message a long time ago, back when Joel called. She has known for seven hours where Marshall Rivers lives.

Alexa takes the phone from my hand and pushes a button, erasing the voice mail.

'Tell me you didn't go over there, Alexa—'

'Shh.' She reaches her hand out to my mouth. 'It's okay. Nobody will ever know.'

I step back from her, put my hands on my head, furiously scrubbing my hair. 'This – this isn't happening.'

'It's okay,' she says to me, lifting herself off the couch toward me. 'I've been planning for this. I did everything right. It looks like a suicide.'

I push away from her and pace in a small circle, passing the movie on the television, the open pizza box with only half a piece missing, cut sharply with a knife.

'It was easy,' she tells me. 'I knocked on the door, and he opened it. I asked him if he wanted some company. He thought I was a – I dressed the part – he thought I was, y'know, a prostitute. A skimpy outfit and a fake blond wig and sunglasses was all it took to get him to open his door.'

I don't say anything, just shut my eyes and listen, my head against a wall.

'I have a Taser. I've always had one. Did you know that?'

I shake my head no.

'It was the easiest thing. I only needed a few seconds. I got him in the neck and he went right down. I dragged him into his apartment and I cut his wrists with his own knife. It looks like he killed himself. It does. I swear it does.'

'Alexa.' I turn, put my hands on my knees like a third-base coach. 'The police are professionals. They're not—'

'What, are you going to tell me about hesitation wounds? I read all about them, Jason. I know that when people slit their wrists, they hesitate first and don't cut deeply. I did all that. I stood behind him and I used his own hands around the knife and I did some shallower cuts first. And I did the left wrist more deeply than the right. I did it perfectly!'

'Even so.' I flap my arms. 'And don't you think the police can look at your Internet searches and wonder why you were reading up on hesitation wounds?'

'What reason would they have to check? I have a really good alibi.'

I let out a nervous sigh. 'And what's that?'

'Look around you.' She gestures with her hands. 'I ordered *Doctor Zhivago* on pay-per-view and I had pizza delivered. Does that sound like someone who went out and committed murder?'

'Oh, Alexa.' I shake my head. 'You could have made a *hundred* different mistakes. You're better off turning yourself in and explaining that you were trying to stop a serial killer. We – we have to go to the police. I'll represent you. I'll do everything I—'

'This man was a *monster*,' she hisses. 'He butchered five women and he wasn't going to stop. I could see it, Jason. I could see it in the way his eyes passed over me when he answered the door, like he was imagining what it would be like to do the same thing to me. Are you really telling me you wouldn't have done exactly what I did?'

I don't confront that question. I'd spent so much time trying to figure out who he was and how to stop him, I hadn't decided on a game plan once I found him. Would I have killed him? I don't have the time or the need to answer that now.

'He's out of the way now,' she says. 'Don't you see?'

He's out of the way. I wipe at my mouth, fidgety, trying to work through this, feeling unmoored, disoriented. *She did this for me,* I think to myself. *She did this so we could be together.*

We are both quiet. She is looking at me, waiting me out, her head cocked to one side, her lips slightly parted.

'How do we even know Joel was right?' I ask. 'How do we even know Marshall Rivers was our guy?'

Alexa reaches into her sweatpants and produces something, a card of some sort.

'Your business card,' she says. 'Sitting next to his computer.'

She holds it out. I walk over and take it. Holding it in my hand, seeing this card on fancy, cream-colored stock, JASON KOLARICH, ESQ. in royal blue, returns me to my law office, to the man in the goofy disguise, pumping me for information, planting a hypodermic needle in my office, plotting to kill women and make sure I knew all about it.

And then it solidifies for me, something for which I'll have to answer someday, a decision: *She shouldn't have to go to prison for this. However messed-up her reasoning may be, she shouldn't suffer for this. Marshall Rivers deserved to die.*

I drop my head. 'I . . . don't even know what to say.'

'Say you'll help me,' she whispers.

I look up at her. Tears have formed in her eyes.

'Because you were right,' she says. 'I did make a mistake.'

107

Jason

I drive slowly, minding the speed limit, gripping the steering wheel with trembling hands, still short on every detail, but the memories coming back. I remember Marshall was violent, sexually violent toward women. I remember a young woman with a baby. Not her name, not every single feature by any means, but I remember a teenage mother. Mexican. Long, kinky black hair, I remember that. An infant in her arms, maybe six months old, not something I'd be in a position to estimate back then. She probably told me the baby's name, age, gender, but I don't remember any of that now.

But I remember she was terrified. I remember that I couldn't use her. If I was going to nail Marshall Rivers, I'd have to come up with something else.

Get me a confession, said Patrick Romer back then. *Get me a confession and we'll prosecute.*

And I did.

I park my car on the 2400 block of West Hampton. Lightner had said 2538 Hampton, and there isn't a 2500 block east – it would be three miles into the lake. So he must have meant 2538 West Hampton. It makes sense, too, this southwest-side neighborhood being the home of an ex-con with minimal job prospects, probably not much money. The area has been completely ravaged by the housing crisis; what was, fifteen years ago, a promising neighborhood has been ransacked by foreclosures and is now riddled with drugs and crime, gang wars and prostitution, con artists and homelessness.

This time of night, in a hood like this, the only people who are walking the streets are looking for trouble. I guess I'm one of them. Yes, in part, I'm here because of Alexa. *I left the Taser there,* she said to me. *I forgot all about it when I was done.* Her fingerprints could be on the weapon. She couldn't very well wear gloves, not in the middle of this blazing heat. Alexa was smart, knocking on Marshall's door, dressed provocatively, knowing that prostitutes occasionally go door-to-door in the seamier neighborhoods – but no matter how much she looked the part, Marshall's radar would have tuned up loudly if she were wearing gloves.

I reach the apartment complex, 2538 West Hampton. It's a brick three-flat, not long ago probably a nice place to live, owned by people with high hopes, sold unrealistic mortgages that put them under water. Now it's a rental building, probably still owned by the bank. Apartment 1 is the garden apartment, five steps below ground. There is a small cast-iron gate without a lock. From the sidewalk, I take one look around me, trying not to look too suspicious in doing so, and cast my eyes upward at the other apartments. No sign that anyone's looking out, no blinds pinched or curtains folded back.

Then I stroll through the gate, covering my hand with my shirt, and walk down to apartment 1 as if I don't have a care in the world. Alexa said the door would be open, she didn't lock it behind her. It could have a lock on the doorknob that will keep me out. But it doesn't. I turn the knob with my shirt again and take a breath.

Don't touch anything, Alexa pleaded with me. *Please don't touch anything.*

The door opens. I walk in and close the door before I do anything else. Then I turn. It's a studio apartment, very small, just one large room with a small kitchenette, a round table for eating, and then a bathroom to the side. There are two pieces of furniture besides the dining table: a small wooden table on which a computer rests, and a dingy yellow couch.

Marshall Rivers is against the couch, tipped over on his right side, his legs splayed out perpendicular to his body. Alexa said she Tasered him and dragged him over by the couch, where she slit his wrists. It looks like she propped him against the couch, sitting upright, but he eventually fell over.

The smell raises bile to my throat. Feces, which is understandable, mixed with the metallic smell of spilled blood.

I ease the backpack off my shoulder. First, I put on the rubber gloves Alexa gave me, small on my hands, but sufficient. Then I walk toward the couch, checking for any marks my shoes might be leaving on the thin, dingy carpeting and finding none.

Then I walk over to Marshall Rivers. I don't get close; I don't need to and I don't want to. But I do want to see that face, turning colorless, mouth gaping, eyes wide open, lying awkwardly on the floor, blood nestling under his cheek and mixed into his hair.

This, of course, is the principal reason I came. I needed to see him, face-to-face, to confirm that he was the man who came to see me in disguise.

And he is. He doesn't have red hair, but rather light brown, cut short and messy. He is wide and muscular, but not fat. So that must have been part of his disguise, the fat suit, the belly flab. There is blood everywhere, a few splatters on his yellow-checkered shirt, probably from when Alexa first slashed the wrists, and then a pool that has migrated to the north of Marshall, up against the wall. The floor is probably uneven, and gravity pulled the blood in that direction.

Those eyes of his, those are all I need to see. This is the man who came to visit me as 'James Drinker.' This is the man who killed five women on the north side this summer.

I give a presumptive nod. He's done. What this will mean for me, I don't know. He said he had a contingency plan if anything happened to him – a safe-deposit box with evidence implicating me in the north side murders. Probably bullshit. But there's nothing I can do about it now. Nothing to worry about at this moment.

I look at the knife, still gripped in his left hand. Alexa said she slashed his left wrist deeper, then the right one shallower. That would make sense for a right-handed person. Is he right-handed? I don't know. Alexa wouldn't know, either. Just one of many things that could raise a red flag when his body is discovered, if it turns out Marshall Rivers is a southpaw.

And is that one of Alexa's knives or one of Marshall's? Did we discuss that? I don't remember. If she was smart, she subdued Marshall and found one of his own kitchen knives to carry out her plan. That's the kind of thing the police can figure out.

I've been planning for this, Alexa assured me. *I did everything right.*

She's been planning for this. She did everything right. Except she left her Taser here.

But – where is it?

It doesn't take me long to pace the room and check the tiny bathroom. I cautiously get down on my hands and knees and look low, under the couch, under the table that holds the computer.

I open some cabinets in the kitchenette, a generous term for it because it's really just a long countertop with a microwave sitting on it. There is a four-burner stove, a small sink full of dirty cups, a plate crusted with ketchup smears, and a pan with remnants of macaroni and cheese. There is a small oven as well. It doesn't make sense to look in these cabinets – there's no good reason why her Taser would have ended up in there – but I look anyway.

In the third cabinet I open, in addition to a few plates and some dishwasher soap and a box of raisins, I find a package of unopened hypodermic needles and two needles sitting inside a plastic sandwich bag, looking as if they've been used.

Just like the one I found a week ago in my law office, taped behind the framed prosecutor's certificate.

No time for that. I close the cabinets, panicking now. It isn't here. The Taser isn't here. Where could it be? I take a breath to calm myself and hold still. The room itself is still, quiet, motionless, save for the screen saver on Marshall's desktop computer, silver asteroids bouncing around the black screen haphazardly, a computer mouse resting next to it on a mouse pad that is royal blue.

I check the bathroom one more time. Nothing. Back into the main room. I gently feel behind the computer, moving the small table slightly when I do so. Nothing back there. No Taser, at least. I take another breath, thinking of how long I've been here, that anyone could walk in at any second.

Could the Taser be under Marshall? Could he be lying on it? It could have happened that way. She sat behind him, worked his hands so he cut his wrists, put the Taser next to him or on the couch next to her, maybe, and it fell to the floor – whatever, one way or the other, it could have ended up on the floor, and when Marshall's body fell sideways to the floor, he covered it.

Am I going to have to *move* him to get it? That, of course, is the very *last* thing I want to do.

I move cautiously toward him. No. Too risky. If I move the body, any talk of suicide goes out the window. But if that's where it is, the police will never think this was a suicide, anyway. Especially if Alexa's fingerprints are on it.

Time is not on my side here. I can't stay here forever. I have to make a decision.

I look to my right, back at the table with the computer.

The screen saver is gone. The black screen, the silver asteroids darting about, have vanished. When I searched behind the computer, and rocked the table while doing so, the mouse must have moved. The screen saver went away.

In its place is a word-processing document, a white background with four lines of text:

Now u finaly know who I am
Now u will never forgit
Number six was difrent
But she was my favorit

A suicide note. Alexa didn't mention doing this. There's no way Marshall could have done it. Alexa wanted Marshall's faux suicide to look more plausible.

466

Don't touch anything, Alexa made me promise.

She didn't want me to see this note.

I've been planning for this, she said to me.

I've been planning for this.

An unintentional slip? It meant little to me at the time, when her revelations were hitting me like a tidal wave, but now those words – they don't make sense. She was planning for what, exactly? How could she have known that I'd leave my phone at her house and she would just so happen to intercept a voice mail to me from Joel Lightner, giving me the name and address of the north side killer? What, precisely, was she planning?

Number six was difrent
But she was my favorit

My blood goes cold. Marshall Rivers only killed five women.

'No,' I say. 'No.'

I reach into my pocket, pat both sides of my pants. No cell phone. Shit. I never got back my cell phone from Alexa. I race through the drawers or cabinets in his apartment. Marshall doesn't have a landline I can see and probably no cell phone, either. He only used throwaways and they're nowhere—

I've been planning for this.

Alexa didn't leave a Taser behind.

I race for the door, a silent prayer echoing in my head.

108

Shauna

9:55 P.M.

I narrow down my list to four rehab centers in the area and start typing notes, questions I want to ask each of them. But with each passing minute, it's getting harder to focus. I check my watch again, think it through again: Jason left after that call at a quarter past eight, and it wouldn't have taken him beyond nine o'clock at the latest to reach Alexa's house in Overton Ridge. And probably earlier than that, this time of night. So that's an hour, give or take, that he's been there. That's not very long. And who knows? He could be on his way back home now. I'm letting this get the better of me.

My phone buzzes and I jump. I grab it off my nightstand and look at the face, praying that it's Jason calling, realizing, at that moment, just how nervous I really am.

It isn't Jason. It's Joel Lightner.

'What's going on?' he says to me when I answer. 'What's up with Jason? Is he having a hard time today or something? He hasn't called me back. I didn't want to bother him, I know he must be going through hell right now, but this is imp—'

'He doesn't have his cell phone, Joel. Or he didn't all afternoon, at least.'

'That doesn't make any sense,' says Lightner.

'Why doesn't that make sense?'

'I left him a voice mail this afternoon. Two o'clock, right around there.'

'Right, but he didn't get it.'

'Sure, he did.'

I get off the bed and pace Jason's bedroom. 'No, Joel.'

'Yes, Shauna. He texted me back, maybe ten or fifteen minutes later. He said he got my message and he'd call me back later. He said, "Give me a few hours. Don't do anything."'

'No.' I shake my head, even though Joel can't see it. 'That's impossible. He hasn't had his phone all afternoon.'

'Then who did? Who texted me back and told me to sit tight for a while?'

Beep-beep.

Next to me in the bedroom, the house alarm pad has gone off twice, the sound of the door downstairs opening. Relief floods through me.

'He just got home, he'll call you back,' I tell Joel, punching out the phone.

I start for the staircase, stopping and realizing something: I didn't hear the garage door open and close. Maybe that was the white noise in my head, drowning it out. Maybe it was Joel talking to me.

Or maybe the garage door *didn't* open and close.

'Hello?' I call out downstairs.

Nothing.

'Hello?' I try again. 'Jason?'

My heartbeat ratcheting up now, I head back into the bedroom. There, on the bed, is Jason's Glock handgun, the creepy black instrument of death.

Take it, I begged Jason before he left. But he wouldn't. *You keep it*, he said to me.

I hear footsteps, from the foyer up to the second floor, heavy, pounding steps. Jason. Jason's hurt again, like earlier this afternoon when he could barely stagger through the door. Struggling to make it into the house, in the throes of withdrawal.

Do I take the gun?

I rush down the stairs, holding the gun away from my body in my right hand, pointed down. I hit the landing and turn into the kitchen.

Alexa Himmel is standing in the living room, walking toward the kitchen. I take a step back and, in a moment of panic, almost fall backward onto the stairs. I'm lucky the gun didn't go off.

'Shauna,' she says, almost sweetly, her feet planted now. She looks like a different person, a more primitive and feral version of the cute, petite woman she is, her face sheet-white except for those dark, wounded eyes that glare at me. She is wearing a gray T-shirt and black sweatpants. Her hair is flat, air-dried, as if she recently showered but didn't touch it with a towel or a comb.

She looks like she was roused from sleep. Except for those eyes that never leave me, those eyes that project such an intense glow. If there is an intersection of despondent and enraged, I am looking at it.

What I'm *not* looking at are her hands. They are tucked behind her back.

'What are you . . . Where's Jason?' I ask.

'Why do you have a gun, Shauna?'

'Why . . . why are you here?' I stutter, a cold wave passing through me.

'Me? I'm just—'

'What do you have behind your back?' I demand.

She takes a step toward me. 'Nothing, Shauna. Put the gun down, for heaven's sake.'

'Show me,' I say, before my throat closes. Then, in a whisper, 'Your hands.'

I raise the weapon, not directly at her but in her vicinity, preparing myself. My hand is trembling, the gun along with it. It must make for a silly pose. I use my other hand for support, which helps steady the weapon. Now if I could only steady my nerves.

It's not that hard, my father, the deer hunter, always used to say about shooting a gun. *Just aim for the middle of the body and squeeze the trigger.*

'I don't have anything behind my back, Shauna. Now *put that gun down* before one of us gets hurt. I just want to talk to you.'

I am cornered against the staircase where it wraps around to the kitchen, Alexa standing in the living room of the open-floor space, but not more than ten feet away. I can smell the heat coming off her, the restrained rage with each heave of her chest.

'Where's . . . Jason?' I manage.

'I said, put that gun down, Shauna!' Her left hand pops out from behind her, poking a finger in the air at me.

Unable to speak, I shake my head, the gun more or less steady in my hands.

She stares at me with those rabid eyes, watching the gun, watching me. 'You wouldn't use it,' she says. 'You wouldn't pull that trigger.'

'I will.' My voice comes alive, something unexpected.

She is quiet, but her mind is racing. It's her resolve, more than anything, that unnerves me. I'm the one with the gun, and yet it feels like the situation is reversed, that somehow she has the upper hand, that she is willing to take the ultimate step and I am not, and each of us knows it.

Then the first hint of pure emotion crosses her face, her face balled up in frustration and rage. 'I heard you earlier tonight, when I called here,' Alexa says. 'Interfering as always. Why do you have to do that? Why can't you just let Jason be happy?'

I don't answer.

'I said *put down that goddamn gun!*' Her throat full, choking, tears forming in her eyes. 'I need you . . . I need you to put down that gun. Please, Shauna, *please*. I'm not here to hurt you.'

I take a deep breath, then another, and speak again.

'Alexa, if you come any closer, I will pull this trigger. I don't want to, but I will.'

'Shauna, I don't have *time* for this.' Her face scrunched up, her hand rotating in the air like a wheel. 'Just – put it down and I swear we'll just talk.'

I don't speak, but I shake my head no.

Her composure continues to melt, her shoulders heaving, her face now streaked with tears, her mouth turned downward in a snarl.

'You don't know what it means to love somebody,' she hisses. 'You like to live in your prim-and-proper little world, but you don't know about real sacrifice. You won't do for him what I did for him.' She pounds her chest with the palm of her left hand.

And then her right hand comes into view, a long knife at her side.

Don't, Alexa. Please, God, don't.

'Don't,' I warn her.

'You think I'm afraid of your gun?' She shakes her head wistfully, almost mumbling the words. Her right hand, holding the knife, rotates in small circles, as if she's warming up, getting the kinks out before she springs into action.

'You don't understand him like I do,' she says. 'You don't understand *us*.'

Her right hand suddenly locks with her wrist, the knife now poised firmly at a sixty-degree angle, as if ready to be thrust upward.

'I don't want to shoot you, Alexa, but I swear to *God*, I will.' I spit out the words, the fear choking my throat, the thumping of my pulse like a gong inside my head. I'm doing my best to keep my outward composure, keep my trembling hands from dropping this weapon. I do the math in silence: No more than four or five strides and she would be on me. Less than five seconds. In that window of time and space, I will have to decide whether I'm capable of pulling this trigger.

I see it in her eyes, in that dreamy way she looks at the weapon in my hand: She is willing to accept either outcome. She is not afraid of death. She is not afraid of anything anymore.

And then, in a movement so sudden that I lurch backward, almost discharging my weapon, she raises the knife and tosses it onto the breakfast bar, a clanging noise that rattles my stretched nerves.

'Do it,' she says to me, raising her hands in surrender, then spinning around, a one-eighty, her back now turned to me. 'You want to shoot me? Do it now, Shauna. Shoot me in the back. This is your chance.'

Relief flooding me, I adjust my posture, spread my feet for better balance.

'Now or never,' she says, and the words are like a siren in my head. She isn't going to stop. She isn't going to let this go. She's made the decision not to act right now, not this moment when I'm prepared for her, when I'm training a gun on her, but I won't always be prepared, will I? Not me, and not Jason.

And not our baby.

She's never going to stop, and every second that I do nothing while she stands there with her back to me, defenseless, every moment that I fail to act empowers her, clarifies for her my lack of resolve, and it's now simply a matter of *when*, not *if*, and then the gun explodes, vibrating through my hands, a single burst, magnificent and exhilarating in its power, its deafening roar, and then everything is different forever.

109

Shauna

10:25 P.M.

The garage door comes to life, cranking upward. A car brakes hard inside the garage. Soon the alarm sings out a *beep-beep* as the side door opens, and Jason is calling out to me as he races up the stairs.

'Oh, no. No.'

I realize only then that somewhere along the line, I have closed my eyes. When I open them, it seems garishly bright, and Jason is hovering over Alexa, not daring to touch anything. Then his hands are on me, his soapy smell invading my space. 'Shauna, I'm so sorry. I'm so sorry. Are you – hurt?'

I shake my head no. I'm deliberately unfocused, holding it at bay, refusing to look directly at it, knowing that when I do, it will change me forever, and not being ready to change forever. Not just at this moment, no.

'I was afraid . . . you were dead,' I tell Jason.

'I was afraid *you* were,' he answers. 'That's why she came here. She came here to kill you. She planned this whole thing, Shauna. She set it up so I wouldn't be here, so she could come here and kill you.'

I break free of him and stand up, my legs unsteady. 'I . . . shot her,' I say. Saying it somehow brings it to life, makes it real, not a dream.

I have killed somebody. I have taken someone's life, someone who was walking away from me as I pulled the trigger. I will always be a person who killed somebody. My daughter or son, the small clump of cells growing every day inside me, will be raised by a killer. I will teach my child that violence is wrong, that thou shalt not kill, and I will know, every time I say that, that I am a hypocrite, that I fully understand the instinct to surrender to impulse.

And yet, I don't remember the moment of surrender. I don't remember saying to myself, *Okay, time to shoot her*. I don't even know if I meant to do it or if it was an accident. How could I not know that difference? Because doesn't that make all the difference? If it was an accident, like one of those tragic stories you see on the evening news from time to time, usually involving a four-year-old or something, two kids playing with Daddy's gun and *it just went off*—

Did the gun 'just go off'? Tell me it did. Someone, please tell me it did.

And yet. And yet, Alexa was going to hurt me and my child. She wasn't going to stop. I could see it in her eyes, those haunting, preda-tory, hate-filled eyes, probing me, appraising me, debating whether to charge me as I held the gun with both hands. Alexa was going to be back. She wasn't going to let anything or anyone get between Jason and her. She was going to take that knife and . . . and . . .

'She was going to kill you,' Jason repeats.

'She was . . . never going to leave us alone,' I whisper.

'Shauna, listen.' Jason grabs me, holds me at arm's length. 'You have to be able to say that Alexa was coming at you with a knife. Somehow she spun around, okay, fine, you shot her in the back. But she came here to kill you, to stab you with *that* knife.'

He rips off a paper towel from a roll on the counter and walks over to the breakfast bar. He picks up the knife with the paper towel and walks over to Alexa.

'What are you *doing*?' I ask.

He turns and looks at me like I'm the one being unreasonable. 'What do you *think* I'm doing?'

'You're putting the knife in her hand?'

'Yes, I am.'

'No,' I say. 'I'll tell them what happened and . . . that will be that.'

'What does that even mean?' Jason says. ' "That will be that"?'

Jason looks over my head, considering everything. 'No, this doesn't work. This – how far away were you when you shot her? *Shauna*.' He snaps his fingers. 'How far away?'

I point to the staircase.

'Okay, so that's, like, ten or twelve feet,' he says to himself, thinking this through. 'You shot her from pretty far away, with her back turned, while she was unarmed. That's the current state of this crime scene. And it's a very long bridge from that set of facts to self-defense. Even if I put the knife in her hand, her back was turned.'

I try to analyze it myself, still in a trance but trusting Jason's analysis as my friend and as a whip-smart defense attorney, unsure of which matters more at the moment. I raise a hand to my face and find it trembling, and then my vision blurs, everything is moving, slow-motion animation.

'It's over,' I hear myself say. 'I'm not going to lie.'

And then I've fallen to the floor in the kitchen. And then my head is in my hands, and tears are flowing, my shoulders are bobbing, a full-scale cry.

'You won't *have* to lie,' Jason says, a firmness to his voice that gives me comfort, a lifeboat in turbulent waves. He grips my arm. 'Because you were never here, Shauna.'

He lifts me up effortlessly, my legs unfolding and finding the floor, Jason's bear-arms wrapped around me. 'Think of the baby,' he whispers. 'Think only of the baby. And you'll see I'm right. Let me handle this. I can handle this.'

'No, it's . . . it's too much, Jase.'

'This is too risky for you, Shauna. It doesn't matter what you and I know. This doesn't look like self-defense. I do this for a living, okay? This is what I do. This isn't first-degree murder by a long shot, but it ain't self-defense, either. This is prison time or, at the very best, probably a trial and the county lockup for you in the meantime. County lockup, Shauna, while our baby grows inside you. You give birth in a detention facility.' He cups a hand under my chin and makes me look at him. 'That can't happen. It won't happen. This isn't about me. This isn't even about you. It's about the baby. You know I'm right.'

I put my head against his shoulder, squeeze my eyes shut, try to mentally will away the last hour of my life. Rewind the clock, let Alexa leave, then call the police, get a restraining order, something, anything other than squeezing that trigger, anything, God, ANYTHING—

'Let me do this, Shauna. I can do this and make it turn out okay. I can.'

'How?' My voice trembling so hard, the word has three syllables.

'Never mind how. It's better you not know. But I promise you, I can do this.'

No, I think to myself, but I don't say it. I don't say it because a part of me is saying *yes*, yes, it's about the baby, he's right, but *no*, it's too much for anyone to do for anyone else—

'Hey.' Jason gives me one good shake. 'It's decided. I've got this covered. So here's what's going to happen. Are you listening?'

I take a deep breath, blinking away tears.

'I need you to clear everything of yours out of here. Your purse, work bag, anything of yours needs to be gone. Can you help me do that?' he asks, pulling my arm.

'I can . . . do that.'

'Good. And then we're going to get you out of here. You were never here tonight, Shauna, do you understand? As of this moment, you were never here.'

110

Jason

10:40 P.M.

Shauna gets into my SUV, inside my dark garage. Next to her, on the seat, is her purse and computer bag, stuffed with work papers and her laptop.

'Sit tight,' I say to her. 'I'll just be a few minutes.'

She nods. Her face is washed out, her eyes vacant. I close the car door behind her. The dome light slowly fades, leaving her in darkness.

I run back upstairs to the second floor, tread carefully around Alexa's body, and stop and think.

I look away from Alexa's face, lying in profile. I can't let sympathy or remorse factor in here. I have to come up with a plan. I need an airtight plan, and I need it right now.

But before my mind even starts the race, it stops. It's right in front of me.

I don't need a plan. Alexa already gave me one.

I've been planning for this.

I squeeze my eyes shut and recite her fabricated suicide note:

Now u finaly know who I am
Now u will never forgit
Number six was difrent
But she was my favorit

She was going to kill Shauna and pin it on Marshall. I'm not sure what was going to be 'different' about the murder of Shauna, victim number six, compared to the other five women he filleted. Using a different knife? Maybe so. Maybe that was it.

But what about *shooting* victim number six in the *back*?

Now *that's* different. And Alexa would be just as much Marshall's 'favorite' as Shauna would have been, each of them a woman close to me, a bloody parting gift to me before Marshall, his mission accomplished, took his own life.

The needle, I think to myself. *The needle that Marshall planted in my office.*

I race upstairs to my bedroom, to my nightstand, to retrieve that needle. Marshall must have injected it into his victims. There's no other possible reason for a needle. But he injected them where? In the neck? The arm? *The neck,* I speculate. Women in the summer always have their necks exposed, and it would be harder to ward off than a needle prick to the arm, an appendage that the victim could move, flap, rotate in several directions. If I had one chance to stab someone with a needle, I'd go for the neck.

It's a guess, but a good guess. And if I'm wrong, then it's another reason the sixth victim was 'different.'

But – *where the hell is the needle?* I put it right here, in the small space under the pullout drawer. There's no way it could have fallen. Where the hell could it *possibly—*

'Oh,' I say aloud.

I'll bet I wasn't the only one who had that idea.

I go back downstairs and walk over to Alexa. She is wearing dark sweatpants, but sweatpants with pockets. I pat her right pocket lightly. Wearing my rubber gloves from Marshall's apartment, I fish into the pocket slowly. I feel plastic. Yes . . .

Yes.

I pull out the small bag I kept the needle in. There's the needle itself, undisturbed, still a small trace of fluid in the vial. Alexa really *had* been planning this. She knew where I kept the needle. She took it, probably the last time she was here. She was going to kill Shauna and inject her with this needle. She couldn't have known when, or even if, we were going to find the notorious North Side Slasher, but she didn't need to. She would have killed Shauna sooner or later, anyway. Either way, whether we had found him or not, she could blame it on the North Side Slasher. Once she listened to the voice mail Joel left on my cell phone this afternoon, she realized she had a small window of opportunity to actually pull this off – to kill Marshall, type a suicide note that referenced a sixth victim, and then kill Shauna and blame it on Marshall. She just needed me out of the way.

I steady my hand, touch Alexa's hair softly. 'I'm sorry,' I say to her, as if a needle injection into her jugular vein is the worst thing that happened to her in the last hour. I'm sorry about a lot of things, and I'll have plenty of time to mourn them, but right now, I have only one goal, and that's to make sure Shauna and our baby are as far away from this as possible.

Once I've injected Alexa with the needle, the vial now empty, I drop the needle back into the plastic bag. This is going to match up very nicely with those other syringes in Marshall's cabinet.

I feel into Alexa's right pocket again. I felt something else in there, I thought, something I need. And yes, here they are.

Her keys. It's not easy getting my house key off her key ring with these rubber gloves, but I'm not risking a print. It's worth the extra effort. It won't make sense to the police when they come here tonight. If I wasn't home when Alexa was killed – as I will claim – and nobody else was, either, then how did Alexa get into my house without a key?

It will clearly put suspicion on me, if it isn't there already. My dead ex-girlfriend, shot in my house with my gun? They probably won't need any extra help. But if they do, the house key, or more specifically the lack thereof, will make me look even worse.

The knife on the breakfast bar? It probably has Alexa's prints on it. That won't help. No. The knife has to go. I will find some sewer and dump it.

I place my Glock on the breakfast bar in place of the knife. It quite possibly has Shauna's prints on it. That's no good. I take a sanitary wipe out of the tube and give the gun a good scrub. I'll blame it on Marshall. He wiped off his prints after he shot Alexa.

I remember one last thing: my phone. Either it's at Alexa's house or she brought it here. It's not in her right pocket. Possibly her left?

The position of her body is such that her left pocket is under her, but I'm able to slide my fingers in there without moving her upper body. It's there. With two fingers, I slide out my phone. I'll be sure that the voice mail from Joel is erased, and I'll check my text messages, too. I know from a drug case I handled that my telecommunications carrier does not retain the content of voice mails or text messages once deleted.

Okay.

I take a moment, assessing everything. Time to go.

The knife, hypodermic needle, and Alexa's house key in tow, I head downstairs to the garage to drive Shauna home.

Then I stop. One more thing. One more cherry on the sundae. I run upstairs and grab it, then head down to the garage.

111

Jason

11:00 P.M.

My ex-girlfriend, my house, my gun.

A good start. Hard not to look at me as the prime suspect.

No house key on Alexa. So no explanation for how she got into my house if, as I will tell them, I wasn't home.

Better. It will be the first lie they catch me in. If I came home and found her dead, how did she get inside in the first place?

Lie about the relationship. Tell them you and Alexa were still a couple.

Even better. It will take them, what, twenty-four hours to get their warrants and see the phone records – her obsessive phone calls to me – and the e-mails, including that horrible one with the letter to the disciplinary board. Line those up with me saying, *Oh, sure, we were doing just swell, Alexa and me,* and you have a liar and a murderer.

Because that is precisely what has to happen. I can't have the cops starting to get all curious. I can't have them saying things like, *Hey, let's take a look at other people close to Jason – like, for example, Shauna Tasker!* Shauna wouldn't hold up under the slightest scrutiny. She'll spill everything if they so much as look in her direction in the next few days.

No, I have to be an obvious suspect right here, tonight. So obvious, so glaringly guilty in their eyes that they stop looking anywhere else.

My girlfriend, my gun, my house, the lack of any house key or means of entry for Alexa, and my lies. It will be enough.

No doubt, they will say. *Kolarich is our guy.*

I'll worry later about how to clean this thing up, how to keep myself from spending life in prison. Maybe the cops will end up putting Marshall Rivers together with Alexa's murder on their own. Maybe I'll give them a few hints. Or maybe I'll wait until trial and spring it on them. It will depend on a lot of things. Things I won't worry about tonight.

I pull the SUV up to the street on which Shauna's condo building is located. It wouldn't be a good idea for anyone to see my car dropping her off. She can walk the half-block.

'You can sit up now,' I say.

In the backseat, Shauna sits up, rights herself. If anyone, God forbid, saw me drive out of my garage, it had to be only me they saw.

'You okay?' I say.

She gives a flat, exhausted snicker.

'You remember what we talked about?'

'I remember,' she says. 'Walk into my building, act tired, don't talk to anyone.'

'Right.'

'Get in bed and don't move. Try to get some rest.'

'Yes.'

'Call Joel and tell him to stand down.'

'Say it exactly, Shauna. It's important.'

She is quiet a moment. I need her for this. I can't call Lightner tonight. The police are about to become very interested in my phone records.

'I will tell Joel that you and I talked, and I'm calling at your request, and he shouldn't do anything about that voice mail this afternoon. And he shouldn't believe what he sees on the news tomorrow.'

Close enough.

'What was on the voice mail he left you?' she asks.

'Later,' I tell her. 'Nothing for you to know tonight. Now, listen,' I say. 'I'm going to be calling you later on tonight. Right?'

'Right.'

'It will be hours from now. Maybe the middle of the night.'

'Yes.'

'And what am I going to tell you?'

She takes a breath. 'You're going to tell me that the police are placing you under arrest.'

'Correct. And what are you going to do then?'

'I'm going to call Bradley and have him go down to Area Three headquarters.'

'Correct. It has to be Bradley, not you,' I say. Shauna is in no position to sit in on an interrogation over the next few hours. The police would get a confession, but it wouldn't come from me.

'Okay.'

'So if anyone tries to talk to you in the next few days, you and Bradley are counsel of record. You're my lawyer.'

'I understand.'

'And you're not going to worry about me, because I have this under control. I'm going to let them think I killed her, but it's not going to stick. I'm going to make sure of that.'

She doesn't speak. I'm not sure she can. I want to reach back there, touch her, but she doesn't need more emotional avalanches right now.

'Shauna,' I say. 'This is all my fault. I'm the one who let Alexa into our lives, and I badly underestimated her. Make no mistake, she planned this tonight. She tricked me into being away from home so she could go to my house and kill you. If I'd gotten home fifteen minutes earlier, I'd have shot her myself. So remember that tonight. I don't care if her back was turned. I don't care if it was tonight or tomorrow or a week from now—'

'She wasn't going to stop.'

'That's right, she wasn't going to stop, Shauna.'

'I get it,' she says quietly. 'I know.'

A police car passes by us, slow and steady. I watch it until it disappears, two blocks down, with a left turn.

'You . . . need to get going,' says Shauna.

'Okay, kiddo.'

She pushes the door open, lifting her bag and shuffling out of the car. She stops before she exits. 'Tell me you know what you're doing.'

'I know what I'm doing,' I promise her. I watch her make the half-block walk to her condo building. It must be the longest and loneliest walk of her life. Finally, she turns in to her building and disappears into the lobby.

Then I pop the car back into gear and drive to Marshall Rivers's apartment.

THREE MONTHS
BEFORE TRIAL
Thursday, September 5

112

Jason

The visitation room at the Alejandro Morales Detention Center is about as nondescript as they come, pale gray walls and an old maple desk, mismatched wooden chairs. Whoever designed the 'Morales Palace' had an eye for soul-crushing blandness.

Shauna, my lawyer and pipeline to the real world, walks into the room. She has visited three times a week – Tuesday, Wednesday, Thursday – often to discuss the case and sometimes just to see me. Three weeks ago, we waived our preliminary hearing, and Judge Judith Bialek found probable cause to send me to trial on one count of murder in the first degree. Then, with a trace of apology on her face, she denied me bond.

The case would normally be in its infancy, but we're on a fast track. Shauna demanded a speedy trial, putting the prosecution on a constitutional clock, and the judge set December 9 for trial.

Shauna moves a chair to the side of the square table next to me and takes my hand. She has brought nothing with her. No major discussion of the case today. We didn't discuss the case when she visited two days ago, either. That was a Tuesday. The day after Labor Day.

That was the day she burst into tears before she even said hello. That was the day she told me that she'd lost the baby.

The spotting on her underwear, then the cramps, then the trip to the emergency room because her doctor's office was closed on

Labor Day. Labor Day – of course it had to be *Labor* Day that she miscarried. It wasn't enough to put that tiny dagger through Shauna's heart, but let's have it happen on Labor Day so we can sprinkle in some irony, too, and remember it every year.

Today, Shauna is different. The mourning is still all over her, the slump to her shoulders, the lifelessness in her eyes, but there is something different in how she addresses me.

'How are you?' I say, my hand on her arm.

'Don't,' she says, tightening up. 'I don't want to talk about that today. It's too . . . it's too much for me. Okay?'

'Sure, okay,' I say. And then I know. I suspected, but now I know.

'I've been thinking,' she starts. 'There's no longer a reason for all of this. There's no baby to protect anymore, Jason.'

Her eyes fill, but her face is strident, determined.

'That was always the justification,' she says. 'We were letting you carry the water for what happened, instead of me, because of the baby.'

I shake my head no.

'I want to tell the truth now,' she says.

'No,' I answer. 'Absolutely not.'

She shakes her head and looks away from me. 'Do you have any idea what this is like for me?' she mumbles. 'Knowing that *I* did something and *you're* taking the blame?'

'First of all,' I say, driving a finger into the table, 'I'm far more responsible than you are, Shauna. Alexa was my doing, not yours. You were put in an impossible situation, and if it weren't for me, you never would have *been* in that situation.'

She chews on her lip, listening.

'And *second*,' I continue, 'I can win this case, Shauna. I can.'

She's heard all of this before. She doesn't look convinced.

'And if you don't?' she asks. 'Who was it who told me that the hardest feat to accomplish in the legal system is to overturn a guilty verdict?'

I never like it when she says my words back to me.

'If I'm convicted, then you can tell your story. I'll back it up.'

She gives me a sideways look. She doesn't believe I'd ever do that.

'Look at it this way,' I say, because I've expected this conversation, too. 'You go in now, today, and spill it to Roger Ogren. What happens? You'll be prosecuted and convicted. And me? Oh, they'll find something for me, Shauna. They'll convict me of something. Tampering with evidence, lying to a police officer, obstruction – something.'

She's listening, at least.

'In other words, we both go to prison,' I say. 'But do it my way, and if I beat this case, we both walk.'

Her eyes rise over my head as she ponders this.

'Think about it,' I say. 'I'm just sitting here now, in solitary confinement. The detox program the county uses is actually pretty good. In a lot of ways, it's easier to get off the pills while I'm in here, free of any temptation. So what's the rush? There isn't any. There's no difference between you giving your mea culpa now versus giving it after I'm convicted, if I'm convicted. But let me have my trial. Give me a chance to win.'

Shauna leans into me. We've had this entire conversation in rather hushed tones – it's a privileged communication and the DOC isn't allowed to listen, but you never know – but now she speaks even more quietly still.

'Convince me you can win this case.'

I touch my forehead to hers. 'Better you not know. We've been over this. I want to keep you clean on this. You and Bradley.'

Shauna is quiet for a long time. Then she asks a question I've long expected.

'Why do I get the feeling that it's not just a coincidence that Marshall Rivers committed suicide at roughly the same time that Alexa died?'

I will credit Alexa with that feat – she pulled off the fake suicide. She had some help, I think, from the police. The way it's been playing out in the press, the police had narrowed their list of suspects and were bearing down on Marshall, and Marshall felt that heat, killed himself before they could bring him in. Me, I don't buy it. I don't think they were close. But I don't know. And I don't care. The suicide theory fits their story line. It makes them look like they were days or hours from solving the crime, they were just about to knock on his door with their guns drawn, as opposed to stumbling upon the killer when he voluntarily ended his reign of terror. It's good press for the mayor and the police department. *Sure, he committed suicide, but only because he felt us coming. We knew it was him. We caught him. We can keep you safe.*

'You have a vivid imagination, Shauna.'

'Jason.'

'Do you want to know if I killed Marshall Rivers, Shauna? If you do, ask me. I'll tell you the truth.'

She makes a disapproving noise. 'I see that the Area Three detectives handled that case. The north side murders.'

'Is that a fact?'

'And I suppose that's why you want me to list every single detective on the Area Three roster on the witness disclosure. Because we're going to be talking about that case, as well as Alexa, at trial.'

I don't bother trying to disabuse her of that notion. It would be insulting her intelligence.

'Jason,' she whispers, 'if you have something up your sleeve, which you clearly do, why not tell Ogren now and get it over with? Why rot in here for three more months?'

'Because he won't let me off until he's sure, and he'll take his time. He'll consider every angle.'

'Every angle,' Shauna says, an edge to her voice.

'Every angle,' I say. 'He'll look at the time-of-death window compared to the time I called 911, and he'll say to himself, *Boy, Jason might have had two, three hours to play with there. Maybe all this stuff he's showing me to prove his innocence – maybe he doctored a few things.* And we don't want that, Shauna. We'll spring it on him at trial, and he'll have days, maybe, but not weeks and months, to react.'

Shauna draws back and gives me a look that a mother gives when she disapproves of a child's actions but also finds them amusing. My mother wore that expression most of my childhood.

But then she grows serious again. 'You think it will work?'

'Probably,' I say. 'You never know for sure. Roger's head is going to explode at trial.'

We are both quiet. The smell of her peach shampoo reminds me of better days. I've certainly had better ones, but I'm starting to break free of the grip that the OxyContin had on me. I'm still lost in the woods, but now I know the path back. I just have to make sure I stay on that path. This incarceration, ironically, has helped. Being deprived of your liberty eliminates options, removes temptations.

I still have the dreams, the night sweats, but the craving, that wicked tugging, has diminished. Everything is on a smaller scale now, still present, but dissipating. The medication they give me helps, but it's talking about it every day that works the most for me, acknowledging it, identifying it for what it is, a sickness, instead of making excuses and keeping the good times rollin'.

'Lightner sends his best, by the way,' she says. 'Talked to him yesterday.'

'About what?' I give her a look.

'Don't worry.' She raises a calming hand. 'Joel isn't talking to me. Or anyone else.'

For obvious reasons, it would not behoove me if anyone discovered that I knew the identity of Marshall Rivers before his death. Joel understands that, too. So he has forgotten about all that work he did searching for the north side killer, which led him to Marshall Rivers. The police interviewed him about me, but they had no reason to ask him anything about Marshall; they asked him about my relationship with Alexa. I assume he told them the truth, that he suspected she was bad news but didn't know much about her firsthand.

They also asked Joel about conversations we had, documented from phone records, but Joel was working for me in my capacity as a criminal defense attorney, so the privilege umbrella extended to our conversations. He kept his mouth shut. And I'm pretty sure that, if a judge forced him to talk, he'd either take a contempt citation or, more likely, make up a story.

But it hasn't come to that. Roger Ogren doesn't consider this a complicated case. His theory is simple: a bad breakup, a grief-stricken woman obsessively tries to reconcile, finally threatening to spill the beans on my drug use, and so I kill her. Marshall Rivers? Or some case I was working on with Joel? They haven't entered Roger's mind. He likes his case, and he hasn't seen any evidence from the defense that would make him think he's wrong.

Not yet, at least.

All the same, I told Shauna that I didn't want Joel visiting me. I don't want to create any ideas in the prosecutors' minds if they look at my visitor sheet. As of now, they will only see on that sheet three people: my two lawyers and my brother, Pete, who has come into town a couple of times already to check in on me.

'Promise me, Jason,' Shauna says. 'Promise me, if you're convicted, you'll let me tell the truth.'

'I promise.'

'*Promise* me. Because if you don't, I'll call Roger right now.'

I detect a tinge of disappointment in her voice. Shauna, I think, wants to confess. Or stated more accurately, she feels wrong not confessing. I think she believes the shooting was justifiable – I hope she does – but hiding it does not sit right with her, regardless of the consequences.

'Shauna,' I say, 'if the jury comes back guilty, I'm going to pop out of my chair and point at you and say, "She did it! She did it!" I swear I will.'

That seems to do it for her. She probably doesn't believe me, and her heart is telling her to come clean, but her brain is telling her that I'm right, that the smartest plan at this stage is to give me my day in court.

I have a good chance, I think. But there's always risk. I've set the table for some Perry Mason revelations at my trial, but you never really know how things are going to work out. Because what I said to Alexa when she told me she killed Marshall Rivers was true: She could have made a hundred different mistakes. I could have, as well, in what I did.

So I will focus on what is most important right now – my recovery – and hold my breath until trial. It's Shauna who has all the worries. She lost the baby and doesn't have me around to help her grieve. She has to live with the fact that, whatever the circumstances may have been, she pulled a trigger and ended a woman's life. And she has the stress of knowing that my fate rests in her hands. A stress that, no matter how much she denies it, was probably responsible for the loss of the baby.

But she *has* to be my lawyer, because it makes it so much harder for the prosecution to try to talk to her. They'd have to disqualify her as counsel, and the judge would push back because I have a constitutional right to a lawyer of my choice. If Roger Ogren really wanted to push it, he could, but he doesn't have any basis for doing so. As long as Shauna is my lawyer, there's almost no chance that Roger Ogren or Detective Cromartie would put her under the lights. If they ever did so, dollars to donuts that Shauna and I would trade places in this detention center.

I touch Shauna's face now. I want to say so many things to her. *We'll have another baby. There's still time for us.*

But I don't. Because I don't know if either of those statements is true. The state of our relationship is not something we've discussed. Everything was so bizarre, after all. Things between us were strained, then she told me she was pregnant and I confessed my drug addiction, and we were together, joined at the hip, maybe forever. And then a few days later, she shoots Alexa and I'm locked up. Quite the bumpy hill.

Can we come back from that? It's not something either of us is ready to explore at the moment. There are too many other things occupying our attention.

So instead, I just say, 'We'll get through this, Shauna. One way or the other, we'll get through this,' and we both pretend to believe it.

PEOPLE VS. JASON KOLARICH
TRIAL, DAY 7
Monday, December 23

113

Jason

The court clerk gavels the mobbed courtroom to order as Judge Judith Bialek assumes the bench. My case is called, and the room goes silent.

It's been six days since Shauna cross-examined Detective Vance Austin. Roger Ogren asked for a continuance of a week, minimum, to consider any rebuttal evidence he might have. Noting that a week would be Christmas Eve, the judge truncated the request by one day, to December 23. That was more than enough time, she said.

During that time, the prosecutors mobilized their extensive resources to try to salvage their case – I mean, seek out the truth. The word is that Roger Ogren tried to reopen the inquiry into Marshall Rivers's suicide, to consider the possibility that he'd been murdered. His argument was simple enough: By the coroner's estimate, Alexa could have died as early as nine P.M., giving me three hours of free time, so to speak, before I dialed 911. Plenty of time for me to have driven to the home of Marshall Rivers and killed him, typed the fake suicide note, planted evidence, whatever, after killing Alexa, or even before killing her. The word I heard back, via Joel Lightner, is that the police detectives told Ogren that his theory was far-fetched, which I find somewhat amusing given that it's exactly what Alexa Himmel planned to do – fake Marshall's suicide, kill Shauna, and pin it on Marshall.

Roger Ogren, in fact, found resistance everywhere he turned. First, the press, more enamored with Marshall Rivers than with me, far preferred the idea that the North Side Slasher had claimed a sixth victim – which meant that I was a *man wrongly accused*, another cause a hungry media eagerly embraced. I was embarrassed to learn that an entire following built up around this idea of me as the victim, including a 'Free Jason Kolarich' website and Facebook page. My role in taking down a corrupt governor, Carlton Snow, which has never been confirmed by me or anyone else, became accepted as fact and Exhibit A in my cause. That's what I've become, a crusade.

James Drinker – the real James Drinker, the one whose apartment door I crashed through, complete with the mop of red hair and the protruding stomach – came forward and told his story of how I accosted him before realizing that I had the wrong guy. That corroborated my story that Marshall had used that fake name. It also showed me as the conscientious defense lawyer who was trying to stop his client, the serial killer, only to realize that he didn't know his real identity. Drinker also said that he'd seen Marshall several times at a burger joint that was located between Higgins Auto Body and the dry cleaner's where Marshall worked. Not hard to imagine Marshall sizing up Drinker, thinking he was roughly the same size, that with a red wig and a belly suit, he could pull off a decent impersonation. Good enough for his purposes, at least.

The police also got around to remembering that, among the thousands of anonymous tips they received, someone had sent a letter to Detective Vance Austin identifying James Drinker as the north side killer. The letter leaked out and became public fare, the words cut out of a magazine like some ransom note in a 1950s mystery movie. There might have been some suspicion that I was the one who sent that letter. But that's not how it all came out. Why?

Because there was one more thing I left in Marshall Rivers's apartment that night, when I fitted Alexa's key on his key ring and placed that hypodermic needle alongside the others he had used. I remembered it just before I drove Shauna home on my way to Marshall's apartment.

It was the *Sports Illustrated* magazine I used to cut out the words for the anonymous note. When the cops first found it, after responding to Marshall's suicide, they thought nothing of it. Marshall just had a copy of an *SI* magazine, no big deal. Compared to the bloody knife and the hypodermic needles and the packets of fentanyl, who cared about a sports magazine? But after they remembered the 'James Drinker' anonymous note over this last week, they searched through the inventory of his apartment and found it, with words cut out of several pages.

This proves it, wrote one columnist in the *Herald* who had taken up my cause. *Marshall Rivers used the same name in the anonymous note that he gave to Jason Kolarich – James Drinker – to throw the police off the scent.*

Roger's other problem was simply the lack of proof to corroborate his theory. He couldn't prove that I knew the identity of Marshall Rivers before his death. He couldn't even prove that Marshall died before I was taken into custody, given the vagueness of the time-of-death window for Marshall, whose body wasn't discovered until August 2. It was possible that he was still alive when the police responded to my 911 call, which would obviously rule me out as his killer. And even if he *could* show that I knew Marshall's identity by then, and that Marshall was dead by the time the cops hauled me in, they had no proof that I had, in fact, killed him. The medical examiner wasn't willing to come off her finding that the manner of death was suicide, and I don't think the police department wanted her to. Even if Roger got the coroner to flip, they would be stuck with her first report, her initial conclusions, which would make her revised opinion open to considerable criticism.

And every step Roger tried to take, he had a county prosecutor facing reelection who wasn't happy about looking like the heavy in this melodrama. A *not guilty* was all but certain now, so wouldn't the county attorney look a lot better if he dropped the charges in light of these new revelations? An elected prosecutor more concerned with Truth, Justice, and the American Way than with mounting another head on his wall?

My biggest fear was that Marshall had followed through on his threat to me, that he was planting evidence at the crime scenes to implicate me, and that the police would now go back and find those clues. I found the hypodermic needle in my office, so I did check Marshall on that one move, but I knew he'd swiped that Bic pen that had my bite marks and saliva on it, and probably other things like used tissues from my wastebasket, anything that might have my DNA. Did he plant those things? I don't know. If he did, the cops didn't attach any significance to them. Or they didn't find them. Or maybe I just gave Marshall too much credit. Or maybe he was waiting until he was done with the killing spree and he was going to put it all at the final crime scene, one gigantic final present to me.

I'll never know. Nor will I ever know when that final day was going to arrive, when Marshall was going to be finished killing women on the north side before lowering the boom on me. I'm not sure that day was *ever* going to come. He was just having too much fun doing it, with the added bonus of torturing me in the process.

'The People move for a dismissal of the charges with prejudice,' Roger tells the judge. He could have given a speech about the interests of justice. Presumably, his boss wanted him to. But Roger Ogren won't do it. He thinks a very clever killer just walked free. So that high-minded speech will come from his boss, on the courtroom steps, a few minutes from now. And Shauna, if she says anything at all, will praise that boss for said high-mindedness.

My case is over. I have been, in a rather sensational way, restored. Not simply *not guilty*, but *innocent*, wrongly accused, a victim myself.

But all is not forgiven. The Board of Attorney Discipline opened an inquiry into me over my drug abuse, which they held in abeyance during my criminal trial, but which will proceed now in earnest. My attorney, a politically connected lawyer named Jon Soliday, is trying to negotiate a three-month suspension from the practice of law. My guess is it will be longer. It should be.

I got addicted to painkillers. I'm not the first and I won't be the last. But I should have stopped practicing law. I should have realized that my clients could be at risk. To this day, I don't think I botched anything or failed a client, but I could have. I could have, and that's what matters. My clients deserved better.

But that's not the worst of my sins. I cheated and perverted and basically pissed all over the criminal justice system. I lied to the police and manufactured evidence and tampered with crime scenes and lied under oath and, in the process, framed another man for murder. Granted, he was a man trying to frame *me* for *five* murders, and yes, he was a sociopathic killer who, by the way, was already dead, so prison wasn't an issue. And sure, I was doing all of this to keep Shauna out of prison. But the last time I checked our lawyers' ethics code, there was no reciprocity exception, no self-defense or *He started it* or protecting-someone-you-love caveats.

I'm a guy who's not fond of rules, in a profession that's full of them. Something's got to give there, yes? And I don't see those rules changing anytime soon.

Three months away from the practice of law could become six months. It could become a year. It could become permanent.

But *permanent* is not a word I'm using just now. Not for anything.

I look over at Shauna, who takes a delicious breath of relief. Today wasn't a surprise, but there is still something about hearing the gavel bang down. I'm out of harm's way.

But here's what's really crazy: Winning this case and avoiding prison doesn't hold a candle to getting clean, to reclaiming my soul. If I had to choose between spending my life in the state penitentiary but being clean, or being free to walk the streets but addicted to OxyContin, I'd take life in prison every time. Because when I was addicted, I was in prison anyway, but a bizarro-world kind of incarceration where *I* held the key, where I was free to leave anytime, where I closed the cell door on myself every day.

I'm six months removed from that tantalizing poison that hijacked my mind and body and I still can't believe any of it happened. I can't believe I let it seduce me and then own me, that I didn't even protest, that I just let it happen. That's the worst part, for me at least, that I didn't even fight for my life.

Not until someone came along and made me fight.

'This is the part where you smile,' Shauna says to me, her breath tickling my ear.

Both of us will have to learn to do that again. We have a lot to figure out. Shooting someone changes you. Losing a child changes you. Spending four months in lockup changes you. Going through addiction and recovery changes you. It's that simple: We aren't the same people we were this summer. I wasn't even sure we made sense together before. Now it's anyone's guess. She's the most important thing to me, as I am to her. There will always be something between us. What, exactly, that will look like, I don't know.

Shauna squeezes my hand under the table.

As if reading my thoughts, she says, 'Now for the hard part.'

Acknowledgments

Many thanks to Dan Collins, former assistant U.S. attorney in Chicago and now a partner at Drinker Biddle & Reath LLP, for answering my numerous questions about federal law enforcement. I am once again indebted to Dr Ronald Wright, forensic pathologist, for guiding me through many issues related to manners of death, causes of death, and estimating time of death. Thank you to my dear friend Beth Weedman for patiently answering many questions about substance abuse and treatment. Neither Dan, Beth, nor Dr Wright reviewed my work for accuracy, and any mistakes are mine alone.

Thank you to my many friends at Putnam, too numerous to list, for all the support you continue to show me and for everything you do to help me shine (or at least not screw up). To name just two: Sara Minnich, you made this book so much better. Ivan Held, you inspire so many authors like me with your commitment and faith in us, and it means everything to me. Thank you, thank you, thank you!

A nod to the Ellis rugrats, Abigail, Julia, and Jonathan, for moderating Daddy's grumpy moods when the words aren't flowing, and for filling his world with indescribable love. And to the lovely Susan, my dream come true, who keeps all of us sane and still makes my heart go pitter-pat.